FACES OF DUPLICITY

Jack Tipping

Fisher King Publishing

Fisher King Publishing Ltd
The Studio
Arthington Lane
Pool-in-Wharfedale
LS21 1JZ
England
www.fisherkingpublishing.co.uk

This book is for
my wife Joyce
for her love
and patience.

In writing this, the first book in a trilogy, I
acknowledge the assistance I received from
my editor and dear friend Marjorie Lawton,
and for the encouragement she gave me to
complete the work. My thanks also go to her
husband, Colin, who steered me through
the sailing of eighteenth century seas
in a square-rigged merchantman.

Chapter One

His long, dark hair hung down and straggled wet about his shoulders like a row of rat tails. With head bowed against the building strength of the gale the man struggled to stay in the saddle. He had hurriedly abandoned his coat and hat, together with his sword, pistols and almost all the rest of his possessions in order to escape his pursuers. His hunched shoulders were no defence against the penetrating shafts of rain, making him shiver uncontrollably as his meagre, saturated clothing leeched the warmth from his body with cold, parasitic greed.

Night was upon him and he was tired from the long chase. His mount had served him well but was now on the point of exhaustion. It walked with a stumbling gait, head down, ears back. He patted it on the neck and spoke in a whisper, knowing well the animal could neither hear nor understand him, "I would walk with you lady," he said. "But now I need your eyes."

The first flash of lightning startled him. At the ensuing crash of thunder the horse tossed its head in a weary gesture, then the flashes of lightning that followed left an image of the way ahead imprinted on his mind. The wheel tracks made by carts and coaches stretched in front with a line of trees breaking the horizon. As he neared the wooded area repeated flashes of lightning showed him where the track disappeared into the wood. He hesitated, bringing his mount to a welcome halt.

Choice was not with him. He had to find shelter. As if to

re-assure himself his hand went to the thick belt he wore, his fingers stroking the bulging pouches that held the heavy gold coins he carried.

Now he could hear the thunderous roar of the wind rushing through the trees. There could be no going back. He needed shelter quickly so he heeled his mount gently to follow the track into the trees.

He entered the wood and was deafened by the awesome roar of the wind blasting through the canopy. It was like a passage through Hell. Leafless trees stretched high on either side of him and the constant lightning silhouetted against the sky a maelstrom of branching tracery whipped to a fury by the storm. He felt as if he were travelling down a fiendish tunnel with the wrath of the Devil directed at him.

Leaves and dead twigs, disturbed and picked up by the gale from the woodland floor, hurtled at him like shot. Branches, torn from the trees, flew past, some striking both horse and rider with jarring, painful blows. The noise was deafening; the crack of lightning bolts and ear-splitting claps of thunder. Numerous creaks and cracks as branches bent and snapped. The occasional scraping, tearing crunch followed by the inevitable thud as a mighty tree succumbed to the storm.

He doubled forward as a large branch struck him, making him gasp and grab at his chest. It had caught him on his right side and he could feel the stickiness of his own blood. His situation was becoming desperate.

Another flash of lightning and he thought he glimpsed movement to his left. Yet another flash and he saw a horse - a rider - a face. Then it was as if his head exploded as he took a tremendous blow from the other side. His senses reeled. He tried to turn to defend himself but his body would not obey his mind. Another blow to his head and he slumped forward and rolled out of the saddle. He was unconscious before he touched the ground.

Chapter Two

It had been a good year for pigs in the village of Nestwith. Not, of course, for the litters bred for slaughter, but for the owners of pigs. It was particularly good for three friends who had gone into a partnership of sorts some years earlier.

Albert Wrigglesworth, known in the community as Wriggly, was an odd-job man who took any work that came along. Even standing in his shoes the top of his head barely reached five feet from the ground. His wife, Gertrude, was a large woman. It was said in the village that she had two very large thumbs and that Wriggley lived under both of them. Their cottage and smallholding, rented from the Nestwith Estate, was situated half a mile north of the village. He, together with Walter Lupton, the blacksmith's striker, who was also a wheelwright and an apprentice-trained cooper, had built a pigsty block and both men subsidised their income by breeding and selling pigs for slaughter. They each owned a breeding sow and kept each litter only until fattened, then sold them for meat. Both sows had now neared the end of their litter-bearing age so it was decided to have them 'visited' by the boar one more time and then sell them at the market at Loylton at better than slaughter price, as sows 'in pig'.

The third of the trio, Adam Gunner, was a big, big man. He was the village blacksmith in Nestwith, following in the footsteps of his father and his father before him. He stood well over six feet but it was the width of his shoulders and his mighty arms - described by one local pundit as 'the size of a fat strumpet's thighs' - that made him stand out from other men. Over the years his Christian name 'Adam' had been dropped and he was known simply as Gunner.

Gunner's pride and joy was an enormous stud boar. The animal was also of huge proportions. It's broad back and great head, covered with thick, ginger-black bristles, gave it a fearsome appearance, but it was the little red eyes, long snout and enormous, stained tusks, together with an unpredictable temper that made even Gunner wary when near the beast. He proudly boasted that he owned the finest boar in the land and named it after the reigning monarch. So the boar became known in the county as King George III, the Second.

Gunner insisted on taking the boar to sows, rather than have 'piggers' bring their sows to be served. This way he would not only obtain money for the services but also a chat on rural affairs and gossip, often a meal and a few tankards of home brewed beer thrown in for good measure. And sometimes maybe even more pleasurable activity.

The boar was housed in a pigsty at the rear of the smithy, the last building at the north end of the village, with a small paddock adjacent to the main village street. In the paddock Gunner had built a ramp to the same height as the rear of his cart. When it came to loading the boar to take it to perform its service, he would open the pigsty gate and stand back. King George III the Second, hearing the sound of the cart being backed up to the ramp and knowing what was expected of him, would rush out of the sty, charge up the ramp and leap into the cart. There he would sit on his haunches, head held high, grunting and snorting, drooling mouth open, in a rampant, expectant mood, his boar-hood unmasked.

For a boar he had very good hearing and his sense of smell was exceptionally keen. But King George III the Second had one very serious fault. He was extremely short-sighted.

His paddock was adjacent to the main village street and whenever a cart passed by King George III the Second would hear the sound of the wheels. His little pig brain would spring into action and convey the message to his nether regions. The message of arousal had such a dramatic impact on his senses that he would prance on the spot, excitement took hold, then grunting and snorting with anticipation he would rush out of the sty, charge up the ramp and with one giant leap would launch himself into space only to discover too late there was no cart. The heavy animal would try to save itself with flailing limbs before hitting the ground with a resounding body-crunching thud. It would then stagger to its feet and shake its whole body, and woe-betide anything or anybody within reach on which it could vent its fury.

Gunner had laid down a thick mat of straw to save the animal from injury but he could not curb its enthusiasm. For the price of a farthing children of the village would take visitors to the paddock, then rub pieces of metal, or wood, together to emulate the noise of a squeaking cart hub in the hope of encouraging the boar to perform. Such was the animal's fame that a landlord in the village seriously suggested changing the name of his inn from The Wheatsheaf to The Flying Boar.

The time had come to sell the sows and a trip to Loylton had proved successful. Wriggley had sold his sow in the morning for a better than expected price and retired to a tavern. Walter had to wait until late afternoon before he sold his, for less than he expected. Unfortunately for him, many potential bidders had left the market because the weather had changed for the worse. Rain was falling and a strong wind gusted through the open market place. He and Gunner then visited the tavern and had to drag the drunken Wriggley out of the arms of an ugly, smelly woman who was hell-bent on separating him from his purse.

With Wriggley singing bawdy songs in the back of the cart they had set off for home. Gunner, leading the gelding, had taken the precaution of putting a flame to a coach lantern but it was a problem keeping it alight against such a wind. As night fell the wind grew to such strength even Gunner, with all his bulk, had to lean into it to stay on his feet. It got worse. Lightning, thunder and lashing rain, now intermingled with snow beat down upon them.

When they reached Black Wood they hoped for shelter of the trees but it was not to be. Gunner walked in one track and led the horse holding the bridle. Walter walked at the other side. Wriggley was still singing in the back of the cart but his voice was drowned by the roar of the storm.

The constant lightning helped them see their way but suddenly a huge flash lit up the way ahead and what they saw brought them to sudden halt.

"What in God's name…" Gunner shouted to Walter. "Is that lantern still lit?"

"Aye it is. It looked like a body, Gunner."

"Get Wriggley out of the cart, drunk or not, and tell him to hold the horse." Gunner had already started forward.

Wriggley was singing about a lass he met and what he had done to her on Waverley Hill, oblivious to all about him.

"Come on Wriggley - we need you - urgent, Gunner says." Walter tugged at Wriggley's coat. But the alcohol he had consumed raised aggression. He pulled his coat back and continued with his song.

"The cart's afire!" Walter shouted at the top of his voice.

The effect was immediate. Wriggley was out of the cart falling on his back on the ground. Walter felt for him and dragged him to his feet and in as strong a way as he could think he told Wriggley to hold the horse and not to move.

The man on the ground was naked. He lay on his stomach; arms and legs stretched out with thin sticks piercing his feet and hands and pushed through into the earth. Gunner could see with the light from his shielded lantern that the man had also been wounded about the head and chest.

"What are we going to do?" Walter directed the question at Gunner, passing responsibility. Then he went on, "we could shove him to one side and let the next folk along have him."

Gunner was leaning over the man. Suddenly he turned and shouted at Walter, "he's alive! By God, he still breathes!"

"Walter," he shouted, "don't pull those stakes out of his feet. If you do it'll pull the muck through the wound. Pull 'em out with the feet and leave 'em in."

Gunner did the same with the hands then he turned the unconscious figure and picked him up as if he were a small child and placed him in the cart. He took off his coat and wrapped it around the limp body. He ordered the other two to take off their sodden coats to cover the man.

"What now?" Walter called.

"To Maisy Pitchforth's, said Gunner.

"Nay, nay, nay. We can't do that. She lost her man and two sons to the pox not six months gone. Now she's tending her eldest from a rock fall in the quarry. We can't take him there."

Walter's shouted outburst got a quick response. "Where else – he'll certain be dead by the time we reach the village."

Chapter Three

Two candles, one at either side of the head of the bed, cast a dim light in the room, assisted by the flickering flames from burning logs in the fire grate. The figure on the bed was dressed immaculately; long, flared coat, ruffled white shirt, knee breeches, white linen stockings and buckled shoes. He lay with his legs tied together with a linen strip and with his arms crossed over his chest. His face was scarred and distorted on the left side and two small, flat pebbles settled on his eyes. A brick wrapped in cloth had been positioned under his chin to keep the jaw closed until rigor mortis set in. A woman knelt at the side of the bed, hands clasped, head bowed, deep in prayer.

Maisy Pitchforth appeared older than her forty two years. Her brow was creased by the ravages of worry and grief and her hair, under her spotless white bonnet, showed streaks of grey. Her eldest son, Jamie, lay dead in the bed, crushed by a rock fall at the quarry where he had worked. She had utilised all her nursing skills for the past fifteen days in an effort to save him but to no avail. He had breathed his last two hours ago, and since then she had busied herself cleaning, dressing and talking to him as if he were still alive. Anything to occupy her mind, to avoid thought of her despair. Now, in the flickering light she was coming to terms with her loss.

Jamie was the last of her family. Her husband Sam and their two youngest sons had succumbed to smallpox six months earlier when the disease swept through the village, taking its toll. Doors had remained closed. The gates of the

Nestwith Hall estate were shut and no persons allowed in or out. Jamie had quarantined himself at the quarry until the epidemic passed and Maisy had thanked God for his mercy. Now it was all over – her whole family gone.

Her shoulders shook as she wept, tears streaming down her face. Having gone through the trauma of burying her husband and two sons she felt she had reached the end of her tether. She was experiencing the emptiness of her loss; the heart-tearing loneliness; the pain that comes with grief. She dreaded the inevitable church service and the burial to follow. She tried not to think of it.

The rector of Nestwith, The Reverend Alexander Butler, would undoubtedly cast aspersions in her direction. His god was no god of love and compassion, but one of wrath and repentance. Just as he had previously told her, 'when God takes the young it is punishment for the sins of their begetters.' There would be no comfort or solace from the Nestwith churchman this time.

She had ignored the sounds of the raging storm but now as lightning burst into the sombre setting and the deafening crashes of thunder shook the very foundations of the cottage, she began to feel trepidation. She imagined God was venting his anger.

She was shaken out of her thoughts by the sound of a knocking upon the door and a muffled voice calling out.

She got up and moved to the door and heard the words repeated, "Maisy. It's Adam Gunner. We need help."

She shot back the bolts on the door and it was pushed from the other side. Gunner entered and closed the door against the storm without allowing the latch to fall.

Maisy, we've found a man bad hurt. He's near to dying. If we take him further he'll surely die. Can we bring him in?"

Maisy Pitchforth knew Gunner well. He had been a good friend to her late husband, so she nodded without hesitation. He had not taken his eyes from her face since he first entered, so when he returned, carrying the near-lifeless man, he stopped in his tracks when he saw the figure on the bed. "Aw Maisy." He repeated, "aw Maisy." He stood, unmoving, the man cradled in his huge arms, not knowing what to do.

"Come on, come on." She beckoned impatiently. "Oh Lord above!" She exclaimed. "Look at his head! And his hands!"

"And his feet," said Gunner as he lay the man on the flagged floor in front of the fire.

Walter came in and closed the door. He was covered in snow.

Seeing the prone figure on the bed he felt acute embarrassment, realising they had intruded on Maisy's grief. "What about Wriggley," he muttered.

Maisy looked up from attending to her patient. "You can't leave him outside in this weather," she said. "You have your horse with you?" Not waiting for an answer she went on, "take it round the back. There's room in the stable, - and a bite of hay – but you let me have back what you use, mind."

Walter left to do her bidding while she and Gunner went to work. He removed the sodden coats and she replaced them with several blankets and a feather quilt. Then, one by one she cut the thin stakes that pierced his hands and feet on the side that had not entered the earth and drew them out. She ordered

Gunner to fetch bricks from a pile in the porch at the rear of the cottage and place them in the large oven. When hot she wrapped them in wads of cloth and placed them on top of the quilt as near as she could to the inert form.

By the time Walter and Wriggley appeared she had bathed the wounds and bound them. They entered shaking snow from their clothes and then looking down guiltily at the wet mess on the stone-flagged floor.

"Don't worry yourself with that. It'll clean." Maisy pushed a huge cooking pot along an overhead slide until it was over the fire. The pot was suspended on a large 'S' shaped hook, one end over the slide the other holding the pot handle. Her hot pot was well known to visitors and it was said it never emptied.

She busied herself, fetching wooden bowls and spoons and when the contents of the pot began to bubble she ordered the three men to be seated at the kitchen table. She then slid the pot off the heat, ladled the stew into the bowls and placed them on the kitchen table in front of each. "Not much meat in it but it's hot," she said.

As the men dug their spoons into the piles of vegetables Maisy stood, looking into the fire, her eyes glazed. She found herself thankful for the company and the fact that she was not alone gave her clarity of mind. After a while she walked to the side of the bed and stared down at the face of her dead son. She then went back to the fire and knelt by the injured man, placing her cheek close to his face. She felt the faint draught of his breath. She held his bound right hand, her fingers poking under the binding. She did the same to the left hand but leaned nearer to examine the fingers more closely.

She got to her feet and with her hands on her hips she turned to the men. They had almost finished their meal and were unprepared for her outburst, "I don't expect any one of you knows just what you have done! Or the danger we could be in." The spoons stopped in mid-air, the mouths, open to accept the food, remained open. Wriggley held his spoon, his arm unmoving, his head jerking back and forth, mouth open, head turned towards Maisy.

"You have done your Christian duty. You could do no more," she said. "But this has to be given thought. That man," she pointed at the still form in front of the fire, "is meant to be dead. Whoever did that to him didn't do it for the good of his health. He was meant to die. You saved him and if he does live – what then?" Not expecting an answer she continued, "what if those who did that to him find out that he lives? Or even if he dies and they learn you brought him here. What if they think he could have come to his senses and talked to you? Maybe he told you the names of those who wanted him dead. And if that's what they think then your lives are in great danger. They may then want to close your lips. And what about me?" She leaned towards them, hands still on hips. "You have put my life in danger too."

As one the three put down their spoons and remained silent, like scolded children. Maisy went over to her son and again looked down into his face. Her lips moved as if she were speaking to him. She then went to the injured man once more. When she turned back to face the men she was wide-eyed, her face flushed.

"I don't like our rector!" She spit the words out. The men looked at each other in bewilderment, remaining silent, not knowing what was coming next.

Wriggley leaned towards Walter and whispered, "she's flipped her coin."

Walter nudged him away. Maisy went on, "he asked my husband to repair the arch at the front of the church. Sam worked four weeks and more, carving, chiselling and putting the stones in place. When it was finished he asked the rector for payment. And do you know what he said? He said payment was God's love for what he had done for His house. Sam got not a brass farthing.

"When Sam and our two youngest died earlier this year, I asked the rector if we could have a plot for the graves at the front or side of the church. And do you know what he said? He said we were commoners and that Sam and the boys had died of smallpox, and disease was God's punishment for sinners. Sinners! Sinners! There was never a better than Sam, and the boys were not old enough to have sinned at anything. We had to bury them in a corner right at the back of the church up against the far wall.

"When it was done I asked him if I could have a stone put up to mark the graves. And do you know what he said? He said others buried there had no kin who could afford a stone and it would look out of place and spoil the look of the churchyard." She paused and then ended, "no, I don't like that rector."

Her expression changed and she waved the back of a hand at them. Well, get on, there's work to do."

"Work?" Wriggley asked.

"Yes." Maisy strode towards the back porch. "There's some spades here. You're going to dig a grave."

Wriggly turned to Walter and in a whisper, "she's going to have us bury the poor bugger alive."

Walter waited until she came back into the room then, with a worried look on his face, said. "We can't do that, Mistress Pitchforth. It's not Christian to bury him. Not while he still breathes."

Maisy stopped in her tracks. She looked at the three, then at the figure on the floor. "Not him you great dolts! We're going to give my Jamie a Christian burial. There's a place I was going to plant a herb garden. I want you to dig a grave there. I know it's not consecrated ground but it will be better than being under the earth at the back of the church with no mark to say he's there. I'll have him with me always. I'll be able to talk with him every day and I won't have to deal with that rector."

"Gunner was nonplussed and said, "I don't like it. We could all be in bad trouble for burying a man without permission of the church." He was sure now that grief had damaged her wits. "And why tonight, Maisy?"

"You still don't see, do you?" She sighed. "Only we four in this room know that Jamie has gone to his maker. So, we give him a decent burial – that's not my Jamie anymore." She pointed to the body of her son. "Jamie died some time gone, when he lost his senses. He's been with his father and brothers in heaven this past two weeks. I've felt it.

"Have you noticed a sort of likeness that fellow has to

Jamie? I know both left sides of their faces are bruised and cut but look further. Jamie's face, chest, hands and feet were damaged in the rock fall and this man has injuries in the same places. The hair is the same colour and they're about the same size. So this is what we do. We bury Jamie then we put that fellow in the bed and who's to know he's not Jamie – still alive. Nobody's going to take a close look. None of us says a word of the truth and all the killers have got is a mystery or perhaps they might think the foxes and badgers have dragged him further into the forest and sated their appetites. Nobody will know the truth but us. But we will be bound to one another and our lips must be sealed."

"But what about him?" Gunner asked," pointing to the man. "What if he recovers? What will you tell him? And what will folk think – and do when it becomes known?"

"I'll cross that river when I get to it." Maisy was adamant.

What if we bury Jamie, as you say, and then that fellow dies. What happens then? Is he to be buried in your garden alongside Jamie?

No. He'll go to the church as Jamie Pitchforth." Maisy shrugged. "I don't know who he is so I won't have to worry where he's buried.

"That's clever, Maisy." Gunner expressed his admiration of the plan.

"That's very clever," said Walter.

"I don't get it," said a bewildered looking Wriggley.

They went out into the storm. The men armed with spades and a mattock. Maisy pointed to where she wanted them to dig and they got to work. She stood with her back to the biting wind, her hooded cloak flapping about her face and body. She held a lantern in front of her, shielding it from the raging blizzard.

Gunner began at one end of the grave, Walter at the other. They wasted no time, working the spades feverishly.

Maisy left them and returned to the cottage where she began to wrap the body of her son in cloth and canvas. When she came to cover his face she broke down, sobbing uncontrollably, saying over and over, "my Jamie. My Jamie. Oh my Jamie."

Chapter Four

The Roulette family had owned Nestwith Hall for four generations. General Sir Montgomery Roulette had been awarded his baronetcy for successful military deeds on behalf of his king and country. Upon his death the title passed to his eldest son George and then on to George's son, Francis.

Francis begot two sons. The eldest, Oliver, did not marry and lived with his parents at the Hall. His main aim in life seemed to be to accomplish as little as possible. He was his mother's favourite and he could do no wrong in her eyes. She gave him money, paid his gambling debts and cushioned him from the despairing rebukes of his father. He was a gambler, a ne'er-do-well, a libertine.

The younger by a mere eleven months, Marcus prospered. As a second son he could not expect to inherit much from his father so while in his teens he had purchased a field. It became a joke in the county that Marcus Roulette was the proud owner of a ten acre estate. But Marcus had the last laugh.

He acquired a herd of sheep, far more than his ten acres would sustain. Each morning he would turn the herd out of the field and, with his dogs, drive them slowly along the highway. The sheep would feed from the verges and by nightfall he would return them to his field well sated. He bought another field and more sheep. Then more. He employed men as shepherds and shearers to clip the wool and so his fortune increased. He ploughed profit back into his business but not speedily enough for his ambitions. To increase his capital, when twenty he married Mary Brook ten years his senior, the youngest daughter of a wealthy family. She was a strange woman and there appeared to be little affection between them but they served a purpose for each other. He received a generous dowry enabling him to add to his land holdings. She wanted marriage and freedom from her parents. She showed her gratitude by giving birth to four healthy children.

Their only son, Totton, was born nine months after the marriage. Charlotte came next fourteen months later. She grew to be talkative child always taking over conversations, though empty chatter found her no lasting friendships. Russet was born five years later and lastly, when Mary was forty years of age, she gave birth to another girl, Katherine.

The family lived well. A live-in tutor was employed for the children's education and apart from the strange behaviour of their mother they had a happy childhood.

Then came news of the death of Oliver Roulette.

Chapter Five

Russet Roulette stood at the window of her father's study looking out on the parkland in front of the hall. She wore a long flowing dress that almost touched the floor. The waistline was raised to a point below her well-formed breasts, pushing them up to bulge above the neckline. A modesty vest of lace concealed her cleavage. Her hair hung in three ringlets at either side; golden brown tinged with lighter hue that glistened in the sunlight as she turned her head. But for any observer it was her face that drew attention, the broad forehead and high cheekbones, straight nose and full lips displaying a hint of a teasing pout. Eyes of the deepest green sparkled with warmth. It was a face of exquisite beauty.

Everything is so green, she thought. The first two weeks of May were, without doubt, her favourite time of the year. Her eyes strayed over the scene before her, the huge park trees, with their massive girths, standing like guardians of nature and now coming to life after a hard winter. They bore newly forming leaves so small she could still see sky through the great crowns. Late born lambs frolicked in groups, their mother ewes, seemingly oblivious to their existence, heads down, munching the lush spring grass. Cattle crowded the shade under great boughs, herded into the parkland to allow the field grasses to grow for hay.

How she had adored the hay harvest. The smell of new-mown hay, she mused, was far sweeter to the senses than any false London scent. Now eighteen, she was expected to act the lady but she longed to go back to her childhood days at her previous home, to mingle with the village children, to romp in the hay.

Up until she was twelve years of age she had ridden her pony astride her saddle but since then, on the orders of her father, she had been compelled to use the uncomfortable side-saddle. 'It was not fitting for a young lady of breeding to be stretching her legs in that fashion,' he had said. What nonsense, she thought. Men know nothing of women and yet we are the underlings and they make the rules. Now she could only watch the harvest sitting uncomfortably on horseback.

She went back to her reverie of childhood. She could see again in her mind the row of men all in line waiting for the order to begin. Then, as one, they would sweep their scythes in an arc, cutting down the long grass. As they brought the scythes back to the original position they all took one long step forward and then, all in time, began the procedure again, taking another swathe and on they went, moving up the field.

Women, dressed in their long, high-waisted frocks, some with them bundled up and pulled from the back between their legs to be tied at the waist like enormous baby's napkins. They would follow the scythes and with short-handled sickles cut down any tuft of grass left standing. Behind would come the women supporting yokes across their shoulders with pails of small beer hanging heavily. They would wander among the workers, dropping their buckets to the ground and ladle the weak liquid on demand to slake parched throats. She had always made a point of getting within hearing distance of the women to listen to their bawdy banter. She had learnt many of the facts of life from their lewd wordplay.

When the hay had dried and the fetching in of the harvest began came the greatest enjoyment for harvesters' children. Playing in hay and helping gather loose wisps of hay the rakers missed and then tossing their bundles onto the hayricks. Then she would sit on top of the loads of hay with the labourers' children, enjoying each bounce as the cart trundled towards the hay barns. The men would hold the horse by the bridle and reverse the cart through the huge barn doorway. The youngsters would slide off the load into the arms of one of the men then stand aside as the hay was unloaded. Two men climbed onto the cart with their hayforks and threw the hay onto the first layer. Two more would then fork it high to the next layer and then up again to finish the stack almost up to the rafters. The men built two giant steps and when they returned to the field for another load the children would delight in climbing the wooden ladder to launch themselves into the air to land on the soft cushion of hay below. Russet had gone a further step. She had climbed up and onto a giant oak beam supporting the roof truss and leapt onto the lower layer of hay. Now, standing by the window she chuckled to herself. None of the boys had dared try it but they all stood below, wide-eyed and calling out, 'do it again Russy, do it again.' Up she had gone and leapt, with her skirts billowing about her, showing her nakedness as far as her waist. She knew well what they could see and she revelled in it but then her father had caught her in the act and she was henceforth banned from the barn.

Only weeks after the hay harvest the sheep would arrive. The huge herds were driven down from the north to feed the great cities of the south. Hollygrove, her old home, with its seven hundred acres had become a stopover for the hundreds of sheep. The herd was split up and turned into the fields to fatten and rest before continuing the trek. Many were full fleeced. These would be clipped by an army of shearers. A number of the fleeces would be retained by the estate as grazing payment and the rest purchased at below market price to give a good income to the estate. Payment to the drovers for wool went to finance the remainder of their drive south to the markets

She brought her mind back to the present and to her new home. Her eyes now took in the 'ride' constructed on the instruction of her grandfather. It twisted back and forth between the trees of the park with the five rail fences put up for the men to jump their mounts and at the side of each a low two rail fence for the ladies. She clenched her teeth in frustration at not being allowed to attempt the high jumps. She looked at the last high fence to the left of a stumpy elm tree. It was almost out of sight of anyone observing from the hall. She was tempted. Yes. Her mind was made up. One day she would jump that fence.

"Damn the fool!" Sir Marcus Roulette thumped his desk in frustration. "My stupid brother was born without a brain."

Russet was startled out of her daydreams and brought her mind back to reality. Her father was directly behind her seated at a desk covered with papers separated into piles, each pile weighed down with a paperweight.

"It is surely not in your nature to speak ill of the dead, Father," She scolded softly.

Ill of the dead! Ill of the dead!" He fumed. "My wastrel of a brother could well have ruined us." He got up from the desk and walked to the front of the huge fireplace. "Look at all those, Russy." He pointed to the pile of papers on his desk. "Unpaid bills. Look at them. Hundreds of unpaid bills." He shook his head. "During the whole of the twenty three months from the time my father died up until his own death, Oliver paid for nothing. The only decent thing he did was to see the workers and servants received their payment. The very first thing he… No, I should not be burdening you with this." He turned and placed his hands on the high mantelpiece and stared into the empty grate.

"I did not want this title. I did not want this house. I did not want this estate." It was as if he were speaking aloud his deepest thoughts. "I did not expect it. My life I had planned - and to some extent the lives of my children. Now all that has changed. The future has been taken out of my hands."

He exhaled a deep sigh. Then for a while he remained silent, deep in thought.

When his wife, Mary, gave birth to Katherine the labour had been long and overly painful. After the birth she had haemorrhaged severely and had fallen into a coma. The doctor attending had given up hope that she would live but to his amazement she survived. When she had eventually awakened her mind was deranged. She knew neither her husband nor her children and because of her strange behaviour she had since been locked in her room and cared for by employed attendants.

As Russet had grown up Marcus had become ever closer

to his daughter, sharing secrets and planning the future. Now he was feeling the guilt of not sharing the truth with her.

Russet came round the desk and stood in front of her father. She looked up into his face. "There is more to this, isn't there Father. I've been wondering why there has been so much secrecy over Uncle Oliver's death. We all know he died in a riding accident and that his neck was broken. But no funeral. Not even a memorial service." She smiled and wagged a finger, then pointing the finger at herself, "I have been your confidante for years, Father, and you mine. I have never spoken of our affairs for other ears but now I am experiencing an uneasy feeling that for the first time you are keeping something from me. What is it that is so inauspicious in Uncle Oliver's demise that you cannot share with me?"

"I will, Russy. I will." He stepped forward and took her in his arms and hugged her to him. "I will tell you but you must first know why I have been so secretive." He released her and turned towards the window with his back to her as if afraid to catch her eye. "I have kept silent and told no one of this unsavoury business. I could not speak a word of it without bringing shame on the family – and the family name.

"It began when I received a note from a London tailor asking for an overdue payment for garments purchased by one Sir Oliver Roulette. I knew nothing of this and it was really none of my business. However, with the family name in mind I followed this up. It seemed a fellow had approached this tailor with a pair of breeches and asked for reward for returning them. Unlike Oliver, this tailor fellow kept accounts and from a number inked into the inside of the breeches this proved to be an unpaid purchase. Not only that but there were many more items of attire tailored for Oliver for which the tailor had received no remuneration."

Marcus took a handkerchief from his cuff, wiped his face with it and continued, "this fellow wanted his money so he checked on Oliver's family and sent me a note and a bill. I employed a man to find Oliver and through him I learned that the breeches were taken from a dead man and that it was most probable that the man was my brother. When I was sure and informed of the circumstances of the death I invented the story of Oliver having a riding accident.

"The truth is, Russy, he was found dead in a sewage gutter in a gambling and whore-house district of the city, dressed only in his breeches with no items of identification on him. The fellow who gave me this information said it was usual for a man who expired in a whore-house to have all his valuables and clothing removed and anything else that would identify him before being taken out and dumped elsewhere – for obvious reasons. Oliver was assumed to be a pauper and he was buried in a pauper's grave six weeks before my inquiry. When I asked where I could find his grave they laughed at me."

"And what of all this?" Russet waved an arm at the crowded desk. "If they are unpaid why can we not pay them and be done?"

"Because, my dear, there is nothing left with which to pay them." Marcus walked around desk, pulled up his chair and sat down. " Before I digressed about Oliver's death I was about to tell you that when he came into the title upon the death of your grandfather, Oliver dismissed the book-keeper. He withdrew monies from the estate accounts until there was nothing left. Not one brass farthing was paid back in. If I sell our old home and the land I could come to an arrangement with the creditors, settle with them, then start again here."

Russet went behind him and stood with her arms over his shoulders, hands on his chest. She lowered her head and put a cheek against his head. "Don't worry, Father," she said. "We can all help. Totton..."

"Totton!" Marcus interrupted. "Huh! He's too busy fighting his imaginary battles with his soldier-boyfriends. All he's interested in is firing muskets and following a career in the military like his illustrious forebear. Apart from being the finest shot in the county and always getting the largest bag of birds, Tott shows no interest whatsoever in a rural calling. But first things first."

Marcus took hold of his daughter's hands and squeezed them gently. "We shall manage, my dear. I have no doubt of that but it's going to be very difficult and we shall all have to give up some of the luxuries of life – for a while. My greatest worry is the missing legal papers. I have lawyers searching for them but so far without success. The deeds must be found, but it would be just like Oliver to have hidden them along with money from the estate coffers in some remote vault where they will be almost impossible to locate."

Chapter Six

The cottage stood back from the highway. A small wicket gate opened onto a stone-flagged path leading to a door with an abundance of flowers of many hues growing in profusion on either side. Further to the left a larger gate gave access to the wide track that ran around the side of the building. The cottage was brick-built and lime-washed to a dazzling white. A thatched roof, dappled here and there with lighter coloured straw, where repairs had been carried out, gave the building a quaint, picturesque appearance.

At the rear, outhouses, fronted with a red brick yard, terraced one side with stables for two horses adjoining a mistal and ending with a small fodder barn. A thatched porch stood out from the rear of the cottage and a thatch-roofed, open sided, walkway led to a covered well. A rustic timber bench was positioned near the kitchen window and to the side an open log shed stacked neatly with split firewood logs and gardening tools. The rest of the area was taken up with a kitchen garden. Row upon row of vegetable greenery ribboned the land as far as the fence. Beyond, a large field bordered by a gully and a running beck.

Maisy Pitchforth lifted an arm and wiped the sweat from her brow with her sleeve. She had finished stacking the firewood that Gunner had brought her and she rested on the bench and let her eyes focus on the struggling figure in the garden.

The face of the man was deformed. The whole of the left side drooped grotesquely, distorting the eyelids and opening the eye to stare in a blood-shot glaze. His mouth was lop-sided, causing a constant dribbling of saliva. Even the beard and moustache he had grown could do nothing to cover his gargoyle-like appearance. His left arm hung uselessly by his side and his left leg trailed behind him when he moved. He held a spade in the right hand. He lifted it and rammed it into the earth. Then, he hopped high and came down with the instep of his right foot onto the heel of the blade, driving it into the ground. With his hand clutching the shaft half way down its length and his forearm against the wood, he levered the soil upwards and turned it. He prodded the soil with the spade to break it up and when satisfied he began the whole laborious sequence again.

Maisy let her eyes wander to the herb patch she had planted. From where she was sitting she could plainly see the different hues of the herbs forming a cross. She thought of her son deep beneath the earth then glanced back at her adopted son. Her mind went back to the strange circumstances that had brought him to her.

The first week had been a sleepless one. She had spent almost every minute of every day attending her patient. The left side of his face began to droop almost immediately and it was touch and go whether he lived or died. Gunner helped her try to feed him but without success. He held him upright in the bed and she had tried to spoon broth into his distorted mouth but he choked on every spoonful. During the second week they managed to get him to take a little mash and from then on things got better – except for the visit of the Reverend Butler and his weird curate.

It was the neighing of a horse that first caught Maisy's attention. She went to the window and spied the Reverend Butler alighting from his carriage followed by his strange companion, Isiah Snufty. With haste she took her patients bound hands and hid them under the blankets then she pulled the material up to cover his body as far as his neck. She turned his head to one side on the pillow so only the distorted side of his face showed. She finished just in time before the door was thrown open and the rector entered. He claimed the divine right to enter any house, invited or not. He was on God's business.

He strode into the room, his cassock flowing. Behind him came Isiah Snufty; always behind, never in front of the rector or even by his side. He stood with his head cocked sideways looking over the Reverends shoulder. He wore the same type of black cassock and on his head perched an ecclesiastical hat, black and wide-brimmed. It appeared far too big for his head and balanced precariously on his two large, protruding ears. His eyes were close together, his nose, of prodigious proportion, jutted to a point above a tiny, lipless mouth. His chin was not to be seen. It vanished below his lower lip and merged with the turkey-like folds of his neck. His eyes darted everywhere. His head made little jerky movements as if a foul smell pervaded the room. Wriggley had summed him up long ago when he said, "he's like a mangy rat sniffing the air to catch the stink of carrion."

"Mistress Pitchforth!" The Reverend's voice had boomed as if he were addressing hard-of-hearing parishioners seated in the back pews. "Mistress Pitchforth, he repeated. "On the last Sabbath you saw fit not to worship our Lord in His house."

"No, I was unable to do so." Maisy uttered the words with humility.

"Unable? Unable?" The rector threw his arms in the air. "The Lord does not recognise 'unable.' If you flout the call of God you will feel the might of His wrath and the punishment of man."

Maisy remembered her distress at the thought of the punishment. Without putting it into words, the rector had threatened the whipping post because that was the customary sentence of the times for persistent absence from church.

"I am sorry Reverend but my son has been stricken down and is near death. I couldn't leave him. But I do get on my knees and pray for His help every hour of every day." She had offered her excuse.

The rector had looked in the direction of the prone figure on the bed. He stepped closer then drew back, a look of horror on his face. "Aaaaah!" He roared and pointed a finger at the distorted face. "That person has been touched by the Devil! Lord have mercy on his soul. Look. He bears the mark of Satan." He backed away, making the signs of the cross, again and again. The curate was at a loss what to do. The rector was walking backwards and calling out. "This is an evil place. A house of evil. We must leave this place. Leave this place." Isiah Snufty was so accustomed to following in the footsteps of his master he did not know whether to dodge round the front, turn round and face the other way, or just continue to walk backwards. So befuddled was he that when he reached the open door with the rector's back bearing down upon him he tripped over the threshold and fell across the path.

"The Lord in his wisdom saw fit to set aside his blessings on this place," boomed the rector. "You, Mistress Pitchforth. You have lost your loved ones because the Lord has withdrawn His favour on you. And you have shown no kindness to your maker..... Oooooh! Oh! Oooooh!"

The rector ended his tirade with a cry of surprise as he stepped backwards into the prone Isiah Snufty. He toppled over the man and landed on his back, legs apart and pointing skyward. His cassock fell about him leaving his nakedness and privacy evident for Maisy to see as she followed him out.

"Ah," she said. "I see your Maker showed no kindness to you in your creation."

She regretted the remark as soon as it came out for she knew she had made an enemy of the Reverend Butler and, therefore of the church.

But, the charade was not yet over. The rector got to his feet using the body of his curate for assistance. He retrieved his hat and with it in hand rushed to climb into his carriage and grab the reins. The curate finally collected himself and collected his hat. He placed it on his head only to find it was the rector's hat and it came down over his ears and eyes. In his haste he stumbled into the carriage wheel as it began to turn. The rector was in no mood to wait and Snufty fell to the ground again. He picked himself up and ran after the carriage. The rector had struggled to place the curates hat on his head but it just perched on the top and blew off to land in the dust of the road. The curate picked it up and the last Maisy saw of the hatless rector was him coaxing his charge to more speed with Isiah Snufty running after the carriage, cassock streaming, waving the two ecclesiastical hats in the air.

When the patient began to come round it was as if he were living a dream. Sight came in a hazy blur for a few seconds and then it was gone. Hours later he began to notice his surroundings. A beamed ceiling, a sense that a fire burned to his left and that someone moved near him. He tried to lick his lips and run his tongue around his dry mouth but it seemed his tongue would not follow the instruction of his brain. He found he could control his right arm and hand and also move his right leg but he had no feeling whatsoever in his left side. When his mind became overtaxed he slept.

"Come on Jamie my love, it's time to wake up." He saw a figure leaning over him. She called him Jamie. How strange he thought when he knew his name was... was... was... It was then he tried to recall his past and for days he searched for his previous life but without success. He finally accepted that his memory was lost. It was if he had been born a grown man in this very bed. Before now there was nothing.

He opened his mouth to speak but no sound came. He tried to shout but could not utter a sound of any sort. He attempted to whisper words but what he intended should be breathed out words were nothing more than a garbled jumble.

He had to accept that Maisy was his mother and that he had three friends called Gunner, Walter and Wriggley, and outside this cottage was a whole new world.

He finished digging the plot and threw the spade towards the log shed then picked up his wooden crutch, hobbled forward to where the spade had landed, put his crutch on the ground then picked up the spade and threw it again. By this means he got it to the shed where he stood it up with the rest of the tools. He then joined Maisy on the bench. With his right hand he took hold of his left arm and placed the paralysed hand on his knee. He nudged Maisy and nodded his head as a signal for her to look at his twitching index finger. He was improving now. It was still going to be some time before he regained control and the paralysis left him but it worried her. Supposing he regained his memory, she thought. What then? She had nursed him and cherished him as if he where her own son and her affection for him had grown into love. She did not wish to lose him. She knew that some day she would have to tell him the truth – but for now…

Chapter Seven

In rural areas, just as in the towns and cities, there existed a class system. At the top of the tree came royalty and the aristocracy, followed by titled commoners. Rurality differed only in that city men of business and the arts gave way to a class of gentlemen farmers, and men of successful rural professions. These were the men along with their wives who received invitations to balls and festivities at the country houses of the wealthy. Below came the gentlemen farmers and then the tenant farmers, those who rented from the estates. Below them were the peasant farmers with tenanted smallholdings who farmed only a subsistence existence. Lowest in rank came the agricultural worker who eked out a meagre living with seasonal work and willing to take on any menial chore. All in the county would keep their stations, to socialise only with their own class - except for one day- the day of the Nestwith Festival.

The festival was held annually on the Nestwith Estate and the proceeds donated to the local church. The occasion had been cancelled the past two years during the reign of Oliver Roulette but Russet had persuaded her father that it would be good for relationships with their neighbours to reinstate the event.

Activities began days before the event with stalls being erected, the turnip shy, the ring-a-hoop, the lucky dip, tossing the horseshoe and many more popular entertainments. Then the physical contests, stone lifting, the tug-of-war, throwing the hammer. Archery butts set up and a musketry range. And, of course, the ale tents.

On the evening prior to the festivities, as was the custom, Sir Marcus donated a young ox and a pig to be roasted on spits. These were slaughtered and the carcasses impaled on stout poles with a farm cartwheel attached at one end. These were lifted on to supports and the fires lit. Wood and charcoal would be added and the turning of the wheel attended by the butchers-turned-cooks slowly roasted the meat to perfection throughout the night.

Early on the morning of the festivities Sir Marcus was seated in his study, eyes closed, slumped in his chair, his arms hanging loosely over the chair arms. A knock on his door made him open his eyes. "Enter," he called.

Russet came into the study. She was dressed in riding attire; the tips of glistening riding boots appearing beneath a long, flared skirt. She wore a figure-hugging black riding jacket, buttoned up the front; a white silk cravat circled her neck, knotted beneath her chin and tucked into the fold of the jacket. Her hair was tied back and fastened in a ponytail beneath a narrow-brimmed hat, worn at a jaunty angle, giving her that cheeky look of impudence her father found so captivating.

"Are you unwell, Father," she asked.

"No, Russy," he sighed. "I am totally, absolutely and comprehensively exhausted." He pushed himself into a sitting position. "Lottie has been here for a whole hour. A whole hour! There cannot be another in the whole of this world that can chatter on as your sister does. For half the time she went on about a friend of a friend of a friend's children, one of whom, she says, is a genius at the age of two. What she spoke of is not one iota of interest to me but you know what she's like. Never could anybody speak for so long and yet say so little. I can see she will live with me forever for I doubt she will ever find a consort to bear such constant gibberish."

"But Father, she has always been like that. She dominates Kate to such an extent the poor girl is terrified to utter opinion on any topic. And she doesn't do mother any good either. Russet paused and then went on, "it is of Mother's condition I wish to speak."

"Oh dear, what has she done now?" Sir Marcus asked, a tone of resignation in his voice. "I understood she had desisted from throwing things at all and sundry."

"Oh she has stopped that." Russet threw her arms wide. "Now she refuses to wear any clothes. She is strutting about quite naked, looking at herself in the glass and imagining she is dressed in some elegant gown."

"Well, apart from keeping her to her room, what do you expect me to do?" Sir Marcus said with exasperation.

"I was wondering if you had invited Doctor Mathews to join our party this day."

Sir Marcus creased his brow "Yes," he said. "He has accepted my invitation and he should be here shortly. I suppose you require that he should examine her. He told me there was not a thing physically wrong with Mary's being. The strain on her brain when giving birth to Kate took her soundness of mind and the good doctor told me there is no hope of a cure. However, I shall do as you wish." He stood and walked to the open windows where Russet joined him.

They looked out on the bustling activities going on in the park. People were already crowding in. Some came in carriages, some on horseback. Several overcrowded hay-carts filled with joyful laughing people rolled along the drive. And then there were those who had travelled on foot. Many would have walked through the night all dressed in the finery of their 'Sunday best'. Clothes that were kept and worn only for church visits had been taken out of closets to be paraded with pride on this holiday occasion.

"You must excuse me, Father. I must leave you." She left his side, walked to the centre of the study and twirled around, letting her skirt balloon. Then as she skipped to the door, "I am to lead the ladies around the course and over the jumps. Wish me well, Father."

By the beginning of June Jamie had made considerable progress. He could almost clench the fingers of his impaired hand and his arm was at last showing signs of movement. His leg no longer trailed as a useless appendage but would not yet support his weight. Gunner and Walter had constructed a leather splint with steel braces that kept his knee straight. He had learned to throw the leg forward with a quick, twisting movement of his body, but there was no improvement in his facial appearance and he could not utter a sound. He was distressed by the way people shied away from him and even those with the best of intentions, attempting to be friendly, would turn away when they realised no answer would be forthcoming. At first, children of the village withdrew speedily upon sight of his face but soon gained courage when they found they were not to be chased and cuffed. They would run alongside the cart, screaming and placing fingers inside the corners of their mouths, dragging down their lips in mock emulation of his distorted face. They called him 'The Oaf'. The misnomer stuck and, much to his disgust, villagers began to refer to him by that name.

On the day of the festival Gunner and Walter were required at the Hall stables to assist with any mishaps; replacing thrown horseshoes or repairs to broken tackle. Wriggley was stationed on the equestrian course at the last jump as one of the stewards; replacing knocked over bars of the jumps and assisting remounts. He had taken Jamie with him, more as an act of friendship rather than the need of assistance and he requested him to find a place well clear of the contestants. Jamie found a place on a small hummock from where he could see the riders start the course before they disappeared over the hill. By turning his head he saw the first rider appear; a lady riding side-saddle, her horse skipping over the low jumps hardly changing stride. His eyes followed her and when she came up to the last jump her horse veered to the right and headed for the high fence. The rider was spurring the horse on but when it reached the fence the animal made no attempt to jump but halted abruptly sending the rider hurtling over the fence. She crashed to the ground and rolled limply towards a large elm tree where she lay writhing with back arched. Jamie found it quite amusing and as it was of no interest to him he remained where he was while others gathered around the prone figure. Then he heard the wail of a woman, followed by screams and shouts of "She's dead. She's dead." With his crutch he pulled himself upright and suddenly he felt a strange sensation of urgency. He began to hobble towards the crowd but it was too slow. He dropped the crutch and hopped on his good leg. Pushing people aside he looked down at a young woman. Her face was blue and she was quite still. He pulled away a woman kneeling by her side and placed the elbow of his left arm on her chin and opened her mouth. He put his fingers inside and felt for the tongue. It was well back but he nipped it and pulled it up. He felt for the pulse in her neck but could feel nothing. She had stopped breathing. Without knowing why he did it he turned her over on her stomach and pressed his hand into her back and pressed. Again he felt for the pulse. Nothing. Turning her he dragged her to him and with his back to the tree he had his good arm about her .He thumped her back. Then he lifted her face and put his crooked lips to hers and blew into her mouth. He squeezed her then blew. He repeated this and kept thumping her back. He felt blows raining down on his shoulders but he kept on.

Charlotte had been following her sister and arrived on the scene to see Jamie holding Russet and apparently kissing her. She had dismounted and with her crop she struck out at Jamie again and again.

"Get off my sister, you oaf!" She cried. "Stop him somebody! Stop him! He's ravishing my sister!

Some went to help Charlotte but then Russet coughed. She vomited. She took in a great breath of air. Her face had turned from the asphyxiating blue to a deathly white - but she was alive. Jamie laid her on her back and signed to the women to take over. He rolled out of the way and went in search of his crutch. Only then did he feel the pain of the blows he had received but it was not the physical pain that troubled him. His mind was in turmoil – how did he know to do what he had just done?

People were now rushing towards the last fence. A carriage was commandeered from a visitor and Russet was gently laid on the seat and taken to the Hall.

Charlotte was indignant at being pushed aside and when Captain Valiant Halgalleon rode up with his fellow officers she waved to catch his attention. He cut a fine figure in his red tunic, white breeches and braided hat.

"What is it about, Miss Roulette," he asked.

"That man," she shouted, pointing to Jamie who had now collected his crutch. "That man ravished my sister. Now she is on the verge of death." She waved her hands excitedly. "Do something Captain. Please do something."

Captain Halgalleon signalled his followers and told them of Charlotte's request. They serried about, pulling on reins, while the horses champed on their bit, as they circled, attempting to get close to their leader to hear his instructions.

The captain broke away and rushed at Jamie striking him with an outstretched foot and knocking him to the ground. Two of the soldiers dismounted and grabbed him. "Take him to the stables," the captain commanded. "They'll be emptied for now. We'll take our pleasure with him there. Never again will this stinkard have interest in the ladies. He will be thrashed within a hairs breadth of his life. Come."

Russet was taken to her bedroom where she lay on her bed fully clothed. Her face was ashen but she was breathing normally. Beads of sweat covered her brow and she remained in a state of unconsciousness. Doctor Jonah Mathews pushed fingers into her neck and felt her pulse. He was a small man in his early sixties and his head, topped by a grey wig, appeared far too big for his body. He wore pince-nez that seemed to balance precariously on the end of his large, bulbous nose and he glared over the top of them when addressing a person. But his face was kindly and one that inspired confidence.

"The beat of her heart is regular," he pronounced, "and there are signs of bruising and abrasions. Can some knowing person explain to me what happened." He turned to Sir Marcus. "This is very strange indeed, sir. I must know the circumstances for this unfortunate accident. Do you have a witness, or better, two? I prefer to hear at least two testimonies to gain an accurate account"

Sir Marcus left the room and returned shortly with a chambermaid and a scullery maid. They had both been helping with refreshments at the end of the course.

"Now," said the doctor, keeping his voice low and tempered. "Can you tell me what happened to Miss Russet?"

The girls looked frightened, holding their clenched hands to their chests. They looked at each other as if expecting the other to speak first.

"Come, come." The doctor encouraged. "Did you see the accident?"

Both girls nodded but remained tight-lipped.

Sir Marcus addressed them. "If you can tell us exactly what happened there will be..." He paused, then, "Half a guinea each for you."

Half a guinea was a great amount to serving girls so both began speaking together.

"One at a time, if you please." The doctor suggested.

The taller of the two then spoke first. "I saw Miss Russet a'coming to the ladies fence but the horse sort of swerved and went at the high one. Then it stopped, quick like, and she went flying over the rails."

"Yes and she were all flailing on the ground with her arms all over." The smaller one butted in.

"She was wriggling, like." The taller one came in again. "Then she went a funny colour – her face went all blue like."

"Blue, you say." The doctor stroked his chin.

"Aye, then she went still. Someone said she'd stopped breathing and she were dead and we all started to weep."

The smaller girl intending to earn her half guinea felt she had to contribute. "Then this cripple comes and knocks me out of the way." She uttered. "He sticks his fingers in her mouth then he feels her neck and then he turns her over and presses his hand on her back"

"Yes." The taller girl took over again. "Then he took her in his arms and started to hug her and kiss her and…"

"Explain that a little more." The doctor held out both his arms in a gesture of squeezing.

"He hugged her, then he kissed her. Oooh, with those lips." She wrinkled her nose. "Then he kept thumping her in the back."

"Yes." The other interrupted again. "Then Miss Charlotte comes up and starts hitting him with her crop and shouting for someone to help her 'cos he was ravishing her sister.

"And he took not one farthing's worth of notice. He just kept on doing it."

"And?" the doctor asked.

"Then she spewed up and came alive again."

The two girls stepped back towards the door, each hoping they had said enough to earn the promised reward.

"Remarkable, remarkable." The doctor strode back and forth, head down, deep in thought. Then he looked at Sir Marcus and said, "I have a friend, you know. He is a surgeon on one of his Majesty's ships of war."

Sir Marcus thought the doctor had a wandering of the mind. "What, sir, has that to with my daughter's plight?"

The doctor continued as if he had not heard the interruption, "his ship was off the coast of West Africa when a fellow jumped ship. He was followed and dragged ashore but was found to have drowned. He had no breath and no pump of the heart. Then along came a black fellow who turned him over and pressed the water from his lungs. Then he beat on his chest and blew air into his mouth. And do you know what? The fellow came to life." The doctor shrugged. "T'would have been better he were dead. Poor soul. He was taken back aboard, sentenced to two hundred lashes for desertion and his life gave out after but half of them."

"What are you saying?" Sir Marcus asked

The doctor stared at him over his pince-nez. "I am saying, good sir, that your daughter swallowed her tongue and but for this... this... cripple, you say?" He turned to the girls who nodded together. "But for this cripple, who somehow knew how to respond. How to retrieve a swallowed tongue. How to blow air into lungs, how to help a sickened heart. But for his fortitude, sir, your daughter would be dead." He paused then as if speaking to himself, "but how could a country cripple know of such things." Then louder he said, "indeed there is no doubt, sir, no doubt at all – your daughter owes her life to this man."

Sir Marcus looked at the ashen face of his beloved Russet. "If that be the truth good doctor, then I owe this fellow a priceless debt." He turned again to the girls. "Where can this man be found?"

Both girls showed reluctance to say more. Sir Marcus took two coins from a pocket of his waistcoat and jingled them in his hand.

Again both girls, spurred on by the promise of payment, began to speak as one. The taller girl slapped the other on the shoulder. "After they took Miss Russet in the carriage, Miss Charlotte went to the soldiers and I heard her say that the cripple had ravished Miss Russet. They knocked him down and took him away.

"What!" Sir Marcus cried out in exasperation. "The foolish, foolish girl. How could I have spawned such fatuous issue! Damned if her mouth must function before her brain." He stopped his tirade abruptly, realising the two servant girls were present. "To where did they take him – do you know?

"I saw 'em. They had him and they were near the stables."

"I must go there at once. Where's Totton?" Sir Marcus headed for the door.

"He's with 'em, sir."

"With who?"

"With the soldiers, sir."

"Aaaaah!" Sir Marcus gave the coins to the girls, threw his arms in the air and ran out.

Chapter Eight

Wriggley stood by helplessly when he saw the soldiers knock Jamie to the ground and then take him away. There was nothing he could have done on his own to stop them. When they departed, dragging Jamie with them, he retrieved the crutch and began to run in the direction of the stables where Gunner and Walter waited idly to offer their services to equestrian needs.

Sir Marcus ran out of the hall entrance and met up with his head forester, Jacob Manley, who was in the process of instructing men to fetch more charcoal for the fires. He explained the situation in a few words and Manley sent men away to gather others while Sir Marcus commandeered a carriage and ordered the driver to head for the stables.

When Gunner saw Captain Halgalleon and his troopers arrive at the stables he thought they were in need of his craft. They all dismounted and then he saw the bedraggled, bloodied Jamie being roughly bundled through a stable doorway. He grabbed his hammer and ran to the stable, followed by Walter. When he entered two of the soldiers were holding Jamie while a third, punched him in the face.

"Leave him be!" Gunners voice thundered and the soldiers turned to see the massive, menacing figure silhouetted against the light of the doorway, hammer in hand.

Halgalleon drew his sword and faced Gunner. "A step further and I shall run you through," he threatened.

"Aye," Gunner stood his ground, the heavy hammer held high. "But I'll take odds on you having a cracked skull a'fore I with a pierced heart."

"Put down your weapons, there will be no contention this day!" Sir Marcus Roulette pushed past Gunner and stood between him and Halgalleon. "You," he turned to Gunner. "See to that man. And you Sir." He addressed the Captain. "How dare you draw your sword in my precinct? You are guests here. All of you." He waved a hand towards the crowded doorway where a multitude of men tried to push their way into the stable. They jostled in the cobbled yard outside, all armed with hayforks, cudgels, spades and any weapon that had come to hand, all there to support the Master.

"Sir Marcus." Halgalleon protested. "We are about your business." He pointed a finger at Jamie. "This is the man who ravished your daughter. We were ordered to take him, so we brought him here to give him the punishment he deserves before he feels the hangman's rope"

"Ravished my daughter?" Sir Marcus spoke with a tone of mock astonishment. "And who may I ask saw this man do such a thing?" There was silence so he continued, "and who, sir, gave you such an order?"

"Why, your own daughter," Halgalleon said, with a bluster of triumph. His elation was short-lived.

"Aaah! And since when did a gallant Captain of Horse take orders from a hysterical woman? Are you not the courageous soldier boy, ready to fight for King and country?" Sir Marcus was now in full flow. "I believe you were named Valiant in the presence of our Lord. Whosoever christened you with that name chose well. What a brave fellow you are. How many battles have you fought, sir. None I'll be bound. Unless we consider the battle of Nestwith where you, the heroic Captain, led your troop into battle against an army of one impaired soul. Fie on you, Sir! Fie on you!" he made to leave but then turned back. "This man." He pointed at Jamie. "This man saved the life of my daughter and I shall remain in his debt unto eternity." He addressed Jamie, "what is your name?"

"He cannot speak. He is a mute." Walter said. His name is James Pitchforth – we call him Jamie."

"Could you take him to the hall. He looks as if he needs his wounds tending."

"We'd best take him to his home, Sir. He'll get no better treatment."

As he left Sir Marcus said, "this was supposed to be a day of enjoyment and happiness. Day of happiness! Huh! It will best be forgotten."

Captain Valiant Halgalleon watched Marcus Roulette leave. His facial expression was one of open hatred. He had been humiliated. Humiliated in the presence of common peasants, but more to his anger, he had been belittled in front of his own men. 'A day best forgotten' Roulette had said. Never. The happenings of this day Valiant Halgalleon could never erase from his mind.

When Sir Marcus returned to the hall he immediately climbed the stairs to the room where Russet lay on her bed. She was still dressed in her riding attire. Doctor Mathews was leaning over her. When Sir Marcus entered he straightened up and shook his head.

"I am afraid she has taken a turn for the worse," he said. "I have done all I can. What she needs now is more care than I can give her.

Oh God in heaven! Please God save my child." The tears began to flow down his cheeks as he looked down on his daughter's beautiful face. It was ashen. Beads of sweat formed on her brow. Her hair was wet and the pillow upon which her head rested was saturated with perspiration. Her whole body trembled as if she were afflicted with ague. Her eyes were closed and she was unconscious.

The doctor took hold of Sir Marcus by the arm and led him away from Russet and the many wailing women who crowded round her bed.

"I know a good lady, a midwife. I think perhaps you should ask her to attend your daughter," he whispered.

"Good God, man." Sir Marcus was nonplussed. "She's not with child."

"No. no." The doctor shook both hands in front of his face. "I have many times before had need of the good hands of this lady to tend the ill and infirm. The person I have in mind would well suit your needs here. She has suffered greatly recently but if she will avail herself to you then it could be a blessing for you will get no better."

"Then get her, Doctor."

When Maisy Pitchforth arrived at Nestwith Hall she was not sure what she had let herself in for. Doctor Mathews had said it was a matter of great urgency and that a daughter of Sir Marcus was gravely ill. Upon entering the bedroom she was appalled at the number of weeping women clustered round the bed. She took one look at the stricken, shaking figure on the bed and took immediate charge.

"Come, ladies. It's time to go." She put down the small leather bag she carried and ushered the women to the door. Some went quickly, others lingered while one remained at the bed unmoved by Maisy's request.

"You." She pointed at one of the women. "You stay. I shall be in need of your help."

A voice behind her said, "can I stay?"

"And who are you." Maisy asked.

"I'm Katherine – Russy's sister."

"Very well." Maisy turned to the patient. "Let's get her out of these wet clothes." She placed a hand on Russet's brow then she said to Katherine, "close that window, no, just leave it a little open...you." She spoke to the woman she had selected to stay. "I want a fire lit in that grate and I want to see the cook. Now!"

The chambermaid hurried out and Maisy began to untie the cravat. It was only then did she realise that the woman who had been nearest to the head of the bed was still there. As she lifted Russet's head to pull the cravat away, her hands were pushed away.

"I do not want you touching her!" The woman snapped.

"And who are you?" Maisy asked. "Did you not hear me say you were to leave the room?"

"I am the mistress of this house," snapped the woman. "I am Charlotte Roulette. My mother is indisposed and while she is so I direct the household. I did not ask you here so will you kindly take your leave."

Maisy was becoming angry. "Well Mistress of the House,

I was asked to come here by the master of the house and his word is above yours. He is my master for the time and I do his bidding so there is only one mistress in this room and that is me."

"I am telling you to leave. Now!"

"Katherine." Maisy's patience was exhausted. "Open that door. And hold it open." Katherine went to do her bidding while Maisy went round the bed, grabbed Charlotte by the scruff of the neck and pushed her through the open door onto the landing.

Katherine stood there wide-eyed and open-mouthed. Never before had she seen or heard anybody get the better of her domineering sister. Even after Maisy had closed the door she remained staring at her with admiration.

When the cook knocked and came in it was like a soul-mate's reunion. "Well, if it ain't Maisy Pitchforth!" The cook bounced into the room her full-bosomed figure shaking like jelly.

"Jossy Makepiece!" Maisy laughed. "I need your help Jossy. I want you to find some warming bricks. Put 'em in the stove until warm – well you know what I want. I need water – just warm – for drinking so it must be clear, and plenty of hot water for washing."

The chambermaid came back carrying kindling, a scuttle holding precious coals and she was followed by a houseman bearing an armful of logs.

When the houseman departed Maisy turned to Katherine and said, "now we can attend to your sister."

The days that followed were traumatic. The three agreed to

take it in turns to get some sleep but all were so desperate for Russet to be well sleep did not come to any of them. The shivering had stopped and Maisy had managed to get her to take water. The choking and spluttering that had gone on in the beginning had now ceased and although her eyes remained tight shut she drank the water they offered.

On the fourth day Russet opened her eyes.

Whispers and gossip travel speedily in rural communities. As a story passes from one another it changes in context. The news of Russet's accident travelled fast and with it the actions of Jamie. But it grew and it grew. The story of her death and of Jamie kissing her back to life was talked about in the market places, taverns, village halls and everywhere that country folk meet. Then came the tale of the golden glow of a halo around Jamie's head as he brought her back to life. One woman claimed she saw angels flying above them. Another said she saw Christ and the Virgin Mary bless them. Nobody seemed to worry that the women who made these claims were nowhere near the scene.

The black eye was but a dark shadow and the swollen nose was back to normal when Jamie took the horse and cart and rode into the village to collect the weekly game that his three friends provided for Maisy's hot pot. Rabbits, hares and any meats that would add to the nutritional goodness of the stew. He would also carry out any errand they required.

He saw the children gathering before he reached the first building and he prepared himself for their verbal onslaught. It was not forthcoming. As he neared them they came out to meet him in silence and walked at either side and behind the cart, some with a hand resting on the cart as if it were some revered object.

As he passed through the village people stopped and stared solemnly. A man made a feeble wave of the hand. Another bowed his head. A woman curtsied. Jamie felt embarrassed at the response. He thought he might have preferred the abuse.

The reverend Butler was in a quandary. With hands clasped behind his back and head down he strode the length of the churchyard with Isiah Snufty close on his heels. As he turned at the end of the path the curate dodged one way and then another to take his place behind his senior. Then he walked close, head bobbing, nose high as if a bad smell pervaded even this sphere of God's domain.

The rector ignored his shadow as if he did not exist. He had greater issues to resolve. 'What can I do to salvage some value from this predicament?' The concentration of his mind bore on his own perplexity. He knew of the accident to the Roulette woman and of the following action by Jamie Pitchforth. He had also been informed of the whispers and speculations that followed. Mistress Pitchforth and her son were barred from attending church on his order and he had preached to his congregation of their sins and how God had forsaken them. He had spoken of their wicked ways and that the son bore 'The mark of Satan' on his face to certify their wretchedness. Now he would have no option but to recant his own accusations of impiety. But how? How? How?

Jamie called at the smithy where Gunner and Walter loaded on to his cart two half barrels of pigswill and some sheaves of straw. He was to take it to Wrigley's holding half a mile down the road. As he approached the church he saw the rector and his curate walking together among the gravestones.

The Reverend Butler could hardly contain himself when he saw Jamie approaching. He hurried through the lichgate and onto the road. He held up one hand and crossed himself with the other. God had come to his rescue.

Chapter Nine

When Sir Marcus was allowed to see Russet he was shocked and distressed by her appearance. She had lost much weight and she lay in the bed, pale and limp like a discarded rag doll. Maisy would only allow short visits and although he spoke words of affection and encouragement Russet was unable to answer him. She smiled and moved her lips but had not yet the strength to speak.

Charlotte and Katherine had come to approve of Maisy and they quickly accepted the authority of the older woman, working together for the good of their patient. The 'Mistress Pitchforth' title was dropped and she became just plain 'Maisy.' The surprise was Charlotte. After being evicted by Maisy her attitude had completely changed and she was quick to obey Maisy's every request. The atmosphere had become one of unity with a common purpose. She was still as talkative as ever but as soon as she began her chatter in the bedroom Maisy would raise a finger at her and she would clamp her lips together like a naughty child.

Jossy was kept busy preparing hot broth, most of which went cold while the women tried to get Russet to take it. This morning she had prepared a saddlebag of food for Totton. After the events of the past few days and the foolery of Captain Halgalleon, his fanatical urge for everything military had waned. Sir Marcus met him as he was leaving.

"Are you off then, Tott?

"Yes, Father." He held the saddlebag over his arm. "I thought I would travel north and meet the herd. As this is the first time we have accommodated them here I thought I would take a rough count of the sheep to shear. We will then know how many workers we'll need to hire and how much of an area of pasture to make available."

Sir Marcus waited on the threshold to watch his son ride away. Totton turned in the saddle and waved. 'At least something good has come of all this,' Sir Marcus thought. 'Poor Russy lying broken upstairs but Tott seems to have taken a new lease on his responsibilities'

When the rector had intercepted Jamie as he passed the church he had asked him to alight and had blessed him there and then. He invited him into the church for further blessing and exorcism in the name of God from the clutches of the Devil, asserting that the blessing and forgiveness applied also to his mother. As the clergyman ushered Jamie out of the church he had stressed that the absolution meant neither he nor his mother were now under the influence of the Devil. They were again accepted as members of his flock.

The Rector was pleased with himself. He had released himself from a tricky situation and now here he was at the door of Nestwith Hall to complete his mission of impunity.

When he was shown upstairs to Russet's room he found the door locked. He knocked. Maisy pulled the door ajar only far enough for her to see it was the Rector demanding entrance. She told him to wait, closed the door quickly and shot the bolt. There was more pounding on the door. Maisy rushed to the bedside and whispered in Russet's ear and silently mouthed "The Rector" to Lottie and Kate. She went back to the door and allowed the rector to enter.

"Ah, the sickened, poorly lady!" He said in his loud sermonic style . "I have come to give you the Lord's blessing and His help to heal your wounds." He moved to the side of the bed and looked down at the pale face. The eyes were closed as she obeyed Maisy's whispered advice and feigned sleep.

"Awaken dear lady!" The Rector commanded. "Awaken and hear the word of the Lord!"

Russet remained unmoved.

"I am the servant of the Lord and I shall hear you confess your sins! Awaken I say!" He leaned closer and Maisy went to stand at the opposite side of the bed.

The Reverend Butler was perplexed. It was said a cripple had brought her back to life and he could not even waken her from sleep. "The Lord has put upon you this affliction as a punishment for your sins. You must repent. Awaken!" He was shouting now and he put a hand to her shoulder as if to rouse her. Maisy caught hold of his wrist but it was Charlotte who came to the rescue.

"Rector," she matched the vociferous tone of his voice. "Perhaps you would hear my confession. And I wanted to ask you of the well-being of Mistress Snowgroot?

"Who?" The Rector looked nonplussed.

"Mistress Snowgroot." The name was a figment of her imagination and the first silly made-up name that came into her head. "She is one of your flock. Does she fare well?" Charlotte now stood in front of the Rector and put her face close to his, the words coming out of her mouth incessantly.

The Rector tried his best to interrupt but to no avail - Charlotte was in full flow. He moved backwards towards the door as she asked him question after question; moving after him, step for step. He felt for the door handle as the endless chatter went on. He opened it but there was no escape. Onto the landing and down the stairs Charlotte kept up her tirade of inane prattle. He backed through the entrance hall and out of the open door. There he attempted to make apologies for his departure as he rushed down the steps to his carriage where Isaiah Snufty waited patiently, reins in hand.

Charlotte closed the door and looked up to where Maisy was standing on the landing. She brushed her hands together, screwed up her face and winked. "Well, that has rid us of this turbulent priest," she quoted.

Very slowly Russet made her recovery. After four weeks she managed to stand and walk around the room but she was very frail and her arms and legs were skeletal. To all involved with her recovery her soundness of mind was an answer to their prayers but when she said she wanted to go out Sir Marcus was apprehensive. He consulted Maisy and the doctor and the answer was that for the present it would be better for her to rest until her strength returned.

The week following was one of the busiest for the Roulettes. Estate workers were brought in from their various duties – foresters, herdsmen, carpenters, horsemen, and coachmen. Everyone was expected to help when the great herd arrived.

Four thousand five hundred sheep crowded through the gateway into the lush Nestwith Hall Estate parkland and fields. They had been driven slowly from the north travelling at no more than four to five miles a day, heads down, feeding as they went.

Now they came in a swirling surge. The bells of the lead sheep clanging, dogs yapping, the shouts, commands and whistles of the drovers all added to the clamorous bleating from thousands of ovine throats. The drovers' route was used by many and was well worn. Cattle, mules, horses and sheep continually gnawed the herbage and feed was in short supply. To the hungry horde the lush pastures of Nestwith Hall Estate came as welcome provender. After all the sheep had passed through the gateway they were followed by a retinue of two covered wagons pulled by oxen, several pack mules carrying food for the men and the pack animals and lastly, a small low cart pulled by a donkey. The cart was open at the top but covered with a wide mesh net. Inside was one solitary pig – a young sow.

The drovers looked forward to the break. The boring occupation of droving gave way to the frenetic undertaking of separating the full fleeced sheep from those shorn before the drive began, then guiding them to the group of shearers waiting, clippers in hand. When all was done and the fleeces bundled several would be set aside as payment for grazing. For the remainder Sir Marcus paid cash.

During the activities The Reverend Butler paid a visit. He insisted on blessing the herdsmen, the workers, the pastures and the sheep but not the dogs. The Rector had been bitten so many times when visiting his parishioners he regarded the canine species to have been moulded by the prince of darkness.

Shepherds live a lonely existence on northern moors and fells. Most were religious men who lived with their God for company. The Reverend Butler took advantage of this fact because it gave him a captive audience for his sermons of righteousness. When he turned up again for the third day of the activities and insisted that tools be dropped to hear his verbosity even the most faithful of the men became impatient.

"And when do you plan to move on," The Rector asked of the head shepherd.

"Och, I think we'll be starting out Sunday." The man turned to his colleagues and they all nodded agreement.

"No! No!" The Rector was adamant. "I am told your sheep will be driven through the village. It would not be fitting for you to do so on the Sabbath. Any day but the Sabbath - for six days shalt thou labour and on the seventh day..."

"Aye, aye, aye." The shepherd shook his head. "We'll be going another day then - if it suits."

The next time the rector turned up, when all was about finished, the herdsmen set their dogs on him. The Reverend Butler and his curate beat a hasty retreat but the Rector was in a furious rage at being spurned.

The shearing over, the sheep well fed and payment in hand, many of the drovers walked into the village to sample the strong ale and spirits at the local inn - and anything else of pleasurable gratification. It so happened that the village sported two very active ladies of easy virtue, Monica Woodcock was the fairer of the two, and she was considered ugly. Her charge of two pence was thought by many to be exorbitant. The other, Tanner Fanny, whose name derived not from any remuneration she solicited for her services, but from the fact that she worked in the tannery. Her work consisted of the scraping and cleaning of fresh hides and the stench of the putrefying matter went with her. She bragged that never had she taken off all her clothes at any one time and never had she taken a bath. She was a big woman, six feet tall and her enormous breasts bulged beneath her loose, stained blouse like huge pumpkins reaching down below her waist. Her head was covered with a piece of cloth tied at the back of her head and what could be seen of her hair was greased and matted.

Her work, of the most menial, brought her hardly enough to buy food so she augmented her income from the drunks in the Wheatsheaf Inn. It was said that nobody sober took advantage of her favours and some even suggested she was still a virgin. Walter Lupton proffered that it took a man ten tankards of the Wheatsheaf strong ale and half a bottle of rum before she even began to look handsome. By the time a man had consumed that amount his sense of smell had deserted him and his physical capabilities non-existent. Fanny would encourage her victims to the barn at the rear of the inn and she would go through their pockets as she resisted their drunken attentions. But Fanny had been caught. She had taken money from a traveller but he had not been as drunk as she thought. She had been before the magistrate and the rector had spoken against her and demanded she be whipped. The magistrate was William Bull, the owner of the Bullington House estate, and he had no love for the Rector of Nestwith. To spite the rector he had shown leniency and sentenced her to twenty-four hours in the pillory. She knew she had been very lucky to get away without a whipping and, although she would have preferred sitting in the stocks, she kept her own counsel.

Twenty-three drovers crowded into the taproom of the Wheatsheaf Inn that Friday evening, all with cash in their pockets. Monica Woodcock was seated in her corner with an eye out for custom when the herdsmen entered. She counted them in and her mind went to work – twenty-three two pence's she thought - that's three shillings and ten pence. Almost four shillings! She had never owned that much money. Monica began her play.

Drink was the first order for thirsty men and the tankards were filled and re-filled. Monica teased the men but when one asked her price she decided to raise her charges.

"Three pence." She said.

The man looked her up and down. "Too much," he said.

Monica did not mind the rebuff; she could always bring her price down. Her opponent, Fanny, was indisposed in the pillory – she had the whole gaggle to herself.

Darkness was closing in when one man rose from his seat and went out of the building to the roadway; a jug of strong beer clutched in his hand. He looked across the village green and saw someone fastened in the pillory. He sauntered across and saw it was a woman. She was so tall she was bent over from the hips to allow her to get her neck in the slot. Her hands were firmly fixed in the holes at either side of her head. He slowly walked around her. Even in the failing light he cringed when he saw her face but he took pity on her and put his jug to her lips. She drank greedily until the man pulled the jug away and strolled nonchalantly back to the inn. He took a seat next to one of the older men, nudged him and whispered in his ear. The drover passed on the message and it went round the tavern causing great peals of laughter and nods of heads. Someone produced a wooden bowl and poured ale into it from his own jug. Others did the same, strong beer was added but when the purpose became known, cheap Dutch gin was donated and poured into the concoction to increase its potency.

A drover carefully carried the bowl as the whole group followed him out, many carrying lanterns as they gathered on the village green where Fanny stood pilloried by the neck and wrists. The contraption was intended for persons of lesser stature and her legs and back already ached and her mouth and throat were so dry she longed for somebody to take pity and offer her another drink. She faced away from the Wheatsheaf Inn and did not see the approaching drovers but when they crowded about her she showed her annoyance.

"Be off wi' ye," she shouted, followed by a string of vulgar profanities.

"Won't ye be wantin' a wee drink then, lovely lady." A drover held the brimming bowl invitingly in front of Fanny's scowling face. "Drop o' the best this is. Are ye to show ingratitude for our generosity?" He pushed the bowl under her nose and when Fanny smelt the brew her attitude changed and she opened her mouth and pursed her lips. The drover tormented her by putting the bowl to her lips and then drawing back before she could drink. Again and again he teased and again and again Fanny stuck out her bottom lip in the hope of a taste but to no avail, and the distortion of her face brought laughter from the gathering crowd. Eventually, the man tipped the bowl and Tanner Fanny slurped the liquid.

"Can ye dance, lady?" The drover with the bowl asked. "If ye dance ye gets another bibble." He held the bowl under her nose. "Come on, lass. Gie' us a dance." A drover took from a pocket a flute-like instrument made from the leg-bone of a sheep and he began to play. A man stood in front of the pilloried Fanny, like a dancing partner he began to dance to the music. To clapping and shouts of encouragement Fanny danced; her great breasts hung below the timber frame and as she lifted her feet in time to the music they flopped from side to side in unison like two uncontrollable bulbous pendulums. Her huge buttocks moved up and down with gusto and as she was awarded more of the brew for her efforts her eyes became glazed, her face fixed in a drunken grin, and her head wobbled like a blown pig bladder afloat on a breeze-stirred pool.

A carnival atmosphere prevailed. Villages came out of their homes and joined the dancing drovers; young girls, old women and their men folk cavorted and laughingly took part in the merriment, and in the middle of all the jollity Tanner Fanny stomped to the tune of the flute and noisily imbibed her reward. Slowly at first her on-the-spot gait began to slow and with aching legs she found it difficult to keep up with the beat of the music. The alcohol took effect and her mind reeled. Her back ached and the muscles of her legs finally gave way as her brain became befuddled. With the weight of her body held up only by her wrists and neck, she began to croak as she fought to breathe.

When the novelty wore off and the performance at an end, the crowd slowly dispersed. The drunken drovers departed to their camp, raucous laughter and the sound of the flute fading into the distance. Monica Woodcock stood at the door of the Wheatsheaf Inn and she was furious. Her potential customers had all left and she found herself alone, with all her hopes of a profitable evening in shreds.

Chapter Ten

The first Saturday of each month saw the travelling market come to Nestwith. This was the monthly excuse for the wives of the rural community to meet for the purpose of listening to gossip and the hearsay of local lore. Their men folk accompanied them to frequent the taprooms of the two local drinking establishments on the pretext of discussing farm prices and anything else that came to mind.

Vendors set up their stalls along the sides of the main street and the fringes of the village green. Whole families of travellers busied themselves erecting the stalls and laying out their wares. Tanner Fanny remained in the pillory and would only be released after her sentence expired at noon. She had already become a target for the visitors' children and was plastered with rotten eggs, fruit, a dead cat and anything else that came to hand. Tanner Fanny was not a happy woman.

By ten o'clock in the morning the taproom of the Wheatsheaf was packed. Men were cramped onto benches around wooden tables packed close to make room for the expected trade. A blue haze hung over the drinkers like a ghostly awning as smokers breathed tobacco through long, curved-stemmed clay pipes. The hum of conversation, the shouts of orders for more ale, the shrieks of the barmaids as many a bottom was pinched in the passing, all added to the good humoured raillery to be found in any country tavern on market day.

Across the road in the Rose and Crown it was a very different scene. Ladies in their spotless gowns seated round linen covered tables sipping camomile tea. Others walked among the stalls looking for bargains, their varied gowns, tailored from linens to silks, almost touched the ground as they paraded their vanity. Those who could afford wore hats of many shapes and sizes; a portrayal of country wealth and status.

Some stallholders shouted the benefits of their wares, their persuasive banter inviting customers to buy. Others remained silent, waiting for custom. One stall bore an array of cheeses of differing sizes, some encased in muslin jackets, others with wedges cut from them for presentation. Honey, jams, hen eggs, duck eggs, bantam eggs, plover eggs and quail eggs, all hemmed-in between the cheeses to keep them from rolling off the display. Some stalls carried vegetables; carrots, turnips, cabbages, onions, kale and potatoes. A covered meat stall; the owner employing two boys with birchwood whisks to keep flies away from the rows of rabbits, hares, and game birds hanging by hooks from a high cross-member of the stall. Cuts of pork and mutton offered for sale lay on slabs with blood from the sweating meat running onto the roadway. Tinkers banged tin pots together to attract attention. Pots and pans, wooden bowls and wooden plates, pewter bowls and pewter plates, stewing pots, knives and spoons made up their merchandise. And to complete their inducement they offered to sharpen knives for free on a pedalled grinding stone as encouragement to purchase. There were stalls with bolts of cloth, skirts, gowns, off-cuts of material and second hand clothing begged, or borrowed, from the houses of the cities' elite and now piled high for the sorting hands of prospective buyers.

Mistress Brookside was a milliner from Loylton and she had set up a trestle table upon which she had placed several straw-filled canvas bags; on each such head a hat of her design and make; a colourful display much favoured by the ladies. There was more, all trading their stock, making up the busy, bustling assemblage of a country market.

Today was a special occurrence for The Reverend Butler. Today he had a captive audience. Today was the day of the month when he could sermonize to the many sinners other than of his parish. He preened himself as he prepared to go forth and Isaiah Snufty fussed about him; clothes brush in hand, grooming his master's cassock. He carefully brushed the rector's hat and handed it to him. Only then did he prepare himself for the morning tour. The Reverend strode out into the road and headed for the village. He walked with his arms swinging away from his body with an exaggerated flourish, more like the swagger of a successful prizefighter than a man of the cloth. The curate ran after him, fastening his own cassock as he hastened to catch up and almost tripping over his own feet as he stooped to affix the lower buttons whilst on the move.

The rector walked between the stalls, greeting people and continually making the sign of the cross. He was in his element. He considered himself far more important than officers of the parish, on a higher level even than the magistrates. He was the messenger of the Lord and on God's business. He stopped to talk to a stallholder. He blessed the man and his goods and said a prayer for him. He moved to the next but a whispered warning passed around the market and stalls became mysteriously unmanned as he approached.

Everyone within a radius of twenty miles had fore knowledge that this day was Nestwith market day. Everybody, that is, except the drovers of the prodigious flock of sheep who were preparing to continue their trek.

The Nestwith Estate was bordered to the south by a river and the impenetrable Black Wood. Sir Marcus had in mind to make way for future herds by felling a swathe of trees to form a fenced route through the woodland. At this time the only way for the vast flocks to travel south was through the village. It was anticipated that the drovers would begin their journey on the Monday but with work done, the sheep sheared and grazed and money in the purse, the head herdsman, not wanting to waste two days made the decision to move.

When the mass of sheep reached the village there was no stopping them. The lead animals, their neck bells clanging, came to a halt at the sight of the thronged marketplace but pressure from the animals behind pushed them forward.

There was near panic among the stallholders and men rushed forward with boards, benches, anything that would form a barrier. They stood in front of their stalls holding the objects in front to funnel the sheep away.

The rector, seeing danger, seizing his chance to lionise himself to his parishioners and the market fraternity, swaggered forward to meet the oncoming mass. He held his hands high and, Canute-like, he commanded them to turn around and return the way they came. He stood his ground but was soon overtaken. The curate was behind him but had to move quickly when the oncoming tide almost swept him off his feet.

Somehow the rector remained standing and as the sheep came on they split into two groups, running on either side of him. This made matters worse for the men who were attempting to keep the creatures to the centre of the road and away from their precious wares. The rector and his curate then became part of the flock as they were driven through the village propelled by the driving force of the throng. Twice the priest fell under the hooves but managed to get to his feet. He lost his hat. He could not free himself and with his dignity in tatters he pleaded imploringly to his Maker for delivery as he was pushed along, out of the village and down the Loylton road.

As the herd moved on past the smithy they were followed by the oxen-pulled wagons, the pack animals and the small cart containing the sow. Unfortunately for the luckless occupiers of the village of Nestwith this young sow had come into season. This young sow was feeling licentious. This young sow was in need of a boar.

King George III the Second awoke from his siesta and sniffed the air. He jerked his head as if his senses played tricks. No, there it was again. He got to his feet and sniffed again. There was no mistake. As his favourite hormonic odour filled his nostrils he jumped in the air, turned a circle and dashed out of the sty. Up the ramp he went and with a gigantic, sexually motivated leap launched himself off the end. Realising his mistake his thick, stumpy legs galloped in protest as he hurtled through the air. In his exuberance he had exceeded his previous leaps, soaring over the straw intended to soften his fall and landed with a body-crunching jar into the mud and filth of his own making.

He grunted with rage. He lifted his snout and sniffed again. It was there. No mistake. A female of his species needed his services - and she was very nearby.

He rushed to the gate and sniffed again. He could see movement but his impaired eyes could not discern what was happening in the road. Frustrated he tore at the planks of the gate. His tusks found a weakness and a board snapped. He tore it away with his teeth and continued until the gap was large enough for him to squeeze through.

He saw the movement of legs - many legs. His acute sense of smell told him these creatures were not the objects of his desire but the aroma came to him again and it befuddled his mind. He had to find the sow. He put down his head and he charged into the mass of sheep.

King George III the Second had very little sense of direction so his charge was not in a straight line. Rushing this way and that, parting the sheep as they stampeded to get out of his way, he zigzagged through the mass and mayhem prevailed.

Trying to escape from the grunting beast the flock split into smaller groups. Some went left, some right. The tinker's stall was the first to feel the unstoppable weight of the crush. Sheep crowded into it until it collapsed throwing pots, pans and all the paraphernalia of the tinker's trade into the road and under the hooves of the rampaging horde. One after another the stalls were brought down. Vegetables were strewn across the road and ignored by the herbivore animals that would normally delight in such delicacies. Men were shouting. Women screaming. The bleating of the sheep added to a cacophonous clamour.

Mistress Brookside attempting to salvage her millinery was mown down along with her trestle display. She held on to her favourite hat but it caught on the curled horn of a passing ewe and the animal disappeared into the crush and only the hat could be seen bobbing among the heads.

The herdsmen were doing their best to contain their charges but many were suffering hangovers from the previous night and others were still drunk.

A misspelled signboard at the open door of the Wheatsheaf Inn welcomed visitors. Sheep poured through the doorway and into the taproom. There chaos reigned. Men climbed onto tables to escape the melee but the tables were knocked from under them by the sheer weight of the animals. Legs went in the air. Bodies were trampled on. Cries of woe rent the air. Screams of the barmaids gave shrill vibrancy to the sustained uproar. Barrels of ale toppled and smashed, the liquid gushing out and spreading over the floor. Men rolled in it. Sheep slipped and fell only to rise, dripping with the wasted beverage. In the space of a minute the atmosphere had changed from a place of peaceful bonhomie to one where men fought men to get out. Monica Woodcock had been soliciting her trade in the Wheatsheaf when the sheep entered. She saw the danger and climbed onto the high windowsill, her feet above the height of the tallest of sheep. From her vantage she could view the chaos and destruction sweeping through the village. She could also see the figure of the hung-over Tanner Fanny, a captive in the pillory. She giggled to herself as she watched sheep collide with Fanny's legs, knocking them aside to leave her hanging by the neck and wrists. She would regain her stance only to have her legs knocked away again.

At the other side of the road the tea-taking women in their finery watched through the window of the tearoom showing polite amusement at the mayhem outside. But the door of The Rose and Crown was also open and a mass of sheep took this route to escape the maddened monster in their midst. In they came. Some took to the stairs. Some went through to the kitchen and others turned and entered the tearoom in a milling, bleating pack. Women screamed and like the men in the Wheatsheaf they took to the tables only to have them turned over. Some ladies climbed onto the low bay windowsill but when the animals pressed toward them they leaned against the frame and the whole window came out and fell onto the backs of milling sheep outside, the screaming women with it.

On the green Tanner Fanny could not escape. With her head and hands firmly locked in the pillory she had to withstand the onslaught. A horn caught her skirt and ripped it. Another tore a piece out of it leaving one ample buttock bare. Horns grazed her legs and then one came close and again her legs were knocked from under her and she was left hanging by her neck and wrists. She howled, bawled and screamed but nobody would brave the chaos to help her.

King George III the Second was becoming increasingly frustrated. He could still smell the scent of female desire but he could not find her. His nose sniffed the air. It was still there, but where? Then he saw it. A great bare buttock. The sow was there for the taking.

Tanner Fanny was becoming very distressed. Her head ached and she felt sick and was beginning to wish she had been whipped and let go rather than subjected to the torment and indignities she had suffered. Nothing could be worse, she thought. Then above the bleating of the sheep she heard grunting. She could not look behind her because her neck was locked firmly between the woodwork. She felt something brush roughly against her bare legs. Then the drooling snout appeared as the boar circled the pillory. She was getting hoarse but she bawled out again for somebody to release her.

King George III the Second's frustration heightened. He grunted loudly and sniffed the air. This was not the one. He turned away to continue his search.

From her position by the taproom window Monica had witnessed the antics of the boar at the pillory and she was beside herself with laughter. Thick, rough textured curtains, dragged down in the confusion lay at her feet. She grabbed one along with a sash and tucking it under her arm she ventured out, easing herself slowly along the entrance hall with her back to the wall. She picked her way through the debris in the road and came up behind the tormented Tanner Fanny She began to grunt and snort and squealed like a pig as Fanny bellowed, hooted and screamed in horror.

Monica could not contain herself and the grunting turned to raucous laughter. She took the curtain and threw it over the huge buttocks, wrapped it round the waist and made it fast with the sash.

"You fancies a bit o' pork then, does you Fanny? She could hardly get the words out for laughing.

"You!" Fanny fumed. "You bitch!"

"Been bored, Fanny, have you?" She held her sides and laughed at her own joke.

"I'm done for, lass." Fanny's voice rasped. "I've 'ad enough."

"Trouble wi' you is your never satisfied!" Monica exclaimed. "Dancin' wi' twenty men last night and the promise of pork today. What more could a woman want?" She started laughing again.

"I mean it Monica. I can't stay round here now – I'll be a laughin' stock. When I get out this thing I'm off to a city. Nobody prattles in cities. Nobody cares. How much longer have I got in here?" She asked.

Monica looked up at the sky. "Bout an hour, I'd say." She turned and looked at the chaotic mess and litter. The sheep had gone and a weird silence enveloped the village in the aftermath as people disentangled themselves from the clutter. The upheaval and clamour was gone and in the litter of the road nothing moved – except for a young sow standing with legs braced to support the mighty King George III the Second who straddled her. He held his head high, his little eyes half closed, emitting low grunts and squeals, oblivious to the confusion about him as he concentrated wholly and solely on maintaining his rhythm.

Chapter Eleven

"I tell you, Tott, we cannot be held responsible." Sir Marcus was adamant. "Once the sheep left this property – once they were all herded out and on to the road our accountability ceased."

Totton shook his head. "The people of the village are our responsibility, Father. They are suffering loss and we should help them."

"We are not in a position to do so." Sir Marcus was showing impatience. "We have a bounden duty to repair any structural damage. I am told that apart from three windows and a small amount of brickwork there is none."

"But Father, the two inns are devastated – wrecked. The ground floors of both will not be in use for weeks. Think of the income lost to the landlords."

"Are you asking that we should alter our agreements with the tenants and take upon ourselves the repair of the interior?" Sir Marcus asked, incredulously.

Well if we are not bound to renovate the damage, who is?"

Sir Marcus now displayed brusqueness at his son's attitude. "Oh for God's sake Tott! We are not obliged to repair damage to the interior. That is the business of the tenant. As for who should be held accountable for the whole fiasco then I suggest the owners of the sheep, or the drovers, or the owner of the damned pig that caused the havoc. Or maybe all three - but not the Nestwith Estate." He thought for a few seconds and then, "I was given to believe that the sheep would leave on Sunday. Why was that arrangement changed?"

"I rode after the flock this morning and spoke with the drovers. I was told that the rector had told them they could move on any day but Sunday." Totton held his hands out in a gesture of helplessness. "We have a priest who acts in the name of God but thinks he is himself God." He paused, then, "can we not assist the people with their costs?"

Totton was standing in front of his father, who was seated behind his desk.

"Sit down Tott." Sir Marcus said, a forlorn tone in his voice. "I thought your intention was to follow a military career but as you now appear to be taking more interest in family affairs it is time you knew the truth regarding your dear Uncle Oliver and the financial legacy he left."

He related the devious actions of Oliver and the true state of affairs regarding the estate finances. "So you see, Tott," he ended. "We must avoid expenditure where possible - until we find our feet." He placed his hands on his face, fingers pressed onto his closed eyes. He slowly dragged the hands downward and opened his eyes with a gesture of tiredness.

"We have at last sold our old home together with the land. With the proceeds we can pay two thirds of the monies owing. I have met with most of the creditors and they have agreed to wait for the other third payment, with interest, of course. We have no alternative but to sell the London house. I had dearly hoped we could hang onto it for the sake of the girls.

The use of the 'we' in place of 'I' had not gone unnoticed. For the first time Totton felt involved, and with a new sense of duty to the family.

Maisy had become part of the Roulette household. She

organised the maids, the housemen, and even the boisterous cook, Jossy, came to her for instruction. The every-day running of the hall had slowly come under her jurisdiction. She arranged the attendance on Lady Roulette and Charlotte had now established the habit of asking advice on the daily menu before passing it on to the cook. Maisy's orders came with encouragement and with praise when carried out to her approval. She refused to be called 'Mistress Pitchforth' and insisted it be 'Maisy.' She was thus addressed but with the greatest respect. A new and happy atmosphere prevailed at Nestwith Hall

Maisy was amazed at the turn of events. Charlotte and Katherine had gone to Loylton on a shopping expedition. Before they departed Katherine had asked if there was anything they could buy for her. She had said there was nothing and Katherine had wished her goodbye and then kissed her cheek. Charlotte had come forward and she too had kissed Maisy, with an added hug.

Maisy had lost her husband and three sons, gained an adopted son whom she loved dearly and also the regard of the three Roulette girls who gave her as much attention and affection as she gave them. It was as if she had lost one family and gained another. Her love and cherished memory of her husband and boys would never diminish but, even though it was so close, but in her mind it seemed so long ago.

Russet had been determined to shake off her debility and venture out. She felt her confinement had gone on long enough and it was time to get back to normality. Her father was standing at the foot of the stairs one day when she came flouncing down with an exaggerated display of well-being.

"I am ready to venture forth, Father Dear." She laughed, a deep chuckle he had so missed.

"Not on your own, you are not," he said in a jovial voice but with trenchant firmness.

"Then I must choose a chaperon, Father."

"No. I shall choose an escort for you." Sir Marcus said. "And you will not walk. You will go in a carriage.

"I want Pitchforth to accompany me then!" She exclaimed.

"Oh no!" He shook his head and waved a hand in dismissal of the suggestion. "If it is to be a man then he must be able-bodied. Somebody able to look after you."

"I don't know how you dare stand there and say that." She stamped a foot. "This man delivered me from death. I am aware of what he did for me. What better an attendant to see to my interest than the man who saved my life?"

"Hold! Hold! Hold!" Sir Marcus held up his hands, palm outwards. "Do not fluster yourself girl. If it be Pitchforth you want then so be it. But, you will have to find him new attire. I will not have you accompanied by a man looking like a peasant – even if he is one." Thus it was decided.

Maisy had helped Jamie into his new livery and now, standing in the hallway while they awaited Russet, she walked round him as he fidgeted, hat in hand, embarrassment showing on his crooked face. He wore black stockings and black boots with polished metal buckles. The costume was brown; knee breeches, a thigh-length jacket, fawn waistcoat and a white shirt. Around his neck he wore a tightly tied cravat and a three-cornered hat completed the outfit

"My, my," she uttered. "Now don't you just look the gentleman." She straightened the cravat and brushed both his shoulders with her hands, as if putting final touches to a work of art.

When Russet arrived, dressed to go out, she too walked round him clicking her tongue as she made an inspection of his new attire. He felt silly and shy and found it a relief to get out of the hall to where a stableman held a pony and two-wheeled carriage.

They climbed in side by side and he took the reins. He lifted a hand and shrugged his shoulders attempting to convey to her his question of where she wanted to go.

Russet pointed to the track running up the rise of the parkland "We shall go over the hill, Pitchforth. Just for a short time. I would go for longer but it would only heighten my father's worry.

Russet made little talk as they travelled but once out of sight of the hall her attitude changed. "When we are away from home I shall call you Jamie and you can call me... Oh I am so sorry." She had forgotten he was mute. "I really didn't mean to be rude." She was quiet for some time then, where the trees ended, she ordered him to stop. He pulled back on the reins and the pony obeyed. She said nothing for a few minutes as she looked to her left, away from him. The gap in the trees gave a surprise view. A river curled through the bottom of a valley. To the right could be seen the dark mass of Black Wood and beyond were hills rising to the horizon, their summits covered with the purple hue of heather.

Russet turned to Jamie. "I want to thank you for what you

did for me." She said the words hesitantly "I have been told you saved my life and I don't know how I can show my gratitude. How can anyone possibly find words fitting for the giving of such a gift."

Jamie waved a hand as if he were wiping clean a slate. He desperately wanted to speak to her or to convey to her in some way that he did not want her thanks.

Russet broke the impasse. "When I was a little girl my grandfather brought me to this place. Just a little further on there is a fallen oak where we would sit and he would point out all the landmarks across the valley. I remember the old flour mill but that was demolished and the new one built that stands there now." She pointed to the large stone building in the valley far below. "They had to build a larger weir to hold back the water to feed the water wheel. That's why the water looks calmer up-river from the mill. See." She pointed again and Jamie's eyes followed her direction.

Then she turned back to him. "Come on, Jamie," she said. "I will show you my favourite seat. We can see more from there."

With the pony tethered she helped Jamie walk to where an oak had succumbed to a gale of years ago. At one end of the fallen tree a tangle of roots spread outwards and upwards like featherless quills of some enormous fossilised peacock. The bark had long gone but the timber of the trunk shone with years of use. Russet took hold of Jamie's hands and sat him down as if he were a child. She took a place beside him and began to point out other landmarks across the valley.

She talked to him incessantly. They went over the hill to

the old oak several times during the following two weeks. She told him of her childhood and would always begin, "when I was a little girl..." She related to him her relationship with her brother and her sisters and how her mother had suffered giving birth to Katherine and that her derangement dated from that time. She told him of her regret that she had no mother to love as she grew up because her mother had no recognition for any of them. She spoke of her great love for her father and how close to him she felt.

His admiration for her grew. It turned to infatuation. As he sat on the tree she would pirouette before him as she told him the most intimate details of her life, her laughter filling the air. He was feeling a sensation he had not before encountered, a sensation that had built slowly but emphatically. Jamie Pichforth was desperately and hopelessly in love. He knew nothing could ever come of it – a lady and a peasant boy. Never. A terrible feeling of sadness came over him but he came back to reality with her next words.

"I can tell you anything I wish, Jamie," she said. "You are my confidant. My keeper of secrets. The treasure trove of my existence. I know my secrets are safe with you. Why, you cannot speak. You cannot read and you cannot write so you cannot convey my innermost thoughts to any."

Jamie frowned at this assertion. She was accusing him of illiteracy. Of course he could read and write. Or could he? He had not given it thought. His mother was illiterate. Gunner, Walter and Wriggley, none of the three could read nor write but all were numerically literate. They could count and they could barter.

When Russet left him at the hall that day he returned the pony and trap to the stables and walked round to the rear of the buildings where a beck wound down from the hills to the north. Careful not to muddy his shoes he crossed the stream to where a sandy tract bordered the waterline. He drew a hand across the surface then with a forefinger he wrote 'James Pitchforth.' He could write.

Knowing he was literate now worried him. How could he, the son of a country peasant come to be so knowing? It puzzled him greatly.

The next day Russet instructed him to drive over the hill to the fallen oak. There she continued with the narration of her life and hopes. She took Jamie's hands in hers and turned them over so she could see the palms.

"I will read the future in your hands so not only will you have knowledge of my past but you will know your own future. I will read your palm as the gypsies do." She paused as she looked at the scars in the palms of his hands. She let go the left hand but looked closer at the star-shaped scar in the centre of his right hand.

"A star," she whispered. She counted the points with a finger, touching his palm. He shuddered with excitement as she said, "a six-pointed star!" Then she dropped the hand and stepped away, a smile on her face. "Jamie Pitchforth, not only do you hold my secrets in the palm of a hand. You hold the heavens in the palm of the other."

She spun around, laughing at her own words. "Do you not think that is poetic of me, Jamie. Perchance upon a day I shall become a renowned Lady Bard."

On the way back to the hall his thoughts were full of what she had said of him. An idea was beginning to form in his mind. He would prove to her he was not just an ugly ignorant oaf. He would write a poem for her.

For days he pondered on what he should write but slowly a verse took form in his head. But how to write it? He possessed none of the materials needed. And how would he present it to her?

The opportunity to write his love poem came sooner than expected.

Sir Marcus had promised Russet he would hold a ball to celebrate her recovery. Invitations had been dispatched to the local gentry and arrangements were going ahead apace. Sir Marcus and Totton were away on business and the girls had gone to Loylton to be fitted for the gowns they would wear for the occasion. Jamie was performing the duties of houseman and seeing to fires that would be lit in the evening. It was becoming colder as the nights drew in.

He entered the study carrying kindling, charcoal and a lighted wax taper. After lighting the fire he rose and looked toward the desk. His brow creased, then he hobbled across the room and quietly closed the door. At the desk he found a newly cut quill, and ink. From a drawer he took a sheet of paper. Quickly he sat down and began to write. When he had finished he sanded the paper to dry the ink and when sure it was dry he folded the paper and using sealing wax he found on the desk put it to the flame of the taper and sealed the note. Taking up the pen once more he wrote on it the name 'Russet' then tucked it in his shirt and left.

Loylton was a busy town. This was the market centre for the area where cattle, sheep, pigs and stock of all shapes and sizes came to be sold under the auctioneer's gavel. Charlotte and Katherine were still with the dressmaker but Russet had made her choices and had left, with the parting words that she would meet them both in the tearoom of the George and Dragon Inn. There she found the room crowded. Espying a gentleman seated on his own at a table for two, she enquired if the seat was free. The man rose hurriedly and bowed. He proffered a hand as an invitation to join him.

It was some half hour later when Charlotte and Katherine arrived to find there were no vacancies in the tearoom. They stood by the door and waved at Russet expressing their desire to depart. She took leave of her new companion who bowed graciously to her. She said nothing to her sisters of her newly acquired acquaintance.

Chapter Twelve

It was the morning of the day of the ball. Russet wanted to help with the arrangements but her offer of help was politely declined. Charlotte firmly told her that as the ball was to be held as a celebration of her recovery it was up to others to contribute.

She felt ill at ease, as if she was not wanted. She called for Jamie and they rode out. This time she directed him to take a new route. He turned north at the stable buildings and followed the stream. When the track came to an end she ordered him to tether the pony and they went further on foot. She helped him with a hand under his arm as they clambered up a hill to where the water of the stream flowed over high rock and cascaded down into a crystal clear pool.

They stood for a while as their lungs heaved from the effort of the climb, then Russet said, "when I was a little girl my grandfather brought me here. Then later when we came to stay at the hall during the summer we would all three come by ourselves. Lottie and Kate would paddle but I would take off all my clothes and bathe. It was magical, Jamie." She hunched her shoulders as she recalled the experience. "It was so cold. I can remember the pain in my shoulders and the back of my head from the coldness of it, but it was wondrous."

She stared at the water. "I wish, oh I wish I was a little girl again."

Jamie gestured toward the pool. She looked him, then at the water. "What! You mean for me to bathe now? In front of you?" She scoffed but he made signs with his fingers and pointed to himself and then down the hill.

Without waiting for her to decide he unbuttoned his jacket, removed his cravat and took off his shirt. He held the shirt and made rubbing motions on his arms and chest, indicating she should use the shirt as a towel.

Russet knew what he was suggesting but her eyes were glued on the broadness of his shoulders and the rippling muscles in his arm as he made the gesture. She had regarded him sympathetically as an impaired cripple and it came as a surprise to perceive his masculinity. She took the towel. "Off you go Master Pitchforth," she ordered. "Out sir! Out of this lady's closet."

She watched him go and then undressed. She stood on the bank of the pool, hesitating to go further. Her hair hung down over her pale shoulders. She held her arms across her breasts, hugging herself as if she could already feel the icy water. She experienced a sense excitement but she also felt very small. Then she took the plunge.

Jamie wound the cravat about his neck and put his jacket back on and waited for her lower down the hill. After ten minutes he began to worry. Suppose she was in difficulty, perhaps a relapse from her injury, but if he went back and she was bathing naked – what would she think of him. He was about to retrace his steps when she appeared waving her hat in one hand, his shirt in the other, as she skipped down the slope.

"It was joyous, Jamie," she called. "But it's doubtless colder than ever." She held out his shirt and he took it from her as she leant forward and shook her head, sending off a fine spray. The shirt was damp with the moisture towelled from her body and as she remained bent over he used it to rub the wetness from her hair. She straightened up and their eyes met. She placed her hands on his shoulders and kissed his crooked cheek. It was a moment he would remember for the rest of his life.

He felt acutely embarrassed but exalted at the same time. His eyes became misty and a tear trickled down his cheek. Russet regretted her action immediately. The thought raced through her mind that it was not lady-like to go around kissing servants – even if this one had saved her life. Then she dismissed the thought – after all, it was only Jamie.

On the journey back, as he negotiated the ford to cross the stream, she said, "when I marry, Jamie, I shall have you as my coachman."

Her words were like a knife twisting in his heart.

Later that evening when the ball was in progress Jamie assisted Jossy and the kitchen staff to prepare the feast for the guests. A great pie had been baked the day before in preparation. First, a standing crust with a thick bottom and sides. Goose, duck and cockerel, cooked and boned previously, were placed inside and round the sides next to the pastry. The centre was filled with raw game, hare, rabbit, breast of woodcock, pigeon and any other game available. This was then topped with large slabs of butter and finished off with a thick, patterned crust and baked slowly for hours. A magnificent, roasted baron of beef rested on a large silver platter. This would be doused in brandy and set alight before being paraded aflame in the ballroom in front of the guests. Sweetmeats of all shapes and sizes to please the lady's palates.

Large iced cakes with moulded sugar columns bearing a decorative domed hood. The kitchen tables stood crammed with food and the staff stood by ready and awaiting the word to convey the provisions upstairs. Far more food had been prepared than was necessary for the guests to devour. When the ball was over the remains of the feast would be taken to the kitchen where another party would take place later. When the drinks where served to the guests the housemen would see that the bottles were never emptied. An amount would remain at the bottom of each and returned to the kitchen for what Jossy referred to as the 'dregs and a drop.' The staff never received extra payment for their efforts so it was the custom to reward them with a late repast.

The strenuous gallop had ended and now an interval was called while the participants rested from their exertions. The string quartet performed their art, playing soft chamber music in the background of the chatter that always occurred between dances.

Ladies occupied one side of the hall while the men gathered at the other —or that was the usual custom. Russet was with the men, chatting and making small talk and holding the attention of the older men with her coquettish manner. She moved closer to her father and when at his side she said, "I see you invited Captain Halgalleon."

"I could do no less," said Sir Marcus. I placed myself in his shoes and I would perchance have taken the same course as he. Had I been he and your sister told me you had been assaulted so, I cannot see that I would have stood aside. I sent him the invitation and through him an invitation to the officers of his choice. I intended it as a gesture of regret and conciliation."

Russet changed the course of the conversation "Just look at Lottie, Father. She is holding court well."

Sir Marcus glanced across the room to where Lottie was entertaining a number of guests. "Humph!" He grunted. "Watch them move away one by one as she keeps up her patter." They watched with amusement as the party around Charlotte diminished in numbers as excuses were made to depart her company. Eventually they had all gone with the exception of a small, fair-haired man.

"Don't recognise that fellow." Sir Marcus stretched his neck to take a closer look.

"I invited him, Father." Russet stood on her toes to see." His name is John Fullerton, I made his acquaintance in Loylton only last week. He is a charming man. I am sorry, I overlooked to tell you."

"Look at the fellow, he looks as if he is taking in all Lottie has to say. Ha! The fellow must be a glutton for punishment. I'll wager a guinea he doesn't last more than ten minutes with her."

"Only a guinea, Father? My. My. You cannot be so sure of your convictions."

Oh! Very well. I would wager five guineas then."

"And I say, oh very well, I accept your wager, Father." She smiled up at him.

"And where will you get so much money to pay such a debt." Sir Marcus spoke to her as he would a small child. "When you lose a wager honour has it that the debt must be paid. I shall end up giving you the five guineas for you to pay me.

"Five guineas you said, Father and I have accepted. Do you renege on your word?"

Sir Marcus laughed at her insistence. He took from his pocket a bulbous timepiece. "Right," he said. "Ten minutes from now."

"Eight!"

"I said ten minutes." Sir Marcus insisted.

"But you have spent two minutes arguing since the wager was laid. So, eight!"

Sir Marcus shook his head and returned the timepiece to his waistcoat pocket. "There is no arguing with you my dear. Eight it is."

Eight minutes passed and Charlotte was still in the company of the newcomer. Russet tapped her father on a shoulder and held out her hand. "Five guineas if you please Father."

"What! What!" Sir Marcus looked across at his eldest daughter, her chin wagging without interruption. "I'll tell you what I'll do, Russy. Make it ten guineas or nothing he doesn't last another ten minutes.

Russet put on a look of dismay. "But that means I shall end up with nothing." Then she quickly accepted before he changed his mind.

Russet moved away to talk with others but she kept an eye on the pendulum clock. After ten minutes she went to collect her winnings.

"Ten guineas please, Father." Her smile made her

irresistible.

Sir Marcus glanced across the room and saw his daughter still talking to the man.

"Come here." Sir Marcus took Russet by the arm and they turned their backs on the guests and faced the wall. "I have only ten guineas on my person. I shall give you a note, you hussy."

"You could give me it now if you have it on you, Father. You will not have need to spend money in your own home."

"I have spent it!" He laughed and took from a pocket a soft leather purse and handed it to her. Russet thanked him, kissed him and departed jangling the purse in her hand.

Sir Marcus returned to the guests. He spoke to Captain Halgalleon. "See that fellow speaking with my eldest daughter. Do you know of him?"

Halgalleon looked across the room to see the subject of the inquiry. "I have not had the pleasure of making his acquaintance, poor fellow," he answered.

"Poor fellow?" Sir Marcus asked.

"Yes. He was a naval man. Retired now. Gunnery Training Officer. You know. Below decks. The guns. Continuous thundering noise. Poor fellow's stone deaf."

For a moment Sir Marcus was speechless. Then, "Stone deaf, you say?" His voice rose. "Stone deaf?" Then louder as he turned away, "Russet!" He bawled.

But Russet was elsewhere.

Jamie was in the kitchen, helping where he could. He was not to be allowed to go upstairs, nor did he want to. He knew his face would not fit and he did not want the embarrassment of seeing the guests turn away at the sight of him. Everybody was ready and awaiting the order to take the food upstairs. When it came they all left, carrying allotted amounts, to play their instructed part.

He was on his own. He touched the sealed note tucked under his shirt and he knew he would never have a better opportunity to deliver it. He hurriedly climbed the servants' stairs to the first landing. It was deserted. He opened the door of Russet's bedchamber and entered. The glow from the fire lit the room and a single candle burned on a table beside the bed. The bedclothes had been turned back so he had no fear that a chambermaid would disturb him. He placed the note on the pillow and moved the candleholder nearer the bed. Then he left.

He went as stealthily as he could along the landing and had reached the top of the stairs when he heard footsteps. He pulled back into the shadows as a figure rushed past and down the service stairs. He recognised the person but had no time to ponder as he sat on the top step and went down quickly on the seat of his breeches. In the kitchen he took up his duties as if he had never been away.

The servants had been allowed to remain upstairs to witness 'walking the beef,' and to assist with the serving of food. Guests and servants were all occupied with one thing or another and soft music filled the air when Lady Mary Roulette made her entrance. She had reached half way down the stairs before she was noticed. The music stopped on a discordant note. The chatter faded away to a strange silence as the lady of the house came to join her guests. She fluttered an imaginary fan in her left hand and held her right arm out to the side as if holding up the folds of a beautiful ball gown. But Lady Mary Roulette had no ball gown. Lady Mary Roulette was completely naked.

The gaiety of the ball was over. People made their excuses and called for their carriages. Lady Mary had been immediately taken back to her room but the embarrassment could not be locked away.

"How in Hell's teeth did she get out?" Sir Marcus fumed. "My God, we shall never live this down. It will be the talk of the county tomorrow and the country the day after that. The Roulettes will be a laughing stock!"

Chambermaids, housemen, kitchen staff, everybody was questioned but nobody owned up to blame. Jamie was sure he knew the culprit but he could not convey that knowledge without giving away his errand of love.

Russet was inconsolable. Her ball was spoiled. It had been intended as a celebration of her recovery and it had all gone so wrong.

The clearing up was carried out in an atmosphere of dejection. The servants were upset. Not only because it was thought one of them had failed to secure the door to Lady Mary's bedchamber, but because of their loyalty to their master and his family. The intended party for the staff failed to materialise. Some took a bite to eat. Some took a glass of claret. Some brandy. Nothing was taken in excess. The spirit was gone.

All the guests left but Charlotte's companion. She asked her father if her new friend, John Fullerton, could stay the night. Sir Marcus was too distraught to argue and too courteous to refuse.

Russet went to her bed unhappy. She undressed and was about to climb into bed when she saw the note. She sat on the edge of her bed and broke the seal then held it nearer the candle flame and read -

For Russet with my heart

The grass is greener o'er the hill

Where fantasies of ego play

That leave me clutching straws of hope

As reason yields to yesterday.

Through dreams I live beyond that hill

In euphoric state of mind,

For you are there beside me

And we as one are blind,

Blind to the seasons numbered mine,

To tides beyond reproof

That scatter hope as gossamer blown

When awake to the sum of truth.

Times cannot join nor balance hold

To meet in entity,

So love is locked within my heart,

Oh, would that it were free!

Alas, reality is but beggar's alms

And the cross that I must bear.

The grass is greener o'er the hill

For I am here, whilst you, my love, are there.

She lay awake, her mind in turmoil. Who could have

written such a poem? It had to be a man of reasonable intellect. She went through a mental list of all the men at the ball but could not choose. Dawn was breaking when she finally succumbed to sleep.

Chapter Thirteen

An air of gloom hung over Nestwith Hall. From Sir Marcus down to the lowliest scullery maid the feeling of dejection was widespread. The housemen had chuckled among themselves at the spectacle of the lady of the house unclothed but with the consequences of their mirth explained to them, the prospect of unemployment wiped the smiles from their faces.

Sir Marcus felt he had to get out of the hall and concentrate his mind on matters of the day so he walked to the stables accompanied by Totton. As they set off John Fullerton came running after them.

"Would it be intrusive of me to ask if I may join you, Sir?" He panted.

"No, no." Sir Marcus, gestured. "We shall be glad of your company. We are but taking the air, with no purpose in mind," he added.

They walked to the stables and all three took a position side by side leaning on a high fence watching horses galloping about the stable paddock. John Fullerton stood slightly apart. Both Sir Marcus and Totton had attempted conversation with him but when answers were not forthcoming they gave up.

"I accounted our income and expenditure on the visit of the flock and I have decided it will not be to our benefit to continue the enterprise. We made nothing from it, Tott. It was a good income when done on a smaller scale but the margin is wrong here. On this acreage we would require the visit of a flock many times the number to cover our overheads - and earn coin. We must contrive to other means."

"Pigs!" Totton exclaimed. He had for some time been trying to find a way to speak of the idea with his father and now the way was open.

"Pigs?" Sir Marcus looked puzzled. "Pigs, you say? I cannot think of any who drive pigs to market past here. And pigs cannot live on grass alone."

"You may remember I rode north to meet the drovers before they arrived here." Totton began. "Well, I stayed overnight at The White Hart in Troffston. There I met with two gentlemen and we dined together. They travelled in opposite directions. One was on his way to Liverpool and the other returning to London. We had the most interesting of conversations. One was a sailor, a Captain Christopher, on his way to take command of a ship. The other, a supply agent for the Admiralty. The topic was food aboard ship on long voyages. The captain complained of the poor supply of salted meats. The quantity and, in particular, the quality. The agent said it was impossible to get regular supplies in quantity because the goods came from so many sources. Dozens and dozens of small pig farms, mostly near the coast. I asked what he thought was the answer and he immediately suggested that his job would be made easier if he could deal with only one large concern."

Sir Marcus nudged Totton and nodded his head, indicating the nearness of John Fullerton.

"That's not a problem Father, the fellow is stone deaf." Totton continued, "I feel that we could be the large concern the agent spoke of and to supply barrels of salted pork to both the King's ships and the merchant fleet."

"That is a tall order, indeed." Sir Marcus mused. "And how many pigs...."

"Thousands!" Totton showed his enthusiasm.

"And where do you think we shall obtain the recourses for such a venture, for I do not have such credit. I see you have thought well of it and I am more than pleased to see you taking such interest in matters concerning the family, but the answer is no. I must first honour the debts my dear brother bestowed on me".

"It is not an opium pipe dream, Father." Totton murmured, both frustration and disappointment in his voice. "I have assessed and planned the whole scheme and if we don't do it now then one day we may come to regret it."

Russet awoke from her short, restless sleep. The poem was running through her mind. She could think of nothing else. Who? Who? Who? She slammed a clenched fist down on the bedclothes then she picked up the note and read the poem again.

"There must be a clue in the writing," she said aloud. "Over the hill. Could that mean that whoever wrote it is over the hill - old? No, it can't mean that because the last line states he is here and I am there. Oh! Tish! Tish! Tish! She threw the bedclothes aside and got out of bed. She read the poem yet again. Then she tossed it on the bed in frustration, "I shall deduce from this that the writer is a coward. Yes, a rake and a coward and I have no wish to know him." She retrieved the paper, scrutinised the poem yet again then folded it carefully and placed it among her private papers in the drawer of her bedside table.

'Love is locked within his heart?' She thought. She stood with her head on one side staring into space. "Oh!" She stamped a foot and said aloud, "I don't care who wrote it! I just don't care!"

Jamie was waiting with the pony and trap when Russet came out for her morning drive. He gestured to ask where she wished to go.

"We shall go over the hill, as usual...." She stopped speaking suddenly. "Over the hill," she said, slowly. Then she was silent and did not speak until they reached the fallen oak. He tethered the pony as she walked across to the log and took a seat. As he joined her she looked up at him, a forlorn expression on her face. "A suitor wrote me a beautiful poem and it was delivered last night." She looked away from him, clasping her hands. Then, "oh, Jamie. It was addressed to me and left in my bedchamber with no indication as to the name of the writer. Oh, I am undone to distraction. It must have been a gentleman attending the ball but I cannot imagine any with such poetic gifts."

'What have I done,' he thought. 'What have I done.' He could not believe he could have been so stupid and unthinking. He could not tell her he had written the poem. Now she was sure some other man had composed his verse. What a mess he had made of it. He had been so besotted with her he could see no further than conveying his love. The consequence of his action never entered his head. He had brought only frustration and unhappiness to her and had accomplished the opposite of what he intended. He wanted to talk to her. To explain. He tried hard to speak but uttered no sound.

They remained on the log for some time. She kept her silence, deep in thought. He sat by her side, his mind wallowing in abject misery.

John Fullerton had accepted the invitation to stay overnight after the fiasco of the ball. The following afternoon he had walked in the gardens with Charlotte. Maisy acted as chaperone keeping her distance discreetly out of earshot some paces behind. They would take a few paces then Charlotte would move in front of Fullerton bringing him to a halt. She would then mouth her words to him with slow, exaggerated movement of her lips. Maisy would stop when they stopped but she could not help smiling at the spectacle. Never had Charlotte been so frugal with words.

John Fullerton accepted Charlotte's invitation to stay another night. Then another. Their friendship appeared to blossom and Maisy was kept busy as their chaperon.

On the fourth day of Fullerton's stay, Totton invited him to ride with him to Nestwith village. Totton declined a carriage for horse and saddle and they rode abreast, Totton turning to allow Fullerton to watch his lips as he spoke. When they reached the Wrigglesworth smallholding Totton pointed out the dilapidation of the ancient building. The thatch of the roof appeared ragged and the walls were patched, with plaster falling away. He waved an arm as if to obliterate the scene.

"I want this eyesore demolished and the stink of pigs with it. It is too near the entrance to the Hall. Not a very fine welcome for visitors to first have the stench of pig waste in their nostrils. I shall, of course, re-house the occupants, for the two who live here are part of my future plans." It was as if he were talking to himself for he was not sure Fullerton had understood a word.

They rode to the village and tethered the horses outside the smithy. Totton introduced John Fullerton to Gunner and Walter. At Totton's request Gunner showed them around. First the smithy and then they moved to the adjacent building where Gunner and Walter Lupton had built the carpenter's shed. Here Walter made the timber furnishings to compliment Gunner's metal work in the building of carts, wheels and barrels.

Totton looked beyond the shed at the adjoining, boggy land. "You do not have much room for expansion should you require it."

"Aw, we got enough room for what we do," said Walter. "Sometimes work's so slack we got more than enough."

They left the horses tethered at the smithy and walked through the village to the Rose and Crown. The Inn was all but empty so they sat opposite each other and Totton told him of his plans, "it is my ambition, John, to have the largest pig farm in the country. I want to breed thousands of pigs to feed the ships of the King's fleet and the merchant ships of this country. I know it can be done. I spoke with a ship's captain not so long ago and he told me of the shortage and the foul trade that goes on in the supply of victuals. He told me of hungry men opening their last barrel of salted pork only to find grit had been deliberately mixed with the salt and the meat had putrefied in its own juices. Of others that found lumps of timber in place of meat. Others who, upon removing the lid, found only sand. Can you imagine what went on in the minds, and the stomachs of those poor fellows? It would seem it is a widespread practice. The Captain knew of two men in Lancashire who were caught and stretched the hangman's rope for their crimes. A joy to the hangman, I say."

"And so say all of us!" John Fullerton broke his silence but Totton realised the man had taken in his every word. He felt encouraged that at last somebody was listening.

"There is a farm on the estate that is up for re-tenancy. The farmer died and he has no issue to take over. His wife is sickly so I want to add that farm to Home Farm and turn it into a piggery. I shall have the very best salt carted from Cheshire. A slaughterhouse, a butchery adjoining it and a salting and barrelling house adjoining that. All in one place. On the land food will be grown to feed the pigs and nothing will be wasted. The guts and offal that is not used will go back into pig feed. We will provide boned meat, which is unheard of. I mean the legs will be de-boned, not the ribs. There will be no waste at all because the bones will be dried and ground to meal and also fed back. I would also require a good agent to buy from the many present suppliers. A man of integrity who would inspect the meat before purchase and would be remunerated at a price per barrel purchased. It could be a welcome good income for such a man."

Totton paused. Then he ended, "I could do all this and make a fortune but for one very important item on which all depends, money! – of which I have none."

"I have some good news and I have some bad news for you, Father." Russet glided into the study. "Maisy is the most remarkable lady and I thank the Good Lord for delivering her to us" Russet faced her father. He was seated at his desk but kept glancing upward at the ceiling. A loud thumping on the floor of the room above resounded through the study. Russet went on, "the very day after the ball Maisy persuaded Mother to dress. Now is that not a miracle?"

"What in the Devil's name is going on up there?" Sir Marcus blurted. "Yes, yes, that is good news indeed," he said, impatiently.

Sir Marcus put his head down to his work as Russet continued.

"The day she dressed she became a mouse."

"He looked up. "A what?"

"Mother thought she was a mouse. She tried to squeeze herself under the bed and under the furniture and she ended crouched under the wash stand and would not come out. The next day she was a cat searching for the mouse she was the previous day. Because she could not find herself she flew into a rage and scratched Molly. Poor Molly says if Mother becomes a tiger she will not go near. "She chuckled. I know it is tragic, Father but it is also very funny."

I do not share you opinion, Russy and I think you should be ashamed of yours...." He was interrupted by louder banging. "What on this sacred earth is that?"

"It is only my unfunny mother," she said with a touch of sarcasm. "Today, Father dear, your wife is a horse!"

All agreed that the turn of mind Lady Mary had undergone

was tragic. In her undressed period she could hold reasonable conversations and obeyed instructions. Now, she brooked no order. When she was a mouse she only ate cheese. As a cat she insisted on eating from a plate on the floor. Down on her knees biting into the food placed before her. Then she would roll over and purr. As a horse it was more difficult to give her nourishment. She refused everything and insisted on hay. She chewed the stalks as if they were some delicious sweetmeat.

Three days later tragedy struck in reality.

The quiet atmosphere of Nestwith Hall was shattered by shrill screams coming from the direction of Lady Mary's room. Molly came running out and down the stairs screaming hysterically. Maisy came out of the dining room, rushed to the distraught Molly and slapped her face.

"What is it, girl?" She shouted.

"It's her ladyship, Maisy. She's jumped out of the window."

Everybody turned and tore through the doorway to see Lady Mary lying crumpled in a pool of blood. She was quite dead.

Molly's nerves were in tatters and she could hardly speak. In the sitting room the tea caddy was unlocked and she was given a cup of the precious, sugared infusion. She sipped it thankfully as Maisy gently coaxed out of her what had happened.

She was running round the room with her arms all a'going. I never thought." She began to cry once more. Maisy quietened her down and she went on, "I got her sittin' on the bed and I couldn't think what to say so I talked to her about

Christmas. I never thought." She stopped again but pulled herself together. "I said we would all have a good feast and she jumped up. Flapped her arms and jumped out of the window. Straight through the glass she went."

Russet went down on her haunches in front of Molly and said, "what was she today, Molly?"

"Today, Miss, she was a goose!"

Chapter Fourteen

Lord Francis Doulain stood with his hands clasped behind his back, feet apart. He stared at the two almost life size paintings adorning the oak-panelled wall above the large, ornate fireplace. The painting on the left was of a very beautiful young woman. She was dressed in white, her hair hung in ringlets below a white lace bonnet. When she posed for the artist she had been looking straight at him and he had captured the wistful look in her eyes. It was as if she was alive and about to step out of the frame to be with him.

The other canvas was of a youth in his mid-teens. The artist had posed him leaning against a desk looking to his right. He was dressed in a golden silk coat and breeches with a white shoulder belt supporting a sword. The young man had his left hand on the hilt of the sheathed weapon with his head held high, as if looking to a distant horizon.

Lord Doulain was a man of great wealth. A banker, financier, ship-owner, slave trader, and merchant. A respected friend of the aristocracy, politicians, and the world of business. Wherever large amounts of profit could be made the Company Doulain had an interest. He dressed in black. Black shoes with black buckles. Black stockings, knee breeches, jacket, and waistcoat. Even the shirt he wore and the cravat about his neck had been tailored from black dyed material. His abundant hair matched his attire with just a hint of grey streaking back above his temples. He was a handsome man in his mid-forties but his face bore the lines of grief.

His late wife was the lady of the painting. She had died

giving birth to his son.

Nine months ago and only days after celebrating his twenty fourth birthday, his son had departed the city to take passage on one of the company ships, the Branston Gold. The ship had met with a tremendous storm in the Bay of Biscay and had gone down with all hands. Lord Doulain had used his wealth to pay for the most intense searches along the western coast of France and the northern coast of Spain but no trace of survivors had ever been found.

For twenty-four years Francis Doulain had lived the life of a recluse. He had been, and still was, so deeply in love with his late wife he wanted no other. In his mind he had blamed his son for her death and had found no love for him. Now he had lost all.

He was roused from memories by a knock on the door. Before he could call out his invitation to enter the door opened and his chief clerk appeared with a folder held under an arm. John Critchley had been with the Company Doulain for over thirty years and knew more about company matters than anybody. His word was law amongst the many clerical staff and he would give praise as well as criticism where either was due. He was respected as a fair man.

"Any news?" Critchley knew that would be the first question his master would ask.

"No Milord. Nothing. I fear we have to face the facts. It has at last been confirmed in Lloyd's List, published this day, the Branston Gold is lost and went down with all hands. I am so very sorry Milord." Critchley bowed his head.

Francis Doulain went to his desk and pulled up his chair.

"What now, I ask? What now?" He buried his head in his hands. When he looked up Critchley was standing opposite him in front of the desk. "Pull up a chair, Critchley, my neck is a'crick looking up at you."

This was a rare occasion. Never in all the years of service to the company had he been invited to sit in his master's presence. He pulled up a chair and placed the folder he had been carrying on the desk.

Lord Doulain began. "My grandfather started this company, my father carried it on and it grew. I have followed their example and I now find myself a man of wealth…

"Immense wealth," Critchley interrupted.

"Yes, if you like – immense wealth." His eyes went to the two paintings. "And yet I have nothing. No man was ever more a pauper than I. There is an empire built but no young emperor to inherit it. "

There followed a few moments of silence. Then Critchley sat up, straightened his shoulders and said, "with the risk of dismissal for my impertinence, Milord, I shall say that you have not yet reached the age of declining virility. You could marry again and have issue. There must be many, many, women who would leap at the prospect of becoming Lady Doulain" He cringed, waiting for the reprimand that would surely come. He was surprised when it did not.

"Oh, I think not, Critchley," he shook his head. "You have not met with the chattering, twittering women who frequent the balls and parties these days. None are looking for the man. They look not for a depth of love but for the depth of a man's purse. I would not wish issue from such." He waved a hand to indicate the subject was closed and pointed to the folder lying on the desk. "What have you there?" He asked.

Critchley opened the folder. "A delicate matter, Milord. Eighteen months ago we made a considerable loan – of some thousands of pounds for which we took possession of the deeds of the owner's estate as collateral should the borrower renege. The loan was to be paid back, with interest, by a certain date but that date came and we received no payment. I made extensive enquiries and it turned out that the borrower had met his end in dire circumstances. Now this is the delicate part. The man to whom we loaned the money was Sir Oliver Roulette. On his death the baronetcy passed to his brother who is now Sir Marcus Roulette – and he is not aware of the situation."

"And what is the situation?" Lord Doulain asked.

"The situation is that we – or should I say, you, are now the legal owner of the Nestwith Hall Estate, together with all buildings, land, and every blade of grass thereon.

Lord Doulain pursed his lips. "I don't see the delicacy. We foreclose, place the property on the market and we either win or lose. If we lose it can't be by much."

"I was not considering the money involved, Milord."

"Oh, were you not, indeed!"

"These are very decent people, Milord. They have been placed in unfortunate circumstances not of their making." Critchley cringed at his boldness.

"How do you know they are decent?"

"Because we have an agent in place who has heard of the family history and the debts the brother left. Sir Marcus is an honourable man. He sold his previous home to pay off the known debts his brother left and I understand he has also ploughed his own personal fortune into satisfying the creditors. If we step in and take the estate now, we will ruin a principled gentleman – and his family."

"What family does he have?" Lord Doulain glanced up at the paintings.

"A wife who was deranged but is recently deceased. A son and three daughters."

"A son." He glanced again at the art. Then, how do you know all this? You say you have a man 'in place' but how could he know such personal detail?"

"He is a man of education, Milord. The fifth son of Sir George Fullerton. He can hold conversations on many topics but he can also mix among people with impunity and hears much that others would not."

"And how, pray, does he do that? Lord Doulain was intrigued.

"His method is simple, Milord. He feigns deafness."

Lord Doulain thought for a moment of the implications then he began to shake with laughter. "I would take pleasure in meeting this young jackanape. Perchance I may use his talents to good effect in other affairs." He patted the file. "Is Fullerton's report in here?"

"Yes Milord, and the deeds. And the written agreement with Oliver Roulette. It's all there."

"I shall peruse it now. Come to me later and we shall discuss my findings." Head down, he was already turning pages.

Critchley halted short of the door. "I ask you to bear in mind my words, Milord."

"What words?" Lord Doulain did not raise his head.

"That you should deign to consider wedlock."

His Lordship said nothing. He did not look up but raised a hand and waved for Critchley to be gone.

When Critchley returned later that day, Lord Doulain had the folder open on his lap, the deeds on his desk. "Ah, come Critchley. I find this report by young Fullerton of interest indeed." He indicated with a hand to the chair.

"You appear pleased with the transaction, Milord. Is it your wish to retain the estate, or sell?"

"It is not the estate that interests me, Critchley. It is the report. It is so detailed. Excellent!" Lord Doulain selected a few papers from the file and separated them from the rest. "It is the subject in here I find fascinating," he patted the pages. "Swine! Critchley, Swine! Who would have thought it? We have always complained about the quality of meat we obtain for our ships. The captains complain. The crews complain and it would not surprise me if the rats complain." He patted the papers again. "Here is the idea of a monopoly for which I well care.

"I shall meet with this Totton Roulette. He looks to have all his mental buttons fastened but is short on finance to execute the project. Well, we can do something about that." He smiled, more to himself than for Critchley's benefit. "You say we own the estate. Well, I see no reason why we should not also purchase a joint or two of the pork."

Chapter Fifteen

A perceptible change had come over Russet. It was taken to be distress at the loss of her mother, but Mary had never been a mother to her. Of the three sisters, only Charlotte had memories of her before Katherine was born, and little memory of a caring mother. Russet and Katherine knew her as the strange lady upstairs and Totton only vaguely recalled his mother before insanity overtook her.

Russet walked about as if in a dream. Her thoughts were not of her mother but of who could possibly have written the poem. She had gone over in her mind every man present at the ball but she could not picture any who had shown her such attention as to warrant a message of love. The concentration and mental search became too much. Feeling as if her head would burst, she summoned Jamie to take her out.

Jamie was also in a dilemma. A great depression clouded his mind, he was full of indecision. Should he tell her he was the cause of her confusion? Or would a confession make matters worse?

When they reached the fallen oak Jamie sat on it but Russet paced back and forth, then around in circles with hands clasped behind her back.

"I shall not repeat to you the words of the poem, Jamie," she said. "It is a confidence I cannot break. It is without doubt intended as a message of affection but how, oh how, shall I ever know who penned it?"

It was too much for Jamie to see her in such torment. His mind was made up. He would confess. He pointed a finger, tapping himself on the chest with it then held out his hand as if holding a quill and adopted an action of writing. Russet stared at him and then clapped her hands together.

"You clever, clever Jamie. Of Course. Why did I not think of that? Now let me see." She began her pacing again, her expression transformed.

"I shall write to all the men who attended the ball. I shall apologise for my mother's behaviour. I shall tell them of her demise and I shall invite them to the funeral in my father's name. They will then surely pen their condolences and I shall compare the writing. Oh thank you Jamie, thank you." She danced with joy and took him by the arm. "Come," she said. "Take me home. I have much to do."

The funeral of Mary Roulette was a crowded affair. Many came to pay their respects but it was respect for the family not for the deceased for few of them had ever known her. Russet had all eyes for the men. She counted them against her mental list of those who attended the ball, looking for a likely suitor. The Rector praised Mary and her good services to the family and as a loving wife. It was as if he quoted from a standard script for the occasion for he had never met with Mary Roulette yet spoke of her as a lifelong friend. True to his style he then sermonised on sinners and God's punishment of those who transgressed, citing the deceased as a sinner in God's eyes; One who had not worshipped in God's house and who now had paid the ultimate price for sinful impiety. Now, in death, she would face the judgment of The Lord for absolution.

Russet was furious that he should speak so of her mother.

She rose from her pew.

"My mother was not a sinner!" She called.

Charlotte tugged at her dress for her to sit down but Russet would have none of it.

"My mother forfeited her sensibility to give life to my dear sister. There was no sin in that."

Every face was turned to her as she persisted. "For sixteen years my mother lived in a hell of her own. How dare you infer that death was God's punishment for her sins?"

Now Katherine joined Charlotte, pulling at Russet to sit down, but to no avail.

"You talk of nothing else but the wrath of the Lord. Where is the love of God in this parish? We hear nothing of Christian love and charity from you!" With that she allowed her sisters to drag her down to the pew.

The Rector was speechless. He grunted and coughed, placing a hand to his face. Then he muttered. "We shall sing the hymn..."

As people left the church to attend the burial there were mutters and nods in Russet's direction. It was said by one old woman that to reject the word of God's messenger was to reject God himself! There would be repercussions.

Everybody at Nestwith Hall attempted to get back to normal after the funeral but Sir Marcus was displeased by Russet's behavior in church. He said he was appalled that a member of his family should openly abuse a churchman in front of his congregation. He told Russet her action was unforgivable but secretly, although he could not condone her action, he was proud of her show of self-assurance and he admired her audacity.

His very next act brought about discord in the household, he dismissed Molly.

Molly was distraught. Jossy tried to console her but she had her hands over her face, saying over again. "I tried so hard. What have I done wrong?"

Maisy entered the kitchen and was told the news. She immediately went to talk with Russet and Katherine. All three returned to the kitchen where, between sobs, Molly told them Sir Marcus had dismissed her for neglecting her duty to Lady Mary. Russet stamped her foot and stormed out of the kitchen followed by Maisy and Katherine. She did not knock on the study door but threw it open and walked in.

"You have dismissed Molly, Father?" Russet snapped the question

"I have." Sir Marcus was surprised by the anger in her voice. "I consider she was negligent. She was tending your mother when the good lady jumped out of the window. She should have stopped her."

"Father!" Russet raised her voice. "Mother was out of her mind. Nobody, and I mean nobody, could read her thoughts for they were insanely irrational. Molly was in no way to blame for Mother's death. I ask you, please, reinstate her."

Sir Marcus shook his head. "No. And I will not be told what to do in my own house. She must go." He rose from the desk and turned to the window.

"Ah!" he exclaimed. "I see we have visitors." He gestured toward the window. "I see we are to receive the company of our dear rector and his curate."

Russet's indignation at the dismissal of Molly faded at the thought of having to face the priest. She desperately felt the urge to hide. Then she was ordered to do so.

"Go on! Out Russy! Sir Marcus spoke quickly. "And keep out of the way. I shall deal with this."

Maisy went into the hallway but Russet and Katherine ran up the stairs to get out of the way. They did not enter any room but hid out of sight on the landing to hear what was said.

Sir Marcus met the rector at the door. "Good day to you Rector," he smiled. It is so good of you to call on me in my time of grief."

"I come to bless you sir and this house and I would have words with your daughter." The Rector boomed, in his singsong way.

"And which daughter would that be Rector? I have three." Sir Marcus bluffed.

"I confess I know not which of your daughters indulged in the outrageous outburst in the House of God, but it is she with whom I wish to communicate."

"I fear I cannot help you there Rector, perhaps you should see all three. Oh, but then, they are not all here." Sir Marcus was quite willing to lie to protect Russet from this reproaching cleric.

"I doubt your word, Sir!" The Rector blurted out the words and immediately regretted it.

"You call me a liar! In my own home!" Sir Marcus shouted, then, "Aaaah! Good morning to you Squire Bull." His voice changed from one of anger to a pleasurable tone as the portly figure of Squire William Bull appeared in the doorway.

William Bull, known to all and sundry as Willye, was a local magistrate. He was a gruff man in his early fifties, of medium height, but with a pronounced paunch. Bushy sideburns adorned his face appearing from beneath a short, dirty grey wig of dubious age. He had a large, bulbous nose and his eyebrows met in one long, bushy line above eyes of piercing blue. It was a face that could be benign or as fearsome a countenance imaginable. He was a well-liked man and was trusted to be fair in all deliberations.

"Good day, Sir Marcus." He looked beyond to where the rector and curate stood. "I see you have other guests, but it is of importance that I have words with you this day."

I am here on God's business Mr Bull. Is your concern of more importance than that?" The rector stood his ground.

"I too am here on a matter of religious consequence. And if you are here to speak with Miss Russet then I advise you not to do so." William Bull snorted as he spoke, then took from a pocket a large handkerchief and proceeded to blow his nose.

"Miss Russet!" The Rector roared with triumph. "I shall speak with Miss Russet, if you please Sir Marcus."

"Rector!" William Bull stood face to face with the cleric. "The common law of this land overrides ecclesiastical law. It spreads its wings far and wide to every corner of this land. Abodes of the most powerful are not excluded. I say you will not speak with Miss Russet for if you persist, sir, then you will be in default of the law.

How could I...." The Rector blustered as he was interrupted.

"Because complaints have been lodged against a member of this family, as you well know. You are a witness to the offence and I have no doubt you will offer your services as a witness for the prosecution. It is not therefore within your legal right to speak with the defendant. Should you do so, after being warned, then a complaint would surely be lodged against you."

The rector understood the threat and made a speedy departure, followed closely by his clinging companion.

"Come into my study, Willye. Sir Marcus opened the door and they entered. "Would you care for a beverage," he offered. "Claret or port – this is an excellent port, I recommend it to you."

Aye, I will take the port, Marcus. But I am here on serious business. Two complaints have been lodged against Russet. The more serious one is of blasphemy. And there is a second of breach of the peace."

"Oh, surely not."

"It is a crime, Marcus. If she is found guilty of the first the consequences could be dire indeed."

"But a cry for the love of God in church cannot surely be called a crime?" Sir Marcus was almost pleading.

"Christianity is a part of common law and blasphemy undermines the law." William Bull was not enjoying being the conveyor of ill news. "Speaking words that vilify or ridicule God, or religion, is a criminal act. A summons will be issued charging your daughter to stand before the court to answer the charges."

"And what if she is found guilty?"

William Bull took a sip of his port. "In the most grievous cases a spell in a penal institution or deportation to the colonies. For lesser charges, a whipping, the pillory, or the most lenient – a spell in the stocks."

"Will you sit for the case?" Sir Marcus asked, sombrely.

"No, no. I cannot. I was present when the alleged offence took place. I was in the church." He paused, then went on, "if you desire, Marcus, I shall offer to be a witness for the defence, but there is further bad news." He shook his head. "The presiding magistrate will be Mr Percy Gavin."

"I know nothing of him."

"No, but your brother Oliver did." William Bull looked grave. "Your brother borrowed a considerable amount from Gavin and did not repay it, so you see, there is bad blood adrift. He is no friend of the Roulettes and I fear he will do his utmost to humiliate your family through Russet."

"You say you will support her, Willye? I would greatly appreciate your good services, for I am at a loss." Sir Marcus filled the glasses. It would not be the last time he replenished his own glass that day.

On the day of Russet's appearance in court, the street outside the Loylton courthouse was crammed with people from all walks of life. Dressed sedately but with a wide-brimmed hat fastened down with a silk ribbon knotted under her chin, she was ushered to the dock where she was overcome with an intense feeling of loneliness. She was a little girl again, desperately in need of protection, and now she began to regret her refusal of legal representation. It was all very well, she thought, to show bravado at home by insisting that she could speak for herself, but here in the solemn precincts of the courtroom she did not feel so brave.

There was a shuffling of feet as the clerk called, "Hats Off! All be upstanding."

Three magistrates entered and stood behind the high bench. They bowed. Officials of the court and all present returned the formality.

When members of the bench were seated the clerk of the Court began. "You are Russet Roulette?"

"I am." Her voice sounded to her ears as if another person had answered.

"And you are a spinster residing at Nestwith Hall in the Parish of Nestwith?"

"Yes."

"Russet Roulette you are charged with the crime of blasphemy."Do you plead guilty or not guilty to the indictment laid to your charge?"

"Not guilty." Her voice trilled as she denied the charge. She coughed to clear her throat. The Clerk went on, "Russet Roulette you are charged with causing a breach of the peace. Do you plead guilty or not guilty to the indictment laid to your charge?"

"Not guilty." She raised her voice.

Russet realised she was trembling. She looked around at the sombre setting of the Loylton courthouse The Chairman of the Magistrates leant forward over the high bench to take a closer look at her as she stood with her hands gripping the brass rail of the dock. His magisterial colleagues, flanking him, also stared at her with equal curiosity. Russet's heart sank; they looked so fearsome.

The prosecuting council, Lawyer Branscombe, was a little man dressed in black with a wig that appeared too small for his head. He approached the dock and stared up at Russet then turned to face the bench. In a voice seeming too loud for such a little man, he began, "Russet Roulette is charged that on Friday, 15th of this month she did stand during a service within the church of the parish of Nestwith. There she did express insult to God, our Lord Almighty, which did distress the assembled congregation. I call a witness, The Reverend Alexander Butler."

The rector took the stand and took the oath.

"You are the Reverend Alexander Butler, rector of the parish of Nestwith?"

"I am. I am a servant of The Lord and a teacher of his scriptures. It is my duty to root out the evil in our society. I speak of..."

"Mister Butler!" The Chairman of magistrates banged his gavel on the bench. "We know now who you are and what you do. Just answer the questions."

Lawyer Branscombe asked, "you were present when the accused allegedly blasphemed?"

"I was. And as a messenger of the word of God..."

"Mister Butler!" The Chairman exclaimed. "Answer the question."

"Now, Reverend," Lawyer Branscombe went on, "in your

own words you may tell the court what you heard and what you witnessed. And I would ask that you stay with your testimony."

The Rector straightened his shoulders and began, I was preaching to the bereaved when…"

"The bereaved?" The Chairman interrupted.

"Yes, Your Worship." Lawyer Branscombe turned to address the bench. "The act took place at a funeral" He nodded to the Rector to continue.

"As I was saying before I was so rudely interrupted…"

"Mister Butler, I will not warn you again." The Chairman was showing impatience. "You are not in your domain – you are in mine. This is a court of law and…"

"There is no law higher than God's law and it is a sin of the greatest magnitude to think otherwise." The Rector had raised his voice to a loud, sing-song chant. "You are all sinners in the eyes of God!" He covered the court with a wave of an arm. "You are all condemned to eternal damnation. You will all burn in the fires of hell. You must all repent your sins. You mus…"

"Mister Butler!" The Chairman used his gavel again and again. "If you are of the opinion that God's law overrides the common law of this land then you are mistaken. The law does not recognise status. Whether a person be a man of the cloth or the daughter of a baron, the law and the sentence of law has equality. I tell you this Rector because I find you an unsuitable witness and you will stand down."

The Rector held out his arms as if enfolding the assembly "I will be God's witness. I will…"

"You will stand down Mister Butler." The magistrate raised his voice. "And if you speak once more I will hold you in contempt of this court." He pointed the gavel. "The punishment for contempt varies but a sentence of incarceration in the pillory is a regular option." He addressed Lawyer Branscombe. "You have written testimony?"

Yes, Your Worship."

"Then read it out." The Chairman relaxed in his chair as the lawyer read the Rector's statement.

The Reverend Butler returned to his seat. The thought of being locked in a pillory appalled him. The thought of the law of this court overruling God's law benumbed his brain.

"Are you not represented Miss Roulette?" The Chairman looked about the court.

"No, Your Worship," Russet answered confidently. "I shall speak for myself, but I have never before seen the workings of a court of law and I have no knowledge of the procedure." She looked up to the three men about to judge her. She cocked her head in a coquettish manner and added, "may I ask you, gentlemen, if you would kindly guide me."

There was a sudden coming together of the three justices. Mumblings, whispers, nods of heads then, "yes, we will help you with procedure, but that is all the assistance we are able to give. The Chairman nodded to Lawyer Branscombe to proceed.

Russet answered all the questions asked and then she spoke in her defence.

"I cannot imagine how a call for the love of God for my mother and the parishioners of Nestwith can be construed as blasphemy. The Rector," She pointed a finger at Reverend Butler, "spoke ill of the dead. He insinuated my mother was a sinner and that she had suffered death as a punishment visited by God. My mother lost her senses when she gave birth to my lovely sister Katherine sixteen years ago. She had to be tended night and day during that time. She was not capable of sin and, distressed as I was at our sad loss, I could not bear to hear the Rector condemn her so."

"One moment Miss Roulette." The Chairman interrupted. "Lawyer Branscombe. This funeral - was this a service for Lady Roulette?"

"Yes, Your Worship."

"Then why was this not mentioned beforehand?" he did not wait for an answer but gestured for Russet to continue.

"The Rector always threatens the wrath of God. He never ever speaks of God's love for any. He bullies everybody with the portent of God's anger, yet shows nothing of, nor proffers, kindness, charity or love.

"He calls us his flock but if that is so, why does he not show the respect and care a shepherd allows his sheep. If a call for my mother to be accepted into the arms of The Almighty is blasphemy, then I am guilty. I ask the court to judge me on the morals I hold dear. I am a God-fearing woman but I also worship God with love and I would never intentionally disoblige Him."

The three magistrates went into a huddle. Again heads nodded, their voices in whispers that could not be defined by others. Then they turned and the Chairman Gavin began, "Russet Roulette you have been charged with blasphemy. On

127

this count we have taken note of the mitigating circumstances and we find you not guilty."

Russet sighed with relief as Chairman Percy Gavin continued, a twist of a smile creasing his lips, "on the count of causing a breach of the peace, we have come to the conclusion that you did cry out and cause a disturbance that brought distress to a minister of God and to his congregation. We therefore find you guilty and you are hereby sentenced to be held for twenty-four hours in the Nestwith Parish stocks.

Chapter Sixteen

It took a great deal of concentration to hold back tears when Russet contemplated the indignity of being imprisoned in the stocks. She really would be the laughing stock of the county. In his capacity as a Justice of the Peace, William Bull had guaranteed her attendance and was to stay at Nestwith Hall until the sentence was carried out. What the magistrate had not stated was when the sentence should begin. It was assumed that William Bull had been authorised to set the date and time and Russet had expressed a wish for it to be soon.

On Friday morning William Bull was with Totton in the drawing room when Russet entered. The two were deep in conversation but ceased abruptly at her appearance.

"Good morning to you, my dear" William Bull performed an exaggerated bow. "I have news for you. Your fine ankles are to be enclosed in the timbers this very day."

"Oh!" Russet gasped, then held her head high. "And at what time am I to suffer this indignity?"

"At ten minutes to midnight you will be locked in, my Dear. You will have paid your debt to society at ten minutes to midnight on Saturday. A time chosen that will not infringe the Sabbath – for obvious reasons." He laughed and held out a hand, palm uppermost, with fingers spread as if balancing an imaginary missile. "We are all looking forward to it." He laughed again. "I have some well-addled eggs and I hear Mistress Pitchforth has some rotten turnips – they should land with a wholesome thump." Both he and Totton laughed loudly.

"And what about a dead hen or two!" Totton suggested

"And – a – bucket – of - cow pats."   William Bull added. He could hardly get the words out for laughing.

Russet was incensed that they should treat her misfortune with such levity. She stamped a foot. "You are neither of you gentlemen. How could you look with such disdain on my misfortune? May God hear your derision and deal with you accordingly."

Both men acted as one. With grinning faces they pointed fingers at her and shouted, "blasphemy!"

With hands on hips, Russet again stamped her foot. She turned about and head held high flounced out of the room, the laughter ringing in her ears. Once away from the men she held her face in her hands. How could they laugh. How could they be so off-hand when they knew she would spend the following day a target for all and sundry. She went in search of Charlotte and Katherine to share her woe but she could find neither. Maisy was not at the hall so she sent a houseman to the stables to tell Jamie she wished to go out.

With Jamie by her side she felt at ease but the thought of suffering her punishment weighed heavily.

"I am to be fastened in the stocks like a common felon, Jamie." People will throw things at me and I fear I shall be severely done by" She spoke to him for the first time as they approached the fallen oak. He felt a great sorrow for her but knew nothing of the mockery she had endured from William Bull and her brother. They alighted and she stood nearby as he made fast the reins.

"I am afraid, Jamie." She looked forlorn. "I am so afraid."

As she began to sob he went to her and placed his arms about her as if it was the natural thing to do. He held her close, his good hand gently patting her back. She did not pull away but put her head on his shoulder and wept.

Quite suddenly she began to feel a strange sensation creeping over her. The weeping stopped and she was trembling. The nearness of him alarmed her but she felt no fear. She felt safe. Then as if knowing she was doing wrong she pushed herself away from him.

"Oh Jamie, I am so sorry. I have acted like a silly spoilt child. Please forgive me." She stood away from him but all her senses were alive. Never before had she experienced such a sensual stirring. Her whole being was quivering with torrid excitement.

Jamie had a feeling of great happiness. It seemed so natural for him to hold her but in his euphoria lived the seeds of dejection. He was so in love with her he would have done anything to ease her unhappiness, but what he wished could never be. He would always be the peasant and she the lady.

On the way back she sat closer to him than ever she had done previously. It was a matter of trust, she told herself. She felt secure when near him. He was the most ugly man with a face drawn down at one side and a straggling beard grown to hide the impairment. He was mute but he had a manner about him that was not the graceless mode of behaviour of a peasant. In the kitchen she had seen him eat, never using fingers but insisting on cutlery which he used with distinct experience. But then, she thought, Maisy had probably worked in the houses of the gentry and had passed on her knowledge of etiquette to her sons. When she alighted from the carriage she thanked him in an off-handed way, as if to say we are now back in the real world and you are the peasant. As Jamie took hold of the bridle to walk the horse and carriage back to the stable she turned before entering the hall and watched him. She smiled at his lopsided walk as he threw his left leg with a turn of his body then skipped forward; the leather and metal splint Gunner had fashioned allowing him to keep the leg rigid. This is the man who saved my life, she mused. Then aloud she said, "for what - to sit in the stocks, to be pelted with every rotten substance imaginable." As she entered the door she added, "and to have an admirer somewhere, nay, perchance a lover - and I know not whom."

Housemen held lanterns on either side as Russet, accompanied by her father and William Bull descended the steps to the awaiting coach. At Charlotte's suggestion she was dressed in white and a silent sombre mood engulfed her. She was more frightened than ever now the time for her ordeal had arrived. William Bull and her father sat next to each other on the rear seat while Russet occupied the other and faced them.

As they moved off she murmured, "I would have at least thought my sisters and my brother could have given me support. There has not been sight or sound of them all day."

"Perhaps they are too shamed, My Dear." Sir Marcus offered, glumly.

The village was alight. Every lantern the villagers possessed was either personally carried or hanging from a prominent position. Russet shut out of her mind a sudden impulse to open the coach door and run away. The two men got out and helped her down. She was amazed at the sight that greeted her, a large dark-coloured marquee had been erected on the green with an enclosed awning leading to a smaller white tent erected over the stocks. It seemed the whole village had turned out to welcome her, for welcome it was. There had been silence as the carriage approached but now that silence was broken with a yelling and clapping such as she had never heard.

Escorted into the marquee she was greeted by Totton and Captain Halgalleon who saluted her. They fell in behind as she was ushered through the canvas-walled awning to the smaller tent. When she saw the interior she felt she was living a dream.

The open top section of the stocks stood vertical, the leg holes padded and covered in red velvet. The lower section had been treated similarly so there would be no chaffing of tender skin. The bench seat had been removed and in its place feather mattresses piled one on another made a bed on which rested quilts partly covered with a counterpane of white silk embroidered with gold needle-work. A backrest was in place holding up several pillows encased in the same white silk embroidery. Coloured silks and velvets draped three of the four walls of the tent, with carpets and rugs covering the ground. Two large, comfortable armchairs and a small table completed the elaborate furnishings. Russet gasped as she took it all in. A humble tent had been turned into a boudoir fit for a queen.

Behind the made-up bed stood four grinning figures, Charlotte, Katherine, Maisy and Molly. They all came towards Russet and one at a time hugged and kissed her. She laughed aloud, with pleasure at seeing them, and with relief that she had not been neglected after all.

The men were told to leave and Maisy pulled back the quilts. Russet lay on the mattresses with her ankles resting in the stock holes. When Bailiff Stamford arrived she was all ready for him. He was a man in his late fifties but looked much older. He wore a grey, curled wig and a blue, braided coat that signified his officialdom. He came to a halt at the entrance with open mouth and eyes seemingly about to pop out of his head. He spoke with a pronounced rustic accent, "I never seen the likes in my life!" He exclaimed. "I never seen the likes in my life!" He walked around the bed holding his jangling bunch of keys. He stopped to look at the drapes. "I never seen the likes in my life!" Taking out a timepiece he said to Russet, "t'is twenty minutes short of the mid of night. Would you have me lock you now? For should I do so t'will be a twenty minutes to the mid of night on the morrow when I do release you from the stock."

"Yes, yes. Please do so now" Russet spoke hurriedly. "The sooner I am locked in the sooner I shall be released."

She slept well. It was not so for Charlotte and Katherine who spent the night in the chairs. As dawn light penetrated the canvas, Russet came awake. Her sisters were already up and about, tidying the bed and placing all the furnishings in order. Russet patted the quilt. "I swear this berth is more comfortable than my own bed." She said. "But one night will be quite enough, thank you."

The landlord of the Rose and Crown provided breakfast and after Charlotte had combed Russet's hair the sisters rolled up and fastened the unadorned canvas wall facing her. The village was a bustle of activity. Two soldiers, resplendent in their scarlet coats, braided three-corner hats, white breeches and knee-length buttoned gaiters, stood guard at each corner of the tent, their muskets held at the ease. The village street was lined with stalls of merchants out to take advantage of the expected throng. Jugglers and tumblers. Charlatans calling out with persuasive insistence the healing properties of their potions. A dancing bear, made to hop by a boy who jerked a rope attached to a ring through the animals nose. It was a bustle of activity; all there to offer goods or to entertain those who came to view a lady of class suffer the deserts of the poor.

By midday the village could take no more; regardless of class, all were allowed into the tent and ushered out when they had paid their respects to Russet. Children, who should have been at work, profited by holding horses for gentlemen who went forward on foot to introduce themselves and to make the acquaintance of the beautiful, imprisoned lady. The landed gentry arrived in splendid carriages; men dressed in the uniform of their station with their ladies on arm magnificently adorned in the fashions of the time.

Russet held court all through the day and enjoyed every moment. She had been introduced to and spoken with far more people than ever she would at tea parties or balls. Everybody desired to know her and by dusk she had become the most famous lady in the county – the notorious Russet Roulette.

Chapter Seventeen

Alexander Butler stood at the church door waiting to welcome his parishioners. His eyes wandered about, looking at the neat line of gravestones and the well groomed, scythed grass that separated them. He looked at the gravelled path that wound to the rectory and the stables beyond. He glanced back into his church and felt a surge of pride; he was lord of all he surveyed.

His thoughts went back to the events of the previous day. Although jollity had been made of the Roulette girls' punishment, she had nevertheless served her sentence and it had shown that his actions were endorsed by the word of God; there was no escaping punishment for sin. All were seen to be equal in the sight of God and there could be no exoneration or recognition of class. He would today preach on this subject and no person would now doubt his authority.

He shivered and hunched his shoulders, drawing his arms to his sides as if to hold in the warmth. His timepiece told him it was late. He wandered down to the lichgate and looked down the road towards the village. Not a worshipper in sight.

Not a single person turned up to attend church. The rector and his curate were alone. Alexander Butler was incensed that he be treated with such contempt but he carried out his duty by narrating his practiced sermon from the pulpit to a congregation of one. Isiah Snufty sat in a pew far from the pulpit, a lonely figure, clasping his hands before him, fingers enmeshed, his head nodding agreement at the priest's every word.

During the following weeks Russet had many visitors. Young men rode up to pay court; carriages arrived carrying reluctant older men escorting their social-climbing wives who wished it known that they knew the renowned Russet Roulette.

Charlotte departed to stay with John Fullerton at his father's estate. Totton had reluctantly agreed to act as chaperon, his mind full of schemes for raising capital to pursue his business plans. Sir Marcus would not entertain the idea of breeding pigs and until the estate began to show a profit had made clear there would be no finance for any fanciful design.

Russet enjoyed her notoriety but her attitude to her family and friends changed. She took on an air of arrogance, speaking sharply to members of the household staff and even Katherine and Sir Marcus became victims of her discordant tongue. She ignored Jamie and when out would summon others to drive the carriage, insisting without argument they dress in livery. Trips to Loylton became a regular occurrence. She would take tea with the ladies of the town and be the centre of attraction, listening to their gossip but always taking centre stage with her new-found garrulous tittle-tattle.

Jamie was distraught at her disregard of him. At first he thought it normal that she should show disdain of a servant in front of others but to wave him away when no other was present hit him hard. When she had another male employee take the reins and drive her over the hill in the direction of the fallen oak, he was heartbroken. But it was Katherine who took the brunt of Russet's pompous manner.

"I do not have time for trivia," she declared to Katherine. "I associate with the ladies of the town who meet to enjoy the pleasure of my acquaintance. I also have so many introductions to young gentlemen of substance. They come forward in droves to solicit my company." She tossed her head as a gesture of dismissal and strode out of the doorway and down the steps to her waiting carriage with exaggerated deportment.

Katherine knocked on the door of her father's study and entered without invitation.

"Who was that I hear leaving?" Sir Marcus was working at his desk. He did not look up.

"Oh, that was only Madam Pomp off to meet her lickspittle friends." Katherine said, sarcastically.

"It won't last Kate." Sir Marcus laid his quill down and put an arm round his daughter. "Perhaps we made too much of her. Perhaps I am to blame for creating her renown. I could not see a daughter of mine confined to the stocks like a common criminal. Willye Bull came up with the idea of making light of Russy's predicament and I agreed. Captain Halgalleon provided the tents and soldiers for protection but nobody thought of the effect it would have on her mind. I will allow it one more week, Kate, and if there is no change in her pretentious behaviour I promise I shall deal with it."

Charlotte was relieved to arrive at Beamstorn House, the home of Sir George Fullerton. The journey had been long and arduous and even though she took the arm of John Fullerton, she had to steady herself as she alighted before the elegant brick-built residence. Sir George himself came out of the building to greet her and he was followed by several of the household staff rushing to attend to the baggage. She curtsied as John introduced her to his father, then she was ushered inside and immediately up the stairs to her room.

"Welcome, my son." Sir George smiled and showed his pleasure. "It is so good to see you." They briefly hugged then he turned to Totton "And this is Mr Roulette I presume." He proffered a hand. "Come inside," he said. "I have another visitor I would have you meet."

The small windows of the house allowed little light to penetrate the room. Totton screwed his eyes to see the tall figure dressed in black coming forward with both arms outstretched.

Introductions concluded, Totton had the uncomfortable feeling that the piercing blue eyes of Lord Francis Doulain were looking straight into his mind. He matched the stare, unblinking. Sir George invited them to take wine and with the niceties over he spoke, "his Lordship is down here looking for swine." He laughed and was prepared to say more when Lord Doulain interrupted.

"George makes it sound as if I am looking for some disreputable scoundrels, but I assure you that is not the case." He came straight to the point. "My company owns a fleet of ships and we are always looking for ways to better feed the crews. Pig meat keeps longer than most, if it is salted properly. You would be astounded at the trouble we have in purchasing quality meat."

Totton was listening intently. "My Lord," he said, "I have great interest in what you say. I have, myself, put my mind to solving such a problem and, with your permission, I would be honoured to converse with you on the matter."

The following morning Lord Doulain and Totton walked together in the large, landscaped garden. They discussed the business of pig breeding to supply meat for ships at sea. Lord Doulain knew most of Totton's plan from John Fullerton's detailed report but listened intently to every word.

Lord Doulain spoke with pretence, "and why, may I ask, have you not proceeded with your plans?"

"Money, My Lord." Totton replied. "We have the land. We could build the appropriate buildings – slaughter house, butchery and casking house. There is a man called Gunner, a blacksmith, who would forge the ironwork and his friend Lupton who, I am told is a cooper. A man by the name of Wrigglesworth, and his wife, have expertise in the breeding of pigs and there is a boar, the likes of which I have never before witnessed....."

"Yes, yes," Lord Doulain interrupted. "Why have you not taken a loan to finance the project?"

"Ah, therein lies the butt, My Lord." Totton said. "My father has recently suffered misfortune financially - through no fault of his own I should add – and he cannot, and will not, personally guarantee a loan."

Lord Doulain clasped his hands behind his back and was silent for a while. Then he said, "finance is my business, Tott." Totton noted the familiarity as the older man continued, "I would not be prepared to offer a loan under such circumstances but as I consider your scheme well worked I suggest to you a three-way partnership. Your father, yourself and I. Your father would provide the land and some of the labour. You manage the business and I provide the money. Other matters can be ironed out later. Well, what do you think?"

"I think well of it My Lord." Totton tried not to sound too enthusiastic. "But it will be necessary for me to consult my father before I answer."

"Then so be it." Lord Doulain nodded. "On second thoughts, I think perhaps it would be a wiser course if I spoke to your father as well. Could you persuade him to invite me to Nestwith?"

Lord Doulain returned to London but left a rider at Beamstorn to fetch him news from Totton. John and Charlotte spent two happy weeks together and it became very clear there was a respectful affection between them. John had suggested prolonging their stay but Totton would have none of it. For him the time dragged. He dispatched a rider to Nestwith with a missive for his father and five days later a rider returned with an invitation for Lord Doulain.

An immaculately dressed rider, attired from head to foot in black, arrived at Nestwith Hall to announce the imminent arrival of The Lord Doulain. The whole Nestwith Hall household, with the exception of Russet who was late dressing, lined the entrance to greet him and they stood nervously as the impressive, hearse-like coach with its four black horses came up the carriageway. Two black-clad men were seated at the front, one holding the reins, the other bristling with pistols and with a sword at the ready. Two armed footmen stood on the low platform at the rear of the coach and behind came four outriders on black mounts, all black attired.

The driver reined in the horses and expertly brought the coach to a halt at the foot of the steps. Then followed a rush of activity. One footman opened the coach door, another unfolded the steps and held an arm out to assist Lord Doulain alight. The guard stood, looking about with his hands on his pistols, ready to defend his master. The four horsemen moved into position round the coach, facing away and ready to repulse any attack. There was no need to take such precautions at Nestwith but it was well drilled and intended to impress.

Lord Doulain stepped out of the coach and was greeted by Sir Marcus who then introduced him to his family.

"I think you are already acquainted with my son, Totton and my daughter Charlotte. He glanced up the steps looking for Russet. "This is my youngest daughter, Katherine." She curtsied. Then as he was about to move on, Russet appeared at the top of the steps and gracefully came down to meet the guest.

At sight of her Lord Doulain gasped. "Helen!" The name came out as a harsh whisper. He pulled himself together. Of course it was not she, but the likeness to his dead wife was incredible.

Later that evening when the ladies had withdrawn the three men discussed Totton's plans. As they made frequent use of the claret jug it was agreed that the scheme would go ahead immediately. Totton could hardly conceal his joy but he wanted to keep his senses about him so he left the two older men to their wine and retired to his room.

Lord Doulain placed his hands flat on the table. "Marcus," he began. "There is a matter I must discuss with you. It cannot wait. It would be unfair of me to keep it from you for a moment longer."

Sir Marcus was puffing contentedly on a clay pipe. "You sound inordinately serious My Lord."

"My name is Francis. My friends call me Frank. I would have you do so. If you will." He was trying to soften the blow he was about to deliver.

"Some time ago a man came to my company to procure a substantial loan. His collateral was his estate and he left with us the deeds of the estate as security in case of non-payment. He also signed papers agreeing that if the loan were not repaid by a certain date the estate would be forfeited. I must tell you Marcus that the date of agreement has passed and the man was your brother Oliver. I assure you I take no pleasure in telling you that I own this house and all of the Nestwith Estate."

Sir Marcus puffed on his pipe and said nothing.

"You seem unperturbed, sir." Looking at Sir Marcus sitting there with a smile on his face, Lord Doulain began to feel uneasy. He had just told a man he had lost his house and his fortune and yet this man was smiling.

Sir Marcus took a puff of smoke and blew it out across the table. "Frank," he began. "You have brought me news of joy. I have searched for the deeds without success and now I learn you have them in safekeeping. I am indebted to you, my friend, but you are wrong in your assumption. You are a peer of the realm and I only a knight, the one thing we have in common is that we are mere tenants of our titles, our lands and all properties appertaining to those titles. That property passes through our sons to their sons in perpetuity. You thought you were giving me bad news but it is the other way about." He emphasised the name as it crossed his mind that the man sitting opposite was visiting not out of friendship but to claim what he thought was rightly his. He went on, "You said you took no pleasure in telling me of my misfortune so I will say the same to you. You have been duped by a sly unscrupulous scoundrel – my dear brother. He had no right to sign away something that was not his to sell. Did you not read the deeds? The clause that states that the estate is the property of the baronetcy? Did you not look for the small writing, as the lawyers say?   Brother Oliver was a tenant of the baronetcy, just as I am, and you know as well as I, Frank, a man cannot sell his landlord's house."

Lord Doulain was silent for a few moments, then he put back his head and he laughed, and he laughed.

Chapter Eighteen

Gertrude Wrigglesworth was mucking out the sties when Totton called. She was a woman of large proportions and but for her enormous breasts the casual onlooker could easily mistake her for a man. Since the age of six, until she married Albert Wrigglesworth, she had worked the river, riddling gravel for the drives and carriageways of the well to do. Even during the coldest winter days she was seen up to her knees in the icy water working to earn only enough to buy food. She had grown to be a hard, tough woman and was known throughout the locality as Gravel Gerty, but none ever dare call her that to her face.

"Mistress Wrigglesworth?" Totton enquired. She had her back to him but straightened up to face him.

"Who wants to know?" She asked. Then before he could answer she recognised him and her fearsome manner changed. "Ah, Master Totton. And what brings you to this neck of the woods?"

Totton took a step backwards. He was tall but he found himself looking up into her face. "I have come to speak to you and your husband. Firstly regarding this property and secondly the business of breeding pigs."

"Then you'd better come inside." She walked past him and he followed. As they entered the cottage she said, "it's not much of a place but we call it home."

Totton glanced around the single room, amazed that humans could live in such squalor. There was no litter about but the furnishings were of the most primitive nature. A large bed occupied one end and on it rough blankets lay crumpled, topped by hessian sacks filled with straw for pillows. A table with pieces of wood nailed to broken legs centred the room. Two rickety chairs similarly fastened with odd bits of wood completed the furnishing. A fire burned in the hearth with an array of pans and vessels propped up against the wall. Several cuts of meat hung by hooks from a beam, all covered with salt-soaked cloth to discourage the hoards of flies that buzzed everywhere. To add to the scene of poverty, the room was full of the smell of pigs.

Totton wondered to himself how people could possibly live in such conditions but he knew only too well that lack of money created this style of living. The Wrigglesworths would barely earn enough between them to sustain themselves let alone afford any of the necessities he took for granted.

"Will you have a bite to eat, Master Totton?" She asked. "We aren't got much but we can always feed a visitor."

Totton wanted desperately to refuse but not wishing to offend her he accepted her offer. She took down a piece of meat, cut off a large slice and cooked it in a black-bottomed pan. Totton could imagine the utensil had never been touched by water. In no time a wooden platter of ham and eggs lay before him on the table. He was not supplied with cutlery so he picked up the slice of meat, prodded it in an egg and took a bite. He was hoping he would not retch but as he chewed his facial expression turned to one of delight. It was delicious.

"Upon my word, Mistress Wrigglesworth, this is the finest ham that ever passed my lips!" Before he could say more Wriggley appeared in the doorway. He was taken aback at the sight of Totton.

"What? What?" He stammered. "Mister – Sir – Roulette."

"Oh come in," Gertrude shouted. Master Totton is trying some of your cured ham, and he likes it."

"I do so, Master Wrigglesworth. It has a rare succulence to it." Totton rose from the unstable chair and said, "I have come to put to you and your wife a proposition that you may consider to be of considerable benefit."

Lord Doulain was enchanted. Russet's physical likeness to his dead wife astounded him but he found her mental aptitude equally identical to the manner of his late spouse. It was as if the clock had been turned back and he was courting her again. At times when in her company he had to temper his words to avoid familiarity. Russet enjoyed his company and the attention he gave her, and was so impressed with being the consort of a lord. She wanted him to escort her to Loylton but Sir Marcus would not agree to it. He knew well that she only wanted to show Lord Doulain off. She did however persuade him to take the reins and drive to her favourite place.

Jamie saw them off. He brought the pony and carriage to the foot of the steps but she did not acknowledge him. He watched them until they disappeared over the hill then he returned to the stables with a heavy heart.

When they arrived at the fallen oak Russet took Lord Doulain by the hand and when seated she said, "why is it you always dress in black, My Lord?"

"Because I mourn my dear late wife." He answered sombrely.

"But that was so long ago." Russet looked at him quizzically.

"Twenty four years, nine months and fifteen days, precisely."

"Then, with all the respect in the world, I would consider you have grieved for long enough. Is it not time you let some colour back in to your life." She stopped, thinking she had gone too far. She was surprised at his next words.

"Do you know, Miss Roulette, I think perhaps you are right." He nodded his head vigorously. "I shall discard my wardrobe and perhaps I may ask you to help me choose my new costume.

"I will with pleasure, My Lord, but you will find no fashion in these parts. I would venture the tailors of London would better suit your taste."

"Then will you visit me at my home in the city to allow me to keep you to your pledge?" He rose and faced her. "Perchance your father will visit also, for I find his company refreshing indeed."

As Russet snuggled down in her bed that night she again read the poem and asked herself, 'what does the future hold for me? Do I wait for an unknown, lovelorn poet, or do I allow the advances of a lonely old peer. His Lordship is wealthy.' Of great wealth she had been told. 'But he must be at least a quarter of a century older than I. *'Lady Doulain,'* it sounded so good in her mind that she repeated it aloud. Then other thoughts crowded in – 'would I be prepared to go to bed with an old man? No, I do not think I would be so disposed. But, I would have wealth, and perhaps for that it would be a burden I could bear? No it would not. I cannot stand to think of it now, it could be a fate worse than I imagine. Father has wrinkles on his brow and his neck. I wonder if older men have wrinkles elsewhere?' She began to chuckle at the thought.

She knew several younger men now but every one of them would be looking for a wife with a substantial dowry. Even bachelors of substance would look to increase their wealth by wedlock. She wondered if the young men she had been introduced to in Loylton would show such interest were they aware that she could not bring in money to a marriage? With a mind in confusion, sleep overtook her.

The following day was taken up with discussion. The three men went over details of the plans for the piggery and the availability of finance. Lord Doulain pledged a sum but only on condition that he supplied a financial director to oversee spending.

"There is a young man working for me in London who has interesting potential. His name is Thomas Chatterton, a fellow of lowly birth but of ready intellect. I recommend him to you." Lord Doulain looked at the other two for assent. "I assure you, my insistence is not a lack of trust. Indeed, I do likewise on every occasion with any partnership in which I invest." He looked from one to the other. "I take it you agree to my proposal?"

The following morning Lord Doulain departed to return to London. Russet was disappointed that she had not been able to spend more time with him and she could not hide her disappointment. In the sitting room in the company of her sisters she acted with obvious false nonchalance at his leaving and turned the conversation to other younger men she knew.

"Robert Graves is a fine young man," she twirled around, waving a fine net scarf above her head. "I met him in Loylton along with many of my other gentlemen friends. He said I was the most beautiful woman in the world. And do you know? All the others agreed with him."

Katherine, who had held her head down as she worked on a tapestry now looked up. "If you think that then you will be obliged to change your wardrobe, Russy."

Russet glanced down at her dress and held it out with both hands. "Why should I do such a thing? Am I not presentable?"

"It is your hats, dear sister." Katherine put on a serious expression.

"And what is wrong with my hats, Kate?"

Katherine looked at Russet closely. "Oh, there is nothing wrong with your hats, Russy. Except perhaps they are now too small to fit such a swollen head!"

Russet stamped her foot. "Oh tish!" She placed hands on her hips and Katherine prepared herself for the retaliation she knew she was about to receive.

"You are one to talk, young lady. I have seen you wide-eyed and all agog when we have the presence of Captain Halgalleon." Russet bent low to look into Katherine's face. "Look at her Lottie. There is the truth. I grant there is a rush of lover's blood, for her cheeks have grown as red as autumn apples."

Charlotte nodded to Katherine who stuck the needle she was holding into the tapestry and stood as if to leave, but

Russet was not yet finished as she worded barbs at her elder sister, "and what about you and your deaf lover, Lottie? I would imagine you have great difficulty whispering your words of love in his ear. Lady luck has certainly shone on both of you. He cannot hear your jabb......"

"Enough!" Charlotte snapped. "Come Kate, we shall leave her to wallow in her own conceit." As they reached the door she turned and said, "the worst thing that could have happened was the attention you received from sitting in those damnable stocks. It was intended as a joke arranged by Willye Bull and Captain Halgalleon and we all fell in with it. None thought it would go to your head in such a way. You are treating everybody as if all are below you. See the way you now treat Pitchforth, the man who saved your life. You ignore the poor fellow and yet you owe him so much. Russet Roulette, take a good look at yourself for you have become unbearable."

As the door closed Russet tossed her head, then looked up and, as if looking to the heavens for agreement, she said aloud, "jealousy makes such poor companions."

Molly was now working at the Rose and Crown. Maisy recommended her and having brought into the world both of the landlord's children he had been hard pressed to refuse her request. Molly had already proved her worth, working as a waitress, a chambermaid and helping in the kitchen. It was a pleasant change from spending the past few years tending the deranged Mary Roulette and she revelled in her new environment. Her life took yet another turn with the arrival of Thomas Chatterton.

Dispatched by the Company Doulain to oversee financial arrangements and general accountancy for the new venture, Thomas Chatterton was a fine looking young man. Slim of stature with straw coloured hair hanging neatly to shoulder length surrounding a handsomely structured face. Only when he opened his mouth to speak did his roots and his class become clear, for Thomas Chatterton spoke with the broadest east London accent.

He took early breakfast each morning then saddled his horse and rode out to Nestwith Hall where Sir Marcus had provided a small room for use as an office. He also spoke with Gunner and Walter who proved to be enthusiastic in their involvement. He spent some time talking to Albert Wrigglesworth and his wife and became convinced of their suitability. It was after a long discussion with Wriggley that he returned to the inn early to find Molly about to set off to visit Maisy. He asked if he could join her and they walked together chatting about his coming to Nestwith.

"I don't particular like the countryside," he said. "I'm 'customed to the smells of the city and the buildings. When I ride out to the hall I feel all the time that I shall become lost."

"You will soon get used to it." Molly laughed. "I grant the country smells is different but..." She sniffed the air. "That smells like something dead." She breathed in through her nose again. "A dead sheep? We should take a look and if it be, then you can tell the shepherd when you next go to the hall." She looked back towards the village and saw two men approaching, leading a horse and cart. Looking down first at her shoes and then at the muddy ground, she decided to wait.

Gunner and Walter where on their way with the monthly load of firewood for Maisy when they saw the two figures in front halt and peer into the bushes at the side of the road. Upon reaching Molly she told how she thought a sheep had died in the bushes. Gunner sniffed the air and went alone to find the cause of the smell. When he returned he was shaking his head. "It's a woman," he said. "Murdered by the looks of it. Throat cut from ear to ear. You better go back and tell the bailiff, Walter – and tell him to fetch a coffin."

Molly had stepped back to the middle of the road, hands clasped in front of her chin. "Do you know who it is?" She looked to Gunner.

"Aye, but I think it no great loss." He wrinkled his nose in distaste, "it's the whore – Monica Woodcock."

Chapter Nineteen

The Liverpool docks were a bustle of activity. Moored ships being loaded and unloaded, beam cranes swinging from decks to pick up cargo from lighters alongside, and then swinging back to deposit the contents through open hatches. Other tackle lifted imported goods from holds to waiting hands to be stacked before being rowed ashore. Men crowded the quayside, all doing their particular jobs; the better dressed with chalk and slates, books or paper lists, ticking off quantities and accounting for each item of freight; Board of Trade officials and customs officers scrutinizing dockets and goods with practiced sagacity, Dockers with heavy loads on their shoulders making their way up and down gangways and, further away from the ships, horses, donkeys, mules and oxen struggled over well-worn cobbles to heave heavy loads in and out of the dock area. Above the teeming interchange of commerce, scores of masts, sails furled, rigging in profusion, like a forest of leafless trees. Further out, a mighty man-of-war lay at anchor, lower gun ports closed but open on the upper gun deck to display a line of formidable weaponry. A multitude of smaller boats served the mighty ship and marines, in brightly coloured uniforms, stood guard on the decks with muskets at the ready to prevent desertions.

Totton and John Fullerton watched the unloading and checking of the first consignment of salted pork. Adam Gunner had driven the first cartload and was talking to a dock official while Jamie Pitchforth, the second driver, waited for his load to be examined and allocated. The pigs that once belonged to Albert Wrigglesworth and Walter Lupton had been purchased, slaughtered and salted for the first run. This exercise had been arranged to learn the procedure for other drivers to follow.

Night was falling when they left the docks. Once the animals were tethered and fed Totton suggested they should celebrate their success.

The tavern they chose was frequented by mariners but away from the docks. The presence of a man-of-war put fear into all able-bodied men and even among this company glances over shoulders were commonplace. Since the arrival of the Royal Navy the press gangs had already taken a toll and drunken merchant mariners disappeared overnight only to awaken shackled in the dark bowels of the King's ship.

The four took seats at a corner table and ordered ale that came served in leather and pitch mugs. A buxom woman brought the ale but in the tobacco smoke haze they took no note of her. She deposited the mugs on the table but she let her eyes dwell in recognition on all four in turn. The next time they ordered, a different ale-wench served them.

Totton, John and Gunner discussed the business of pig meat while Jamie listened to their conversation. More ale was ordered and the mugs refilled, and refilled again. The evening wore on, then there was a sudden movement in the room as men rose hurriedly from their seats leaving half-filled mugs of ale as they rushed to get out. Some went out the back way while others rushed through the front door and into the night, in groups for safety.

John Fullerton appeared unperturbed. "Don't worry

yourselves," he assured them. "I am on the reserve list and still hold the rank of Lieutenant. If it is the press-gang they will not touch us."

They finished their drinks and prepared to leave for their billets. As they reached the street they were pounced on by a group of men. Gunner took a blow to the head and fell as if pole axed. John Fullerton was also hit on the head and fell before he could protest. Totton put up a fight but was overwhelmed and also beaten unconscious. Jamie was grabbed as he appeared in the doorway. He was thrown to the ground and his wrists and ankles bound and a sack pushed over his head before being thrown into a cart along with the inert figures of the other three. The cart trundled along at speed as some men pushed and others pulled the cart with ropes while several ran alongside. As the troupe disappeared into the darkness a lone figure came out from the shadows of a doorway. She jingled the coins she held in her hand, her face contorted in an evil smile. It had been a profitable night for Tanner Fanny.

The village of Nestwith did not mourn Monica Woodcock. It was whispered a good riddance for the fair name of the village. Rumour had it that Tanner Fanny was responsible for the death, but nobody could recall having seen her for weeks prior to the murder. Some insisted it had to be one of the military from the garrison in Loylton. Others, that it was the work of a band of cutthroats roaming the district, but the popular belief was that a customer took his pleasure and killed her to avoid payment. The official verdict was that it was a murder committed by a person, or persons, unknown.

Only one Nestwith resident had revelled in the occasion – The Reverend Alexander Butler.

"The Lord hath retribution on the sinner," he bawled from the pulpit. "You are all sinners in the sight of God. The Lord has shown his might. Vengeance is mine sayeth the Lord." He went on as if the hand of the Almighty had guided the assassin's knife.

"The man is an idiot!" William Bull took a sip of his wine and looked across the drawing room at Sir Marcus. "Whosoever ordained that creature must have had his snout deep into the communion wine." He took another sip, then, "you look very pensive, Marcus, are you not well?"

"I am thinking it is time my son made an appearance. It is almost three weeks since the departure of the wagons. It does not take so much time to travel to the port of Liverpool and back. I have an ill feeling something is amiss." He was about to say more when he was interrupted by a knock on the door. "Come in!" he called.

A houseman opened the door and said, "there is a gentleman to see you, sir. Captain Halgalleon."

"Show him in, show him in." Sir Marcus said.

Captain Halgalleon entered, resplendent in his military uniform. "Gentlemen." He bowed to both in turn but addressed Sir Marcus. "I have come to pay my respects to you and your family, sir. To thank you for your hospitality - and to bid you farewell."

"Farewell?" Sir Marcus looked puzzled.

"Yes, sir. We are to leave within the next few days for the

American Colonies. We are to strengthen the garrison at Boston in Massachusetts."

"Then you must take a glass with us and we shall drink to your health, your safe return, and to the success of your mission." Sir Marcus went to the huge sideboard that was adorned with an array of decanters, glasses and silverware. He took hold of an ornate claret jug, poured a very generous helping of the wine and held it out to the captain. He held his own glass high. "To you, sir, and to the brave young lads under your command."

There followed a few moments of silence then Halgalleon said, "I would not wish to depart without taking leave of your daughters, Sir Marcus. They have shown such kindness to myself and my fellow officers....."

"Of course." Sir Marcus rang a hand bell and sent for his daughters.

Russet came in with a flourish. Upon hearing that the captain had called she had hurriedly sprayed herself with perfume and now she came up close to the captain for him to breathe the aroma. A subdued Charlotte followed her.

"The captain is about to leave us for pastures new." Sir Marcus said.

Russet took a chance. "You are going oe'r the hill, Captain?"

"No, Miss Russet. I am going over the seas" The captain frowned.

"Where fantasies of ego play?" She put her head to one side, quizzically.

Captain Halgalleon shook his head and smiled. "You play

with words, Miss Russet. I am not clear to what you refer." He turned to Charlotte but before he could utter a word Russet spoke out, "you will get few words from my usually talkative sister, sir. She is mourning the absence of her Mister Fullerton. Her mind is elsewhere."

The door opened and Katherine entered. She wore a wide-brimmed straw hat held by a chiffon scarf that bowed the brim on either side. The scarf went under her chin and was tied at one side, the other side bore a delicately, sewn on badge of the Roulette coat of arms. She fiddled with it but at the sight of Valiant Halgalleon she stopped, hand on the door handle, eyes wide, open-mouthed. Her face reddened. "Oh!" She exclaimed with surprise.

"You will have to excuse my little sister," Russet said, sarcastically. "Any man in uniform affects her to the extent she will swoon on sight...."

"Russet!" Sir Marcus shouted. Then he lowered his voice. "What has got in to you child?"

"I am not a child."

"Then stop acting like one."

Russet turned to the captain. "I will bid you goodbye, Captain Halgalleon, and I wish you well." With that she strode out of the room, leaving the door open. She climbed the stairway and went to her room, closing the door behind her. She stared at herself in the looking glass and aloud she said, "whoever wrote the poem it was certainly not he."

Charlotte engaged in small talk then asked to be excused. Katherine was over her shock at seeing the captain and he was now giving her his undivided attention. There was a shaking of hands as Halgalleon prepared to depart. He went down the steps to where his horse was being held by a trooper. Katherine followed him and as he was about to mount she took off the chiffon scarf and held it out to him. "Here," she said. "This is for luck."

Captain Halgalleon laughed. "Sweet Kate, when I come back – if, God willing, I do come back - you will be a grown woman and perhaps married. But if you are not married then perhaps I may even bend a knee to you."

"You will come back! You will!" Her voice shook with emotion as he turned and rode off waving the scarf high in the air. Katherine went her room, tears streaming down her cheeks. She threw herself on the bed her body trembling as she sobbed.

Sir Marcus and Willye Bull were once again alone. Sir Marcus filled their glasses. "I swear I do not know what has got into Russet," he said. "She was the most witty, adorable creature and now she takes the role of a harsh-tongued vixen."

Willye Bull settled back in his chair. He lit a pipe of tobacco, took a gulp of wine and said. "Women! Women! We men will never understand them, Marcus. They're different to us, you know. Oh, I don't mean the obvious physical attributes – it's up here." He tapped his head. "They supposedly fall in love with a man and as soon as the church knots are tied they start to undo them. I never spoke of this to any man because I would be ashamed to do so, but on the night of my marriage I was shunned – denied my marital rights, by George! My new wife said she was not going to perform the disgusting actions of the beasts of the field. She hasn't done to this day. As far as

I know the woman is still a virgin – and so would I be had I not been introduced to certain bawdy haunts in the city. The Lord God bestowed man with amorous propensities, Marcus - desires that must seek satisfaction from time to time. Can't grumble though – I got the money to buy Bullington House so it was not such a great sacrifice. When her family pass away, she tells me, their wealth will pass to her – and so to me." The wine was having effect as he went on. "She is a sickly creature and takes more and more to her bed. When I look at her now after all these years I begin to realise what a wise woman she was – or is. Ha!" he drained his glass and indicated with his eyes that he required a refill.

"My only regret is that I have not begotten issue. Nobody to carry on at Bullington when I am dead. My good lady wife is not long for this world and I just hope she outlives the rest of her family. Tight-fisted! That's what she is." His voice was becoming slurred. "I know what I'll do. I shall leave it to your issue. When my wife dies I shall make another will and when I depart this mortal world it will become part of the Roulette estate. How about that, my friend?" He pushed himself up and, as if regretting what he had said, wagged a finger. "Not a word, Marcus, not a word. I shall now go home to my favourite fare. Fresh shot duck, not hung, roasted then the breasts dipped in beaten eggs and breadcrumbs and fried in duck fat Aaaah!" He belched loudly. Then, "not a word, Marcus."

Sir Marcus put a finger to his lips. Wine was doing the talking. "A confidence is a confidence, Willye. I would not dream of back chatting." He rose and again filled the glasses.

"You say you know of secret haunts in the city?"

Willy Bull again put a finger to his lips. "Not a word Marcus."

"Not a word, Willye. But I would welcome your directions. It is sixteen years since Katherine was born and I have not had the pleasure... They both burst into raucous laughter.

Chapter Twenty

Jamie squirmed on the hard wooden deck. Slowly, pushing at the material a bit at a time, he managed to nudge the sack off his head. His hands were tied in front and he lifted them to his face but the blackness was so absolute he could see no movement. He began to work on the rope that bound his wrists, but to no avail. He was on a ship, deep inside and just above the bilges. Water sloshed about below but that noise was almost obliterated by the constant, thunderous crash as the bows mounted each wave and pitched down into the next trough, making the timbers creak and squeal as if the vessel was about to break up. He turned on one side, feeling with his tied hands, like a blind man seeking his way.

Gunner lay next to him, the barrel chest and huge biceps unmistakable. He noted with relief the rise and fall of the chest. Totton and John Fullerton lay beyond. All were alive. He struggled to remove the sacks from their heads to make their breathing easier. Even though handicapped by the ropes binding his own wrists and legs he managed to undo the ropes binding theirs. He was crawling back over Gunner when the big man moaned and stirred. Suddenly Jamie found himself crushed by the great arms, squeezing the breath out of his lungs. He tried to shout but nothing came out. He struggled but the grip only tightened. At last, when his chest felt as if it would burst he let himself go limp and immediately the arms opened. He took in a great gulp of air and rolled onto the boards where he lay gasping, breathing life back into his aching lungs.

"I think I got one of 'em." Gunner croaked. There was no answer. Then, "oh, my head." A pause, then grunts and sighs, followed by, "where in God's name am I?"

Time passed before all three came to their senses. A few seconds of touch and talk took place before they were satisfied that all four were together.

"We have been pressed into the King's service." Totton murmured. "What a mess."

"This is not a fighting ship." John Fullerton's voice sounded hollow. "It could be an auxiliary or supply vessel. My bet is that it's a private merchantman. The captain has probably lost some of his crew to the press gangs and has tried to make it up by grabbing us. He's in for a surprise if he thinks he's captured the services of four mariners."

"God, I feel sick!" Totton retched.

Time dragged but none of them knew for how long.

"We are definitely on a merchant ship." After what seemed an age John Fullerton's whispered pronouncement echoed in the confined space. "Had we been taken by the navy we would have been fed by now. As it is we may be kept here for some time without food or water to make us submissive. I have seen strong, arrogant men confined in isolation on the lower deck for days in the darkness only to be brought out whimpering, servile wrecks. But don't worry, we have each other…"

Jamie was the first to be released. He was still suffering from the might of Gunner's arms as he was dragged out down a narrow gangway between stowed merchandise and thrown onto the open deck. He lay there dazzled by his sudden emergence from the darkness. When he attempted to stand he toppled over, unable to balance with his one good leg against the roll of the ship.

When Gunner appeared from below he walked unaided, none daring to lay hands on his mighty frame. He put a hand to his brow to shield his eyes and saw Jamie prone on the deck. A man with a belaying pin in hand stood over him, nudging with a boot and shouting for him to stand. Gunner rushed to his aid shouting, "leave him be. Can't you see he's a cripple?" The man turned on Gunner and lifted the belaying pin as if to strike. Gunner caught the man by the wrist and held it in a grip of steel. Their eyes met and held. For a few seconds it was impasse. A voice from the poop deck called, "belay there bosun!" With eyes locked the man made an almost imperceptible nod. Without blinking Gunner released him.

John Fullerton and Totton were brought out and they too screwed their eyes, dazzled by the sudden light as they joined Gunner and Jamie. Behind, a number of the crew stood in a line across the deck laughing at the antics of the four as they endeavoured to remain upright. The ship was under full sail and, after their close confinement with legs bound, the roll and the pitching of the vessel made it difficult to stand. Jamie was hauled to his feet by Gunner and winced as the great arm circled his already aching chest.

A voice from above called out, "you are aboard the Branston Silver. I am Captain Christopher and on this ship - my - word - is – the - law!" He paused between each word to allow the significance of his statement to sink in.

"You!" He pointed a finger at John Fullerton. "In which ships have you served?"

"Many ships, Captain. I am Lieutenant John Fullerton, a serving officer in His Majesty's naval service. You, sir, have abducted an officer of the King and I am sure you are aware of the potential consequences of your action." John Fullerton did not disclose that he was merely on the reserve list.

"And you." The Captain appeared to be unconcerned at the threat and moved on.

Totton was becoming accustomed to the light and he pointed a finger. "Did you say your name is Christopher?

"Captain Christopher! And who are you?" At the sound of Totton's cultured voice his initial arrogance changed.

"My name is Totton Roulette. I am the son of Sir Marcus Roulette of Nestwith. If I am not mistaken, sir, we dined together some months gone in the White Hart Inn at Troffton. You may recall we discussed the merits of salted meats." Totton was beginning to feel confident. "When last we met I believe you mentioned you were employed by the Company Doulain. If that is so, is this a Doulain ship?" Not waiting for an answer Totton said, "if this is a Doulain ship I must inform you that I am a business associate of Lord Francis Doulain, and you, sir, have not only abducted a colleague of his Lordship but you have disrupted important business matters I was conducting on his behalf.

The captain was silent for a few seconds then he bawled, "Bosun! To me!"

When it became clear that Jamie was not only crippled but also mute, the captain could not contain his fury. He had lost two experienced officers, a clerk and five newly signed members of his crew and the bosun had 'recruited' inexperienced landlubbers.

Captain Christopher retired to his cabin followed by the bosun. A few minutes passed then John Fullerton was summoned. He bowed his head to enter the dark cabin and could make out the captain seated at the head of a table. At his side stood the bosun. The captain had removed his hat and wig and did not cut so impressive a figure without the trappings of rank. He was bald, thin-lipped, but with a strong, jutting chin. His nose was small and a darker shade than the rest of his face. Even at a distance John Fullerton could see the myriad of tiny veins covering the protuberance in a purple map-like tracery. His eyes were deep-set below greying brows but the creases lining out from the corners on either side stretched as far as the temples and down either cheek. He was a man who could be stern when needs must, but the signs were also indicative of a humorous frame of mind.

"Mister Fullerton," the Captain said, "you have arrived aboard my ship in the most unfortunate circumstances, for which I apologise most humbly." He pointed to the chair at the opposite end of the table. John Fullerton took the seat as the Captain went on, "I lost two officers, a clerk, and a number of my crew in extraordinary circumstances. I presume the press gang got them but it is strange that when I enquired, the naval authorities were reluctant to comment. So, you see, it was with great urgency that I ordered my bosun ashore to recruit, not to abduct, new members for my crew. He took the word of a strumpet that you and your company were experienced sailors and she told him you would resist, hence the method used.

John Fullerton interrupted "Are you telling me we are here on the word of a harlot?"

"Who else?" The Captain smiled, his thin lips spreading across his face. "T'would be no good asking a high class madam of the town to choose my crew. She would not know a sailor from a midden dipper. On the other hand, a harlot has an eye for a seafarer – she knows a lass-starved tar when she sees one." He shuffled in his chair. "Enough! Mister Fullerton, with your experience and rank I am appointing you my First Mate."

"I cannot accept, Captain. And what is more, I demand we be put ashore with all haste."

"That is not possible Mr Fullerton, and you know that only too well." The captain was beginning to lose patience. "I sailed on the tide without a full complement but I have every intention of completing my mission. I will say only this. You have been appointed and that is an end of the matter."

"And if I refuse?"

"Then that would be accounted mutiny, sir." The Captain leaned forward. "Regardless of your rank, while I am captain of this ship - my - word - is - the- law!" He repeated his previous inference. "If you refuse, naval man or not, you will go back below deck and remain there until we return to England – or die." The Captain smiled. He had recruited his First Mate.

Totton and Gunner received no option. Regardless of their protestations Totton became a member of the deck crew and

Gunner was assigned to the master carpenter. Jamie was a problem. The Captain made clear that he would not carry passengers and, those who did not work, did not eat. Because of his incapacity he was looked down upon and became a subject of mockery by members of the crew and consequently was allotted the most menial tasks. The bosun, Billy Dibb, took pity on him.

"I got to find you sittin' down jobs," he said. "There don't be many of them on board a ship, lad. You's goin' to 'ave to stitch sails an' such and the worse labour of all – pickin' oakum"

Jamie soon found out what 'picking oakum' entailed. He was provided with short lengths of old rope and instructed to unwind the rope, strand by strand, down to each individual fibre. It would have been intricate work for a man with two hands but for Jamie it was almost impossible. He began by holding the rope ends between his teeth to unwind the strands, but the muck and salt encrusted in the rope made his mouth and lips sore. Eventually, sitting on the deck next to a raised hatch, he trapped the rope against the woodwork with his good knee and continued the laborious process until he had a pile of loose fibres beside him on the deck.

As he worked his mind became detached from the present and wandered back to Nestwith and to Russet. Would he ever see her again? Would she remember him? He remembered the kiss on his distorted cheek after she had taken a swim. His mind went back to the fallen oak and then to his poem. She would never know he had written it. His thoughts were far away when a sudden gust of wind lifted the pile of completed fibres and blew them high in the air and over the side of the ship.

He watched in dismay as his work disappeared into the blue. His mind came back to reality as he heard nearby laughter.

One man cried out "You better put an anchor on 'em next time, cripple."

Another, "they're for hammerin' 'tween boards wi' pitch, not feedin' fish."

"If we springs a leak, be Jaisus, we'll a'ter plug it wi' part o' you – and you know what part – unless that's crippled too!"

Jamie began to chuckle at his own misfortune. His mouth was sore, the ends of his fingers cut and bleeding, and now he had to begin all over again. 'It serves me right,' he thought, 'for not concentrating.' He picked up a piece of rope and as he did so a crewman passed and picked up some of the rope. Another walked by and took a handful. Others followed until only three short pieces remained. As Jamie finished the remaining three, the men came back. One had a bulging canvas sack. He held it open for Jamie to see the separated caulking fibres inside. The man said nothing but dropped the sack, winked, and walked away.

The days passed as the ship headed south. Totton was not happy at having to climb the rigging. When ordered out onto the yards to furl sail he was terrified, but helped and encouraged by the crew he gained in confidence and began to enjoy his new environment.

The captain confined himself to his cabin and was rarely seen, which meant that John Fullerton was virtually master of the ship. He had noticed the armaments as soon as he was brought from the hold – five 9-pounder guns each side, nothing like the huge familiar 32-pounders of a ship of the line. A small calibre bow-chaser situated forward, and three small swivel guns mounted on the rails at each side completed the armament. Although classed as an armed merchantman, the weaponry was in place for defence against small-time piracy and buccaneers hunting for a 'prize'. The guns were in a state of neglect with rust beginning to bubble the surfaces. He handled the ropes and found many wanted renewing and splicing. The runners and sheaves required greasing; the heavy wooden blocks needed stripping, cleaning and oiling. On every one he found the firing vent blocked, making the guns unusable. When he searched for rammers and sponges to service the guns he was appalled to discover none existed and consequently the guns could not be loaded. He checked below decks to find large quantities of gunpowder in stock but only ten cannon balls. He was also surprised to find there were no canisters of grape included in the arsenal but counted many crates of musket balls and long wooden boxes marked 'Muskets'.

From the very first day of his appointment he organised gun drill with each crew responsible for the upkeep of their weapons. Only the Captain and Jamie were excused. Galley cooks, riggers, carpenters, sail makers, every member of the crew had to attend gun drill. At first it was laughable. Men fell over each other and laughed at their own antics, until the bosun threatened them with flogging. The attitude of the men changed with competition, helped by John Fullerton's promise of tots of rum for each member of the gun crew that produced the tidiest weapon and put up the fastest, most efficient effort, at the end of each week.

Jamie felt left out. Seated on deck he was cleaning turnips for the evening meal when the bosun slumped onto the deck beside him."I want you to know I'm right sorry I got you into this." He removed the cloth from his head and wiped the sweat from his face. "I been watchin' you. It's bad enough tryin' to keep balance wi' two legs on a rollin' deck, let alone one." He took hold of a turnip and began to clean it. "They tells me you come fro' the countryside." He gave Jamie a sideways glance. "I never been there. I started work runnin' errands on the docks when I was four years old and went to sea when I were ten. That's thirty two years gone. Think on it, thirty two years looking at nowt but water. When I was a little 'un I saw a paintin' of a house standin' in a green field. There were cows and sheep and a black pig and a rustic in a smock sittin under a hedge suckin' a piece o' grass. I never forgot that paintin'. When I've finished wi' the sea that's what I'd like to do - live in a little house and stand in a field. I never stood in a field in me life. I seen 'em on land and on top o' cliffs as we sail by, but I never stood in one. All those years back I 'ad a mind to save me money and get a place in the country when I leave the sea – but it's not goin' to be. I'll never make enough coin – unless we captures a prize – but there's fat of a chance o' that." He finished cleaning the turnip, then with a sigh he said, "when you've finished these the Captain wants 'is cabin cleaned. Better see what you can do. And be careful – he don't think you're worth your salt so watch your one-legged step, m'hearty."

"Hell and damnation!" The loud exclamation from within made Jamie hesitate as he was about to knock. He waited a few seconds then quietly rapped on the cabin door.

"Enter!"

He opened the door slowly and hopped inside. The Captain was seated at a desk, quill in hand, his fingers covered in ink. He looked up and glared expectantly as if waiting for a spoken reason for the intrusion. "Well?" It was only then he realised who had entered. "What do you want?"

Jamie made a rubbing movement with his good hand indicating cleaning.

The Captain glared. "God in heaven!" He turned his head from side to side as if looking for something the crippled man could do. He turned and fixed his eyes on Jamie. "What I need is a clerk and I am sent a one-legged, one-armed, illiterate peasant."

Jamie hopped forward and looked at the ink-blotted paper on the desk. He pointed a finger at his chest then made the motion of writing. He pointed the finger at himself again, hoping to be understood.

"You? Write?" The captain stood, put a fresh piece of paper on the desk and signalled for Jamie to be seated. Captain Christopher was a desperate man. Among those of the crew who had disappeared was his newly acquired clerk. With no scribe he was at a loss. His own handwriting was almost undecipherable and his spelling atrocious. He was willing to clutch at any straw. "Write what I say," he ordered.

The Captain strode backwards and forwards with his hands

clenched behind his back. "To whom it may concern," he began. "I have taken on board an illiterate cripple who I, Captain Christopher, have ordered to write down my words with immediate effect. On this ship my word is the law, so he had better not be wasting my time or he will taste the sweet bite of the bosun's rope." He turned to look at Jamie who was sitting looking back at him, pen poised.

"Damn you! Of course you cannot write. Get out! Go on. Out!"

Jamie rose as the Captain came at him and he urgently gestured toward the paper.

The Captain snatched it and perused his own dictated words. His expression changed from anger to one of incredulity "The Lord be praised! He exclaimed. "That is as neat a hand as I have seen in many a year."

Chapter Twenty One

Sir Marcus struggled to break the seal on the note from Liverpool. He had dispatched Thomas Chatterton to find out why Totton and company had not returned and now his fingers shook with anticipation as he fumbled to open the folded paper. He read the note three times before lifting his head to look at his daughters, who waited patiently for news.

"Chatterton says he has found no sign of Tott." He paused. Then went on with sadness in his voice. "The animals and the carts have been sold to pay for stabling and fodder, as is the usual case in these circumstances."

"What circumstances?" Russet interrupted.

"Well, if one leaves animals in the care of another for a length of time and no payment is made, then the stableman has the right to sell them to offset the cost of keeping them. That is what has happened. Chatterton goes on to say that there was a naval ship in port at the time and that a press gang was active." Sir Marcus began to walk back and forth, holding the note, reading it yet again.

"I cannot believe they were pressed," he said. "John Fullerton was, and I suppose still is, a naval officer. He would not be pressed. Chatterton has dispatched a rider to London with a note asking Lord Doulain to use his influence with the Admiralty for information. We can do nothing but wait for an answer to that. However, he says here," he waved the note, " a woman has come forward to say she knows the whereabouts of four men who vanished about that time, but wants an extortionate amount of money to tell."

"Then you must pay it, Father." Charlotte confronted him. "Tott's life may be in danger – what is money compared with that?"

"I have a better idea," Charlotte said. "I would think this woman would be better dealt with by another woman. I propose to go myself and ……"

"I shall go also!" Russet proclaimed enthusiastically.

"No you will not." Charlotte was adamant. "I shall deal with this.

"Stop! Stop! Enough of this tittle-tattle. I shall go to Liverpool myself." Sir Marcus lost patience. "There is another note here with the Doulain seal. It is addressed to me but concerns you all." Placing the Chatterton note down he picked up the other and said, "we have all been invited to London by his Lordship…."

"Oh how lovely!" Russet pirouetted, all thought of her missing brother gone. "I shall need new gowns, Father. And shoes, and all the things a lady needs to be the talk of the town."

"Hold there, my dear." Sir Marcus was astounded as Russet selfishly dismissed all thought of Totton.

"I cannot possibly go to London at a time like this. I…..

"Then I shall go alone." Russet stamped her foot. "If Lottie can go to Liverpool, I shall go to London.

"You will do no such thing. What sort of a father do you take me for? I will not allow any of my daughters to travel alone, particularly to places with such sordid reputations. I already have a son gone astray, I am not such a fool as to place the rest of my family in jeopardy. For the time being that's an end of it."

Russet stormed out, followed by a subdued Katherine.

"Now we are alone, Father, I have news I must tell you." Charlotte held her head high. "Before he left for Liverpool, John Fullerton spoke to me of marriage. I told him that with your permission I would be happy and honoured to do so. I Am sure he was about to ask you to allow our marriage when he left to accompany Tott. So, you see, I shall go to Liverpool. If I go with you, I shall feel more at ease, but if not then I shall go alone, and before you complain and lay down the laws of parentage, I must tell you, that if needs be, I shall disobey you."

Sir Marcus opened his mouth to speak but was lost for words. He had been resigned to Charlotte being a spinster forever and had not imagined any man willing to put up with her constant chatter. Now he realised his eldest daughter was no longer a little girl to be commanded. At last he spoke, "Charlotte, you are of an age that compels me to advise you in matters of life, rather than bid you comply. If it is your wish to marry John Fullerton, and he appears to me to be an honest upright young man, then you shall have my blessing. I would, however, require to know more of his means. You have been brought up well and I could not allow you to marry a man unable to support you in a like manner."

"Thank you, Father. Oh thank you." She threw her arms around his neck and hugged him. "We had better leave for Liverpool tomorrow," she urged, "but there is another I would have accompany us."

The wet, cobbled streets glistened with reflections from

the amber glow of candle-lit windows on either side. Even the inclement weather could not bring a halt to the exuberance of an English port. Sailors with their women of the night, dockers, clerks, and people from every working walk of life bustled through the street seeking enjoyment. None took notice of others, each concentrating on their own search for escape from the drudgery of every-day life.

Thomas Chatterton led Sir Marcus and Charlotte to the tavern where he had arranged the meeting. The three walked side by side with four attendants a few steps behind. Between the two groups, as if alone, a very tall person kept pace. When they reached the tavern Chatterton entered alone. The tall figure broke away from the group and took up a position outside the tavern door.

Fanny was seated at a table on her own; a flickering, single candle cast light through the smoky haze onto her expectant face. She was about to receive more money than she had ever owned at any one single time in her life and with her eyes locked in space, she fantasised on how she would spend it. She came out of her dream world as the door opened. Through the smoky gloom she recognised Thomas Chatterton and signalled to him.

Chatterton took a seat at the table opposite her. There were no niceties. He began immediately, "tell me what you know, woman," he ordered.

"You got the money?" Fanny whispered.

"Tell me what you know." Chatterton insisted.

"If I tells you, how do I know you'll gi' me the money?"

"If I gi' you the money how do I know you'll tell?"

Chatterton imitated her. He said, "you're the one selling, I'm the one buying, so I want proof of the puddin' afore I agree."

"Show me the money, Fanny insisted."

He looked around at the crowded room. "You don't think I would show money in here." He stood. "Come on," he said.

"'You got the money on you?"

"What do you take me for madam?" If your story is worth it you will get what's coming to you." With that Thomas Chatterton walked out into the street.

Fanny followed but stopped with one foot across the doorstep, mouth agape, as she caught sight of the huge figure in conversation with Chatterton. Frightened of violence she was about to turn back to the safety of the alehouse when thought of the money took precedence. "Who's he?" she asked pointing at the tall one.

"My minder." Thomas Chatterton replied. "I was brought up in the streets of London. You don't think I would come to this place without protection. Certainly not with the amount of money involved."

They walked to the docks, crossed an open space and Chatterton came to a halt where new development was taking place. Fanny had obediently followed, with the minder bringing up the rear. All was quiet here, away from the bustle. Chatterton took a purse from a pocket and weighed it in hand, moving it up and down in front of Fanny.

"Now," he said. "If you want this you tell me everything."

"I want the money first." Fanny said, but there was not the demand in her voice as there had been in the crowded counter room.

Chatterton returned the purse to a pocket. "I think you've brought me here to chase wild geese. I don't think you know anything. Come on." He waved an arm, signalling for the minder that he was about to leave.

"No, no." There was desperation in Fanny's voice.

Chatterton stopped and then took the purse from his pocket and handed it to the minder. "If you won't tell me what I want to know, then perhaps you would rather tell my minder." With that parting shot he walked away but stayed within sight.

The minder held the purse out but took it back as Fanny reached for it and stood without saying a word until Fanny broke the silence, "I do know what happened to them men from Nestwith but I ain't telling till I get the money. You don't know me but when I says I'll do something, I keeps me word."

"But I do know you." The minder removed the hat that had seemed to perch too high on the large head. Hair that had been bundled up now cascaded down over the broad shoulders as the minder said, Fanny Bottomly isn't it? Or would you best be known as Tanner Fanny?"

Fanny stepped back with surprise. Then, with hands on hips she circled the large figure. "And I know you – Gertie Wrigglesworth, aint it? Or would you best be known as Gravel Gertie?"

"Aye, 'tis me. My friend Adam Gunner is missing and if you know where he's about you're going to tell me. I'll give you the purse when you've told me where Gunner is. If you don't tell, I might just break your fingers, one at a time till you does tell."

As Gertie held the purse, rattling the contents, Fanny

blurted out all she knew, including her betrayal of the four. She emphasised that she was getting back at the folk of Nestwith for what had been done to her and that it was unfortunate that Gertie's friend Gunner was involved.

When she had finished she held out her hand for payment but Gertie threw the purse on the ground. As Fanny bent to pick it up Gertie planted a foot on her buttocks and gave her a hefty push. Fanny, purse in hand, lurched forward and with a cry of alarm plunged over the edge of the dock to land spread-eagled in deep, filthy soft mud, the purse still clenched firmly in her hand.

Gertie joined Chatterton. "Good job the tide was out." She laughed. Then she held out a purse. "She told me it all and I would think Sir Marcus will be pleased to get this back."

Chatterton shook the purse. "I thought you gave her the money."

"I gave her a purse."

"I saw that, but if this contains the money, what did the other hold?"

"Gravel, sir. "She laughed heartily. "But only the very best of gravel."

The following day, during the return journey to Nestwith, Thomas Chatterton spoke to Sir Marcus and Charlotte and told the full story of the events leading to the disappearance of Totton, John Fullerton, Gunner and Pitchforth.

"The ship, Branston Silver belongs to the Company Doulain. His Lordship named six ships after his late wife. She was Helen Branston before she married so there was the Branston Gold, which was lost with all aboard. The rest are the Silver, Diamond, Sapphire, Ruby and Pearl. They are all merchantmen and slavers but only a small part of Doulain shipping. That woman could only have knowledge of your son being taken aboard – nothing of how he fares. We do now know, according to the agent at Liverpool, the Silver left with a cargo of goods for the port of Loango in Africa. There her Captain will barter the goods for slaves to be transported to Jamaica. He is then to take on a cargo of sugar, rum and sail to Virginia, one of our American Colonies. There he will take on baled cotton and tobacco to fill the holds, then return to Liverpool. It is a well-known trading triangle with ships carrying three paying cargoes." He paused then continued, "a fair length of time could pass before they get back, but a message could be dispatched to Jamaica aboard a direct sailing, to reach there before the Branston Silver.

Sir Marcus listened intently. He was relieved to hear that Totton was alive and he considered a wait a small price to pay to have his only son back. It had crossed his mind that if Totton died, the line of Roulette would be broken. The baronetcy would then pass to the eldest son of his eldest daughter. Should she not bear a male heir then it would move to the eldest son of his second daughter, and so on.

It was a tiring journey and they arrived at Nestwith Hall with sighs of relief. Katherine came down the steps to meet them, a look of consternation on her face.

"Don't fret yourself, dear Kate," Sir Marcus comforted. "Totton is alive and aboard a ship bound for Africa and the colonies. He alighted from the carriage and took his daughter in his arms. "Come," he said. "We must tell Russy."

"Oh Father," Kate began to sob. "Russy is not here."

Thinking Katherine's tears where of joy at hearing the good news, Sir Marcus laughed. "We shall tell her the glad tidings when she gets back."

"She said she would not be coming back." With tears running down her cheeks she said, "Russy left two days ago. She took the grey coach with a coachman and two footmen and she said she was taking up his Lordship's invitation to stay with him in London."

Chapter Twenty Two

The sails hung limp like dormant beasts awaiting the elixir of nature to bring them into life. The sea shone like a mirror of glass with not a ripple or break upon its surface; the heat oppressive; not a single cloud breaking the dazzling blueness of the sky. The ship lay becalmed with not a whisper of a breeze to unsettle the serenity or to stimulate movement. From horizon to horizon a scene of tranquillity prevailed and apart from the occasional lazy groan from the timber hull and, now and then, a creak of tensioned rope, there prevailed an eerie, uncanny silence.

For Adam Gunner, seated, legs astride the forward starboard bitt, it was a time of his life that seemed unreal, as if he were living a dream. What in this world, he thought, was a village blacksmith doing in this vast realm of nothingness. He looked across at Totton who was sitting on top of the rope-grooved larboard capstan and who now took off his shirt and wrung the sweat out of it before putting it on again. He, like Gunner and other members of the crew, wore a tightly bound handkerchief about his head, the material brought together and knotted above the nape of his neck. His mind was running on the same lines – why me? Why has the Lord seen fit to place me in this ridiculous position? Why? When all I wanted to do was sell a few barrels of salted pork and then go home? Home. His mind wandered to thoughts of Nestwith. He felt a tinge of self-pity, knowing well it would be a long time before he again set eyes on the green acres of home.

The ship, close hauled, had battled its way out of the Irish

Sea and, keeping well to the west of Biscay, eventually found the Portuguese trade winds. Fair headway south followed; finding the northeast trade winds and taking a course west of Madeira and the Canaries the ship ran easily, with wind mainly on the larboard quarter. Winds could always act irrationally and approach from an unexpected quarter. After steering a passage east of the Cape Verde Islands the winds lessened to a breeze and finally ceased altogether. The sea became placid. Forty-four days out they had reached the Doldrums.

Rank and status aboard had completely overturned, Totton assigned to the starboard watch as a member of the crew, was now the lowliest of the four; John Fullerton had a position of unquestioned authority; Gunner, the skilled smith, bunked with the idlers and apprentices next to the galley along with the chief cook, the sail maker, the carpenter with their underlings and apprentices. Then there was Jamie who had become the captain's clerk.

The captain was not a happy man. He had made a hasty decision to embark upon the voyage without a full complement and was now contemplating how he could possibly have managed the ship had not John Fullerton been pressed aboard. It was usual for the two watches to be taken by the first and second mates - one allocated to oversee the starboard watch and the other mate the larboard watch. As matters occasioned, the captain had no alternative but to take a watch himself. Like many merchant captains he relied a great deal on dead reckoning, calculating course and speed, and taking an occasional sight of the noonday sun to confirm his position. He had never learned to take stellar sights at dusk or dawn and he had always found difficult the complicated mathematical calculations involved in the art of navigation. But no seaman knew better than he the ocean currents and the trade winds.

It was a simple matter to take a sight with a cloudless sky and a becalmed ship. Captain Christopher did so and returned to the great cabin to determine the ship's position. He placed his prized John Henry chronometer on the chart table then took a piece of paper from Jamie's desk and wrote down his observations. As he turned to put away his sextant and pour himself a generous glass of claret, Jamie glanced at the figures and began to scribble. He then stood and hopped to the chart table where, with square and compass, he plotted the ships position.

"Get back to your desk, Pitchforth." The captain shouted. "You stick to your clerical work and leave the business of navigation to me." He snatched the paper and began his own calculations. Ten minutes later, after several attempts, he put down his pen and plotted the course and position. He looked closer at the chart, then pulled Jamie's piece of paper next to his own – the results were identical. He turned and looked at Jamie who was bent over the desk mulling through the ships papers. He turned back to the chart, checked again the two calculations and with a look of bewilderment on his face he again let his eyes dwell on his clerk. Then, as if returning to reality from a daytime reverie, he straightened up, grabbed his hat, and walked out of the cabin.

John Fullerton was on the poop deck when the captain

appeared.

"That fellow Pitchforth," the Captain began. When the mate did not reply he went on. "I was told he was from ignorant peasant stock - that cannot be."

"On my word, sir, he is a peasant." John Fullerton insisted. "I know well he is the son of a peasant woman who works at Nestwith Hall for Sir Marcus Roulette. I understand he worked as a quarryman but was badly injured in a rock fall and since that time he has not spoken a word and has no memory. It is said he saved the life of the second Roulette daughter for which he was rewarded with a job on the estate as a handyman. He came with...."

Captain Christopher interrupted. "That man is no peasant! The fellow is a scholar! Damn it, I have just witnessed him calculate our position from my own figures in less than a quarter the time it took me. I tell you, that fellow has been well schooled." He began to descend the companionway, muttering to himself. "Peasant! Peasant indeed!"

Upon returning to the cabin he took out a clay pipe, stuffed it with tobbaco and puffed away while contemplating Jamie's broad shoulders, noting how badly clothed he was. It was only after a long silence that Jamie, with a sixth sense feeling of being under inspection, put down his quill and turned to look over his shoulder. The captain moved his pipe to the corner of his mouth and without taking it out he said, "it would appear I have a man of mystery aboard my ship." He paused as if mentally searching for words. Then, "I am informed that you suffer from loss of memory. Is that so?" Jamie nodded and the Captain continued. "Then how is it that you remember how to write, how to read and how to calculate the position of this ship with such dexterity?"

Again Jamie shrugged.

"You, young man, are not what you seem."

Jamie took up his quill, dipped it in the ink and began to write. When he had finished he blew on it to dry the ink, then rose, hopped to the chart table and slid the paper across the surface. The Captain picked it up and read…

'Sir, I cannot understand why one part of my mind can recall certain aspects of knowledge, yet another part remains dormant and without thought. My mother is a midwife and I was a stone worker but I have no memory of what went before my injury. I wish to thank you, sir. You are the first person in my recallable memory with whom I have conversed in this manner.'

After reading the note the captain placed it back on the table. Then as if speaking to himself he said, "I am fifty three years of age and I have spent most of my life at sea. I have been a master for fifteen years and I am now beginning to tire of it." He shifted his position, took a deep intake of tobacco smoke and blew it out slowly to form a moving blue cloud that billowed out and spread across the cabin. "It's this having to take a watch that's wearing me out. Four hours on and four off. When I was younger it was normal, I thought nothing of it. Now I commit for one watch but have to keep a weather eye open during the other. Damnation to the navy's press gangs! But for them I would have a full crew."

Jamie returned to his desk and began to write…

May I be so impertinent to suggest, sir. – Promote bosun

Dibb to second mate. Promote junior bosun to senior and give Dibb the responsibility of selecting a new bosun for the larboard watch. Dibb cannot navigate but he can steer a course and knows the wind and trim of sail as good as any man. He has the respect of the crew and as our captain you are the most important personage aboard and in need of rest. A ship cannot afford a tired captain.

I have studied the Articles of the missing crew and I am of the opinion that the signature of both mates and the clerk were penned by the same hand – different names but signed by one man. I checked further and it would appear the clerk signed all three. Perhaps a check on the contents of our cargo may be appropriate.

Captain Christopher was aghast at the suggestions. Not that he objected to Jamie bringing them to mind but at what he now considered could be a dereliction of duty on his own part. He had waited months for a ship and when command of the Branston Silver was offered he took it and boarded the ship with a full crew already aboard. He had assumed and took for granted that all crew credentials had been checked and approved by his predecessor. He should have checked. He had followed the normal procedure that when in port the loading, checking and stowage of cargo is generally left to the mate, but the captain shoulders the final responsibility.

"What is done is done." Again it was as if he spoke quietly to himself. Then, "Mister Fullerton!"

Jamie was startled by the ferocity in the captain's voice as he bellowed for his first mate. When John Fullerton appeared he was asked to summon the bosun and return immediately.

Billy Dibb was a fearsome looking man. He stood before the captain in duck trousers and a sleeveless shirt open to the waist. An intricate pattern of tattoos decorated his arms and chest. His shaggy beard begirt a long, gaunt face criss-crossed with scars; trophies of many a tavern room brawl. His nose was twisted and hooked but the benign blue eyes seemed out of place amongst the coarseness of his general bearing.

"Gentlemen." At that pronouncement Billy Dibb looked about him, not believing that he was being included in such a term of respect.

"I have decided to make a few changes aboard this ship," the Captain got to his feet and stood with legs apart, hands on hips. "You, Mister Dibb, will from this moment take up duty as second mate with officer status. You may move your sea chest to the appropriate cabin.

"No, no. Not me Captain." Billy Dibb looked abashed. "I always been one o' the lads. It would not go down well with the......

"Mister Dibb, on this ship my – word – is – the law. You have a choice – take the second mate's berth or get off my ship – now!"

Both Jamie and John Fullerton turned their heads to hide their smiles.

Billy Dibb fidgeted and then said; "Aye, aye Captain. I'll have my chest shifted, slick and hasty like."

As Billy Dibb moved to leave the cabin the Captain shouted after him, "we'll have to get you into some decent clothes. And get that damn beard trimmed. You look more like a privateer than an honest merchant seaman."

Out onto the deck with his usual shoulder swagger, a seaman nodded at him and said, "alright Billy?

"Don't you Billy me."

Realizing he was in no mood for friendly banter the man offered, "sorry Bosun."

"And don't you bosun me either – it's *Mister* Dibb to you." And off he went, the old boson swagger more exaggerated than ever.

It was a time to cool overheated bodies and overheated minds. Members of the crew threw roped buckets over the side and dowsed the decks to cool caulking tar that was rapidly softening in the heat. Occasionally there would be cackles of laughter as the crew threw water, attempting to catch each other off guard. But tempers flared. Trivia became magnified in the heat and squabbles increased as the morning wore on.

"Give them something to do, Mr Fullerton." The Captain ordered. "Give them another taste of gun drill."

Covers were speedily taken off the guns and tampions removed. Fastenings were loosed and the gun crews took their places. There had been keen rivalry among the men during previous drills and now boredom and the discomfort of the doldrums gave way again to competition.

They ran the cannons into the firing position and coiled the ropes neatly to allow them to run through the blocks without hindrance. At a signal from John Fullerton the five crews went through the motion of firing and then ran the gun back to simulate recoil, men heaving on the ropes as fast as they could; through the motions of worming, sponging, loading the charge, loading imaginary cannon balls, ramming home the final wad then running the gun to the firing position and holding up their hands to signify completion. As they finished John Fullerton shouted out their times. At the next drill they were expected to improve.

While the starboard watch went through their drill the larboard watch stood on the hatches, up on the yards, and any other vantage point from where they could see the action. Cheers, jeers and lewd banter from those watching accompanied the shouts and commands of the gun captains as they urged their team to greater effort. When it came to the turn of the larboard watch to go through their drill the positions were reversed. It all turned into a carnival atmosphere but when it ended the heat and effort took its toll as men lay exhausted about the deck, crying out for water.

Captain Christopher had been a keen spectator from the poop deck. John Fullerton joined him.

"Next time I think we shall try them with live rounds." The Captain said, thoughtfully. "We can afford to waste a few cannonballs I think.

"I can find but ten, sir."

"Ten!"

"Aye, we have powder a plenty, not a grape canister to be found and only the ten balls. We have musket balls by the box and many a crate of muskets.

The Captain shook his head. "There should be three hundred and ten cannonballs. I know the inventory by heart." He stared at the sea and the horizon, his mind dwelling on Jamie's suspicions. "Have all hatches opened, Mr Fullerton. I shall look for myself."

The check confirmed his suspicions. The number of bolts of cloth appeared correct, but on closer scrutiny it became clear that was not the case. The material had been cleverly built up in such a way that left a hollow space inside each stack. A count proved exactly one hundred bolts short of the number supposedly stowed. The Captain pointed to the crates of muskets and ordered that one be opened. Gunner prised a lid with a hammer and marlinspike and stood back as it was lifted off.

"Well, that solves the problem of the missing cannon balls." John Fullerton took a cannon ball from the crate and weighed it in hand. There is much amiss here."

All three hundred muskets had been taken from the thirty crates and replaced with three cannon balls in each. Canvas packed grape shot had been slotted between each ball to hold them in place.

"Thieves!" The Captain fumed. "The artful damnable thieves!"

Back in the after cabin he was in a state of agitation. "Mr Fullerton, he began. "This is indeed a grave situation. The military in England is in the process of changing to a new musket and the company purchased quantities of the old weapons to sell to the Africans. Some say a dangerous action, but it is a profitable business transaction and a good source of barter for purchasing slaves. Now we might struggle to buy enough of them to make a profitable cargo – not only a reduction in the number of slaves we carry but the price we get for them in Jamaica may not purchase a full cargo for the return to England. It is a sorry state of affairs indeed."

"Well, at least we have the cannon balls." John Fullerton said.

"Cannon balls! Cannon balls!" The Captain fumed. "We can't barter cannon balls. What good would they be to Africans without guns and powder?" He paused and stroked his chin. Then he spoke in a whisper; his practice of thinking aloud, "I suppose we could sell 'em a couple of our guns."

"Would that not be irresponsible?" John Fullerton shook his head. "It would weaken our own defences. Our force of eleven guns will have all on to match the fire power of any piracy or prize hunters we may encounter."

"Mr Fullerton, until a few moments ago we had but ten cannon balls to defend ourselves. Now we have three hundred and ten. If we parted with two guns, a small parcel of powder and ten balls we still have greatly more firepower than we thought we had."

Jamie was seated at his desk and now he wrote on a piece of paper and held it out to the Captain.

"The muskets? The cloth?" The Captain smiled wryly. "I would hazard a decent wager that the cloth was sold to finance transportation of the muskets to Ireland. The three absconders with whom I had acquaintance had Irish accents. I believe the theft was well organised and the mates and clerk were nothing more than part of an organised gang of thieves – or rebels." He paused as if to contemplate his next order. "Gentlemen," he said. "My words to you this day will not leave this cabin. This must never happen again and to that end

I shall appoint - what shall I say – a Master of the Purse - who shall be responsible for all matters appertaining to cargo, and every other conceivable purchase, sale and issue aboard this ship. He will be a junior officer of my crew with status equal to that of a second mate, and from this day he will be addressed, with respect, as *Mister* Pitchforth."

The talk was interrupted by a shout of urgency. John Fullerton rushed out and returned almost immediately. "We have signs of a change in the weather, sir. Clouds sighted directly aft as we bide." He left but returned immediately. "Perhaps you may wish to take a look, Captain."

Chapter Twenty Three

"Colonel Ronald Ingrham and Mrs Emily Ingrham."

The call of introduction did not invite interest sufficient to bring about a turning of heads. The assembly continued to converse; men stood at one side of the room while the ladies, separated from husbands and partners, occupied the other. It was a colourful occasion; the men, uniformed army and naval officers of high rank, some wearing powdered wigs, gloried in their silver-buttoned, gold-braided finery. The conversation was of victory and glory, and the possibilities of future battles. Lavishly dressed ladies with bouffant wigs of elaborate proportions, prominently displaying their dress and jewellery in hope of outshining their peers. On a raised platform at one end of the room a quartet of musicians played. The two violinists and cellist performed mellow background music while a harpsichordist, seated at the instrument, awaited his turn to play.

"Rear Admiral Sir Percy Rawcliffe and Lady Rawcliffe."

Guests were still arriving to be greeted by the party-giver and host Mrs Emma Fitzhamilton. She ushered them in and passed them on to presentable ladies in her employ to be escorted and introduced to other guests with mutual interests.

Bewigged flunkeys, dressed in immaculate livery, moved among the guests, replenishing glasses from ornate wine jugs. Others carried trays of sweetmeats to tempt the ladies. Everything was planned to a detail; Mrs Fitzhamilton's success as a hostess was based on her insistence that the personal interests of male guests be researched, allowing those with reciprocal interests to be introduced. Their ladies looked for friends and acquaintances and were left to meet with those of their choice.

"Major Crawford Whitley and Miss Mary Van Dyke."

It had become a symbol of status to be invited to a social gathering hosted by Mrs Fitzhamilton. She was a professional party-giver, and although it was well known that behind all her soirees there was both a sponsor and a purpose, discretion demanded secrecy for both. Her patrons comprised gentlemen in need of business introductions; gentleman desiring the acquaintance of a lady, or for any other reason requiring what would appear a fortuitous encounter.   Should a potential sponsor ask a price for her services he would meet with immediate refusal, leaving eligible only those of prominence and wealth.

Some of her clients wished it known they had financed an event and Emma Fitzhamilton would make it obvious by the attention she bestowed on them during the course of the evening. Others required anonymity; so it became a guessing game among guests as to which of them had opened his purse. On this occasion, on the day before the event was to take place, the patron had withdrawn to give way to what he described as 'a personage of note' while insisting the guest list remain the same. It was too late to cancel her investment but she had received assurance that no expense should be spared and that all financial matters would be honoured.

"Lord Doulain and Miss Russet Roulette."

The hum of conversation ceased and all eyes turned toward the entrance. The unsociable Lord Doulain? The man in black. - Surely not.

Lord Francis Doulain was a mystery to most. Known as something of a recluse but of immense wealth he was rarely seen and avoided society except when involvement in business or politics required his presence. As he entered with Russet by his side there were gasps of surprise. He was dressed in colourful attire; long silk jacket of royal blue edged with silver and gold braid. His waistcoat was of rich brocade with a threaded design of glistening gold and silver yarn. He wore no wig and had his long, dark hair drawn back and tied with a thin blue ribbon, matching the colour of his jacket. If eyes dwelt on him with surprise they were soon diverted to the beautiful lady by his side. Russet looked the complete embodiment of perfect womanhood and she was dressed completely in black.

The gown was of her own design and not at all like the high-waist- fashion of the times. The slimness of her body and the outline of her breasts appeared accentuated by the many layers of material that billowed out below her waist. Around her neck she wore a single black ribbon above the heart-shaped cut of the neckline that fell to a point where her cleavage began. She wore elbow-length gloves to match her dress, adorned with identical diamond brooches at the wrist. Single diamond earrings sparkled as she walked, as did another elaborate diamond brooch in the shape of a snake that appeared as if the reptile was creeping over her shoulder. Her russet hair was swept back above her ears and fastened back with a single, wide black ribbon, tied in a bow.

Mrs Fitzhamilton went to meet them and this time she did

not pass them on to one of her ladies, but remained to introduce them into appropriate circles. Lord Doulain was soon in conversation but found that military men talked of military matters and men of the sea spoke of ships. Discreetly he moved away and joined Mrs Fitzhamilton.

"My God, Emma!" he exclaimed. "I know now what I have been missing this past twenty-five years, if 'missing' be the operative word." He let his eyes wander over the crowded room. "Where is my dear Russet? She is new to all this and I fear she will feel out of place." He need not have been concerned; Russet had joined a group of ladies and she held them spellbound as she related the experience of her day in the Nestwith stocks. She ended, "so you see ladies, you are in the company of a notorious criminal." There were shrieks of unladylike laughter and other women pushed in to become part of the gathering.

"You need not worry about that one, Frankie." Emma Fitzhamilton smiled. She used her familiar name for him and, having obtained from him a loan to establish her business, they had, over the years, become firm friends.

"I wish you would refrain from addressing me so, Emma." He shook a finger, reprovingly.

"I just want to thank you for stepping in to save me with such little notice." She touched his arm.

"I am not aware that I have done so."

"Oh come now, Frankie. I know it is you." She touched his arm again, a little harder this time.

"Emma, I received your invitation some days ago, and, just as on previous occasions, I was about to decline when Russet came into my charge. I then thought your assembly would entertain her greatly. Look at me! She has me dressed like a popinjay. She has been here three days and had tailors and dressmakers working their fingers to the bone for this night. She is the reason for my presence. I assure you I have not been approached to be the benefactor of this assembly."

"Then who could it be?" Emma Fitzhamilton had been so sure Lord Doulain was 'the personage of note,' she now became worried. She had obeyed the original request to 'spare no expense' but had no knowledge of the identity of her sponsor. She expressed her concern.

"Then account to the first one." He took her hand and squeezed it gently to reassure her. "Tell him it was too late to cancel. I shall help you with that if necessary. Do not worry, Emma. Enjoy the evening."

Russet joined them just as one of the lady usherettes came rushing towards them in a most inelegant manner. Mrs Fitzhamilton waved a hand to indicate to the woman she should slow her pace. She came up and whispered in Emma's ear. Mrs Fitzhamilton blanched. She looked one way and then the other and then said, "oh God in heaven! Come!"

Russet thought she was being asked to follow as Mrs Fitzhamilton, head high, calmly left the room. When in the entrance hall she ordered the ballroom doors closed. Two large uniformed men stood to attention on either side of the main door as a man entered. He wore a red jacket bearing insignia; a fashionable, curled, powdered wig topped his head. Russet noted his sloping forehead and large mouth but she had no idea of the man's identity.

Mrs Fitzhamilton went down in a deep curtsy. "Your Majesty," she uttered.

Russet was frozen to the spot. She felt her knees trembling as she curtsied. 'It can't be', she thought.

King George came forward. "Pray forgive this intrusion, Mrs Fitzhamilton."

"We are deeply honoured, Your Majesty."

Russet bit her lip and felt ill at ease. She did not know what to do or how to act in the presence of a king. But he appeared to be enjoying the surprise.

"I hear good words spoken of your enchanting evenings." He spoke to Emma Fitzhamilton but his eyes dwelt on Russet. "Please be good enough to have me announced." His eyes smiled as he said, jokingly, "you may tell your congregation Mr King has arrived," He put out an arm and Emma Fitzhamilton placed her hand on his. "And who is this fair lady?" He asked.

Emma Fitzhamilton blushed. She had been so taken by surprise. "May I introduce Miss Russet Roulette, your Majesty. Miss Roulette is chaperoned by Lord Doulain."

Russet had by now regained her composure. She curtsied and bowed her head. As she looked up she saw The King was holding out an arm. She glanced briefly at Mrs Fitzhamilton to see if this was in order. She saw the almost imperceptible nod and she placed her hand on the King's other arm. The doors of the ballroom were thrown open, "His Britannic Majesty King George The Third."

The quartet played and there was the hum of conversation as the King entered the room. Many thought it a prank but when they saw King George flanked by Mrs Fitzhamilton and Russet, the murmurs ceased, the music faded, and a spontaneous applause broke out.

The King dropped his arms, as a sign of dismissal, leaving Emma and Russet to find the company of Lord Doulain. He then wandered among the guests, followed by members of his entourage, speaking to officers and their ladies and making small talk.

Lord Doulain was as surprised as anybody at the appearance of the monarch. It explained the all-armed-forces gathering and also the exclusion of diplomats and politicians. He had already taken note of the fact that he was the only person present without military or naval connections. His brain raced. That explains, he thought, why a sponsor withdrew and yet the guest list remain the same. He was allowing his mind to ponder the implications when King George approached.

"My Lord Doulain." The King waved an arm with an exaggerated flourish. "How good it is to see you."

Lord Doulain bowed "Your Majesty," he said.

The King nodded toward Russet. "And where, tell me, did you unearth such treasure?" Before His Lordship could answer the King went on, "may I remind you that all discovered treasure in this realm is the property of the crown." He laughed at his own joke then turned to Russet. "Do you perform," he asked. "Do you entertain?"

"Russet was speechless. She thought for a brief moment she was being propositioned.

"Can you play?" He asked. Do you sing?"

With a sense of relief Russet answered, I play the harpsichord a little, Your Majesty – but not very well. And I sing a little – but not very well."

The King took her hand. "Well we shall see how good not very well is, shall we." People moved quickly aside leaving a clear passage way as he led her across the room to the stage. Russet was terrified. She was trembling as the King, still hold of her hand, helped her as she mounted the step. She had no idea what she would play or sing. She turned and curtsied. What could she do? It was as if she had suffered a mental pause. What song should she sing to a King? Then it came to her. She would sing her favourite, the one she had practised since childhood. The harpsichordist moved aside and she took his place.

The King had moved back several steps and stood in the middle of the room. The guests moved up behind him, keeping their distance but crowding to form an audience.

Russet played a short introduction and then began to sing Green Sleeves.

She accompanied herself and sang the lyrics to the end. Then she began the song again. Her voice was so clear and strong her audience stood in awe. She indicated to the harpsichordist to take over and for the other musicians to join in. She rose and stood with arms stretched towards the King and her eyes on his. She sang to him as if he were the only person present.

While all eyes were on Russet, a member of the king's entourage entered He trod softly until beside Lord Doulain. He whispered in his ear then spoke with Mrs Fitzhamilton, who nodded. She took Lord Doulain by the arm and they followed the man out of the room. Mrs Fitzhamilton returned alone.

Russet ended her performance and made a deep bow to the King. There was a silence that seemed to last an age. The King lifted his arms then spreading them wide he brought them together in a huge clap. He repeated the action but speeded the movement until he was clapping his hands together with genuine enthusiasm. The guests joined in the applause. Cries of 'huzzah' and 'encore' echoed around the room.

The King stepped forward and took Russet by the hand. "You are a delight, my dear, a delight." He helped her from the stage and walked her through the applauding crowd to where Mrs Fitzhamilton stood alone. "I return the nightingale and I hope we shall see and hear more of her." He then said, "this has been but a fleeting visit and as I have many kingly duties to perform, I shall bid you all farewell. Thank you, madam, for your kind hospitality." He turned to face the guests and raised his voice. "I have been enchanted with your company but unfortunately I must leave you now." There were murmurs of disappointment from his audience as he ended, "a very good night to you all." With that he walked with great dignity towards the door, nodding his head in acknowledgement of the bows and curtsies as he passed.

He entered the entrance hall and the doors of the ballroom were closed behind him. He was ushered across the hall and into to a room where Lord Doulain waited alone.

The King raised a hand. "I shall be brief, Francis." Lord

Doulain was taken aback that the monarch should address him so. The King went on "What I am about to say is for your ears and no other" He touched the side of his nose with a finger."

"I am plagued by small-minded politicians and their despicable spies who dwell on my every word and then misconstrue them for their own ends." He looked briefly over his shoulder, then, "I wish to speak with you in confidence because as a banker, merchant and shipper, you well understand the fundamental importance of protecting our shores, our trading routes and our merchant ships."

Lord Doulain was about to speak but The King held up a hand.

"This cannot be a debate so hear me out." He continued, "we have a shipbuilding programme that is not sufficient to our needs. I have spoken with members of the Navy Board, shipbuilders, architects, surveyors and men of the sea, and all are in agreement that a large part of our naval strength is aged and in need of replacement. The information I have gathered indicates that most of our shipyards are engaged in repair of old vessels and that our naval strength is augmented by the use of prize ships – mainly captured from the French – that are of poor quality and usually in bad repair. I know that Sir Thomas Slade, Surveyor to the Navy, is appalled at the situation and he has conveyed to me his concerns. But tell that to my Government and they snuff and puff and decide they will think about it - and that is as far as it goes. The French and Spanish shipyards are building ships of new design and if we do not sustain our strategic naval strength then we shall surely find ourselves hard pressed in future times. Should things remain the same, God forbid, then not only could we be placing our merchant fleet in danger, we may well completely lose our advantage on the seas.

"I give you a possible answer to the problem. Would you - or should I say, could you, - offer or determine to finance the building and equipping of a seventy-four gun ship of the line. Were this is done as a private venture, with open knowledge of purpose that it would be presented as a gift to the nation when complete, then I feel sure it would shame Parliament to action. I am aware I place an enormous burden on you, but perhaps you could persuade and encourage other bankers and shippers to contribute."

I ask you to give the matter consideration. What I have said is not a royal command - it is a royal plea. Now I must leave. I repeat that what I have said this night must remain in confidence. I have never spoken to you on this matter. To all others, this meeting did not take place.

The King went to the door and knocked once. There was a pause, then the door opened and he was gone.

Chapter Twenty Four

The chambermaid had already been into the room and drawn back the curtains. Russet lay in her bed staring at the ceiling, wondering if all that happened the previous evening had not been just a dream.

"I met the King." She whispered to herself. "I sang for the King. Me - Russet Roulette – I sang for King George. I can hardly believe it."

It did not cross her mind that her performance was cleverly designed, by King George, on the spur of the moment, to highlight his visit as one of a social nature. That did not detract from the fact that she had made a great impression on those who witnessed her performance. By mid-morning two invitations arrived for her to attend functions. By noon a further three notes were delivered with more requests for her company.

Russet opened them and laid them out on a table. Some dates clashed so she spread them out and began to select which to attend, before she could make up her mind, Mrs Fitzhamilton was announced.

"You must be very careful, my dear." Emma Fitzhamilton warned. "There are those who desire your acquaintance only for use as a corridor to others, and there will undoubtedly be some with evil thoughts in mind. This is not a rural community where everyone knows everyone else's business. There are devious characters at large in the city and they will not hesitate to take advantage of naivety." She read the invitations and pushed them away. "I can only advise you that there is not one respected name amongst the lot. I am sure you already know that you cannot, under any circumstances, go unescorted. Etiquette dictates that a lady must have a male escort if she wishes to accept invitations.

"His Lordship will accompany me." Russet said, haughtily.

"I am afraid His Lordship will be away for several days. He left early – I called to see him in the city and was told he had departed for the dockyards at Deptford and Woolwich - something to do with building more ships. But don't worry, he asked me to see to your needs and I shall advise you with the wisdom of experience. As for your entertainment, well, I'm sure I can provide a suitable hireling." Emma Fitzhamilton knew there would be a sharp response.

"And what, may I ask, is a hireling?"

"A hireling is a man who is willing to act as an escort to a lady – for money. There are many women – widows of officers who would otherwise be lost to society, spinsters who wish to socialise in hope of finding a husband, and ugly ladies, those who cannot attract a suitor. It is even said that some hirelings are willing to bed their benefactor – for a price." Emma Fitzhamilton teased.

"I think not." Russet looked aghast. "I could not possibly offer my company to a person of such depraved morality. They must indeed be men of lowly character."

Emma was trying hard to suppress her mirth. "You will shortly see for yourself, my dear. The chosen one is invited to attend you this very morning. Ah! I believe he is here now."

A maid knocked, then opened the door and announced Mr Tarquin Willoughby. He entered, bowed to Emma and then to

Russet.

"Your servant, ladies. I understand I am to accompany Miss Russet Roulette - at her direction." He bowed again.

He stood tall. Russet guessed he would be well over six feet. He was well dressed but it was his face that caught her attention; fair hair swept back from the top of a high forehead; straight nose with a thin wispy moustache that spread as far as his cheeks. His eyes were deep-set and vividly blue. Russet wondered how such a man could lower himself to have intercourse with elderly, or ugly women, and ask reimbursement for it. He could be nothing more than male whore.

Russet stepped towards him. "Mr Willoughby, is it true that you bed the women you escort?"

"Only the handsome ones, Miss Roulette." His eyes looked into hers without blinking, as he added, "I assure you, *you* will be quite safe."

Russet took a step back. The reply was unexpected. "You have an impertinent tongue, sir."

"Impertinent questions warrant impertinent replies." His voice purred.

"How dare you speak to me so!" Russet stamped a foot.

"I see no daring in speaking truth Miss Roulette."

"You are to be paid to escort me wherever I wish to go, and I insist you keep your incautious tongue to yourself." Russet placed her hands on her hips defiantly.

Tarquin Willoughby sighed. He glanced at Mrs Fitzhamilton and shrugged. Then he turned to Russet. "I feel you are under a misapprehension, Miss Roulette. I have attended this house to ascertain *your* suitability for *my* company. Now, having met you, I find I must decline the invitation."

He addressed Mrs Fitzhamilton. "I have a chair awaiting me and as I see no point in prolonging my visit, I shall bid you both a very good day." He bowed again and departed.

"That was not a very wise thing to do." Emma Fitzhamilton said.

"I do not consider your choice of escort appropriate." Russet answered.

"Mr Willoughby was not my choice. Lord Doulain instructed him. And I can tell you that no more an honourable man will you find in the whole of London." Emma huffed. "I hope you have brought embroidery and needles with you," she said. "For that is what you will now be about for the rest of your stay,"

Russet stamped a foot." Oh tish!" she exclaimed. She ran to the door, calling, "Mr Willoughby, Mr Willoughby." She reached the doorway to see two men carrying a sedan chair. "Oh, Mr Willoughby." She called again, but her voice fell to a whisper.

As the men carried the sedan towards the open street gateway, four figures, all carrying cudgels, appeared and attacked the carriers. The two men promptly dropped their load and fled. The attackers turned their attention to the sedan, heaving it over onto its side. They proceeded to open the door and then stood back with cudgels held high, ready to attack the emerging passenger.

With no thought for her own safety; all decorum gone,

Russet grabbed a walking stick from the hall stand, bundled her skirt and petticoats up above her knees, took the entrance steps two at a time and sprinted down the drive brandishing the walking stick and whooping at the top of her voice.

Tarquin Willoughby burst upwards through the open door of the fallen sedan. As his head appeared he took a glancing blow to the face that knocked him back. He grabbed one of the attackers and held him close, using the man as a shield.

Russet swung the walking stick in a great arc and brought it down on a man's head with all the force she could muster. As he fell she turned on a second who came in too close for her to flail the stick. He grabbed hold of her frock at the neckline and attempted to throw her to the ground. She wriggled free but his hand held the material, tearing it from neckline to waist. She thrust the stick into his midriff. He gasped and went down on his knees. She struck again across his back and the two men staggered to their feet and scurried away. She ran around the sedan where Tarquin was having difficulty fending off the other two attackers. Again she swung the walking stick, catching a third attacker on the side of his neck. He reeled away and quickly followed the other two into the street.

Tarquin was standing in the open doorway of the toppled sedan, blood pouring from his nose. He held the fourth attacker by the lapels of his tattered coat. To Russet's amazement he took some coins from a breeches pocket and gave them to the man, then let him go. The wretch touched his forelock several times as he muttered and backed away.

Russet stood gasping, her chest heaving. Her frock was

split down to her waist and she was unaware that her left breast was openly visible.

What did you give him," she gasped.

"Sixpence."

"What in this world for?"

"Bread." Tarquin stepped from the sedan. "Those men are not professional footpads, they're starving wretches. All they wanted was to get what articles of clothing they could from me to sell and buy food."

"Suddenly her face broke into a smile as she looked at his blood-soaked face. "You do not look a pretty sight," she said.

"I may not, but you certainly do." He was admiring the fullness of her breast and could not take his eyes from the upturned pink nipple that peeped from beneath her torn frock.

Russet glanced down. She let out a cry of surprise, and hurriedly covered herself. "You could well have looked the other way," she reproved.

"Who am I not to admire such a beauty?" He laughed, but his laughter ended abruptly as blood gushed from his nose.

"Come on," she said. "We had better do something about that. You could well wake up tomorrow with a red nose and two black eyes."

As they reached the house Russet said, "in the stories I read, when I was a little girl, it was always the prince who rescued the princess – not the other way round."

Emma Fitzhamilton stood in the doorway, backed by several housemen who had conveniently arrived when the violence ended. She took one look at Tarquin's bloodied face and turned away, insisting she could not stand the sight of blood. Her commercial brain was already considering how she could benefit from the events of the last few minutes. From experience she was aware that exaggeration bred exaggeration. She would add a little spice to the occurrence, knowing her words would be passed on for the incident to gather momentum and be magnified at each telling.

During the following days, the name of Russet Roulette was the main topic of conversation at ladies' tea parties, and also among men, in the many coffee houses across the city. Russet was becoming known as the beautiful 'friend' of the King who had fought off a gang of footpads and brought off a daring rescue. There was little mention of Tarquin Willoughby.

The day after the fracas, Tarquin arranged for a coach and horses from the house stables. He accompanied Russet to see the sights of the city. She was enthralled to see the magnificence of the buildings but when they approached the river she pinched her nose to escape the stench.

"That is the most repulsive smell I have ever known," she mumbled. "What is the cause?"

"The cause is humanity." He screwed his nose. "This is the beautiful River Thames, Russet. Up river it has the sweet smell of the countryside where it truly portrays a picture of beauty. Here it is the open, stinking sewer of London. I wanted you to see and smell it to show you that all is not honey and roses in this great city." He gave instructions to the coachman and they set off for Hyde Park.

They were seated opposite each other and Russet remained silent for a while as she took in the sights. Then she said,

"Lord Doulain asked you to act as my chaperon. Is he a good friend to you or is it that….."

"He is no friend!" Tarquin interrupted. "Quite the reverse. That is why I was at a loss to understand why he should have requested *my* services to act as your chaperon. Our dislike of each other was the reason for my reluctance to accept his offer."

"I do not understand." Russet said. "I have found His Lordship of good grace and, indeed, kind and generous."

"Oh, he would be to you. I have heard that he is looking to marry again and is searching for a presentable young woman to bear him an heir for his ill-gotten gains." He smiled at Russet and lifted his eyebrows, mockingly. "I must admit, I can but admire his impeccable choice."

"Me?" Russet had been sitting forward and now she slumped against the backrest. "I fear you are under a misapprehension, sir. I have no wish to become the wife of even the richest of men if it means I would be expected to be merely an heir-producing creature. Nor have I been asked to do such a thing."

"Where Lord Doulain is concerned you would have no choice. No man is more devious. Once his mind is made up he will go to every means open to him to get what he wants. I have known him go to unbelievable lengths to overcome refusals in business and anyone who gets in his way. I see no reason to believe he would not use those tactics to enhance his private life."

"You sound very bitter." Russet wanted to hear more. She added, "why do you dislike him so? What has he done to you?"

Tarquin looked away. "It is a long story. I have no wish to bore you with it."

"I'm listening." Her interest was roused and she wanted to hear what had brought about such animosity."

Tarquin shuffled, moving his position to find more comfort. "It goes back some years," he went on. "It began just before my eighteenth birthday when my father, who got himself into inextricable debt, shot my mother and then reloaded his pistol, stuck it in his mouth and blew his brains out. I was studying in Bristol and had no option but to call a halt to my education for lack of funds. I was penniless and I had to find work to sustain myself. I took the first job I found, a position on a merchant ship as a captain's clerk – little reward, but three meals a day. What I did not realise until it sailed was that it was a slaver. Am I boring you with...."

"No. No. Please go on." Russet was becoming intrigued.

We voyaged to the African Slave Coast, to the port of Ouidah where we bartered the cargo for slaves. As clerk, I had to count them on and I was as shocked at the degradation of those people. All were shackled, at the wrists and ankles but they every one held high his head. They were from a tribe called the Yoruba, a very proud people, and I was astounded at their deportment and dignity. At this time they were not cowed – that was to come later.

"You smelt the river today. Let me tell you that is sweet compared with the stench of a slaver. Humans packed like herrings in a box. So cramped they touched each other as they lay. The first layer were encamped on the deck of the hold but the fitting of shelves meant there were layers of slaves above them. When weather permitted groups were allowed on deck but when the weather turned they had to remain below. Can you imagine the sheer horror of it. The human body must keep working and those above would urinate and worse on those below. I can barely believe that one human society could treat another so cruelly and with such indifference.

"But that was not all." To Russet it seemed he was struggling to speak. He continued, at Ouidah we took on six black women. I was told it was not profitable to trade women as they only brought a fraction of the money a healthy man would fetch. I wondered why they should bring any. I was soon to find out.

"On the first night out I could hear the mumbled chatter of the enslaved men but these were drowned by the shrieks of the woman as they were used for the benefit of the crew. One, a girl of no more than twelve or thirteen, was abused in the most sordid and gross manner. Over and over again, day in day out, for forty-six days they were all used for fornication, including sodomy, and every possible form of depravity. Three days out from Kingston the sea was calm with almost no wind. Members of the crew were amusing themselves watching sharks chase smaller fish that scavenged the ship's discarded waste. Two members of the crew dragged the youngest of the females on deck. She was naked and horribly swollen and bleeding from the abuse she had suffered. Without any hesitation, they tossed her screaming over the side and cheered as she was torn to pieces by sharks. They had finished with her. She was no more use to them so her life meant nothing to them. The sight of that poor child will remain with me for the rest of my life."

Russet was about to speak but she saw the tears in Tarquins eyes so she refrained and he went on.

"I left that ship in Jamaica and worked my way back to England aboard another. Since then I have been an abolitionist and in opposition to your dear Lord Doulain. Three generations of the Doulains have built their wealth on the slave trade. Since my return I have opposed him at every opportunity, but he has both wealth and power so it is a difficult task I have taken on.

"Fortunately I am not alone in my quest for the abolition of this abhorrent trade. There are many men of note who are only too willing speak out, and we shall eventually succeed." He opened his arms. "Oh Russet," he said. "I must have spoiled your day with my ranting. I do apologise. I shall say no more."

Russet lay in her bed that night, her mind pondering on what Tarquin had told her. She thought nothing of his adventures, or of the slaves. Her thoughts dwelt on the tale of Lord Doulain looking to find a wife for the sole purpose of giving him a child. "Well he can look elsewhere," she said aloud to the ceiling. "I will not be a child-bearing animal for a middle-age man in a loveless marriage. Wealth or no wealth." Her thoughts returned to Nestwith and the poem. 'I do wish I knew who had written it.' She sighed, deeply. 'To Russet with my heart.' She quoted silently. 'Somebody out there must love me.' She closed her eyes, and slept.

Chapter Twenty Five

The Branston Silver lay easy at anchor. With all sails furled she looked like a great monster at rest, replenishing energy for the next prodigious foray. The vessel looked at ease, but aboard was a buzz of activity. Hatches had been open since dawn and samples of the cargo had been handled out and lay stacked neatly on deck, ready for inspection. All was about ready to welcome aboard the local merchants. No money would change hands; goods would be valued against the number of slaves considered of equal worth.

During the past weeks a strange rapport had built up between the Captain and Jamie. The Captain spoke and Jamie wrote his answers and comments. For one it was a meeting of minds; conferring with a person of equal, if not superior, intelligence. For the other it was a revelation; communicating in question and answer discussion for the first time in his short memory. To converse in this manner they were compelled to sit near to each other and the Captain was now in the habit of pouring two glasses of wine and 'Pitchforth' had become 'Jamie Lad.'

The tropical sun had passed its zenith when the merchants came aboard. One was a large man dressed in white and adorned with the pelt of a leopard, the animal's head worn over his own head suggesting a crown of authority. The forelegs of the pelt fell over his shoulders with the main body of the fur hanging down his back like a shawl. As he came aboard an attendant held the tail like a ceremonial train. Two soberly dressed merchants, together with a retinue of attendants, followed him.

Jamie was intrigued by the method of barter. The Portuguese held power here and most of the slaves were shipped to Brazil. Only through the influence of Lord Doulain, through his trade with Portugal, was a British ship allowed to do business here.

Neither the Captain nor the merchants spoke the others' language and all accounting was done by sign; fingers of hands spread wide to signify multiples of five. A wave of the hand, palm down, signalled 'no', palm uppermost, 'yes.' A single finger pointed upwards was to lift the price, pointing down indicated the merchant thought the price too high. A deal done was by a touching of hands. All goods were valued against a number of slaves; humanity the only currency.

Carried on a chair by two members of the crew, Jamie followed the captain, ticking off goods bartered, and accounting each sale. When it came to the bolts of cloth he interrupted and began his own silent barter. All three merchants stood back and seemed hesitant to deal with him. He touched the cloth, rubbing it between his fingers, inviting the buyers to feel the quality and pointing a finger upwards to indicate quality. He turned what had been single sale offers to an auction, with the three merchants bidding against one another.

He wrote a note for the Captain and an empty musket crate was brought from the hold and laid before the merchants. Jamie gesticulated and all three merchants burst into laughter.

"What's he doin', Billy. A seaman asked.

Billy Dibb turned on him. "Mr Dibb to you, lad." He

turned away to watch the sale, then, "look at 'im, lad. He's crippled and can't talk a word but e's just bartered them empty boxes - as coffins, good as like – and look see, they've taken 'em."

Before nightfall the merchants were entertained then left the ship to be rowed ashore. Captain Christopher was elated with the outcome. The increase Jamie had obtained from the bolts of cloth and his sale of the crates had almost made up for the goods stolen.

The following day was for inspection and selection of the human cargo and agreement to be reached on quality before any goods left the ship.

While the captain and Billy Dibb went ashore to select the slaves, the ship was restocked with food for the voyage, and the huge fresh water butts filled to the brim. Citrus fruit, carcases of wild antelope and pigs were given priority, to feed the crew for the first days of the voyage. Carcases of monkeys were offered but declined. Bales of dried beans and peas, loaded aboard at Liverpool, would be the main diet of the slaves and this was supplemented now by taking on quantities of yams and rice.

It was another two days after the selection process before the boarding of the slaves began. The decks were cleared and the bartered cargo loaded into boats and taken ashore where hoards of porters waited to carry the goods to inland markets. The empty musket crates, now with long handles affixed, were loaded and lifted onto shoulders of porters to be taken away. The carpenter and his crew toiled and sweated in the hold, fixing bedding boards and erecting shelves. Shackles were taken ashore and the first batch of slaves brought out to the ship.

John Fullerton was familiar with the strict Royal Navy discipline and seeing men in irons did not astonish him. Jamie felt a sense of guilt and shame at the sight; black, naked men, their skins glistening with sweat, eyes wide with fear, struggling to climb aboard. Shackled at wrists and ankles they shuffled forward, heads bowed, to be ushered through a hatchway and into the hold.

"They look like condemned men knowing they are about to die." John Fullerton spoke to the Captain.

"You'd look frightened in their place." The captain said. "They'll be from an inland village and never seen sea nor ship. Poor devils have a life of hell in front of 'em."

"Do I hear a tone of compassion in your voice, Captain? Do you not think them inferior? Good only to be slaves?"

"No. I regard them as people, like us. They may have different colour but in the eyes of God they are just as much His creatures as we." The Captain had been leaning on the fore poop deck rail, now he straightened up and faced his first mate. "Billy Dibb has sailed with me for many a year and he knows the ropes. I will not have them ill treated aboard this ship. They must remain shackled, for without being chained they could easily overpower the crew. But that does not mean to say I agree with fettering men.

"Two meals a day and a pint of water with each meal. When weather permits we have them up on deck in groups and sluice them down. You soon find out which of them can be trusted and those that would be rebellious - given the chance. Billy Dibb, has a merciful streak in his nature. He will look after them; kind, when kindness warrants, hard by, when merits must. He threatens with the rope but I have never known him use it." The Captain began to climb down the companion ladder but stopped. He looked up at John Fullerton. "What is the point of cramming slaves into a hold, to starve and beat them, only to have a number die? I know captains who have ordered dying slaves thrown overboard for fear of disease spreading amongst their crew, when some of the poor creatures suffered only from sickness of the sea. What earthly purpose is there in ending a voyage with a quarter less than started?"

He was about to continue his descent but lifted his head. "Mr Pitchforth is of the same opinion. He urges that the slaves be kept active and not allowed to brood. He says we should use incentives for good behaviour – extra food, or water."

"With all due respect Captain, you seem to treat the words of this peasant with undue respect." John Fullerton spoke with scorn.

"With the greatest respect, Mr Fullerton." The Captain raised his voice. "Say what you will, but Mr Pitchforth is no peasant. I have questioned him on many subjects and his knowledge astounds me. From Greek mythology, English history, mathematics, even Latin, he is far more the learned than I."

"I can assure you, sir, the man is from peasant stock." John Fullerton was adamant. "I know his mother who is a midwife and also works as a housemaid for the Roulettes at Nestwith Hall. Ask Totton Roulette."

"So you have said before, but I need ask nobody on this score." He took a step down the companionway, then said, "you ask yourself this, why would a peasant lad – a quarry worker, I am told – have need of knowledge to navigate a ship. And how, tell me, could such an uneducated person be able to quote the teachings of Plato, Aristotle and Socrates. Peasant indeed! He is no more a peasant than King George himself. I tell you Mr Fullerton, the man is a scholar"

He descended another two steps and halted again. "He has no memory of how he gained knowledge. He has no knowledge of his early life. He writes that he awoke after an accident, of which he has no recollection, for his mother to nurse him back to health. He cannot understand why he can recall what he has learned but not how, when, or where he studied the subjects." The captain took the remaining steps and disappeared into the aft cabin.

For the first week after leaving the Slave Coast all went well. It was during the second week that the stench of enclosed humanity began to permeate everywhere. Seasickness was a major problem with fettered men vomiting over others, causing tempers to flare. Cleaning became a priority and it was a detested chore. John Fullerton told of navy men claiming they could smell a slaver downwind for a distance of three miles, and he believed. Captain Christopher kept to the aft cabin as much as he could and with the company of Jamie continued their discourse.

Whenever the weather kept fair the hatches were opened up. The morning began with the duty watch on their knees scrubbing the deck, working from forward to aft with wet sand, holystones then swabs. As soon as all was shipshape slaves were brought out in a group of no more than twenty at any one time. They were dowsed with seawater before being returned and another batch ushered out. This ritual went on throughout the day and when all had been 'swilled' the first group would be brought out for a second time, and so on. Cleaning the holds was the most hated chore and a strict rotation of the crew was enforced.

"Egad, this is the most direful matter I have ever known." John Fullerton said. He stood on the poop deck looking down at the naked bodies, men, hampered by the chains of their fetters, desperately attempting to clean their bodies with the seawater that was being thrown over them. "When this voyage ends I shall become a landlubber. Never shall I seek another ship as long as I live." He spoke to nobody, but made his pledge to the skies.

Totton had the worst of it. He emerged from an open hatch, his cleaning duty done. "Never did I imagine a Roulette shovelling up the shit of others. By God! I swear my nostrils are so impaired I will never smell the sweet country air again." He stood with legs apart, dressed only in ducks, while members of the crew bucketed water over him. He gasped as a bucketful took him in the face. "Why is it we have to do this? Why not release some of them and let them clean up their own mess."

"That is for me to decide." The captain's voice thundered from the poop deck. "You may be the son of a baronet, but here you are a seaman and you will do the work of a seaman." He turned his back on Totton, the interchange over.

Gunner had witnessed Totton's emergence from the hold. "Have you never mucked out a pigsty, Tott?"

"Not personally, no." Totton wiped the flat of his hands down his chest and followed the water down his body to wipe them on the duck breeches he wore. "I have mucked out horses more times than I can remember," he said. "But nothing could be as bad as that." He jerked his head, indicating the open hatch. Screwing his nose he looked up to the skies. "Never again shall I visit a seaport. Never again shall I leave myself open to be pressed. Never again shall I leave the green acres of dear England. And, when all this is over, never again shall I set foot on the deck of a ship."

Chapter Twenty Six

Russet peered at herself in the mirror. Moving closer to the glass and turning her head, she ran her fingers gently down her cheek. Standing back, a smug look on her face, she spoke to her own image, "I would hazard, Russet Roulette, that many women would risk death itself for such perfection." She remained in front of the glass, turning this way and that, admiring herself in differing poses.

"Tonight I shall be the femme fatale. I shall bewitch them all." She twirled round and round, seeing herself in the glass at each turn and laughing happily at the prospect of another of the Fitzhamilton soirees. She was in the process of dressing when a chambermaid knocked and entered.

"There is a gentleman and two ladies to see you, ma'am. He has announced himself as your father." The maid curtsied and left the room.

Russet was aghast. She stamped a foot. "Oh damn and damnation!" she exclaimed. "This is going to spoil everything."

Sir Marcus Roulette was in no mood to be greeted lovingly by his wayward daughter. He waited in the reception room with Charlotte and Katherine. All three had declined to remove their travelling coats.

"Father dear!" Russet bounced into the room, all smiles and with arms outstretched.

"Don't you dare 'father dear' me," Sir Marcus fumed, his face reddening with anger. "How dare you leave home without my permission? How dare you come to live in the house of a person, no matter whom, without my permission and without a chaperone of my choosing?"

"But you did say you would accept Lord Doulain's invitation." Russet knew she had been impetuous but could only defend herself by attempting to put the blame for her flight from Nestwith onto her father.

"I don't know what has got in to you, Russet. Do you not think there are times when you could consider others above yourself? I have been sick with worry at the whereabouts of Totton, and when I return home from Liverpool I find you gone. You can pack your bags, you are coming with me."

"But I cannot, Father," she implored, "I am to accompany His Lordship this very evening to an assembly of his choosing."

"I care not what you have arranged, you will do as I say." Sir Marcus picked up his hat. "Go on with you. I will order the maids to pack your clothes, if you are not of a mind to......."

"I will not go!" Russet stamped a foot and stood her ground.

"Then I shall take you forcibly."

"And what will society think of that?" Russet pouted her lips.

"I don't give a damn what society thinks!" Sir Marcus was furious.

Russet put her head on one side and said, "you might not, Father, but what about the reputation of His Lordship. Tongues will wag. People will say, or assume, that impropriety on the part of His Lordship has compelled your action. Imagine, a father dragging a young girl from the house of a peer of the realm. Lord Doulain is a very powerful man and I would consider retaliation and the protection of his good name would be at the core of his thoughts. And what would you do to my reputation, Father. Russet Roulette, an acquaintance of King George. The King asked me to sing for him.......

"Ha!" Charlotte laughed and Katherine joined her. Both held hands in front of their mouths to hide their mirth.

"It's another of her egotistical stories, Father. Sang for the king, indeed. What next?"

"You may have to eat those words, dear sister. But no matter what you say, I shall not leave." Russet was very pleased with herself, but the feeling of success was short-lived.

"If you do not come with me now, I shall disown you." Sir Marcus stamped a foot, in imitation of his daughter.

A knock and the entrance of a maid broke the impasse.

"A Mr Willoughby to see Miss Roulette," the maid said, timidly. It was as if she realised she had interrupted. "I have shown him to the sitting room. Shall I ask him to wait?

"No, no." Russet replied quickly. "Show him in – at once." As Tarquin was shown in Russet turned to her father. "Mr Willoughby has been my escort. Lord Doulain appointed him for my protection. He has shown me the sights of London and has looked after me so well, even fighting off the threat of footpads and villains." Her last words were spoken loudly hoping Tarquin would realise her dilemma. Then she added, as an afterthought, may I introduce you to my father, Sir

Marcus Roulette, and my sisters, Charlotte and Katherine."

He bowed to Charlotte and Katherine, "Ladies," he said. Then addressed Sir Marcus. "Your servant, Sir. I am honoured to make your acquaintance."

Both Charlotte and Katherine stood wide-eyed at the sight of this tall, handsome man. Sir Marcus had no time to weigh up the newcomer. "Mr Willoughby." Sir Marcus was hesitant. "I understand you have been looking after my wayward daughter during her stay here. I must tell you she is here without my permission and you sir, have acted inappropriately in accompanying her."

Tarquin smiled. "But you were not here to give me instruction, sir. Would you have had me leave her to fortune in this wicked city?"

"No, no," Sir Marcus stammered. "I suppose as you are a friend of Lord Doulain…"

"I am an employee of His Lordship. Tarquin corrected. "His Lordship is no friend to me, nor I to him. However, when we walk the same plank our diversities swim as one." He turned to Russet. "I come with a message from His Lordship. He has arranged his business commitments and he will escort you to Mrs Fitzhamilton's assembly this evening. When I spoke with him I am sure he knew nothing of the arrival of your father and sisters, but I am sure Mrs Fitzhamilton would be delighted to have their company, and I also suggest that His Lordship would expect you to remain here as his house guests." He bowed all round, then added, "I doubt the King will attend this evening but I am told he enjoyed your company and I am sure he will invite you to sing for him again another time."

Russet felt herself thrill at his words. She had a great urge to throw her arms about him. He excused himself but as he was about to leave he glanced briefly at Russet. There was a slight hint of a smile on his lips and a twinkle in his eyes. He had come to her rescue – he had repaid a debt.

Sir Marcus accompanied Charlotte while Katherine entered on the arm of Mr Willoughby. Marcus was surprised at the number of nobility and political leaders in the company, many apparently, with no female companion. He was enchanted with Emma Fitzhamilton and was unable to hide his pleasure. Then came the announcement, "Lord   Doulain and Miss Russet Roulette."

The murmur of conversation ceased abruptly and all eyes turned towards the entrance. As Lord Doulain appeared with Russet on his arm a burst of applause rang out. Russet gently waved a hand in acknowledgement.

"She might have met the king but now she's acting like the queen." Charlotte whispered.

Tarquin stood behind Charlotte and Katherine. He leaned forward and placed his head between theirs. "She is the queen in this company," he whispered. "She is greatly admired." He straightened up and moved to Katherine's side. Again he leaned down to speak in her ear. "It may be my misfortune to act in a discourteous manner. I may have to leave you from time to time. I must keep my eye on Russet to see she is not overwhelmed by unwelcome company."

"Unwelcome company? Here?" Katherine looked up into

his eyes.

"There are many who would seek her acquaintance and I must rescue her from their clutches when needs must. Miss Roulette."

"My name is Katherine – my friends call me Kate." She waited for a reply but he did not offer one. He was looking at two men who were approaching Lord Doulain.

"Ah! He exclaimed. I see Lord North is here, and that young man with him is young Charles Fox, if I am not mistaken. Now why would His Lordship invite such men of note? I know he has sponsored this soiree so their presence must be for some benefit to him. He is a shrewd fellow, our Francis Doulain. I would not wager against him being up to something."

"Mr Willoughby," Katherine said, sharply, "I do not have an inkling of your meaning. I know none of these people, so you speak to me in words of little context. Perhaps you could enlighten me as to the identity of those with the names you utter.""Tarquin." He glanced quickly at her, ignoring her request. "Call me Tarquin – Kate." He then excused himself and made his way over to where Lord Doulain and Lord North were deep in conversation.

"A very fair evening to you Francis, I trust you are in good health." Lord North bowed his head in greeting as he spoke. "I do not think you have the acquaintance of Charles Fox." Lord North introduced his companion and went on, "he is the son of Henry and a bright young prospect." He stepped closer. "What's this I hear of you going into the business of building ships?"

"Ah!" Lord Doulain, smiled. "Like all politicians, your assumption that tittle-tattle is the truth is somewhat tardy. I would have you know, my family has been in the business of building ships for the past three generations."

"Yes, yes." Lord North lowered his voice to a whisper and leant across Lord Doulaine's shoulder and spoke into his ear. "I have it on good authority that you are to build a ship of the line. Is that not a strange thing for a merchant to do?"

"I have informed the Admiralty of my intention, and when it is built and fitted out I shall present it to the admirals to use as they see fit, for the service of king and country."

"But why?" Lord North questioned. "Why would a private citizen go to such expense when it is the business of government to make such decisions?"

"Because there is so much hot air surrounding parliament it creates the fog that blinds your vision. My view as a man of business is very clear. We are a country of trade and our routes of trade must be protected. I have recently paid a visit to naval shipyards and I have sent others to see what goes on elsewhere. Are you aware, Frederick, our shipyards are almost all fully engaged in repairing prizes. Mostly French ships we have captured. They are of poor construction compared to our own and have been built to a flimsy design. They have forfeited sturdiness for speed and some have been known to break up while at sea. What advantage do we get from that? Are you prepared to send our seamen out in such vessels, when the designs of our own architects and surveyors are far superior?"

"It is a case of cost, Francis....."

"Of course it is!" Lord Doulain felt he had won his point. "That is why as an Englishman I am prepared to finance this venture."

"That is very noble of you, My Lord." Charles Fox intervened. "But I hear you are not to finance it alone but are asking around for donations to your patriotic cause."

"So I am." Lord Doulain grinned. "Perhaps you gentlemen would care to offer your generosity to my - patriotic cause?"

Tarquin had been unable to get near enough to hear the conversation so went to the rescue of Russet who was surrounded by admirers. He found her declining requests to sing.

"I only sing for kings," he heard her say. "I see no royalty here." She put a hand to her brow and pretentiously looked around the room.

"Mr Willoughby." Lord Doulain approached, using the etiquette of formality. "I would be pleased if you would call on me at ten tomorrow morning. I have a proposition that may be of interest to you." He gave Tarquin no time to refuse the request, but added, "it is of the utmost importance you observe promptness," he then turned away to speak to Emma Fitzhamilton.

Charlotte and Katherine were amazed at the way Russet commanded attention. They watched her move from one group to another, and wherever she attended laughter ensued and sometimes gasps of astonishment at her repartee.

At ten o'clock the following morning Tarquin entered the Doulain building with apprehension. He was ushered up the marble stairway and into a large oak-panelled room. Lord

Doulain was seated behind a large desk strewn with piles of papers. As the door closed he looked up.

"Ah, my dear boy. Do take a chair." He addressed Tarquin like a friend of long standing. "The proposition I spoke of may be of interest to you" He pointed to a table and two chairs. As he rose from his desk he rang a hand bell. Before the ringing ceased a servant appeared so quickly Tarquin thought he must have been standing by the door awaiting the call. Lord Doulain nodded and another servant appeared with a tray.

"Coffee, Tarquin?" His Lordship asked.

Tarquin felt a sense of disquiet. The familiar use of his first name made him wary.

Lord Doulain sipped his coffee, then he said, "you will no doubt have heard that I am to finance the building of a seventy four gun ship of the line. I am doing this for selfish reasons in one respect - for the protection of my own merchant ships - but I am also going ahead with this project because I believe the politicians are blind to the need to protect our trade routes.

"I have the resources to finance one ship but intend to ask merchants, bankers and business people in all walks to contribute towards the building of other ships of war. I also believe we need foreign investment and in particular, help from the colonies. I cannot ask the Americas because they are taxed to the limit already. But I feel it is in order to ask plantation owners in the Indies to contribute. After all, trade is a two way bridge and although they pay their taxes I consider they should also be liable for the protection of their products."

He paused and took a sip of coffee then continued, "that is where I need your good services. I want you to go to the Indies as my emissary to get what you can in the way of contributions from plantation owners.

Tarquin shook his head. He was astounded at His Lordship's apparently facetious request. "Nothing in this world would induce me to act as your emissary abroad. Why should I help you in any way? You and I have been at drawn swords for some time and I am not prepared to sheath mine. I wondered why you asked me to escort Miss Roulette. Now I know." He rose from the chair to leave.

"No, no." Lord Doulain, pleaded. "Hear me out, Tarquin. I admit I used Miss Roulette to gain your credit, but I can think of no other who could serve this cause so well. You will be paid well and I will make a promise to you. If you do this for me – and for England – when you return I shall stand with you in your fight to abolish the slave trade."

Tarquin laughed, scornfully. "Now I know this is a trick. You, an abolitionist, Ha! You have made your wealth out of slavery." He was standing half turned towards the door, and with a wave of his arm he said, "but for the enslavement of your fellow men, regardless of colour, you would have none of this." As his arm encompassed the room, he noticed the portraits on either side of the fireplace.

"My God!" He stared at the paintings. "How did you get..."

"It is not of Russet." Lord Doulain interrupted. "It is a portrait of my wife – my late wife - Helen. The likeness is astonishing."

"I would have sworn..."

"So would I." His Lordship cut in. "When I first saw Russet it was at Nestwith Hall. She came down the steps toward me. It was as if I had been struck by a bolt of lightning. Helen died twenty-five years ago but for a brief moment I actually thought Russet was she." His eyes looked dreamy as he stared at the portrait. "Helen was – how could I put it – demure with a quiet dignity about her. Russet is more, er, bold. The extraordinary likeness is probably why I am so disposed towards her."

"Well, I must bid you good day" Tarquin reached for the knob of the door.

"I wish you would reconsider." Lord Doulain spread his arms for one last plea. "I know you have a poor opinion of those who make profit from the trade in humanity. I do however believe that many have a wrong picture of what goes on. White traders do not go running into the forests of Africa firing muskets and wielding swords to capture the natives for enslavement. They are already enslaved by their own people and we are but the transporters." Tarquin was about to speak but His Lordship continued, "oh, I know what you are going to say and I agree with you – if we were not there to do the transporting. But it is six of one, half a dozen of the other.

He turned and went to his desk. "One year, Tarquin. One year. That is all I ask, and I promise I shall keep my word."

"You promise to be an outspoken abolitionist and yet carry on with the transportation of those poor creatures?"

"No." he shook his head vigorously. "You misunderstand me. I shall give orders for all my ships to cease slave transportation immediately. What is more I shall give that order whether you accept my proposition or not."

Tarquin moved back to the table. "One year, you say?"

"One year."

"Then I shall do your bidding. Not because of any respect I have for you, but because I wish to see conditions in the Indies."

"Good, good." Lord Doulain picked up a folder from his desk and joined Tarquin at the table. He opened the folder and took from it several sealed documents. "This is a note from the Admiralty to the captain of HMS Brimham. She is at this moment anchored off Chatham. These," he placed four sealed notes before Tarquin, "are letters of credit, in your name, to be drawn on the Company Doulain Bank in Kingston. And this is for the captain of Branston Silver." He added the last note to the others on the table. "The Branston Silver is expected at Kingston with a cargo of slaves. You shall take passage on the Brimham, a frigate with more speed than a merchantman, so you should arrive first. The Brimham has orders to sail for English Harbour in Antigua but this note from the Admiralty supercedes the original orders and the ship will go to Kingston. She leaves on the morning tide the day after tomorrow, so I suggest you pack your chest and leave for Chatham as soon as you are able." He went back to his desk and opened a drawer. From it he took a polished wooden case. "I have a little something here that may be of use to you in these troubled times." He opened the case and Tarquin found himself looking with interest at a pair of pistols. They were of the highest quality with ornate silver plates, intricately engraved and secured with tiny screws to each. Machined lead balls, each settled in their own impressed bed, lay in a row across the length of the velvet-covered base. A ramrod and wadding, together with a small powder flask, completed the contents. Tarquin closed the lid and thanked His Lordship. He then took the notes and turned them over one by one. "These already bear my name," he said, cautiously. Then his eyes widened as he ended, "damn it! You knew all along I would accept."

"I may be an evil slaver, Tarquin, but that does not debilitate my judgement of a man's character." He took Tarquin's hand and gripped it firmly. "Good luck to you, my boy, and God speed."

Chapter Twenty Seven

The roar of rain striking the roof, muffled hoof beats; the crunch of iron-tyred wheels along the rutted road and the swaying, jerky, motion of the coach made the journey one of immense discomfort. This was the third day of travel after leaving the capital and Russet was suffering the irritating itching of fleabites acquired from her bed at the last overnight stop. She could see that her sisters also suffered and she made a mental note never again to lodge at that particular inn.

She was bored. Conversation had diminished and finally ceased. Sir Marcus and his three daughters sat in silence, each lost in their own thoughts. All four were suddenly awakened by a resounding crack. The coach lurched to one side and dropped as if about to topple over. Katherine came out of her seat and fell on to her father's lap. Charlotte was pushed against the door, while Russet slid down the bench seat and ended pressed up against her father. There was much shouting outside as the coachman fought to control the horses. A door was opened and a voice called out that the coach was in danger of falling over and advised the passengers to alight.

Russet was first out. She wrapped a shawl about her shoulders but it was meagre protection against the incessant downpour. As the others were helped from the coach they all peered at the collapsed rear wheel. Several spokes had broken and the rim settled across the hub. It was irreparable.

Sir Marcus cursed. "Where are we?" He asked the coachman.

"About half way through Black Wood, sir." The man

removed his hat to address his master. Sir Marcus waved a hand, indicating he should replace it.

"We are all but home then?"

"Aye, sir. Would you care to take the horses while we....."

"No, no." Sir Marcus was annoyed with himself for ordering that the grey coach be retained in London. Had he ordered that both coaches return to Nestwith together, the breakdown would have been no problem. He would have had no qualms in taking the outriders' horses had Russet been his only companion. Glancing at Charlotte and Katherine who stood huddled together looking bedraggled and miserable he was momentarily at a loss what to do. There was an embarrassing pause, then Russet suggested, "why do we not take shelter at Maisy's cottage? It's only a short way and I'm sure we would be welcome."

Sir Marcus gave orders for one of the two mounted escorts to go on to Nestwith Hall and return with another coach. The other escort and the coachman would remain to guard the baggage.

Russet had already set off along the track. She skipped in and out of the water-filled ruts, then halted and lifting her arms high with head back, her face presented to the pouring rain, she cried, "it's raining! It's raining! Is it not wonderful!" Then she set off at a run along the track.

"Her brain is addled." Charlotte uttered words of disdain. She shivered as the rain penetrated her clothing to dampen her shoulders and trickle down her back. "Our silly sister will never grow up. Look at her, she actually enjoys discomfort. It would not surprise me should she find herself in Bedlam."

"Oh my shoe! My shoe!" Katherine bent to retrieve her footwear and slipped, going down on her knees in the filth of the track. As Sir Marcus and Charlotte helped her to her feet she began to weep. "I hate this," she cried. "I hate it. I hate it, I hate it."

Back on her feet she struggled to replace the shoe. "Russet is a fool, Father. She has never grown up. How could anybody take joy from such a direful predicament."

Sir Marcus shielded his eyes from the rain and looked down the track to where Russet was still dancing and splashing. "Your sister flourishes on adversity, Kate. She is never more happy than when challenged. She may at times display anger but it is always short-lived. Where we see misery she sees only happiness. It is a gift from God, and I would not have her any other way."

Russet reached the cottage and hurried round the back. There she entered the porch and banged her fist against the kitchen door.

The bolts were drawn, the door opened and Molly peered out, "What in the world are you doing here, Miss Russet?"

"Waiting to be invited in, Molly." She chuckled at her own answer. "Is Maisy not here?"

"Yes she is." Maisy's voice called reassuringly from within. "Come in, my dear, come in." Russet entered, dripping water onto the stone-flagged floor. "Oh my lovely, you must get out of those wet clothes." Maisy began to rummage among a pile of clothing on the kitchen table. "These are Molly's, just washed and dried. You'd look like a sack in mine." She selected a frock and tossed it to Russet. "Drop your dress and we'll rub you down." She stopped suddenly, then, "what *are* you doing here, Russet?"

"My father and my sisters will be here shortly. We have suffered a mishap." Russet was about to explain when heavy thumping on the front door heralded her father's arrival.

"Mistress Pitchforth, er, Maisy" she heard her father say. "We find ourselves at the mercy of misfortune and we are in the veriest need of shelter. I would not impose our company upon you but for the inclement weather and my daughters' discomfort."

Maisy invited them in and they stood in the entrance as Molly helped them out of their sodden coats. Charlotte and Katherine looked a picture of misery and they stared in disbelief at Russet who was standing in front of the fire holding up her frock with her bare buttocks to the heat.

"Russet! Cover yourself at once!" Sir Marcus turned his head away.

"Father dear, this is sheer heaven." She wiggled her hips. "You should drop your breeches and try it." She giggled to herself as she imagined her puritanical father following her suggestion.

Sir Marcus was embarrassed. Charlotte and Katherine were in the process of removing their clothes and he knew not where to look.

"Molly," he said, quickly. "It is not my way to admit regret to those I dismiss, but to you I offer my sincere apologies. I am aware of the care and compassion you gave my dear wife and it was remiss of me to act as I did."

"It is of no matter now, sir." Molly answered. "I have work

at the Rose and Crown Inn and I am very happy. Had I still been at the Hall I may never have met with Thomas Chatterton, and as I am to become his wife, everything has happened for the best."

"He asked you?" Russet whooped and took her own question as answer. She straightened her skirt and came away from the fire to throw her arms about Molly. "Oh Molly, I am so pleased for you." Charlotte and Katherine shook Molly by the hand and congratulated her.

Sir Marcus looked bemused by it all. "Does this mean you will leave to live in London when Thomas Chatterton completes his work here?"

"Oh no, sir." Molly went across to the fireplace and heaved the great pot along the slider to warm the contents. "Thomas says that when his work here is done he will leave the Doulain Company and find work hereabouts. He says he won't ever go back to London. Says it stinks there and there's too many folk."

"So." Sir Marcus stroked his chin. "I shall have words with Master Chatterton."

"Oh sir!" Molly exclaimed. "I should not have said. Oh please, don't you be telling him I told you. He will be angered with me. It was rash of me to speak my mind."

"Do not distress yourself, girl." Sir Marcus reassured her. "No words shall pass our lips. Many a hasty word is said in happiness, and in anger." Then as if as an afterthought he added, "and in grief."

The deluge ceased as quickly as it began. The coach arrived and the party were transported to Nestwith Hall. The sisters were still attired in Molly's clothing and while the girls chatted Sir Marcus had hardly spoken a word. He sat in pensive mood, deep in thought. His first act upon arrival was to dispatch a message to Thomas Chatterton.

When Thomas Chatterton was shown in to the study early the following morning, Sir Marcus was astonished at the change in the man. Gone was the sallow-skinned city clerk and the drab trappings in which he had arrived. His cheeks now displayed a rosy sheen and he dressed as a country gentleman.

"Good morning to you, Thomas." Sir Marcus deliberately addressed him by his first name. "You look in eminent good health"

"It is the country air, I am told." Thomas said. "It enters the lungs and brings the flush of life back to the very soul."

"You will miss it when you return to London." Sir Marcus forayed.

"Return?" Thomas looked aghast. "Are my services here at an end?"

"Good gracious no!" Sir Marcus was pleased with his ploy. He went on, "the time will come when you will return and we shall miss you, Thomas"

"I shall not return to the city, sir. I am taken with such a liking for the country and country ways. I have a mind to remain where I can find space away from crowds and deal with honest country folk."

"But if His Lordship requires your services in the city...."

"Then I shall leave his employ, sir." Thomas showed his determination. "I shall find work, I have no doubt of that."

Sir Marcus could hardly contain his pleasure. "If ever that should happen, Thomas, we have a vacant position here as Estate Manager. There is a house to go with the job but I doubt the position will fetch as much as His Lordship is likely to pay you. However, as Estate Manager you would have a reasonably high standing in the community and your station would demand respect."

"I – I." Thomas stammered. "I don't know what to say, sir."

"Say you will think on my words, Thomas. Give it some consideration and then let me know your decision."

"An offer like that don't need no thinking on. I am shortly to be married, so I would be honoured to accept, sir."

"Then I ask for your discretion, Thomas. Say nothing of this conversation and you will leave the employ of his Lordship prior to officially accepting the position here. I would not have His Lordship thinking I was poaching his protégé."

Later, Russet and Charlotte accompanied Sir Marcus as Thomas Chatterton showed them around the new enterprise. The slaughterhouse was almost complete and the adjacent butchery was taking form. The rows of pigsties, in various stages of construction appeared as if a small town was being erected on the site. To the side of the main building stood a larger sty complete with yard and small, adjoining paddock.

"What is that one for?" asked Russet of Thomas Chatterton.

He laughed. "That is the palace of his majesty, Miss."

"His Majesty?"

"King George III the Second, Miss. He's the great boar. We moved him from the village and he appears particularly content in his new surroundings."

"Haaa! This I must see. Come Charlotte, I will introduce you to Royalty."

When they reached the sty Charlotte complained about the stench and the mud. "I do not like this, Russet," she said. "The place stinks of pigs."

"Well what do you expect it to stink of?" Russet looked over the sty wall to see the huge boar lying on its side apparently asleep. The animal was snorting erratically as if enjoying some erotic dream.

"Just look at him, Charlotte. Is he not magnificent?" She leant over the wall and addressed the beast, "good day your majesty," she said. "I have had the honour of meeting your namesake." The boar grunted and lethargically pushed itself up to a sitting position and remained on its haunches staring at Russet with its little pink eyes. She curtsied and said, "I am at your Majesty's service. Do you have any request of me, sire?"

"I have had enough of this stupidity!" Charlotte turned to leave. "You are out of your mind, sister." With her parting words she heaved up her skirts and set off to find her father.

"Father," she said, upon joining him, "I fear Russet has the makings of mother. She has gone completely mad and will surely have to be locked in her room. Just look at her."

Sir Marcus screwed his eyes and looked at Russet who was standing in front of the sty with arms outstretched. "What in this world is she doing?

"She is singing, Father. She is singing Green Sleeves – to a pig!"

When they returned home a housemaid met them in the hall. She was holding a bundle of clothes. She spoke to Russet, "these are the clothes you came home in yesterday. They are washed, dried and flat-ironed, but Maisy has left for home and forgotten to take 'em."

"Don't worry." Russet took the bundle. "I will take them to her. I think Molly will be in need of them. I have to visit Maisy. Father promised her a butt of pork and some rabbits for her hot pot – we ate her out of house and home yesterday."

"Father says you are not to go out alone." Charlotte reminded her.

"Oh come on." Russet argued. Maisy walks here most days and then walks home. Nobody has threatened her. Father is thinking of what happened to that whore, Woodcock. The one that had her throat slit. Well, I am not a harlot, Charlotte." She laughed at her own rhyming words. "I shall take a loaded pistol if that pleases you."

When Russet arrived at the cottage Molly was about to leave driving Maisy's pony cart. "I am sorry, Miss Russet, I cannot stay to speak. I usually go to the inn later to serve the evening fare, but there is a tea party. They need me there to serve."

"I am returning the attire you so kindly loaned my sisters and me." Russet called after her. She then alighted from the carriage and led the horse to the rear of the cottage.

Maisy was delighted with the meat for her pot. Russet had added a hare because it had been hung for some time and was becoming too ripe for her taste. Together they prepared the meats. Maisy skinned the rabbits and the hare while Russet cut the pork off the bone. All went into the pot along with vegetables and herbs. Time passed as they talked. Clouds accumulated and dusk came upon them unnoticed.

Russet glanced towards the window. "Oh, my lord!" she exclaimed. "Time does pass so quickly. I must go. Father will have a touch of the vapours if he knows I am so late out on my own - it will be dark before I reach home."

Maisy held the gate while Russet drove out onto the roadway. She shut the gate and returned to the cottage. As she closed her door a lone horseman, dressed all in black, and lurking in the shadows of Black Wood, heeled his mount.

Russet had pulled a shawl over her head and across her shoulders. She heard only the sound of her pony's hooves. Suddenly she was grabbed and dragged from her seat. She cried out and lunged for her pistol but it was out of reach. She was held dangling against the horses flank, kicking and screaming, but the grip on her tightened.

The attacker held on to her with one arm and raised a knife. He held it in his fist like a hammer and brought the hilt crashing down against her head. She went limp in his arm and he let her fall to the ground. He tethered his horse out of sight then returned for his victim and pulled her unconscious into the bushes. He half-carried her roughly through the undergrowth; dragging her across a small, water-filled dyke to a flat, scrub covered area. There he lay her down, lifted her skirts and had his way with her.

When he had satisfied himself he adjusted his clothing then took out his knife. The sky was now overcast and darkness enveloped them. He was on his knees, his legs between her thighs. Now he leant forward to feel for her head. Then straightening up he slashed viciously at her throat – once – twice. He fingered the flow of blood, wiped his fingers on her clothing, then got to his feet and walked away.

Chapter Twenty Eight

Sir Marcus slapped the table in frustration. "How is it I cannot have those of my family in residence seated at the table in time for the meal?" He spoke to Charlotte who sat well away from her father.

"Katherine has washed her hair, Father. "Charlotte shrugged. "Her hair is so thick it takes such a length of time to dry. She is on her knees in front of her fire with towels to rub and hurry the drying. I fear she will be some time before she shows her face."

"And Russet. Where is Russet?

"Oh, she will be preening and admiring herself in her mirrors. I do not know what has become of her. She was such a joy but now she thinks only of herself and her appearance. She does such silly things…….."

"Lottie!" Sir Marcus raised his voice. "For the sake of sanity stop criticising."

"Well she has turned into a shrew…."

"Methinks it is others who should look in the mirror, young lady. They could well see a shrew staring back." He immediately regretted what he had inferred and tried to soften his words, "every person I meet outside this hall has a good word to say of Russy. Everybody I speak to seem to like her and vie for her acquaintance. She is very popular in London and known for her kindness here in Nestwith. Why then do I not hear complimentary words of her from you? Could it be jealousy, Lottie?"

"No, Father. It is not jealousy it is a pining spirit." It was

Katherine who answered as she entered the dining room. "My dear elder sister is pining for her long lost Mr Fullerton."

"And you for your dashing Captain of Horse." Charlotte answered, tartly.

"What is this?" Sir Marcus asked. "Is there a matter here I should know of?"

"She has a yearning for Val Halgalleon, and can think of no other." Charlotte laughed.

"Well at least *he* can hear what I say." Katherine slumped into a chair.

"I do not doubt that. He is so far away and you so loud of mouth." Charlotte snapped.

"That will do. That will do." Sir Marcus threw his napkin onto the table and rose to his feet. "God blessed me with the gift of three daughters. Could I have had a choice I would have had all sons for then I could administer a cuff about their ears to keep the peace. With daughters I find myself at a disadvantage - huh!" He walked towards the door. "I shall have peace. I shall have dinner served in my chamber. Goodnight to you."

Charlotte occupied the first floor bedchamber overlooking the front of the building. A chambermaid crept into her room at dawn to draw the curtains silently along the rods to avoid awakening her mistress. She peered out of the window and down towards the stables. Her eyes rested on a horse, harnessed to a carriage but wandering free with no attendant in sight. She remained at the window watching the animal bend its neck to feed on the lush grass as it moved about aimlessly. She was trying to make up her mind whether she dare awaken Miss Charlotte, but she had been a victim of Charlottes tongue on previous occasions so she tiptoed to the door and left the room.

Sir Marcus was always an early riser and as he came out of his bedchamber the chambermaid was leaving Charlotte's room.

"Sir." The woman spoke in a hissing whisper

"Good morning to you." Sir Marcus headed for the stairs.

"Sir. Sir" The maid rushed towards him. There's a horse and carriage outside...."

"And so there should be." He laughed as he interrupted her. "We very rarely fetch them into the house."

The girl ignored his joke to say, I think it is Miss Russet's carriage – the one she went out in yesterday and there's nobody with it."

Sir Marcus descended the stairs unhurriedly. He went to his study and looked out of the window towards the stables. The chambermaid had followed him and she stood at his side.

"It is the one Miss Russet took. I saw her go." She spoke in a timid way, as if interfering above her station.

"It is well you told me." Sir Marcus stood with a furrowed brow. "It is not like Russet to neglect an animal so. It has always been her nature to put the well-being of animals before herself." He turned to the chambermaid. "Go to her room and awaken her. No. I will go. Come." He took the steps two at a time and burst into the room with the maid panting behind him. The curtains were drawn to but enough light was seeping through for him to see the bedclothes neatly folded back. The bed was empty. It had not been slept in.

"Where did she go? Do you know?" His voice now held a tone of urgency.

"She went to see Maisy – Mistress Pitchforth."

Sir Marcus ran down the stairs, called to a houseman and ordered him to run to the stables to have a horse saddled and brought to the house immediately.

People of the village of Nestwith, going about the business of starting their day, stopped what they were doing to see the master of Nestwith Hall coming at full gallop down the main street. Some got out of the way, others shouted abuse, their voices fading when they realised whom it was. They all stood as if glued to the ground watching his back as he sped away along the Loylton road, not knowing, but wondering, what urgency drove him to such haste. At the cottage he reined in the horse, tethered the sweating animal to the fence and ran to the door.

"Mistress Pitchforth Maisy. Maisy. Are you there?" He shouted and kept on calling her name until the door opened.

Maisy stood before him, holding a shawl about her, her hair loose and hanging about her shoulders. "What is it Sir?" She knew instantly something was amiss.

"Is Russet with you?" Sir Marcus was inwardly praying the answer would be 'yes'

"She left for home just before dusk yesterday."

Well, she didn't arrive, Maisy. We found the horse and carriage but there was no sign of Russy.

"Oh my God!" She lifted both hands and covered her cheeks. "Oh no, no, oh no."

The search was organised on a massive scale. Every

villager turned out. The doors of the Wheatsheaf Tavern and The Rose and Crown Inn remained closed. Shops, stalls and businesses of all kinds closed down and the proprietors and workers alike headed in droves for Nestwith Hall. On the estate the head keeper took charge and organised drives along the shoot beats. These covered the whole estate where the routes had been defined for decades. Others were dispatched to search premises and outbuildings. Many were divided into small groups to search roads, tracks, lanes paths and verges. Squire William Bull mustered his workers and, together with residents of the hamlet of Bullington, searched the land on his side of the river before crossing to add numbers to the Nestwith contingent.

Sir Marcus had changed horses and rode from one group to another, his hopes fading as the day wore on. Charlotte and Katherine joined the beaters, both declining to search on horseback.

By four in the afternoon, with no sign of Russet, the searchers were going over ground they had previously covered. Albert and Gertrude Wrigglesworth met Walter Lupton at the smithy. They had been searching lanes and outbuildings and were racking their brains to think of some that could have been overlooked.

"There is that old barn the other side of Black Wood." Walter stroked his chin. "You know, it's off the Loylton road. In the old days it was used to winter cattle but since they started using the land to grow grain, it's been empty."

"Somebody will have taken a look," Gertrude said. "But we could always look again and we could do a second search of the verges as we go."

They set off down Loylton Road, Gertrude standing high in Gunner's pig cart while Walter and Albert searched the verges on either side. After a while Gertrude called a halt.

"Look!" she exclaimed, pointing to her left.

Walter come running up and climbed into the cart. "What is it, Gerty?"

"See the folk searching the parkland on the other side of the hedge?"

"Aye." Walter could see the heads of a line of people bobbing as they moved forward.

"Well, we searched the verge as far as the dyke and I thought they'd search the strip beyond from the other side. It doesn't look as if they have done." She climbed down and added, "come on." Upon reaching the dyke she went down into it and, without hesitation, waded the water and climbed the opposite bank with Walter in her wake.

"You go that way, I'll go this," she said.

Walter set off but had not gone far when he heard Gertrude's cry of anguish. He rushed back to find her kneeling by the side of Russet's prone and bloodied body.

"Is she alive?" he cried.

"I don't know. I can't feel any beat of her heart. She's so cold. So cold.."

Russet was lying on her back with her head against a fallen branch, forcing her chin to rest above her left breast. Gertrude moved her head to see where the blood had come from and gasped. "God in heaven!" she exclaimed in horror as she saw where the knife had dug into the flesh.

Walter had visions of the night he, along with Gunner and Wriggly, had found the man in Black Wood. With urgency in his voice he suggested, "let's get her to Maisy Pitchforth – she's only down the road."

Gertrude took Russet in her arms and waded the dyke. She ordered her husband to go on ahead to warn Maisy of their coming and with the tailboard of the cart removed she rested the inert figure on the boards and walked behind, holding her steady as Walter led the horse. Maisy was ready for their arrival but not prepared for the sight she beheld as Gertrude carried the stricken Russet into the cottage.

"Oh my poor lovely," She cried. "Oh my poor lovely." When she saw the extent of the injuries she began to weep. They laid Russet on the floor in front of the fire and vivid memories of the night they found Jamie returned to both Walter and Albert. Maisy had no thought for anything but the present and although in a state of agitation she issued orders abruptly, "Gerty, you go and get Doctor Mathews. Walter, you go and tell Sir Marcus – but no one else. We don't want crowds milling about here. Albert, You go with Walter and tell the searchers she has been found. Don't tell them where she is or in what state. Now, go."

On her own now, she pinched Russet's nose and placed her cheek near her mouth. She could feel the weak exhalations and sighed with relief. On her knees, Maisy lifted the skirts. She gasped and for a moment could not move. Then she pulled herself together and fetched water and cloths and washed Russet thoroughly. As she hurried to complete her task she kept glancing towards the door, hoping she could finish before the others got back. She dried her and pulled the skirts down.

"It might not take," she said to herself. "It might not take. Nobody must know." The signs were that Russet had been raped and in these times an unmarried young woman who had been molested held little chance of attracting a young man of substance. She turned her attention to the knife wounds and again tears streamed from her eyes at the sight.

Maisy washed the wounds and was attempting to remove clotted blood from Russet's hair when the door burst open and Doctor Mathews entered, followed by Gertrude. He went straight to Russet without saying a word and made a brief examination of her wounds. He had difficulty bending and had to be helped on to his knees where he began by lifting her skirts and taking a good look to see if there had been interference of a sexual nature. Seemingly satisfied there had not, he turned to the wounds.

"Who found this woman? He asked.

"I did." Gertrude answered.

He moved Russets head from one side to the other. Then he asked, "in what position did you find her – the head, I mean?"

Gertrude thought for a few seconds and then said, "she was lying on her back and her head was resting on a fallen branch – sort of pushed forward onto her chest."

"Yes, Yes." The Doctor nodded his head. "You see this." He spoke to Maisy. "My assumption is that she was attacked in the dark and her head was to one side and on her chest, as the lady here says. It was intended that this young woman should die. The attacker slashed at her throat intending to kill her. Because her head was turned to the left and forward he missed her neck and did this." He demonstrated, as if holding an imaginary knife he brought his arm down twice to emulate the act of causing the two enormous wounds that scarred Russet's left cheek. One gash ran from the corner of her eye and ended by cutting through her lips. The other was even longer and began at her temple and split the length of her cheek and across her chin.

"She has been in the open for some time and flies and insects have penetrated the wounds" The doctor put out his arms and was helped to his feet.

"There is nothing else for it," he said. "I shall have to cauterise the wounds. Better I do it while she is out of her senses,"

"Will she live, Doctor?" The tears were running in rivulets down Maisy's cheeks.

"I know not. Apart from the facial lesions she has taken a knock to the head. We shall have to wait and see if time heals" He took a cauterising tool from his bag and pushed it between the bars of the fire. "I am saddened for one thing," he added. "If she does live, the poor soul will carry those hideous scars for the rest of her life."

Chapter Twenty Nine

Tarquin Willoughby peered through his telescope at the approaching ship. He had been watching it since first the topgallants then the topsails appeared over the horizon. It was as if the ship was growing out of the sea as the mainsails came into view and then, gradually, the hull completed the picture. He could make out the tiny figures moving out on the yards, their feet sliding along the footropes in unison, and then the awe-inspiring spectacle of furling the sails, likening the ship to some great monster having given its all and now slowing to a welcome rest at anchor.

He had arrived in Kingston three days ago and spent his time trying to contact Isaac Critchley, an assistant to the Doulain agent, but without success. He had asked if any knew of his whereabouts but was greeted with shakes of the head and wry smiles. A visit to bankers, where he presented one of the letters of credit, ensured his finances were in order and he had hired a boat and oarsmen, ready to meet the ship.

"Ahoy the Branston Silver." The boatman called out, his singsong, accented, voice directed at members of the crew who lined the rail and stared down at the boat. "Prepare to receive Mr Tarquin Willoughby with letters for the captain."

Tarquin threw a leather strapped satchel over his shoulder and climbed the slatted rope ladder the crew had tossed over the side. When he stood on the planked deck his nostrils flared at the fetidness coming from the open hatches and, although he had been prepared for it, when the stench reached him he turned his head in an effort to avoid it. He was shown to the aft cabin where Captain Christopher welcomed him and, in the custom of the times, he was invited to partake of a glass of claret. As they toasted the king and wished each other good health, Tarquin noticed they were not alone. A man seated at a desk beneath a squared window was looking directly at him, as if weighing him up. The man lounged in the chair with a leg stuck straight out along the side of the desk and the part of his face that could be seen, beneath a straggly beard, made him appear to be wearing a grotesque mask.

Tarquin took a letter from his satchel and handed it to the captain. Captain Christopher broke the seal and unfolded the paper. Another sealed note fell out and onto the deck. He picked it up. "This one is addressed to Tarquin Willoughby Esquire." He passed the note to Tarquin who opened it and they both began to read. The captain grunted as his eyes went down the script and when he had finished he tossed the note onto the desk.

"It would seem, Jamie lad, that we are to take our orders from Mr Willoughby here." He gestured towards Tarquin. There was a note of displeasure in his voice as he went on, "it would also appear that I have been relieved of command of this vessel and that I should hand over my seniority to Mr Willoughby."

Tarquin finished reading his instructions and now he corrected the captain. "That is not so, sir." I am charged with the direction of this ship for one year only. Not with the command. You are captain of this ship and I hope you will remain with this ship and continue to serve in that capacity."

Then as a sop he said, "I shall be in great need of your help and your advice."

Captain Christopher pointed to the note that Jamie held. "It states in there that I am not to put forward my cargo for sale but to take instruction from you as to its disposal. I wonder, sir, how am I to free my ship of this humanity and its unhealthy stench. Do I release them to their fate? Or just have my crew toss them over the side for the sharks," he added sarcastically.

From a waistcoat pocket he took a silver snuffbox and, taking a pinch placed it on the back of his hand. He lifted it to his face, put his left nostril to the powder and made a noisy inhalation. While everybody looked on in silence he repeated the act with his right nostril. Then with a large handkerchief he blew his nose with great zest. He offered the snuffbox "Snuff?" he asked.

As there were no acceptors, he continued, "I do not consider, Mr Willoughby, you have knowledge of how members of the crew of this ship receive due monies for this voyage. We are not paid by the day, the week, or the month. We all take a percentage of the profit, scaled by rank. Are you suggesting that we gain nought from this cargo and that we have sailed the seas merely for the love of it?" The captain was walking backwards and forwards as he spoke, anger growing with his every word.

"No, Sir," Tarquin said, calmly. "The slaves are to be taken to the Doulain plantations where arrangements will be in place to make them free men. I shall come to an agreement with you as to the worth of the cargo and you will be paid accordingly. You will go about purifying this ship and making it suitable to carry clean cargo for trade between those islands of the Indies under the protection of King George. My own mission is to speak with plantation owners and managers as an emissary of His Lordship on matters of his concern." Tarquin paused then went on, "we are destined to be bed fellows, you and I, so for the next twelve months it would be folly indeed should we disagree on our course at this early stage.

The captain was deeply committed to his own course. He had planned to take on cargo and depart for England with all haste. Now he was being ordered to spend a year trading as a lowly island hopper. He tried once more, "sir," he said to Tarquin, "there are four members of the crew who wish to return to England with all possible haste. Failing the Branston Silver, they would I am sure, seek passage on another ship. Without my first officer and my master of the purse," he gestured towards Jamie, "I do not see that we can sail at all. These four came aboard in unfortunate circumstances. The other two are Adam Gunner and Totton Roulette who I am sure......"

"Roulette?" Tarquin interrupted. "That is an uncommon name, sir. Could this fellow be one of the Nestwith Roulettes?"

Jamie slapped his desk and nodded vigorously as the captain said, "I believe that is so. You know of him?"

"It could be that I am acquainted with his sister." Tarquin went on, "only as a casual acquaintance, I might add. If it can be arranged, I would take pleasure in meeting this gentleman."

When Totton appeared Tarquin could not imagine, at first sight, that this scruffy individual could be the brother of the elegant Russet Roulette. His clothes were patched and tattered. He wore a beard and his hair straggled loosely about his shoulders. Gunner was next to enter the cabin and he too was unkempt. Clothes that he had on when taken aboard ship were now worn; garments held together only by a patchwork of sailcloth. John Fullerton was the last to be introduced and was the smarter dressed of the three, his borrowed brass-buttoned jacket hiding the threadbare shirt he wore.

Captain Christopher addressed them, "Mr Willoughby here has given me instruction from the masters that we are to remain hereabouts for a period of one year under his direction. I know you will all wish to return to your homes but, as you are aware, this ship would be hard-put to sail out of this harbour without the services of Mr Fullerton. I would be hard-put to run the every-day matters concerning this ship without the services of Mr Pitchforth. Mr Gunner and Mr Roulette have also become valued members of the crew and so I must ask you what is your wish. - To stay with the ship for the coming year or, to leave me and my ship floundering while you return to England by any passage you may find?"

John Fullerton answered first, "Captain, sir. I am already in the employ of His Lordship and if his instructions are to remain with the ship, then so be it."

Totton said, "I shall return home. There is business to which I must attend and it is business that is also of concern to His Lordship. I doubt I shall be missed, for my part onboard has been of little value."

Gunner thought for a few seconds before answering. He had the smithy to see to but other than his business there was no urgency to return. He turned to Jamie and nodded his head. "What about you, Jamie? Do you wish to return to Nestwith?"

Jamie had made up his mind. Why should he return to the life of a peasant labourer when his work was now appreciated and he had won the friendship of Jacob Christopher. His thoughts were of Russet and a longing for her, but to return would not raise his station in life and there was no possibility of him realising his dreams. He pointed a finger at his chest and then at his desk.

"You will remain with the ship?" The Captain's question was more of an answer. Jamie nodded and a huge grin spread across the captain's face. "Then that is three." As he announced the obvious all eyes turned to Totton.

"I should go back." Totton mused. He stood for a while, biting his lip, trying to un-scatter his thoughts. "I have business to attend to," he insisted. "My father will have a mind for my well-being. I must relieve his anxiety. I am his only son. Then there are the pigs...." He looked at the faces staring at him. "Why should any man wish to remain cloistered up with a filthy, foul-mouthed crew. Run up and down rigging, risk life and limb on the yardarms, drink putrid water, eat salted meat until the salt crystallises into a ball in the stomach, and spend his life down on ulcerated knees, holystoning decks. All this when he could be wearing a clean, un-sweat-stained shirt and fashionable garb, sleep between silk sheets, taste the delights of a fine table – oh what I would give for a haunch of venison! You are asking me to forego all this?"

They all listened in silence to his tirade, then the captain said. "I take it you'll stay with us then?" This brought guffaws of laughter that faded to silence as they waited for the answer.

Totton stroked his beard. "No, sir. However much I shall miss the delights of your company, my duty lies at home. I will help with the unloading and distribution of the cargo but then I must seek the first available passage."

"Well that is settled, then." Tarquin rubbed his hands, a smile of satisfaction on his face; he would have preferred Totton to remain but he considered the first part of his task accomplished. "I shall take my leave now," he said. "I will go ashore and make arrangements for the disembarkation of your cargo. However, I cannot make contact with the agent, Freeman or his assistant, and that means I have a journey inland of twenty miles to the nearest Doulain plantation. The manager is a man by the name of Ridley, Simon Ridley. He knows nothing of your arrival, Captain, but I am given to believe he is an upstanding fellow. I hope I shall find him helpful"

"I do not have the aquaintance of the man," the captain said. "I have been here but once, and never did I journey further than the town. From my experience of that visit, I must warn you that it would be folly to travel alone. I suggest you take a man-at-arms to guard your back."

"I shall, Captain." Tarquin cast his eyes around the company. "It is not my intention to venture forth on these unfamiliar tracts without company, so I shall be pleased to ask one of you to come with me." He gave no time for anyone to volunteer, and quickly said, "Mr Gunner, I would be obliged to have your presence at my side."

Gunner had not been on horseback for months and after ten miles his buttocks, thighs and calves felt as if they had been seared with red-hot irons. He stood for a while in the stirrups to ease the pain but gave that up in favour of sitting back in the saddle with legs splayed. Tarquin rode ahead as they wound their way down a rutted track between fields of tall, leafy sugar cane. Occasionally they came across groups of black women carrying bundles of goods and men, some in pairs, others alone, walking in both directions, seemingly without purpose.

As they approached their own destination they came across the first dwellings since leaving Kingston. It was a village of timber and mud huts roofed with thatch, as if the whole cluster had been uprooted and transferred from Africa. Neatly dressed women carried water buckets, older women squatting in front of their homes worked on dressmaking. Others mixed foodstuffs in carved, wooden bowls. Small children played together. There was no sign of shackles, and no sign of men.

They rounded a corner and came across the plantation house. It was of wooden construction with thatched roof and fronted by a long veranda that stretched the length of the building. A man seated on the veranda rose to meet them. He signalled to servants to see to the horses.

"Good day to you, gentlemen. To what do I owe this pleasure?" He came down the few steps to meet them. "Simon

Ridley, at your service."

Tarquin shook his hand and said, "Tarquin Willoughby, emissary of Lord Doulain. My companion is Adam Gunner." He smiled as he continued, "do not judge him on his appearance, sir. Or should I say the appearance of his attire. My friend suffered a misfortune and is the owner of only that in which he stands before you."

"Come." Ridley gestured at the veranda. "You will no doubt have a thirst upon you after your ride. We have a special beverage you must try."

They all took seats about a rustic table. Ridley spoke to a manservant who then hastened away and shortly returned with three large glasses filled to the brim.

"We have a deep well at the rear that keeps water fresh and cool. We lower sealed jugs of lemon or limejuice into it. Mixed with rum and a little sugar it makes the most refreshing drink."

Tarquin explained the situation and that he would need assistance to get the slaves to the plantation. Simon Ridley thought for a while. "Twenty miles is a long way for men who have been incarcerated for months. The skin on the souls of their feet will have softened. It would be needlessly cruel to make them walk that distance. I shall have to arrange transport. We have plenty of sugar carts not in use at the moment. When are we to move them?"

"The day after tomorrow," said Tarquin

"Hmm." Simon Ridley took a sip of his drink, then, "we have never taken so many all at once. It will take some organisation to get them all billeted. There are two other

Doulain plantations and then there is Mrs Dickinson. She will be thankful of some men – if she has not to purchase them."

Tarquin looked puzzled. "Mrs Dickinson? I have not heard of the lady. Her name does not appear in my directive."

"No, it would not." Simon Ridley went on, "Ralph Dickinson owned the plantation to the north. He and his wife were drowned in floods four years ago. Their son Michael took over the plantation and then he married Tilly Morrison. Three months after the wedding he too lost his life, in a riding accident. Tilly inherited the place and has tried her best to keep it going. It is difficult for a woman to sell her produce; there are unscrupulous men about more than ready to take advantage of a lady. I took it upon myself to help her, with agreement that she sells her crops through Doulain. I market her cane and tobacco and pay her the purchase value - less a commission for the Company."

"Why did she not deal with the Doulain agent?" Gunner asked.

"Aah! Now there's the rub. Freeman is the official agent but he has been ill and frail for years. He keeps his position by employing assistants to do his work. His present assistant is a toper by the name of Critchley. He lives in his own rum-hazy world and he is a dangerous fellow if ever there was one. He has been pestering Mrs Dickinson of late so we have placed a couple of armed men with her, to see to her safety. I now have no truck with the fellow and I have personally taken on responsibility to act as agent for the Doulain plantations. From what I hear of Critchley, the drink has deranged his mind. He is now out of control and is to be taken into custody

– when he is found"

"Then why is he still in His Lordship's employ?"

"I doubt if London know of the rogue. Freeman would not inform them for fear of losing his own job." Simon Ridley raised a hand and the manservant came forward and replenished the glasses. "I have written three notes to London regarding the fellow's inappropriate behaviour and downright incompetence. I have received no reply and the man is still in his position. If or when you ever come to face him you would do well to temper your words for the man has been known to take offence at a genial inquiry as to the state of his health. Watch him. He will welcome you with his right hand and stab you in the back with the other." He rose and went to a dresser where he produced three clay pipes and a jar of tobacco. Gunner was relieved at his next words, "I hope you will accept my hospitality for the night. A ride to Kingston is far enough. To ride here and back again in one day is too much for any man's buttocks."

At dawn the slaves were wrist shackled and taken ashore in batches. There they were pushed into the cane carts for the journey inland. Totton and Gunner accompanied the first two carts and when they arrived at the plantation in the afternoon Simon Ridley directed them to take their charges to the Dickinson plantation where, he assured them, quarters were being prepared for them.

They continued on and were met by two armed white men who offered to accompany them to the billets. Totton and Gunner went on to the plantation homestead and as they dismounted in front of the house they heard a cry of alarm; a woman's voice calling for help. Totton ran inside to find a giant of a man holding a woman in his arms. She was struggling to get away from him. Totton grabbed the man and tried to pull him away but he swung round, threw a fist at Totton's head and another to his chest. As Totton staggered back Gunner came through the doorway and, without hesitation, struck the man a glancing blow to the jaw. He dropped to the ground but before Gunner could catch him he staggered to his feet and ran out of the house and away.

The woman straightened her clothing and smoothed back her dark hair with both hands. "I am in your debt, gentlemen," she said. "The fellow is unendurable and becoming altogether more than one can bear."

Gunner was intrigued. It had never entered his head that Mrs Dickinson would be anything but white skinned. She was an extraordinarily handsome woman; her skin was like fawn coloured velvet, signifying a part-white ancestry. Her nose was slimmer than her African ancestors and her even teeth glistened white against her lips.

"Your arrival could not have been better timed. Your friend – where is he?" She stopped abruptly and looked towards the open door. Gunner let his eyes follow hers, and then hearing a moan, he spun about to see Totton lying prone in a corner of the room. His eyes were glazed and blood trickled from a corner of his mouth; a circle of crimson was spreading slowly across his shirt from where the hilt of a knife protruded from his chest.

Chapter Thirty

"There are absolutely no eyes of needles available in the legality of the transaction?" Lord Doulain addressed the three young lawyers standing before him.

"Well, there are many facets to our findings, My Lord." The middle one of the three, who appeared to be the senior, spoke out, "we have searched every avenue and in some aspects we find you have favour absolute, in many others our findings are that you do not have favour absolute."

"Meaning?" Lord Doulain questioned.

"A legal phrase, My Lord." The lawyer smirked and moved his head from side to side. "It's means that the agreement signed by Oliver Roulette is valid, but we have grave doubts gleaned from our searches regarding some of the appurtenances. These we will explain to you. Then it is your prerogative to decide on what action you wish to take."

"Can I take possession of the Nestwith Hall Estate?"

"Well, there are some items in need of clarity, My Lord. And that may take a little time" The lawyer on the left spoke in a squeaky monotone, his words flat and without expression.

"Time! Time!" Lord Doulain stretched his arms towards the three men. "You mean money! Time indeed! Why is it that you in the legal profession always use the words 'it will take time' instead of being truthful and saying it is going to add a considerable amount to the fees you will ask of me?"

The lawyer who had remained silent now began, "my Lord, you purchased the Nestwith Estate some time ago from Sir Oliver Roulette...."

"I am fully aware of that." Lord Doulain said. "Good Lord in heaven am I to pay you for telling me something I already know?"

"My Lord, may we be allowed to report our findings." His Lordship shrugged and the lawyer continued, "your ownership of the Nestwith Estate came into being on the default of a loan made by you to Sir Oliver Roulette. The loan, according to your records, was for a period of six months. The question arises, was Roulette alive or dead when the time for repayment arrived? If he was dead at that time, did the loan die with him or, did the responsibility for the debt lie with the Estate?"

"The Estate." Lord Doulain stressed with alacrity.

"Not necessarily, My Lord." The lawyer spoke with a tone of indignation at Lord Doulain's emphatic conclusion. He continued, "at the end of the loan period, that is, at the end of the six month term, we do not know if Oliver Roulette was alive or dead."

"What difference does that make?"

"If he died shortly after taking out the loan it could be argued that he was ill at the time of his request for a loan, and that he was of unsound mind. It could also be argued that because the sum of the loan was but half the estimated land value of the Nestwith Estate, at the time of the loan agreement, the Company Doulain acted sharply."

"No, no, no. I will not have that." Lord Doulain thumped a fist onto his desk. "It was a straight forward loan and it was not honoured. I am in possession of the deeds and the signature of the recipient of the loan. That cannot be construed as sharp practice. I have the proof. What more do I want?"

"Well, My Lord, with all respect may I say that, according to law, in this case you do need more. May I define our findings?" He went on without waiting for permission, "the actual time of the Estate passing into your hands is in question. Did completion of the transfer of the Estate from Oliver Roulette to you transpire at the date of the time limit set on the loan? Or, because the loan was not honoured, could it be argued that the transaction came into force six months previously, when Oliver Roulette accepted monies, on promise of the Estate in lieu, at the date of the signing of the loan agreement?

"That is for you to tell me." His Lordship was showing impatience.

"As far as we can ascertain, My Lord, there could be dissension on this point because it is not clear when Oliver Roulette expired, so the date of completion on the property cannot be defined."

Lord Doulain slumped in his chair. "I am beginning to wonder why I ever asked for this search."

"That is not all My Lord." The Lawyer continued, "if the transaction is proved in your favour then the Estate came into your possession *'as is'*, or *'as was'* in this case. By that I mean you became owner of the Estate in the condition appertaining either at the time of the agreement or at the end of the time limit on the loan."

"Cannot you lawyers ever speak in simple layman terms? Surely you could make your words a little more understandable." Lord Doulain understood well but was attempting to stall the conclusion.

"What I am trying to explain, My Lord, is that if the Estate has passed to you then it became your possession at the time of the agreement – or thereabouts. At that time the Estate was in a state of dilapidation. I do not refer to the land, for there was little depreciation there, but to the buildings and in particular to the ongoing business of the Estate. Oliver Roulette had neglected his duty to the Estate. Not only had he allowed deterioration during his tenure, he had incurred enormous debts."

"I feel I know what you are about to say."

"Yes, My Lord. If it comes about that you correctly came into possession of the Estate at that time, then it can be argued that you also inherited responsibility for the debts of the Estate. I would add that my learned friend here has taken advice from the lawyer who acts for Sir Marcus, and for – er – 'a fee', we have had sight of much we needed to know of matters appertaining to Sir Marcus Roulette and the Nestwith Estate. The lawyer, who shall be nameless for obvious reasons, has received no instruction regarding the transfer, neither is he aware of Sir Marcus having knowledge of these matters.

Lord Doulain interrupted. " I did mention this to him personally and told him I had possession of the deeds. He would have none of it. Talked of hereditary ownership. But if it is a matter of informing him of the facts, then that is not a problem."

"Ah, if it were all so straight forward, My Lord." The

lawyer shook his head. "Since taking possession, Sir Marcus has all but paid off the Estate debts. According to information received he has sold off all his other properties and invested the accruals from these measures, together with his own fortune, in the Estate. He is also successfully putting the business back on its feet."

"Are you telling me what I think you're telling me?"

"I am suggesting to you that if you were the rightful owner of the Nestwith Estate at the time Sir Marcus claimed his inheritance, then it could be argued that it was *your* debts that he settled."

His Lordship leaned forward. He slid an elbow onto the desk and stroked his chin. "This is getting all very complicated," he said. "Paying off Roulette is no problem. How much does it come to?"

"We do not yet have the exact figures, My Lord. That would be for Sir Marcus to provide, but it will certainly be greatly in excess of the original loan. There is also the matter of reimbursement for increased business, property renovation, stock purchases and many sundry items, all paid for by Sir Marcus. The fact that you did not inform him in writing, but allowed him to continue unknowingly improving your investment, would not look good before the court, My Lord."

"I have no intention of going to court."

"No, My Lord, but Sir Marcus Roulette most certainly will, if the matter comes to a head."

"Then what are you suggesting?"

The middle one of the three spoke out, "it is not in our brief to suggest, My Lord. We were asked to search for facts and derive conclusions. The facts we have laid before you. Our conclusion is this, should you persist in your claim of ownership the matter would, without doubt, be settled in the courts." The lawyer smirked again and swayed his head in a know-all, supercilious manner. "Gentlemen of the legal profession acting on behalf of Sir Marcus would revel in the fact that the money was lent under dubious circumstances. That you knowingly kept from Sir Marcus the fact that he was not the legal owner, but nevertheless allowed him, unknowingly, to put money into your investment. This would no doubt be brought before the courts as downright fraud. The broadsheets would make hay of the matter. They would do all they could to smear the Company Doulain for having acted with impropriety. With no disrespect to your good self, My Lord, I would hazard that no Peer of the Realm would wish to be dubbed '*The Noble Usurer*.'"

His Lordship was about to answer but the lawyer continued, "we are of the opinion that the case would be indefensible. It would be a waste of your money and, may I say, unwise on your part to ask us to continue with the chase, when the hare is already jugged."

Lord Doulain placed the palms of his hands on his desk and pushed himself to his feet. "Thank you gentlemen," he said. "You say you have 'got at' Sir Marcus' lawyer. From what I have just heard I would consider it the other way about. You sound as if you are instructed by my opponent rather than myself."

"My Lord!" all three exclaimed, indignantly.

"Well, you appear to have placed all the birds in his cage."

The three lawyers edged towards the door as Lord Doulain came round his desk towards them. He rounded on them, "you come here and tell me *I* am in the wrong. You have the gall to call *me* a usurer. You say *I* owe Roulette because he has paid debts on my behalf which I believe *I* have not incurred. You hold that I am in the wrong on all counts in this matter."

Two of the men had already slipped out of the room and the third was holding the door as Lord Doulain bore down on him.

His Lordship raised his voice, "a man borrows money from me and I am accused of wronging his brother. What sort of law condemns a man for that? You come to me and tell me another has paid *my* debts - debts I have not incurred. God in Heaven! You will be telling me shortly that I should kneel to the fellow and beg his forgiveness. God damn me, I have heard it all!"

As the last of the lawyers pulled the door to, he stammered timidly, "well not quite, My Lord. There could be a claim for - for - er - good will."

"Begone! Out!" Lord Doulain put a hand to the door and slammed it shut.

He was chuckling to himself as he took hold of a chair and positioned it in the centre of the room and sat down. Once seated he stared up at the painting of his late wife. He remained there for some minutes, concentrating on the face in the picture. He smiled and nodded, as if he had received a spiritual message, then he stood and replaced the chair. Without resuming his seat he picked up a hand-bell from the desk and rang it.

John Critchley knocked once and entered.

"I shall take coffee, Critchley. And see there are two cups."

Critchley gave the order knowing that the request for a second cup meant his presence was required.

"Come here, Critchley." Lord Doulain ordered. He went to the rear of his desk and gestured to his chair. "Please sit down," he said.

"In your chair, My Lord?"

"Yes, Critchley. Please be seated."

Critchley tentatively lowered himself into the chair.

"Do you find comfort in your position, John?"

John Critchley was befogged. He had no idea of the meaning of the situation, nor why he was being addressed by his first name. He had been 'Critchley' all his working life; His Lordship's familiarity unsettled him.

"Mi'Lord?" He was asking for guidance.

"Is the comfort of the chair to your satisfaction, John?" Lord Doulain was enjoying the moment. "Does the position behind the desk suit you."

"Mi'Lord?" Critchley had not grasped His Lordship's inference.

"Well, John, if it does not comfort you then you will have to make it so, for I shall have little use for it in future. I intend to retire from my responsibility for the everyday running of the Company. I have it in mind to spend more time in the enjoyment of my own pleasures. Sir Marcus Roulette invited me to fish his stretch of river. He told me it was exceeding good for trout and grayling, and fishing for eels at night, he said, is exciting and full of jollity." He tapped a finger on the desk. "You will run the business from this desk, John. How does that suit you?"

John Critchley was silent for a few moments, his bottom lip twitched as if he were fighting for words. At last he spoke, "I am indeed grateful and honoured that you think to put so much trust in me My Lord."

"I have trusted you and your good judgement for more than twenty years, John. I shall, of course, keep an eye on matters and will expect you to keep me in touch with any new concerns of importance." He smiled as he continued, "there will naturally be substantial increase in the emolument as befitting your position. I shall shortly visit Marcus Roulette and I shall send Chatterton back to you. I would presume by now Sir Marcus has done with his efforts." He chuckled. "Poor Chatterton. He will no doubt be delighted to get back to the city. It must be hard on a poor fellow who is city born and bred to have to live among, and deal with peasants and country yokels." He then changed the subject, signifying the promotion was done. "How is that wayward son of yours getting on?" he asked.

"Stepson." Critchley corrected. "He is not of my blood. He was my late wife's son from her previous marriage. It was she who insisted he take my name. She died in suspicious circumstances and, the miscreant that he is, he tried to blame me for her death. Fortunately, I was in conference at the time of her death and there were many notable witnesses to my presence there."

"Where is he now?" The whereabouts of Critchley's son

was of no interest to Lord Doulain, but he asked out of kindness.

"He found himself in trouble, for what, I do not know, and do not wish to know. And what is more, I care not." Critchley spoke unashamedly as he carried on with his distressing tale, "he had the audacity to come to me for help. I would not have raised a finger to assist him but, for the memory of my dear wife, I obtained and paid passage for him to the Indies. I have heard nothing of him since. Nor do I wish to hear. When the fellow is in drink he becomes a maniac and a danger to all. It would not surprise me, My Lord, should he have already felt the knot of a hangman's noose, and if that was the case, I would not shed one single tear."

His Lordship again changed the subject, "have we had any word of the Branston Silver?"

No. We shall not hear for some weeks. Mr Willoughby should be in Kingston by this time but I doubt he will have anything to report. I believe you instructed him to advise you if young Roulette and John Fullerton are aboard and in good health. He will no doubt inform you by letter on the first available ship."

Coffee was brought and His Lordship took a seat facing his manager. They were both quiet for a few seconds, then Critchley said, "you mentioned you were to fish the river at Nestwith. What is to do with our interest in the Nestwith Estate?"

Lord Doulain laughed. "It would seem we have waded out of our depth, or at least, out of time. Those three young lawyer fellows I instructed took great delight in telling me I had no chance of recovering either the loan or the estate. They even had the impertinence to accuse me of fraud. I shall require the Nestwith deeds but the loan agreement with Oliver Roulette can be filed. Better it is kept, one never knows when dusted records may come to be an advantage."

"And what of the deeds?" Critchley asked.

"Have them copied and then file the original along with the loan agreement. I shall present a copy to my friend Marcus and say no more of it." Lord Doulain put down his cup then rubbed his hands together as if wiping the slate clean. "We cannot win this one without lengthy court procedures, but there are other ways. With the odds against us we shall cut our losses and, as one young lawyer said to me earlier, for the time being, put it all down to good will.

"And your time? Apart from fishing, how will you spend that? If I may be so bold to ask." Critchley added the last sentence fearing he had overstepped the mark.

"I shall visit business acquaintances and speak to the prosperous and see how generous they are when it comes to helping their country. England needs fighting ships and I shall do all I can to see she has them. As for the rest of my time, well, I shall a'courting go. There is a lady I have a fondness for, so I have decided to take your good advice at last, John. The time has come for me to consider marrying again."

Chapter Thirty One

When it did happen it was as if the very walls of Nestwith Hall were convulsed with distress. It was a desperate, heart-rending cry from the core of a woman's heart. It was a scream of horror, of anguish, of pain, of dread, of utter despair. It went on, penetrating, battering every wall until even the stones seemed to shiver.

Sir Marcus was at his desk and he sat frozen in his chair. Charlotte and Katherine were together in the withdrawing room and they both gasped and each remained motionless, hands covering mouths. The chambermaids stopped what they were doing. Cleaners held dusters and mops and stood like stone statues. In the kitchen, the cook paused, her fists embedded in the dough she was kneading. Even the cellar man, deep in the bowels of the building could not escape the piercing screams as the sound echoed and re-echoed throughout the building.

In the bedchamber Russet sat on the edge of her bed, holding up clenched fists and screaming uncontrollably, her scarred face distorted, her whole body trembling in a delirium of mental agony. The floor was scattered with shards of shattered glass and the broken frame of a hand mirror leaned crookedly against a leg of the washstand. Molly had accompanied Maisy this day to help nurse Russet, and now she was on her knees on the bed holding Russet's shoulders and whispering unheard words of comfort. Maisy took hold of Russet's wrists and shook her, but to no avail, she was in a world of her own, a world of hysteria. Finally. Maisy let go of one wrist and brought the flat of her hand across Russet's right cheek. The screaming stopped abruptly. Russet looked up into Maisy's face, her eyes wide, whites dilated as if they were about to burst out of their sockets. She gasped for breath, filling her lungs and wheezing noisily with every inhalation. As her breathing eased she began to sob. She put her arms around Maisy's waist and clung to her.

"Come now, my lovely. Come now, my lovely." Maisy placed a hand on Russet's head and held her close. With the other she patted her gently on the shoulder. "Come, my lovely," she comforted. "It's not as bad as it looks now." She lied to ease the pain. "It will get better with time. You see. Come now, my lovely, let's just have a little lie down." She nodded to Molly who eased the bedclothes back while Maisy lifted the stricken Russet and helped her into the bed. "I think some warm milk and a drop of the master's brandy." She indicated with her head toward the door and Molly went to do her bidding.

When Molly reached the stairs Sir Marcus had almost reached the top. Charlotte and Katherine were at his heels.

"Is she....? Is she...?" Sir Marcus was lost for words.

"She is all-right, sir," Molly assured him. "Maisy has calmed her and is trying to get her to sleep." She looked at Charlotte who was pushing past her father. "It would be better you don't disturb her. It could start her off again."

"What started it in the first place?" Charlotte asked, haughtily.

"She saw her face in a mirror, Miss." Molly answered. "It unbalanced her mind. Better leave it be for now, Miss

Charlotte. Unless you wish to feel the wrath of Maisy's tongue?" Charlotte backed away, remembering her first confrontation with Maisy .

When Molly returned with the milk Russet was calm and breathing normally. She lay with her head on the pillow, the wounds, bearing the black brands of cauterising, stood out in ugly contrast against the ashen pallor of her skin. Maisy held Russet's hand in the cup of her own, gently stroking it and murmuring, "that's right, my lovely, that's right. Everything is going to be all right. "She whispered words of comfort, offering the security and love a mother would to her own child. "There, there, that's the way; close your eyes, time to sleep. There, there now."

Sir Marcus was returning to his study when William Bull arrived.

"I have come to offer my condolences, my dear friend," he said. "I am at a loss for words. I can only say how sorry I am."

"Thank you Willy." Sir Marcus gestured toward his study. "I am in need of a friend at this time and I am indeed glad of your company. Come. You will take a glass with me?"

"I shall be pleased to do so, Marcus, for I too have suffered family loss." Willy settled himself in a chair and sighed. "Yesterday my dear wife succumbed to her desire to be with God. She passed away in the afternoon, and I do not know whether I should grieve or rejoice."

"I am sorry to hear that, Willy. I know not what to say, other than offer you my most sincere condolences." Sir Marcus looked quizzically at his guest. "When you said you too had suffered loss were you inferring that I also endured a bereavement?"

Before he could go on William Bull said, "it is rumoured that poor Russet was found dead"

"No, no, Willy. She is alive but she has suffered dire injuries."

"I am so sorry my friend." William Bull shifted his position and appeared embarrassed. "One hears rumour and gossip, and stories grow in such profusion a man knows not what to believe. I hope I have not distressed you, my friend" He began to rise.

"Sit down, Willy." Sir Marcus tipped a claret jug and filled two glasses. "Russet had an accident," he lied. It appears she fell out of her carriage, how, I know not. Perhaps a wheel went over a rock, we shall never know. I can only surmise that she struck her head and tore her cheek on branches before rolling into a dyke where she was well hidden."

"And what does Russet say of the incident?"

Sir Marcus thought for a few moments. He considered it prudent to keep the truth within the family. He answered, "she knows nothing of it. The blow to the head has completely erased her memory of the event. But what of you, Willy? Will any of your late wife's family wealth come to you?" At least that would ease your grief somewhat."

"I acted with haste when I married Agather Mather." William Bull said. "The dowry bought me Bullington House and the estate, but there was promise of an inheritance coming to her from an aunt. There was not one word of truth in what she told me. It took a long time to discover the falsehood, and when I did it was too late. All those years that woman duped me. I was fooled with the promise of wealth coming to her from a family member who did not exist. I have scratched and scraped to keep Bullington solvent. All those years she said 'do this for me', and 'do that for me', and when it comes to the rub she has taken me for a fool and used me like a lackey." He took a great gulp of his wine, emptied the glass in one go and thrust it forward to be refilled. "I shall drink to your health just one more time then I shall repair to Bullington House to partake of my favourite fare. I have asked my keeper - poor old Baker, on his last legs, you know - to shoot a brace of ducks. My cook roasts them, fresh shot and fries the breasts in breadcrumbs Aaaah." He drained the glass again and held it out to be refilled.

An hour later an unsteady William Bull negotiated the steps down to the drive and made several attempts to mount his horse before being helped on to it by a houseman. He waved and swayed precariously as he rode away. Sir Marcus stood on the topmost step and laughed at his friend. 'I suppose we have to thank the Lord his mount is sober' he thought.

Not more than twenty minutes later the Reverend Butler arrived. He alighted from his open carriage and climbed the steps with Isiah Snufty close behind. He walked straight in without invitation. Sir Marcus had been informed of the rector's arrival and he dreaded an encounter with the priest.

"Sir Marcus!" The Reverend Butler called out. It was not a request but a demand. "A word with you, Sir Marcus." The rector opened the dining room door but when he saw the room was empty he went to try another door.

"Rector. How good it is of you to call." Sir Marcus

appeared from his study.

"I have come to bless this house and offer you the consolation of the church." The rector blustered. "Your daughter is at peace now."

"Well, I hope she is, Rector."

"It comes to us all. Those who have sinned in the eyes of God are those whom God sees fit for redemption before entry into His kingdom." The tone of his voice rose and fell as if he were addressing a congregation. "I shall go to her now and absolve her of her earthly sins......"

"She sleeps." Sir Marcus interrupted.

"Ah, sleeps, sleeps. Yes, she sleeps in the arms of the Lord." The rector was in full flow now. "The Lord giveth and the Lord taketh away. He who......"

"She," Sir Marcus corrected.

The rector ignored the interruption and continued, "he who puts his trust in the Lord shall..."

"She." Sir Marcus was beginning to enjoy the confrontation. He had realised the rector thought Russet was dead.

"Sir, when I refer to 'he' I refer to all humanity," the rector stated haughtily. "Man is God's creation, women are but man's chattels. God created man in his likeness. He then took a rib from man, and from this created woman - to lift and carry for her master."

"Does not the bearing of children come into the Lord's equation?" Sir Marcus was guiding the rector.

Yes, yes. That is so."

"And with pleasures of fornication for both in the

conception? Sir Marcus was chuckling silently, trying to keep a straight face.

"No, no. There can be no pleasure in the begetting. In the eyes of the Lord pleasures of the flesh are profane."

Then why, when the Lord created us did he include these pleasures? Sir Marcus felt he was winning this discourse.

The rector blustered. "Er, to try us. He put the Devil in our minds and we must resist." He paused, took a handkerchief from a pocket and blew his nose. Having given himself time to think, he went on, "the Lord created man to suffer. He gave us the power of sinful pleasure so that we may fight against it in His name. Man should desist the sins of the flesh. He...."

"Desist, Rector?" Sir Marcus fought to keep a straight face. "You mean we should not take pleasure in the making of love? That fornication should be forbidden and abandoned?"

"Hmmph, humph." The Rector took out his handkerchief again. Behind him Isiah Snufty emulated his master and they both blew their noses loudly.

"Are you really advocating the abolition of all pleasures of the flesh, Rector?"

"Pleasure of the flesh is a paramount sin and cannot be tolerated in the kingdom of God." Isiah Snufty nodded vigorously at his master's words. His nose upturned, sniffing over the rector's shoulders alternatively.

"Were that ever to come to pass then you would condemn humanity to extinction, for there would be none of us left to hear your gospel of perfection."

"Perfection. Ah, yes. How true, how true." The rector turned towards the stairs. "I shall now pray over your daughter, Sir Marcus. Where is she?"

"Up the stairs, Rector." Sir Marcus was having to bite his lip to contain his composure. "But if you go up there you are a brave man," he added. "Even I am not allowed near."

"Ah but you are not a man of God, sir." The rector said, sarcastically.

"Man of God or no, Mistress Pitchforth I will not have my daughter disturbed.

"That woman!" The rector exclaimed. Then as if Sir Marcus' words repeated in his mind he said, "disturbed? Disturbed? Only God can disturb the dead."

"My daughter is not dead, Rector. She is indisposed and is not receiving visitors. You are mistaken in your assumption of Russet's disposition, she is very much alive.

"Alive!" The rector jumped back, bumping into his curate who was lurking behind him. "Alive!" he said again. Behind him Isiah Snufty was up close and poked his head over the rector's left shoulder. The Reverend Butler turned to chastise him but Snufty had gone. He was now looking over the rector's right shoulder. When the rector turned his head to the right, Snufty went left. This continued until Sir Marcus could no longer contain himself. He burst into a fit of laughter and placed a hand against the wall to steady himself.

As the two men of the cloth departed, the rector paused on the steps. "Strange," he said. "Very strange. I was sure she was dead."

As the weeks passed, the cauterising scabs came off, leaving two wide, vivid red furrows that scarred the left side of Russet's face from temple to chin. The eyelid drooped, giving it a sleepy appearance, her lips puckered slightly at the corner. She allowed only Maisy and Molly in the room and she herself had not once left it. Charlotte and Katherine showed their annoyance at not being allowed to see their sister, but Russet was adamant. All mirrors had been removed at Russets insistence and the curtains were open only enough to let a glimmer of light into the room.

"You can't keep yourself locked up forever, my lovely" Maisy brought the brush down in one smooth stroke through Russet's hair. "You are too young to deprive yourself of company. Only old hags like me shut themselves away."

"You are not old." Russet spoke with a lisp, still finding it difficult to speak through her damaged lips. She was seated in a chair near the window while Maisy combed her hair. "I shall make a veil," she said. "A double thickness on the left should cover my ugliness, but I feel I never want to be seen ever again."

Sir Marcus got up from his desk and looked out of the window. It was a dark, murky morning. Mist engulfed the parkland. Drizzling rain formed droplets on the windows that joined with others to trickle down the glass in rivulets. He did not see the rider arrive, and it was not until Thomas Chatterton knocked and entered that he found he had news from London. He gasped as he read the note.

"My Lord Doulain has graciously invited himself to stay with us." He says he will be here shortly and that he has good news for me. Damn! Why cannot the man produce a date for his visit? Shortly, he states. That could mean tomorrow, next month or Cumknuckle day. We could have done without his company at this unfortunate time. Good news he says. I wonder if the news is of Tott?" He read further and then said, "it seems he requires your services in London, Thomas."

"Yes, sir." Thomas waved his note. "He has written to me on the same lines. I have been with the Doulain Company since a boy so it'll be a wrench to tell him I have no intent to continue in his employ.

"My offer still holds," Sir Marcus said. "You must face him first and tell him of your intention, then leave the rest to me. We shall presume that as far as I know you are to return to London, and I shall show my regret." He returned to his desk and sat down. "Now Thomas," he said. "How does our pig flesh business fare?"

"It fares well, sir." He came forward and stood in front of the desk. "I am sure your son, Master Totton, chose the right people. What Gertrude Wrigglesworth doesn't know about breeding swine is not worth knowing. She makes the workers keep at it and allows for no slack work. I heard her telling a labourer to get on with the job in words I cannot repeat to you, sir. Albert, her husband is no mean persuader. He has nearly every farm in the district breeding pigs and he keeps that great boar mightily happy. We send three cartloads of salted pork a week to Liverpool, and all is taken up. Gertrude has plans to double this in six months' time, and then she has her eyes fixed on the port of Bristol."

"And what of other estate business? Sir Marcus asked.

"We had a buyer wanting to buy the mature oaks at the north end of Black Wood. He offered a silly price so I sent him packing."

"How do you know his price was silly?"

"Because part of my work in London involved the acceptance of invoices. His Lordship purchased oak and elm for the building of his ships so I know the dockyard prices well. Work back from the invoiced price by subtracting the cost of felling, loading and carting, with respective margins of profit, and you have the price given for the standing timber. I tell you, sir, the man was a fraudster."

Sir Marcus smiled and nodded. "I am coming to believe it will be a clever man indeed that gets the better of you, Thomas."

Seven weeks had passed since the attack on Russet and she had not ventured forth from her self-imposed confinement. Maisy came slowly down the stairs, an expression of resignation on her face. She knocked on the study door and was bidden to enter. Sir Marcus was standing with his back to the blazing logs in the hearth.

"Good morning to you, Maisy," he said. "I hope the reason for your presence is to bring some light into the darkness engulfing this household."

"I have not yet found that light, Sir." She stood before him and a single tear ran down her cheek. "There is something I must tell you, though it grieves me beyond all reason to be the bearer of ill tidings."

Oh, not more bad news, Maisy?"

She clasped her hands and began, "when Gertrude Wrigglesworth and Walter Lupton brought Russet to me I sent them off to tell you, and to fetch Doctor Mathews, When

I was on my own I examined Russet and could see she had been interfered with. Before Doctor Mathews arrived I washed her to make it look as if nothing had happened and he seemed satisfied that the attacker had not had his way with her. But I knew different. I thought it better to hold my silence because it might not have taken – if you see what I mean.

"She was due for – er – a visit from Captain Scarlet but he did not arrive. He has not paid her a visit this month either." She shuffled her feet and put the back of her hand to her cheek to wipe away the tears that were now beginning to flow. "I am sorry, Sir Marcus. Very sorry, - Miss Russet is pregnant."

Chapter Thirty Two

Totton lay on his back on the bed, bleeding profusely. He was unconscious and his breathing was laboured. With each breath blood sprayed from the wound in his chest and blood also trickled from a wound on his head where he had struck the corner of a sideboard as he fell. Gunner had removed the knife and, because of the loss of blood, was now thinking perhaps he should have left it in to be dealt with by a qualified physician. Mrs Dickinson hurried in carrying cloths. Some she threw on the bed and another she pressed against the wound.

"We can do no more," she said. "I have sent a carriage for Mbungi. He will know what to do."

"Is he the local doctor?" Gunner asked.

"Oh, he's a doctor all right – of sorts." Tilly concentrated on stemming the flow of blood. "Do not judge him by appearance. Mbungi is a clever man."

Gunner was prepared to see a scruffy individual but when the carriage returned he was surprised to see a tiny, frail old black man being helped to alight. His total attire consisted of a pair of baggy knee-length trousers and a folded blanket draped over one shoulder. He walked leaning forward, as if the crooked stick he held was the only means of keeping him upright. His ribs were defined like a skeleton and his limbs bore little flesh, the outlines of the bones clearly visible. His body skin sagged limply, scoured and creased like the dried-up surface of a sun-baked waterhole. White thinning hair sprouted above his ears, accentuating a shiny bald pate. His chin was covered with white bristle and toothless gums allowed his bottom lip to almost reach his nose. Eyes as black as night and a nose that spread wide across his cheeks made him look as if his crumpled face had remained the same since birth.

He murmured to Tilly as she ushered him to where Totton lay and she answered him in what to Gunner sounded like an unintelligible series of moans and grunts.

"A chair." She gave the order to her black servants and they hurriedly obeyed.

Mbungi threw off the cloth from Totton's chest and as blood sprayed out he took the lips of the wound between his thumbs and forefingers and nipped them together, at the same time exerting downward pressure on the chest. Then he began to chant, constant mumblings that merged into one long ululating sound. He breathed through his nose and uttered the sounds from his mouth, his chanting ceaseless, never halting to take breath. A servant pushed a chair behind him and he sat down.

"Could not a qualified doctor see to him?" Gunner asked.

"Really," Tilly said mockingly. "Where would we find a doctor of quality in this locality? The nearest is Kingston and your friend would be dead before any could get here. Mbungi will remain until he recovers or dies. That may take some time and both your friend and Mbungi will take only water until one or the other comes about."

Gunner blushed at his own unthinking naivety. "I am sure it will take time, as you say, Ma'am, but I cannot stay with him. I would be glad of a bed for the night but come the morrow I must return to the ship. I shall come back as soon as may be."

"There is no hurry, he will be here for weeks. A punctured lung, loss of blood, and God knows what else, will keep him to his bed for many a week - if he lives." Tilly slipped an arm through Gunner's and walked him out of the room. "We must leave him now to fate, "she said. Then added, "and to Mbungi's healing spirits.

The following morning Gunner was mounted and about to leave when Tilly called out to him. "Is your friend a seaman? An officer? A captain?" She opened her arms in a questioning gesture.

Gunner laughed. "He's not much of a seaman Ma.am. He is Totton Roulette, the son of Sir Marcus Roulette of Nestwith - but a fine friend for all that."

"Thank you Mr Gunner," she sang out, as Gunner heeled his horse to a canter.

When he arrived back at the harbour cleansing of the ship had begun. The crew manned pumps to draw out the filthy water from the bilges and then pumped in clean seawater. This was to be continued until the water came out clear. Holystoning and swabbing the hold where the slaves had been kept was a laborious task also the boards on which the slaves slept were brought on deck to be scrubbed and limed.

Gunner did not return to the ship immediately. He sought out a tailor and was measured for a coat, shirts, breeches, stockings and a hat, then returned to the ship to tell of the misfortune that had befallen Totton. He asked the captain if the name Critchley was known to him.

"I know of John Critchley, a gentleman if ever there was one. He is the chief clerk of the Company Doulain in London. I know of no other."

The Captain was not happy at having to spend more time than necessary at anchor. Seamen always became restless at seeing the shore so near, yet not allowed the pleasures a seaport offered. The captain feared that if he let them go ashore there would undoubtedly be trouble, and some might not return. As Tarquin Willoughby was away visiting plantations and not expected back for several weeks he conceded to allow no more than five ashore at any one time. The aim of the men was always to get blind drunk, making getting them back to the ship after dark a hopeless task. At John Fullerton's suggestion the groups were rowed ashore at dawn. He knew from his naval experience their order of preference would be rum, women, and back to the rum. By mid-afternoon he, along with Gunner and Billy Dibb, went ashore and rounded them up. Most would be legless, some unconscious but they were piled into the jollyboat and rowed out to the ship. There they were hauled on deck and left to the care of their mates.

Totton came out of his coma, vaguely hearing the drone of Mbungi's chanting. As he gathered his senses the noise became louder. He opened his eyes and saw the wizened black face, eyes closed, head rocking to and fro. He felt pain in his chest and began to remember the events leading up to being stabbed. Who was the man who stabbed him? Who was the woman? She was a mulatto, her skin tawny; she could not possibly be the plantation owner – or could she? His question was answered as Tilly came into the room and leaned over the bed.

"It is comforting to see you are still in this world, Mr Roulette." She held a spoon, dipped it in a water container and put it to his lips. Not until he tasted the liquid did he realise his thirst. He nodded his head for more.

The chanting went on for five days and Totton felt he would die of starvation rather than fall foul to his wound, but Tilly would allow him only water. At the end of the fifth day the chanting stopped abruptly. Mbungi removed his hands from the wound and fell across the bed, head resting on Totton. Tilly called for help and the old man was gently and reverently lifted and carried out of the room.

"I thank the Lord for the old man's silence," Totton said, weakly. "My head is in torment with the constant dissonance."

"You should be thankful to Mbungi, Mr Roulette." Tilly's voice held a tone of reproval. "He has given the last five days of his life to save you."

"Oh, I shall thank him, when I rise from this cot." Totton was beginning to feel very tired. Now the chanting had ceased he wanted nothing more than to close his eyes and sleep.

Tilly threw a linen sheet over the bed and said, "you will have to thank him in your prayers."

I will do that," Totton said, wearily. "But I shall shake his hand and thank him personally."

"That would be difficult in the extreme, Mr Roulette. Mbungi is with his spirits."

"Spirits?" Totton opened his eyes wide.

Tilly sat on the edge of the bed and said, softly, "when Mbungi first saw you he did not hesitate to help you. He decided immediately that you were worth saving and there was no thought in his mind other than giving you life. The chanting you so scornfully dismiss were prayers to his spirits to transfer life, from his body, to you. That is what he did. You should be forever grateful, Mr Roulette. Mbungi gave his life that you may live."

Gunner looked the part. He came out onto the street in his new attire hardly recognisable. He wore black, buckled shoes, white stockings, black breeches, a white shirt, open at the neck, and a long maroon coat with flap pockets. A wide sash encircled his waist into which were stuffed two pistols. A leather band hung from his right shoulder and crossed his chest to hold a sheathed cutlass by his side. His hair was tied back in a plaited pigtail and his beard trimmed to a point. On his head he wore a three-cornered hat, turned-up brim forward. He was a fearsome sight and people moved aside to let him pass.

It was time to do his rounds of the taverns and brothels to find the five crewmen allowed ashore that day. It did not take him long to find the drunken seamen and with one over his shoulder and another under his arm he trundled down to the beach where Billy Dibb had arrived in the ship's jollyboat. He fetched the other three and they set off back to the ship.

"I don't think bad of 'em for drinkin' their senses blunt," said Billy Dibb. "I was one for doin' the same, until I got to be bosun. Then I doesn't want any to see me in that state. Drink yourself daft, and daft you be in everybody's eyes, even when the demons depart and you gets to be sober. It loses respect. That's what it does to a man. A bosun or an officer can never afford to be one o' the lads."

John Fullerton was distressed at the news of Totton's injury but Captain Christopher would not allow him to leave the ship, except for fleeting visits to the town. He too had purchased clothes and felt more at ease in well-fitting garb. Because of the boredom of being at anchor he had increased the gun drill and encouraged rivalry among the gun crews of each watch, with a day-to-day trophy and rum as the prize. The men were becoming very proficient, but this was mere practice; how they would apply themselves under fire, should the occasion arise, was another matter.

Gunner stood with John Fullerton looking at the bow chaser. "It is a waste of weaponry, Gunner," John Fullerton said. "It faces for'ard. A chaser is a weapon of attack as its name suggests, but not one bit of use in defence."

"Are you saying we should forget it?" Gunner was trying to read John Fullerton's mind.

"No. I'm not. But it is very unlikely that our captain would wish to attack another ship. More likely we would make a run for it if attacked, and use our guns only to defend ourselves."

"Then what do you suggest?" Gunner looked about. "Shift it down onto the lower deck?"

John Fullerton leaned over. He handled the coils and rattled the blocks attached to the gun. "Aye to shifting it, as you say, but not off the forecastle deck. What say you Gunner to fetching it about to face at ninety degrees to larboard and add to the armoury on that quarter." He stroked his chin, then he added, "better still, mount it facing part astern, say forty five degrees to the hull."

Gunner could see the sense of this. Any ship trying to come alongside to attempt boarding would have to come into the firing line of the chaser.

"You are assuming that if we are attacked then it will come on the larboard quarter," he said..

John Fullerton was silent for a few moments as he again stroked his chin and let his eyes wander across the deck planking. He began to take strides from one side to the other, and back again. Then he said, there is room enough to make fast the gun for use on both quarters. How long will it take to manhandle the weapon from one position to another if we could make it fast on either side." Gunner was about to speak but John FuIIIerton answered his own question, "three minutes at the most if we get the holdings at the right angle. Then the way the men are framing up, say another three minutes to have it ready to fire. Hmmm. Not bad. Yes. We can do it."

Two weeks after the stabbing Totton got out of bed. He staggered a few paces and was amazed that his legs felt so weak. He was humbled by the sacrifice Mbungi had made on his behalf knowing it was irrelevant whether he believed in the little man's spirits or not. Mbungi believed, and was prepared to forfeit his own life to save a man he had never before met. He was trying to untangle his mind and come to terms with such a sacrifice.

"Would you care to walk with me in the garden, Tott?"

Tilly had already shortened his name and as their friendship grew he began to sense the feeling of familiarity creeping into their relationship. As they strolled, he with a stick and she with her arm through his, supporting him, she asked about his home in England.

"My father lived almost all his life in Jamaica," she said, "but he always referred to England as home. I have never been there but I remember well the stories he told of that green, green land. He longed always to go back, but it was not to be. Mr Gunner mentioned you live in a hall – is that in the countryside?"

"It is, Tilly," he answered. "I too miss my home and look forward to my return. I shall, as soon as I get well and find a berth."

"Oh dear. Then I shall be left here, all alone again?" She clutched his arm tightly and turned to him, puckering her lips in pretence of petulance. Then she added, "I presume people in England would frown on me? Perhaps, for the colour of my skin?" she teased.

"You presume too much, Tilly." Totton felt comfortable in her company but inwardly he admitted that her strong firmness of purpose caused him concern. "I wonder you could assume such flummery," he said, "when a gentleman of colour has just given his life to save mine."

They talked to each other, telling of their early lives and the environment in which they were brought up. She gave him every attention as she nursed him back to health. As the days passed he became stronger. As the days turned to weeks they drew closer, each deriving pleasure from the company of the other.

Tilly Dickinson had a note delivered to the ship telling the captain of Totton's recovery and that it would be many weeks before he would be fit to rejoin the ship. She also wrote that Critchley had not been seen again in the vicinity. Gunner wished to visit Totton but his presence was needed, along with Billy Dibb, to keep the crew from rebelling and to fetch the drunken sailors back to the ship after their revelries.

On a day when almost all the crew had taken their turn to go in to the port, Gunner and Billy Dibb could find only four of the five they had brought ashore that morning. They rowed the four back to the ship, then returned to seek the missing sailor. They searched for two hours but to no avail, darkness closed in as they returned to the ship to face the captain.

"I knew it! I knew it!" Captain Christopher stormed. "Give men and inch and they'll take a yard." He strode back and forth in the aft cabin. "To keep a ship at anchor with an idle crew is naught if not a butt for trouble. Keep men idle, they get restless and you always get the one or two who take matters into their own hands." He turned on John Fullerton, Billy Dibb and Gunner who stood before him, hats in hand. "Who's idea was it to allow them ashore? It was not mine I vouch."

"Had we kept them aboard without hope of a little freedom, we would more than likely have had a revolt on our hands." John Fullerton faced up to the captain. "There are but five more to be given leave to go ashore, then that is the full complement."

"No! The Captain snapped. "One man jumping ship is

enough. I can't afford to lose any more of my crew."

Jamie had been writing as he listened. Now he handed the paper to the captain who read it. "Hmmm," he mused. "Jamie lad thinks the five should go ashore tomorrow. If not we really could have a revolt, as you say, Mr Fullerton." He nodded to Jamie and addressed the others, "I will allow the last five their spell ashore but that's an end to it. We shall then await the return of Mr Willoughby."

The following afternoon Gunner could again find only four of the seamen. He and Billy Dibb searched again until nightfall but without success.

"Did I not tell you what would happen." The captain shook a fist. "Now I am two men short when if I had stuck by my guns it could have been but one."

"Captain," Gunner said, ruefully. "It may not be so. They may be a'bed with some woman who desires their company for…"

"Don't make excuses for them." The captain was in no mood for compromise. "If and when they return they will feel the sting of the bosun's strap."

It was the following afternoon when uniformed men of the Governor's guard came alongside the Branston Silver.

"Ahoy the ship." An officer stood in the boat and called out. "Is your crew in full complement?"

John Fullerton answered, "we are without two men. They are ashore and have not returned. Have you news of them?"

"Aye, we have two." The officer called. "I would be pleased if you could furnish a man who knows them well, to see if they are yours."

Gunner and Billy Dibb took the jollyboat and followed the guardsmen. Ashore, they followed the officer for more than an hour until they arrived at a sandy beach. Several uniformed men stood about and came to attention as they appeared. The Officer took Gunner and Billy Dibb further along the beach to where two naked bodies lay prone on the sand.

"I am afraid your mates have been victim to some sort of ritual, by the looks of it." The officer said. "African's have their own gods and spirits, sacrificial rites have been known before."

As Billy Dibb went forward to identify the bodies, Gunner stood back aghast. Memories flooded back. Black Wood - the storm. – the finding of Jamie. He took a few steps forward to take a closer look. One seaman had been killed by what looked like several blows to the head and the other had his throat cut. It was not the manner of their death that took Gunner aback, but the position in which the bodies lay. Both men lay face down, arms stretched wide. A slender stick had been thrust through the flesh and between the bones of each hand and each foot, pegging the men to the ground.

Chapter Thirty Three

In the study, Sir Marcus Roulette sat at his desk, head in hands. He had been in that position for some time, trying to come to terms with news that Russet was pregnant. He was disturbed by a single knock on the study door and Charlotte entered.

"Well, she's done it this time!" Charlotte exclaimed.

"Done what?" Sir Marcus said wearily.

"Got herself with child, Father"

"Oh, Lottie, how could you say such a thing. You know well what happened. Russy knew nothing of it."

"Whether or not, she should not have been out on her own at that time, and now she brings shame to this house and to the name of Roulette.

"There is no shame in her." Sir Marcus felt angry at Charlotte's inference.

"There will be shame if she gives birth to a bastard."

"What do you mean 'if'? Has something awry been kept from me?"

"I am told there is a woman in Loylton who can rid...."

"I will not hear of it!" Sir Marcus retorted, angrily. "I am not prepared to even think about putting Russet's life in danger." He got up from his chair. "Let me tell you this, young lady, any decision on the matter will be down to Russet, not you, not me, nor anybody else." Sir Marcus paused, and then he asked, "how do you know of this abortionist?"

"I asked, in Loylton." Charlotte stated haughtily. "Better it is done quickly…"

Sir Marcus interrupted her, "Charlotte, I doubt if tact will ever come to you. I always hoped that the feathers inside your head would blow away with the winds of time." Sir Marcus sighed with a tone of resignation. "You talk about Russy shaming our name while you go out and tell the world you are looking for some woman to abort a Roulette infant." He sighed again, and then added, "do you not ever think before you speak? Do you not realise that gossipers will have a heyday with such news. It will not be long before everybody in the county will know something is amiss in the Roulette household."

"Well, I shall be out of it when John Fullerton returns." She turned to leave. "I shall marry him and live elsewhere."

"You will marry no man without my permission." Sir Marcus was losing patience. "You say Fullerton asked for your hand but he has not approached me."

"We spoke of marriage at Beamstorn. I told you that before we went to Liverpool looking for him."

"Yes, yes. I know that, but what words did he use when he asked you to be his wife?" Sir Marcus knew more than he was prepared to say.

"Why are you probing so, Father?" Charlotte began to fidget, clutching her hands and rubbing them together. "We spoke of marriage and it is a foregone conclusion that we shall wed when he returns."

"He has yet to ask me for your hand." Sir Marcus gave Charlotte a questioning glance. "Did John Fullerton go down on one knee when he made his proposal? Did he ask you be his wife when you walked with him? Did he actually use the words 'will you marry me Charlotte' when he made his appeal?"

Charlotte hesitated, then, "well, yes."

"Are you sure Charlotte?" Sir Marcus uttered the question with gravity. "I have it on good authority that John Fullerton is not all we thought him to be."

"What authority?"

"I spoke with Thomas Chatterton – not about your relationship – but about matters in general. He told me that Fullerton was employed by that shrewd devil Doulain, and had been for six months prior to his arrival in Loylton. Chatterton told me he had never met Fullerton but had noted the name and payment of fees in the Company Doulain accounts. I know more than I am able to tell at this time, but I am sure John Fullerton was sent here to spy on this family and to discover much about the situation here. I must give credit to the man, who better to give him the information he sought than my chatterbox daughter."

"It cannot be true, Father." Charlotte looked incredulously at him. "All the loving things he said to me – I do not believe for one moment that he was anything but sincere."

"I am truly sorry, Lottie." He went towards her and took her in his arms. "The man was doing the job he was sent to do, but he will answer to me when he returns. It was dastardly behaviour to take advantage of you to gain his objective. It was not the act of a gentleman."

Sir Marcus knocked once on the door of Russet's

bedchamber and attempted to open it. He pushed, but something was wedged against it.

"Hullo!" he called. "Russet, open this door at once!"

Maisy answered from the other side, "Miss Russet insists the door be kept closed."

Sir Marcus took a few steps backward then charged at the door. His shoulder slammed into it and it burst open. Pieces of a flimsy bedside chair, used to wedge the door, scattered across the floor as he lunged into the room.

"Enough of this!" He bellowed. "I will not be told by my daughter or by a serving woman where, and where not I am allowed in my own home." He went straight to the bed where Russet sat, knees up, covered by a linen sheet and holding a pillow up to her face to hide the hideous wounds. He grabbed the pillow from her and tossed it across the room "And enough of that too! You cannot hide yourself from the world forever, Russet." He sat on the edge of the bed and put a hand up to her chin and turned her head to view the scars. Russet had only once before seen her usually mild mannered father act with such resolute authority and she meekly gave in to him.

"Now let me see," he said. "It is much better, Russy. Yes. Yes. Much better. They have healed well." He turned her face this way and that as he inspected every inch of the healed wounds. "I last saw you after you were found and the cauterising made it look much the worse. The scabs have gone and the skin is not as red. The swelling and discolouration gone." He looked around the room. "No looking glasses, Russy? When did you last take a look at yourself?"

"I have no wish to look at my ugliness, Father."

"But you are not ugly, my dear. The scars may be a little unsightly but you are still my beautiful, beautiful daughter."

"Oooh," she cried, and threw her arms about him.

"Come now." He turned to Maisy who had been standing away from the bed. "Fetch a mirror," he ordered and waved a hand, dismissing her.

When they were alone he said, "Maisy has told me the fiend left you with child. I want to know your intention and whatever you determine I shall yield assent. I understand there is a woman in Loylton who can abort it." As Russet was about to speak he carried on, "I cannot approve such behaviour but the decision is yours."

"I have done little else but think of it," she said. "I have decided that I shall give birth to the child. It may be that half of it is the seed of the devil, but the other half is part of me – of Roulette blood. With Maisy's help I shall give it existence, then I shall decide what life it shall lead."

Lord Doulain arrived at Nestwith Hall in his black carriage with his usual retinue of black-attired footmen and armed outriders. A horseman had been dispatched to advise of his arrival and the Roulette's, with the exception of Russet, went down the steps to greet him. He had discarded colourful garb and was again dressed in black. He held a bundle of papers under his arm and once the salutations were over he was shown into the reception hall.

"A word with you, Marcus, if you please." He nodded,

indicating the papers he carried. "I have here the deeds of the estate and but one hour ago a rider overtook my carriage and delivered to me a letter containing news of your son. I opened it and read it before my arrival. Perhaps you would also wish other members of your family to hear it what it reads."

Sir Marcus could hardly contain himself as Katherine went to tell Russet but returned on her own.

Lord Doulain began, "as well you know the four men were abducted in Liverpool and it was by people employed by my company – members of the crew of the Branston Silver. The four were pressed into service and, may I add, this is a normal and legal procedure when a captain is short of men to crew his ship. At this point I should tell you that all four are alive." He was about to carry on when the door opened and Maisy entered.

Lord Doulain lifted an arm and flicked his hand, indicating that Maisy should leave. "This is private business. Please leave."

"No, she will not leave." The voice came from the doorway as a veiled figure appeared. Russet wore a veil of dark muslin thrown over her head; her face masked from view. "My Lord, this is Mistress Pitchforth," she said. "Her son James Pitchforth accompanied my brother. She has every right to hear of his circumstances."

His Lordship stared at Russet, then he went back to the letter. "According to this letter from the captain of the Branston Silver, Totton worked passage as a common seaman, climbing rigging and scrubbing decks with the rest. It would seem from this note he has become quite accomplished. However, he was wounded in a fracas in Jamaica and is at present making a recovery and is being nursed back to health." He looked to Sir Marcus. "It states no more, so we must presume your son is no danger of losing his life." He placed one sheet of the letter on the desk and went on to the next.

"It states little of Adam Gunner, other than to say he is well. I shall read on as it is written. - It could only have been with good fortune that John Fullerton was fetched aboard. I appointed him my first officer and his Royal Navy experience has stood the ship in as good a stead as may be. It is his wish that his regards be passed on to Sir Marcus Roulette and family.

There was a gasp from Charlotte and she clutched her hands with joy.

His Lordship went on, "if it was good fortune that Mr Fullerton was aboard then it must have been the wish of Neptune himself to allow me the company of James Pitchforth. His good fellowship made the voyage bearable to a degree."

"He cannot possibly be referring to the son of Mistress Pichforth." Sir Marcus shook his head. "With all respect, the man is a peasant – the son of peasants – with no education and cannot speak a word. How can one gain fellowship from such acquaintance?"

"I am reading what is stated in this message." Lord Doulain waved the paper. "I can only relate the written word. I am not in a position to give an opinion." He looked at each in turn, then addressed Maisy, do you wish me to continue?"

When she nodded he went on, "your son is as well as can be expected considering his disability." Lord Doulain waved the letter again. "The captain pens a message from Pitchforth. The man wishes me to convey his affection to his mother and says he looks forward to his return."

After dinner Charlotte and Katherine withdrew, leaving Sir Marcus and Lord Doulain at the table. Sir Marcus dismissed the staff and produced brandy, clay pipes and a tobacco jar.

"Is your visit one of a business nature, Frank?" Sir Marcus said. "Or is it merely to return the deeds of the estate?"

"Tomorrow I will speak with Chatterton of the salted meat business. I will not bother you with that, Marcus." He puffed on his pipe, putting his head back and blowing out a cloud of smoke that hovered like a blue mist above his head. He went on, "I must tell you that I shall require Chatterton to complete his work here and return to London as soon as he can make possible. My business there is in need of his talents, and I would hazard that he will be pleased indeed to get back to his roots.

"I shall be greatly saddened to see him go." Sir Marcus played the game as he continued, "not only has Chatterton occupied his mind to the provision of pig meat, he has given great assistance to me in bringing to date the backlog of estate matters. I thank you for the notice of his departure; it gives me time to seek another. I shall appoint an estate manager in Chatterton's place. When do you say he is to leave?"

The conversation went on, discussing many topics and then Lord Doulain said, "and what of Russet, Marcus? I got your note telling me she had suffered an accident but I am surprised she did not greet me better when I arrived."

"If I told you other than the truth, you would no doubt learn the truth later." Sir Marcus sighed deeply. "You would then regard me as a liar so I must tell you all." He told of the attack, and that Russet was not found until late afternoon of the following day. He described the horrendous wounds to her face, the cauterising, and the opinion of Doctor Mathews that the attacker meant to kill her. Then he added, "the man, if he be such, not only had intention to take her life, but had his way with her while she was out of her senses. Now we find that Russet is pregnant to the beast."

Lord Doulain was silent for a few moments. With an elbow on the arm of the chair he held his nose between thumb and forefinger and moved his head up and down, deep in thought.

He eventually lifted his head. "I have a great fondness for Russet." He paused as if trying to find words. Then he said, "I would be willing to give Russet my name, Marcus." He paused again and then continued, "when Russet has the child it will be looked upon as a bastard and she a woman of low morals." Sir Marcus was about to interrupt but Lord Doulain lifted a hand. "People have short memories. The facts will be hidden and the truth stretched to suite the tongues of gossipmongers. I am prepared to marry Russet and claim the child as my own. Should you and she agree then we could go through the ceremony here in the parish church as soon as the banns are read."

"Of course you have my permission Frank." Sir Marcus was astonished at the proposal. "I am honoured that you would wish take my daughter's hand." He bit his lip and then said, "you know what a headstrong girl she is. I think perhaps it better I tell her of your offer before you ask her yourself – to test the water, so to speak."

Lord Doulain waited in the study while Sir Marcus put the proposition to Russet. He felt like a teenager having asked a father permission to attend his daughter. He was contemplating his own position when the door opened and Russett entered. She wore a white shawl draped over her head and shoulders and held the material halfway across her face to hide her scars.

"Russy." Lord Doulain went to meet her and took her hand in his. "Your father has spoken of my suggestion?" She nodded and he went on, "would that I could ask you in different circumstances, my dear." He fought to find the right words. Then he said, "I would regard it as a great honour if you will accept my proposal and become my wife." He waited for an answer but Russet remained silent, looking into his eyes.

"Well, will you?" he began to feel embarrassed.

"No, Frank, I cannot," she said.

"What!" His Lordship was taken aback. "You turn me down?"

"It would be remiss of me to take advantage of your gracious charity." He still held her hand and now she squeezed his. "You will always be my dear, dear friend, Frank, but I am not the one for you. How would it be for either, living together yet knowing our marriage came about from such perfidious beginnings? It would always be with us and though I love you dearly, it is a love of friendship, not of passion." She smiled, the one half of her face that was visible lighting up, her eye twinkled as she added, "and there is another, is there not, *Frankie*?" She took her hand from her veil and wagged a finger at him. "I have seen the way Emma Fitzhamilton looks at you. She adores you, Frank. And what better lady could a Lord of the Realm have for a wife? She is charming, witty, known and liked by men of substance and the aristocracy, and has no equal as a hostess. Think of it, Frank, think of it." She let go his hand and turned to leave then turned back, dropped the shawl about her shoulders, exposing the scars. She stood on her toes and kissed his cheek. "I shall never forget your kindness and I shall remember you always as my dearest friend."

Lord Doulain met with Thomas Chatterton the following day. They walked the garden paths; feet crunching on finely riddled gravel.

"So you feel it is going to be a profitable business? His Lordship asked.

"I do Milord. Master Totton expected it to be up and running in a year but it will take three or four to come to peak. Pigs breed quickly, but not so quickly."

"Well I hope this business will thrive without you." Lord Doulain turned his head to see Thomas Chatterton's reaction as he went on, "John Critchley is in need of your services and you will return to London. You have one week to finalise your business here then you must be gone."

The two walked on for several paces without speaking then Thomas Chatterton said, "I am most grateful for the opportunities you have given me, Milord, but I have no wish to return to the city."

"But you must. - I command you." Lord Doulain said with finality.

"No sir. I am to marry and I have no wish to take my future lady wife to live in that gin pit of a city. I have come to enjoy the open spaces here and I consider any man a fool to give this up to go back to the filth of London. I see no alternative but that I must terminate my employment with you, Milord."

"Oh come now." Lord Doulain had been taken by surprise. "You are to be promoted, with good money in your pocket. If you refuse me, what will you do here for a living?"

"There are banks and businesses in Loylton. I would not have trouble finding work."

"I am truly sorry should I lose your services and I know John Critchley will regard you sorely missed." Lord Doulain took hold of Thomas Chatterton by the arm and turned about. "I must be getting soft with age, or perhaps it is the influence of the Roulettes. A year gone I would have put every obstacle in your way, but let me ponder on this a while."

They walked back along the path for some distance. Then Lord Doulain said, I told Sir Marcus you were to return to London and he showed disappointment at the news. He also said he would be obliged to set some person in your place to manage this estate." He stopped and placed himself in front of Thomas. "Would you consider taking up that post? It would place you in a position to see to my interests here – for a substantial fee, of course - and there may be accommodation included. I could have a word with Sir Marcus and my influence may sway him in your favour."

Thomas Chatterton was smiling inwardly as they walked through the garden to the front of the hall. Sir Marcus had just dismounted and a groom led his horse away. He stood with one foot on the lower step as he waited for the two to join him. As they came together a workman came running towards them. He stopped and with his hands on his knees gasping for breath.

"What is it man?" Sir Marcus asked.

"I bring news, sir." He gulped air

"What news. Come on, out with it."

"It's the king, sir. The king is dead."

"Oh God Almighty!" Lord Doulain exclaimed. "I shall have to leave for London with all haste." He turned to climb the steps but Sir Marcus caught him by the arm.

"The King?" Thomas Chatterton said. "Are you sure?"

"Aye, King George..."

"How did he die?" Sir Marcus interrupted

"Ee were doin' business..."

"What business?" Lord Doulain said, seriously.

"You know – business – fornicatin' like." The man was beginning to get his breath. "Ee were doin' too much on it, if you asks me. It were't fourth one today. He was doin' it when ee just moans and falls down dead."

Lord Doulain was aghast at the news. "Oh my God. It will be a scandal throughout Europe – perhaps the world. I really must go. I shall be required to help with funeral arrangements..."

"Wait Milord." Thomas Chatterton could not contain his mirth. "I believe the fellow speaks of a pig – a great boar. It is, or was, named after his Majesty. They called it King George III the second"

"A pig!" Lord Doulain gasped.

The man was still there, hands on knees, nodding his head and looking in amazement as the three fell about laughing.

"Doing the business!" Sir Marcus could hardly get the words out.

"The fourth today! Can you imagine the King…" Thomas Chatterton was bent over, his hands on the stone steps.

"Fornicating like!" Lord Doulain spluttered. "Funeral arrangements for a pig!

"A scandal throughout Europe!" Thomas Chatterton added, pointing at his Lordship.

"But what a way to go!" Sir Marcus held his sides.

The laughter eventually died and all three sat on the stone steps to regain their composure. Then Lord Doulain stood and lifted his arms. He called out, "the King is dead – God save the King!"

Chapter Thirty Four

Fanny Bottomly held a piece of paper in her hand. She put it up to a plaque on the door scrutinising the wording and comparing it with what was written on the paper - 'APOTHECARY'. Not being able to read she compared the shape of each letter until she was certain this was the right place. She knocked and stood back.

The door opened slowly and then stopped as safety chains tightened. Only half a face became visible in the space between the door and the jamb. A large nose and a single eye, peering over the top of pince-nez, stared out at her. "Yes?" The voice was muffled "What is it you want?"

"I seek some balm for a boil. I was told you could oblige me." Fanny stood quite still and she could almost feel the eyes searching her body as if she were naked. After a few seconds the face disappeared and she could hear chains being removed from their sockets. The door creaked and groaned on un-oiled hinges as it was drawn back. There was no invitation to enter but she climbed the two steps and brushed past the man into a dark, mysterious room. The only illumination came from a small, barred window; it took a few moments for her eyes to become accustomed to the gloom. Two of the walls were shelved to the ceiling with bottles and jars arranged neatly. She could see what looked like a lizard preserved in spirit. As she perused the labels, not knowing what was written on them, she saw a bottle of white balls and on closer scrutiny realised they were eyes. Further along the shelf an array of preserved objects, some of which looked very familiar to her.

She could not mistake the human anatomical parts, pickled for eternity. She began to feel uneasy.

"What sort of a boil?"

Fanny came out of her preoccupation and turned to look at the apothecary. He was a tall, lean man, with stooped shoulders. His back was so bowed he appeared to have a hump between his shoulder blades. The 'hump' lifted his shirt and waistcoat, to make his apparel appear badly fitted, as if the garments had been tossed loosely about him. His face was gaunt; the nose, supporting his spectacles, had a huge Roman hook as if nature had created the protuberance to balance his frame against the hump on his back. He was bald except for a tuft of hair at the front, slicked down against his furrowed brow. His eyes were so deep-set they looked like black holes against the pallor of his skin and were topped by a single bushy eyebrow that bridged the nose and straddled his face.

"What sort of boil?" The man repeated.

"Just a boil – how many sorts is there?"

"There are boils and there are boils, Good Lady." The apothecary opened his arms and gestured with his hands. "I make some balms for little boils and some balms for big boils. I make cures for dead-eyed boils, blind boils, festering boils and gumboils. I mix ointments for spots and rashes, ulcers, suppurating cankers, warts, pimples, carbuncles and corns. Now, which sort have you got?"

"I don't know."

"Then you had better give me sight of this unknown affliction." Two seconds after uttering the request he regretted his words. Fanny was standing in the middle of the room and now she spread her legs and lifted her skirts up in front of her face to show her naked body.

The apothecary was taken aback. He got a whiff of the foul smell from the movement of her clothes. He bent his humped back to take a closer look at a suppurating canker oozing pus and another, less inflamed protrusion in her groin.

"Yes, yes. I see. You may drop your skirts, madam. And stay in the middle of the room. Do not whatever you do wander about." He could not hide his disgust but turned away from her and retired behind a counter at the far end of the room.

"Why must I not move?" Fanny asked.

"Because," the apothecary stammered, "because you must remain motionless while I mix the balm."

"Why?" She asked again.

"Because of the spirits, madam." He was thinking of any excuse to keep her in one place. "If the spirits be wrong then the balm will not cure your ailment." He began to mix powders in a mortar, added a little oil then ground it with a pestle until it formed into a thick paste. This he transferred to a small, ceramic pot.

Fanny had remained motionless and silent while the man worked but now she said, "do you want that I should lay down?"

"Lay down?" The man looked baffled

"So's you can put the balm on."

He looked down at his hands, an expression of disgust on his face. To touch any part of this vile woman was repulsive to him, but to lay hands between her thighs on that pus-oozing canker appalled him.

"I, er, I..." For a brief moment he was lost for words. Then it came to him, "I only provide cures and pain relief for self-administration. This balm," he banged the pot on the counter, "is for self-application only."

What?

"You put it on with your own hand, Madam."

"But I can't see down there," she bent her head, demonstrating her inability to see the sores.

"I am a qualified apothecary, madam, not a physician." His voice held a tone of exasperation. "I prescribe potions and balms – I do not administer them."

"But I can't see where to put it."

"Then *feel*, madam. *Feel!*" The apothecary lost patience. "That will be three pence for the balm and three pence for my diagnosis.

Fanny dropped her skirts. "Dia – what?"

"My diagnosis, madam. That is the price I charge for giving you my professional opinion of your affliction." Realising she did not understand he added, "I tell you what is wrong with you."

Why should I pay you three pence when I already know I've got a boil?"

"Two." The apothecary corrected.

"Two pence?

"Two boils. You have two, and they are not boils." He came around the counter with the jar of balm. "Now, do you want this or not?" His patience now exhausted he began to open the door and held out a hand. "Six pence please."

What if I 'as it without that dia-whatsit? How much then?"

"Five-pence ha-penny."

"You said three-pence."

"Ah yes," the apothecary put on a wry smile. "The extra is for the receptacle. If you take my diagnosis I throw the pot in for no charge at all."

"I still saves a ha'penny then?"

"And then there is the charge for professional service...."

"Here, I've 'ad enough of this." Fanny was baffled. She struggled with a fold in her dress and produced some coins. She counted out six pence in pennies, half pennies and farthings and put the money into the outstretched hand. "There," she said." Now tell me what ails me."

The apothecary ushered her to the door. "Madam," he said, quickening his voice. "You are beset with an acute measure of syphilis. Now, I wish you good day." With that statement he pushed her out onto the street and slammed the door. Now on his own he went to the middle of the room and began to jump up and down, slamming his boots onto the floor to kill any fleas that may have fallen off his clients' clothes He was about to sprinkle lime on the infected area, when Fanny knocked again.

After being ushered out, Fanny stood for some moments, mouth open. Then she turned and banged her fist against the door. It was opened, again to the length of the chains and the hooked nose and one bespectacled eye appeared in the narrow space. "Yes?" The unseen mouth uttered the question.

"You say I have syphilis?" Fanny asked.

"Yes," came the muffled reply.

"Does that mean I'm going to die?"

"Yes, Madam. Without doubt."

"Then what can I do. What can I..."

"Madam," the apothecary interrupted. "You can do three things. One – apply the balm. Two – do not practise fornication. And three – seek out a coffin maker with all haste." He then slammed the door shut.

Fanny walked as if in a dream along the cobbled street. She was going to die. She kept repeating this to herself and passers by stared at her as if she were a woman deranged. She came to a square with a stone trough in the centre. The drinking font was encircled with horse droppings, evenly spaced the length of a horse away from the water. It reminded Fanny of stories she had been told as a child, of witches' circles, magic spells, and the witches' power of life and death. She stepped over piles of dung and seated herself on a corner of the trough. Looking down she saw her clear reflection in the water and spoke to her own image, "well, Fanny Bottomly, what do I do now?" She ran her fingers through the water and, as tears began to fill her eyes, she watched her reflection waver and become distorted on the rippling surface. Then, quite suddenly a thought came to mind. 'No fornication' the man had said. That could mean only one thing. She was going to die but, until that time, she herself held the power of life and death. The water in the trough settled and her image became clear once more. She began to cackle as she again spoke to herself, "well Fanny my lass, if I'm going to die, who am I goin' to take with me...?"

Chapter Thirty Five

"Is your mind irretrievably fixed, Tott?" John Fullerton asked. He was seated with Totton Roulette and Tarquin Willoughby on the veranda of Tilly Dickinson's homestead.

"My mind is made up. Never have I been so determined on any issue." Totton coughed and put a handkerchief to his mouth. He took several breaths and then said, "Mrs Dickinson has been my saviour and I am indebted to her. That apart, I find her company pleasurable indeed. She could take a berth on any ship but Captain Christopher has promised her a cabin and if that comes to pass then I can think only that it will be your misfortune to forfeit your cabin, John."

"That is the usual procedure when a lady comes aboard for a voyage." John Fullerton said, resignedly. "It's always the mate who suffers eviction. I shall most likely be required to bunk with Billy Dibb – not the most inviting proposition."

"So Mrs Dickinson has set her mind on going to England?" Tarquin said.

"Yes." Totton paused to cough. Then he went on. "I too will travel as a passenger for I hazard I shall not have strength to holystone decks, or man the yards. It is good fortune that I still have money received for the salted pork delivered to Liverpool." He paused, then said, "I am grateful to the honesty of the crew for not relieving me of my belt when I was brought aboard."

"Ha!" John Fullerton laughed. "That was not honesty, Tott. It was fear of the bosun's belt were they found to be thieves."

"And what of Mrs Dickinson's assets here – the

plantation?" Tarquin asked.

"Simon Ridley is to set a man of his choice to manage it" Totton said. "But that is a long way forward. According to you," he said to Tarquin, "we shall be here for some months yet."

"You may well weigh anchor sooner than you think," Tarquin said. He got to his feet, stood behind the other two and continued, "for reasons of which I am not yet aware, I have been sent here chasing a wild goose when the goose I chase is safely sitting on its nest at home. I was dispatched at the behest of Lord Doulain to speak with plantation owners, or their managers, to request donations for the building of ships of war to protect the trade routes. Now I find that all plantations of sizable acreage are owned either by nobility, or men of wealth, living fat in their country houses in England. Yes, they have managers, but they are men who do not have authority to dip their fingers into their master's purse on my say-so."

"Are you saying we have been kept here for no reason?" John Fullerton got to his feet. He did not give Tarquin chance to answer but went on, "the ship is commissioned to your command for a year. What of that?"

"I have a good mind to leave Jamaica within the week and sail for Antigua." Tarquin made the statement forcibly. He added, "so if you and your lady friend intend to join the ship you had better put your affairs in order with all haste."

News of the departure from Kingston spread among the crew and there was excitement aboard at the prospect. Captian Christopher ordered the loading of cargo; sugar, tobacco, molasses, rum and coffee. There was great jollity the night before sailing. Men danced the hornpipe on the forecastle deck to the tune of finger-whistles and a fiddle. Rum was allowed on board and allocated, apportioning only as much as would keep a man on his feet. The usual bartering, and payment of debts, meant some drank more than others. Certain crewmembers were deliberately fed more and then encouraged to perform well-practised feats that brought applause as if witnessed for the first time.

The following morning a baggage boat arrived at the ship and Tilly Dickinson's effects were hauled aboard. After this came Tilly herself, accompanied by Totton with Billy Dibb at the tiller and men of the Branston Silver manning the oars. A slatted ladder had been lowered over the side but Billy Dibb shouted for the bosun's chair to be sent down. This consisted of a wooden plank with ropes attached to each end, chiefly used for supporting men working on the hull.

Totton was hauled aboard and then Billy Dibb helped Tilly as she tried to balance her buttocks on the plank. Her skirts spread as men on deck heaved her upwards.

"Eyes down!" Billy Dibb commanded the oarsmen. "Keep your eyes down. Any man as lifts 'is 'ed will feel my belt across 'is back... Buckley!" He called out to one of the oarsmen who seemed prepared to risk the mates wrath, "I said keep your eyes down." The man immediately dropped his head but it appeared the threat did not apply to Billy Dibb himself. He raised his head and his eyes widened as he glanced up, to see Tilly's shapely legs, as far as her thighs, dangling above his head. As he lowered his eyes he saw

Buckley staring at him, his face creased in a knowing grin.

Shortly, after all were aboard Captain Christopher gave the order to weigh anchor. Men manned the forward starboard capstan and with a chanting rhythm they circled the vertical drum to the constant clicking of the ratchet. As the cable came in the great anchor was dragged from its grip on the harbour bed and before it showed above the waterline the ship began to move. The light wind was in the right quarter to give steerageway so kedging was not needed. With only the topsails set the Branston Silver moved slowly out of the harbour.

Early in the morning of the second day out of Kingston came a cry from the lookout at the masthead. "Ahoy the deck. Sail dead astern."

Billy Dibb was on watch and he sent a man to inform the captain. John Fullerton was first up onto the poop deck, half dressed, telescope in hand. He put a knee against the taffrail to support himself and put the glass to his eye.

"I can see nothing yet, "he said and lowered the telescope. He put his head back and hailed the lookout, "keep her in sight, lad. Give me her bearing when you have it."

A tense hour passed. The captain had been warned of pirates in the vicinity and amongst the crew, from the oldest hand down to the youngest cabin boy, there was a rising feeling of apprehension.

"I have her now." John Fullerton was now fully dressed but he felt the chill of the morning air. He called to the lookout, "can you see what she's about yet?"

"Aye, sir," the man replied. "She's in full sail. Was bearin' across our course but she's come about now. I sees her fore an aft so she's lookin' to join our wake."

The captain looked glum. He was a merchant seaman not a battle-hardened naval mariner. He moved near to John Fullerton and murmured quietly so no other could hear, "Mr Fullerton," he whispered. "If yon is a pirate ship then we are in trouble. We weigh heavy and she will no doubt be upon us by mid-afternoon. I confess I have no experience of such encounters." He came closer and whispered. "I am not such a fool as to let pride come before a fall so I am willing to relinquish command to you for the duration of this encounter. What say you, John?"

"Aye, sir." He said nothing more to the captain but called for Billy Dibb and Gunner. When they arrived he told them of his plan, "we shall bear to starboard so they cannot see what we do on our larboard side. When I give the command the larboard gun crews will uncover their guns and double charge with grape. They will not run the guns out but have the coils ready to do so. The guns will then be covered. Keep the men quiet and lay them low until the time for action." He turned to Gunner. When we return to our course load the bow chaser with double – no, treble grape, move it to the new larboard setting and have it ready to fire. And take grappling hooks for'ard to the forecastle and have them coiled and at the ready."

"What makes you think they will come at us on our larboard beam? Billy Dibb frowned.

"Because that is what we will make them do, Mr Dibb. When we are ready we shall change course from east to east-north-east. They will not follow in our wake but take the shortest route to us, and God willing we shall have them to rights. We must catch them off their guard - make them think we are an easy prize. When they near, we'll strike our colours as if to surrender. The starboard watch will man the yards. On my order they will reef the mainsails and the topgallants but they will stay on the yards awaiting my order to set them again with all haste."

Billy Dibb was about to pass on the orders when John Fullerton added, "tell the men what I have said so all know what is to happen. Tell them also that, God willing, we are about to take a big fat prize."

Tarquin Willoughby took the six muskets that comprised the small-arms weaponry. He loaded all six and left them at the ready in the companionway near the poop break. Cutlasses and knives were handed out to the crew and when John Fullerton gave the order to alter course the plan went into action. Covers were removed from the five guns. The crews worked silently to load them, keeping low to avoid being seen. Blocks were set, coils ready and covers replaced. The men then crept back into hiding

John Fullerton saw the puff of smoke from the bow of the closing ship and he took out his pocket watch. He said nothing but when the cannonball struck the ship it took everybody else by surprise. It came in with a whine and struck the stern with a resounding thwack. Splinters of timber shot skyward but the taffrail shielded the deck and the fragments fell harmlessly into the sea. A moments delay, and then the report of the gun was heard. Those on deck remained motionless, nerves tingling, fright showing in their eyes. All, with the exception of John Fullerton, who stood, legs apart, looking aft, timepiece in hand.

"My God!" the captain exclaimed. "They'll sink us."

"Not they, Captain. They're after the ship and its contents." John Fullerton kept his eyes on the following ship. "That was a warning shot. I don't think it was intended to strike us. If it was, then at that range they must have a master gunner aboard. I tend to think Lady Luck aimed their gun, not good judgement. They will no doubt have another go at us. Keep an eye on them and tell me when you see smoke from their bow chaser."

Totton and Tilly Dickinson appeared on the quarterdeck to see what had caused the commotion.

"Please return to your cabin Ma'am. Now. Unless you wants your 'ead blowd off." The tone of authority in Billy Dibb's voice sent her and Totton scurrying for the companionway.

"Now," the captain called. "I see the smoke of their gun. They've fired at us again." The ball landed well short and plunged into the sea creating a clearly defined spout.

"Ha!" John Fullerton laughed. "Not only can they not aim true, it took them over eight and three-quarter minutes to reload their gun." He shouted down to Billy Dibb, "tell our lads it took them nearly nine minutes to reload." A few seconds later he could hear nervous, but derisory guffaws, followed by orders to remain quiet.

After loading the bow chaser, Gunner disappeared for a while then came out on the deck dressed in his new garb.

"You need not be looking at me like that, Billy Dibb," he said. "If I'm going to die, then die I will, but dressed to be proud." He had his cutlass sheathed at his side, the two pistols bought in Kingston stuffed into the sash that girded his waist, and in his left hand he held a large hammer complete with metal shaft. With hat on head at a jaunty angle he looked a frightening sight.

"God a'mighty! Gunner," Billy Dibb exclaimed. He looked Gunner up and down. "Keep yourself hid, man. If they sets eyes on you, they'll run a league."

"Strike the colours!" John Fullerton gave the order.

"Reef mains'ls, royals and t'gallants." Billy Dibb shrieked the command.

Men scurried up the shrouds, feet dancing on the ratlines and out onto the yards, sliding along footropes with practiced precision. On deck others undertook their part with equal dexterity.

"Two points to larboard." John Fullerton ordered the helmsman. He looked back towards the pursuing vessel. "Aye, another two then." As the ship changed course, almost imperceptibly, the pursuers changed course to follow, taking a more acute tack, as if to head off their prey.

A great cheer could be heard from the pursuing ship as the pirates lined up along the starboard rail of their ship waving pistols, muskets, and cutlasses to signify their victory, acceptance of surrender, and their readiness to board.

"Be prepared, Mr Dibb." JohnFullerton, head down, shoulders hunched, was doing his best to appear dejected and defeated. As the ships began to draw level he shouted, "now,

Mr Dibb!"

The gun crews came out of hiding and scurried to their positions. Ports were dropped. Hands went to the coils and guns run out. Blocks laid. Ropes fastened. Gun captains standing by, blowing ash from their slow matches to expose a glow. Men, kneeling or standing in their practiced positions. Waiting... waiting... waiting.

"Fire as she comes to bear." John Fullerton gave the gun captains their last order. He wanted sporadic fire, not a broadside that could strain the timbers

The first gun to be fired went off with a thunderous roar. An orange flash burst from the muzzle and the gun carriage recoiled across the deck at a murderous speed. The gun was brought to a standstill by the breeching, the dull thump of the stretched rope lost as a second gun went off with an ear-splitting crash.

The crew of the first gun to fire went into their practised drill. Sponging, worming, ramming home the charge followed by a wad, the thick, flannel-wrapped charge of grape, another wad rammed home and the gun run back into position, coils laid, blocks set, men standing clear of the recoil path, the gun loaded and ready for the touch of the gun captain's match.

It was a frantic scene, a cacophony of the sounds of battle, thunderous blasts of cannon, the crack of musket and pistol fire, smoke, the acrid smell of burned gunpowder, shouts of command, cries of the fallen - and blood spilt all around.

Gaps appeared in the ranks of the pirate crew who lined the starboard rail as the grapeshot tore into them. Some had gone to their guns, but so confident where they of taking a prize, they had not loaded them. Musket fire was now raining in and the crew of the Branston Silver began to take casualties. Men fell and were dragged out of the way to lie on the deck, some moaning, some screaming for help, others silent in death. There was no time to tend the wounded.

Tarquin was on the poop deck and he was joined by Totton. Each held a musket to shoulder, aiming at figures standing by the wheel. Tarquin fired but the rolling deck spoiled his aim. When Totton fired a man fell to the deck. He turned away to reload only to come eye to eye with Tilly who carried two of the loaded muskets. She passed them over and returned for the other two. With sleeves rolled she then lay on the deck, a ramrod clamped between her teeth as she reloaded the muskets. Totton touched the trigger and another man went down. Whenever others tried to get to the wheel they came under Totton's accurate fire. The continuous, thudding recoil against his shoulder affected his wound and began to take its toll. He coughed, and spit blood onto the deck. Yet still he kept on, until no man daring to take hold of the wheel, the attacking ship was out of control.

At a nod from John Fullerton, Billy Dibb signalled to the men above and the mainsails came billowing out to be pulled tight as crewmen heaved on ropes with such urgency even their hardened hands blistered. The sails took the wind and the ship was driven forward.

"Hard a'larboard." John Fullerton cried. He went to assist the helmsman. Tarquin put down his musket and rushed to help. They heaved and turned the wheel until it would go no more. The ship came about, the bow turned towards the privateer until the timbers almost met. John Fullerton grabbed a slow match and ran to the forecastle where Gunner and his mates had the bow chaser at the ready. At John Fullerton's command men came forward and threw grappling hooks and lines to bring the vessels together. Pirates came up to counter them but as the stern of the Branston Silver moved away the bow chaser came into line. John Fullerton peered along the barrel then he stood aside, blew on the slow match and put it to the touchhole. It went off like a clap of thunder, the glimpse of an orange flash immediately hidden in a cloud of smoke. The gun recoiled and leapt high in the air to be brought up by the breeches. Three charges of grape went off down the length of the deck of the pirate ship like spreading shot from some enormous fowling piece. The carnage they wrought was deadly; where men had stood they now lay, some still, others moving. Cries of pain and pleas for help filled the air.

Gunner stepped back, waited until waves lifted the ship to take the deck higher than the forecastle deck of the pirate ship, then he lunged forward and jumped the gap. As the lines of the grappling hooks tightened and the ships came together Tarquin followed him along with some of the more agile members of the crew.

Those of the pirates who had escaped the grapeshot crowded to larboard. Gunner charged down on them, cutlass in one hand, hammer in the other. He roared at the top of his voice as he struck right and left. Slashing. Hacking. His face red with the exertion, hammer cracking skulls, his cutlass cutting swathes through the men as if he were cutting a jungle path. He took a cutlass wound to his arm but continued mowing his way along the deck until the few left on their feet broke and fled.

A great cheer went up. It was all over. The few pirates that were still alive gathered by the poop break and threw down their arms.

On the Branston Silver John Fullerton went up to the captain, I think it time now to relinquish command, sir." He walked to the edge of the poop break and looked down on the scene below. Five of the crew lay dead on the deck. Another five sat against the after hatch, their wounds being tended by their mates as best they could. "We could be hard pressed to crew both ships," he said. "I would hazard our best bet is to keep course for Antigua. Saint John's harbour is as good as any to lick our wounds and we can register our prize with the Royal Naval Establishment there and leave it in their hands." He expected an answer but when he looked at the captain he could see the man was in shock.

Jacob Christopher was not a timid man but the happenings of the past few minutes had unsettled him. Had he been giving orders, or occupied in any other way during the conflict his mind would be steady. As it was he had remained on deck with nothing to do but watch the battle and see his men die. He peered over the rail at the dead crewmembers.

"We lost four, then…"

"Five, by the looks and five wounded."

A seaman poked his head above the deck. "That cannonball they shot at us hit the aft cabin and went right through." He came up the steps and stood before the captain, "it done damage, sir. It hit Mr Pitchforth... if he aint dead, then he's hurt real bad."

Chapter Thirty Six

Captain Jacob Christopher was jolted back to reality when told that Jamie was hurt. He rushed away from the poop deck down to the aft cabin. The cannon ball had struck between two of the square, stern windows, leaving a jagged hole half the beam of the ship. Splintered timbers, shards of glass lay scattered about, furniture broken, the bulkhead breached, and Jamie lay spread-eagled, eyes closed, blood from a head wound forming a spreading pool on the cabin deck.

He was extracted from the debris and carried out unconscious to be placed face down on the quarterdeck. Tilly had been doing what she could for the wounded seamen and now she knelt by Jamie. "He is alive, but I can only try to stem the bleeding," she said. "This man needs better attention than I can give him. I have no experience of head wounds."

With the sails reefed on the captured ship, a count aboard showed the captain and his officers had been killed in the action, mostly on the wheel deck by Totton's accurate musket fire. Four of the pirates lay badly wounded, while the five who surrendered were put to work separating the wounded from the dead. Billy Dibb had them take all clothes and personal belongings from every corpse and as each was stripped, he said a short prayer and the body was then heaved over the side to a watery grave.

An hour after the capture a sailor searching the holds came back up on deck. He spoke to Billy Dibb, "there's men down there," he said. "Poor buggers look like they've been starved."

The first man to be brought on deck climbed out of the

hold, screwing his eyes, attempting to take in the situation. He held a battered leather bag close to his chest as he struggled to stay on his feet; his emaciated legs hardly able to bear his meagre weight. Red hair, matted and filthy, straggled his shoulders, and his thick beard could not hide the signs of suffering. His clothes were worn and soiled; yet he had a proud bearing about him.

"Water," the man croaked, hand to mouth, gesturing as if drinking. "Water, he repeated.

Gunner put an arm about the man and helped him to sit on a raised hatch. "Who are you?" he asked.

"Water." He requested again with urgency.

A seaman brought water and the man gulped it down until Gunner took the ladle from him, "Steady now, more later." Gunner leant forward to look the man in the face and he asked again, "now tell me, who are you?"

"Are you an English ship?" The man coughed to clear his throat.

"Yes, we are." Gunner replied.

"Well thank the Lord in heaven for that." He coughed again, then said, "I am Surgeon Lieutenant Jack Battle of His Majesty's Royal Navy." He began to get to his feet but as Gunner gently pushed him back he said, "there are men down there. Men who have lived through hell. In God's name get them out."

The following half hour was traumatic for even the most hardened mariner. Five men were carried up out of the depths of the ship. Their skeletal frames no more than skin and bone. Cheeks drawn in, eyes sunken into their sockets, heads more like the fleshless skulls of the dead than of living mortals. What was left of their filthy, tattered apparel was still distinguishable as military uniform. They were given water and an awning erected to shield them from the sun.

A boat was lowered and John Fullerton and several members of the crew were rowed across to the pirate ship. When he came aboard, his first concern was to inspect the damage. He found the superstructure pockmarked and splintered from grapeshot but the ship itself was seaworthy. He kept Billy Dibb on board and sent Gunner, Lieutenant Battle and the five emaciated soldiers, together with the five, now securely bound prisoners, back to the Branston Silver. Another four wounded pirates remained on board.

The ships' carpenter began immediately and worked throughout the night to make the aft cabin habitable. Jamie did not regain consciousness so the following morning he was taken to the mate's cabin where Tilly Dickinson kept watch over him. Lieutenant Battle, rested and fed, began a round of the injured crewmen, gouging out musket and pistol balls and stitching gaping wounds. The air was rent with the moans, cries and screams as he probed deep into flesh to dislodge and remove offending metal. When he paused to rest, Tilly asked him to take a look at Jamie.

"A head," he said, with a grin. "I like heads. Much more of interest than sawing off limbs and sewing wounds." He let his fingers wander over Jamie's head, prodding here, stroking there. He shook his head. "The knock he received should not have rendered him unconscious for this length of time, but there is an old wound here." He parted the hair and looked closer. "Yes," he mused. "Yes. There is a depression. This fellow has had a knock before and he has a depressed fracture of the skull. Interesting. Interesting." He mumbled as if talking to himself. "I shall need all his hair off and the skull shaved before I make a final diagnosis." He straightened up and addressed Tilly, "I shall need plenty of brandy – rum would do. Two large bowls, washed clean with seawater. And I shall want light. It's too dark in here. I shall need cloths – plenty of them - and clean mind." He faced Tilly. "I will do my best, but I must be truthful and offer that never before have I been charged to perform with such intricacy on a living human, so there can be no guarantee of success. I would be unsure of the outcome even were I to operate on dry land. Here on a rolling ship the chances of saving him are slim indeed."

"And if you do not try?" Tilly asked.

"He will die anyway. Of thirst and starvation, I hazard, rather than the knock to the head. Try to feed him or quench his thirst and he'll choke. I have heard of the unconscious being fed and watered, but I have never been able to do it."

Jamie was carried into the aft cabin where the ship's carpenter and his assistants were occupied with repairs. The captain ordered a halt to the work. The dining table was damaged but still intact and Jamie was lifted onto it, face down, with light from the one unbroken window illuminating his head. The surgeon poured rum into two bowls and placed instruments taken from his bag in one of them, in the other he put some pieces of cloth. Gunner helped with cutting Jamie's hair and Tilly carefully shaved his head.

The surgeon washed his hands in rum then rubbed a rum-soaked cloth over Jamie's head.

"Why do you do that?" Tilly asked.

"I don't really know." The surgeon kept his head down, his fingers probing once again at the depression. "I was told by a fellow surgeon that in the orient, surgeons there use fermented rice. They distil it and use it on wounds to help stop infection. I have used the method ever since, with brandy or rum, and in some cases it seems to work. Don't ask me why, because I don't know."

He carefully cut down to the skull and folded back a flap of skin, holding it with a stitch to the scalp. Then he began to scrape at the bone. "See this," he said. This piece of bone has been knocked inward. Whether it's putting pressure on the brain or not, I am not sure." He wiped sweat from his brow with his sleeve. "What I am going to do is weaken the end of the broken bone, where it's fused to the skull, then use that as a hinge and lift the shard to fit its original position." He scraped away for some time, then he said, "I do not have equipment here to perform this as I would have it done. I have no gut and I can think of no way I can attach something solid to the scalp."

"You have me lost," said Tilly. "Perhaps you could be more explicit for a simple woman."

"If I was ashore, I would thread a length of gut under the piece of bone and pull it back to its original place. Before beginning I would have shaped whalebone and drilled holes in it through which I would pass the gut. Then I would stitch the whalebone to the scalp and that would give me a solid base to hold the gut. Gut will fuse with the bone whereas here I shall have to use yarn and there is a risk it will rot. I don't like doing it like this but there is no other way."

"Gunner asked, "what sort of gut?"

"Catgut, you know, the stuff fiddle strings are made of. Unfortunately for this fellow, I do not have a musical aptitude." The surgeon continued scraping the bone. "Good job he is out of his mind with his senses numbed – otherwise the pain of this would drive him to distraction, and we would never keep him still."

Gunner and Tarquin left the cabin and shortly returned. "We have a fiddler aboard," said Gunner. "He has kindly donated his strings to our cause." He did not tell of the threat he had used to make the man give up his prized possession.

Tarquin opened a box and took out one of the ornate pistols given to him by Lord Doulain. "This may be of help," he said.

The surgeon looked up aghast. "I want to cure the poor devil, not shoot him."

Tarquin turned the pistol and pointed to the silver plates at each side of the stock, fastened to the polished walnut by a number of silver screws.

"Good man." The surgeon nodded. "I can think of nothing better. Will one of you take off a plate and straighten it. Leave a slight curve to fit the shape of the head."

An hour later the operation was over and Jamie was swathed in bandages, only his mouth and eyes visible. With the silver plate stitched to the scalp and the gut threaded under the shard of bone, through two of the screw holes, and tightened, everything was in place. Tiredness was overcoming the surgeon as he stepped away from the table, his job done. He staggered and almost fell. "A bunk would be a most welcome," he muttered. "I fear the heat must have the better of me."

In the evening Lieutenant Jack Battle was roused by Tarquin. He washed; dressed in clothes provided and went to the aft cabin to join Captain Christopher and Tarquin. Jamie occupied one end of the cabin; strapped to the dining table, face down, his wrists tied to the table. The three men took seats at a makeshift trestle. The captain passed round the claret jug and asked of Jack Battle, "you were obviously a prisoner but how is it you appear in more robust health than the soldiers?"

"Before I answer that question, Captain. May I ask what is your intention regarding the captured pirates?"

"I shall see they are handed over to the Royal Navy authorities at Saint John's when we reach Antigua. I have no doubt they will be dealt harsh punishment." The captain sipped his wine contentedly, as if that topic was now concluded.

"You should give them a hearing then hang them from the yards." Jack Battle thumped a fist on the trestle, making the glasses jump. Before the captain could answer he continued, "as captain of this ship you have the authority to do what you wish with pirates. These men are not privateers or buccaneers working in an underhand manner for some foreign government. They are out and out criminals, robbing and killing for self-profit." He paused, then went on, "let me give you the whole picture, Captain. And what I say now I trust both of you will keep your silence." Again he paused, then he took a breath and began, "the ship you have captured is the Brierley Maid, built as a slaver, like this very ship. She was leased to the Admiralty as a supply vessel and was also used for the transport of troops to the American Colonies. Her captain was on his maiden voyage as master but was not, in my opinion, a man for the job. He was a good, pious Christian fellow who relied on persuasion rather than discipline; a man who believed passionately that all men are equal; a man who craved the love of his fellow man rather than their respect and obedience. It was a decision of disastrous proportion to appoint that man master of a ship.

"We departed Portsmouth for Boston but two weeks out we encountered a wicked storm and we were blown off course. Eighteen days later we found ourselves battered by another fierce gale. The first mate and the bosun were washed overboard, and by that unfortunate incident we lost our navigator and our disciplinarian. The captain navigated the ship by dead reckoning but it is my opinion that he was a long way out with his calculations. We were more than four weeks adrift our expected position and running short of water. Apart from the crew we had a hundred or so troopers destined for the colonies and we were each rationed to a pint of water per day. There had been no spreading of canvas during the storms to collect rainwater and when land was sighted the captain put in to a cove regardless of who had right of presence. He sent men ashore to find fresh water and they were accompanied by a troop of soldiers. He allowed the crew gin to celebrate the landing, and that night he posted no lookouts.

"The ship was taken during that night. I know not how but I presume men swam out to the ship where she lay at anchor. I was captured and I expected to be killed, but when I told them I was a surgeon they locked me in a cabin. I was fed once every three days and given water. I was allowed out every now and then, but only when my captors found themselves in need of my services. It was from the men I treated that I learned that when far from land all the other members of the original crew, including the captain, were heartlessly tossed over the side, alive."

The surgeon took a sip of his wine, then he went on, "the plight of the soldiers left aboard was horrendous. They were caught as they slept in their bunks and locked into the aft hold. There were forty-one men down there and they were given neither food nor water. Several of them succumbed but the others made a pact." He looked at his two companions in turn, then he said, again I ask you not to mention a word of this." He paused, then as if reluctant to tell he lowered his voice; "They agreed that when any of them died the bodies should be devoured by the others."

"Cannibalism?" The captain looked aghast.

"They would call it survival." The surgeon continued. "Can you imagine the horror those men went through. Locked in darkness eating a part of a comrade, raw. And what is more, not knowing what part you were eating? On top of that, they suffered the contempt of the pirates for what they did. There are but five come out alive and I am concerned, not only about their physical condition, but their state of mind.

"Now I come to why I am sure you should hang the pirates. If you hand them over when we reach Antigua, they will, no doubt, talk to save themselves. If it becomes common knowledge how the five men survived, those honourable Englishmen will be forever vilified. They will have no future and will be pointed out as the cannibals – the lowest creatures imaginable."

"I could not bring myself to hang a man." The captain shook his head. "I shall have them handed over and let the Naval authorities be the judge."

"Aaaaaaah."

All three men turned and craned their necks to look at the prone figure on the dining table.

"Aaaaaaa." Jamie let out another sonorous moan.

"Well that is a sound of joy to a surgeon." Jack Battle clapped his hands.

"It's a sound of joy to anybody," the captain said. "Even more so to me. That is the first utterance I have ever heard from him."

"What do you mean – ever?" Jack Battle looked puzzled.

"Jamie lad is a mute," the captain said. "Never a sound did he utter. We communicated by the use of my voice and his writing, but never a verbal conversation as such."

The surgeon rose from the table. "Nobody told me that," he said "I could see for myself the muscle wastage down his left side and his facial disfigurement was obvious, but I was not told he was without speech." He went down on one knee and looked into Jamie's face. The eyes were closed. "Making a noise, even a moan, is good. Yes. Very good." He was nodding his head in satisfaction when a knock on the cabin door brought an end to his observations.

Tilly Dickinson put her head round the cabin door. "Could the surgeon please attend Mr Roulette." There was a note of urgency in her voice as she said, "I fear he is near death."

Chapter Thirty Seven

In the light of a full moon the Nestwith parish church stood silhouetted against a cloudless, starlit sky. A gaunt figure placed a finger stick against the lichen gate and leaned over the top rail to rest. Tanner Fanny was a shadow of her former self; syphilis was draining the life from her body and her clothes hung about her feeble frame like pleated sacking. She wore a shawl draped over her head; the material pulled together to hide her pockmarked face. Her dress trailed the ground and was bundled together about her middle, stained with matter that oozed through the cloth from the ulcerated rash that covered her body.

She had been born and baptised in Loylton and her befuddled mind could think only of returning to her roots to die in the place where she had been given life. Her purse held the last of her coppers; enough to buy a meal of broth and dumplings at the Wheatsheaf Inn, and perhaps a pot of ale or gin. Feeling for her stick, she pushed herself upright and set off. She concentrated only on placing one foot in front of the other as she hobbled down the village street. So occupied was her mind she almost walked past the inn. Pulling herself together she went through the stable archway and entered the taproom through the back entrance. She paused at the door and looked towards the barn. A smile creased her haggard face as memories returned; she had romped with many a man on the straw in that place. It brought back to her Monica Woodcock's summing up of their trade, 'you got it, you sell it, and you still got it. It don't eat nothing. It don't cost nothing.

You just makes it handy and sets it to work.'

She was still smiling at her thoughts as she sat at a corner table and looked about at the few others in the room. She recognised only one man. He stared at her, then he made his way between tables towards her.

"Is it Fanny? He said. "Tanner Fanny?"

"Aye, t'is."

"God, I hardly recognise you, woman." He looked at her with disbelief. "You look bad."

"I am bad." She sniffled and wiped her nose on a dirty sleeve "Is Monica about?

Who?"

"Monica Woodcock, you know."

"Nay, lass, thi' won't be seein' 'er again." The man shook his head. "She got her throat cut on the Loylton road, by some buck who didn't like 'er charges, they say."

Fanny spooned up her broth and dumplings and spent her last coins on a mug of gin. She left the inn the way she came in, by the back entrance. Out on to the street, she looked across towards the green, her eyes resting on the stocks and pillory, plainly seen in the light of the moon. She smiled silently but the smile turned to a low chuckle as she recalled the time she had spent pilloried with Monica teasing her and the drovers making her dance for drink. The chuckling ceased and sadness came upon her as she remembered Monica was dead.

She struggled painfully down the Loylton Road and when she reached Maisy Pitchforth's cottage she leant over the side gate to rest.

Glancing up at the sky she realised that she must have slept. The moon had moved across the heavens and scudding clouds blocked the moonlight. She sighed deeply as she felt for her thumb stick and set off along the track through Black Wood. Every now and then she would rest with a hand against the bark of a tree. Her gait became even slower as fatigue set in, every step a tortuous agony. She had reached a stage where the pain was too much and she cared not whether she lived or died. Only her determination to reach Loylton kept her going.

The sound of hoof beats came to her ears but it did not register danger. As the sound became louder she moved to one side of the track to let the rider pass. She felt a sharp blow to her head and fell to the ground.

Awake but feeling no pain she attempted to rise but hands grabbed her and she was roughly dragged off the track and into the woodland. Thrown onto her back she sensed hands fumbling with her clothes. Against a background of the woodland canopy she saw the bulky figure of a man astride her. She began to chuckle as she felt him between her thighs. Her laughter turned to a harsh cackle, becoming louder and louder. She felt a stinging blow to her face but she was past caring and her laughter continued. Then she felt the tickle of a blade beneath her ear followed by a sharp pain as the knife bit into her flesh. Still she laughed, until it ended abruptly in a gurgling dissonance as the blade cut through her windpipe.

The man wiped the knife on her dress then stood and adjusted his clothing. He went to his mount, climbed into the saddle and rode away.

Chapter Thirty Eight

"Now, let me see. What do we have here?" Surgeon Jack Battle held up a lantern, allowing its flickering light to fall on the body sprawled on the bunk. The man lay with eyes closed. Blood, escaping from his mouth, dribbling across his chin to form a gory stain down the front of his shirt.

"Tell me what happened to this fellow." Jack Battle lifted the soiled shirt to check Totton's chest. He saw the wound and asked, "what's this?"

"He was stabbed," Tilly said.

"I shall want to know the details – and I mean every detail. Not like the other fellow. Nobody informed me that he was a mute. Do you know what happened, Mrs, er…"

"Dickinson." Tilly offered. "Mrs Tilly Dickinson. And yes, I was there when it happened. She related how Totton came to be stabbed and by whom. She told of Gunner withdrawing the knife and of Mbungi's sacrifice.

"And what exactly did this Mbungi do?" Jack Battle asked

Tilly told him of Mgumbi holding the wound and keeping pressure on it for several days, and of his chanting to the spirits.

Totton cried out with pain as fingers gently pressed the scar tissue. Then the surgeon whispered, as if talking to himself, "well I'm afraid the witchdoctor has done more harm than good. These people mean well but they deal only with surface wounds. What goes on beneath the skin they leave to their spirits, and unfortunately their mythical physicians have not studied human anatomy. This man has a broken rib, perhaps cut with the thrust of the knife - and it has pierced his lung. Keeping downward pressure on the wound has left the broken bone facing inward. Movement has kept the wound open since then and it has not had a chance to heal." He glanced about the small cabin as he went on, "can he walk? If not he must be carried to the aft cabin. Might just as well have all the wounded in one place."

"Will you want rum, as before?" Tilly asked.

"We shall both be in need of rum, Mrs Dickinson. Myself for cleansing, and he for partaking, - and plenty of it. Opening a man's chest is a painful business and by getting him deep into his cups and out of his mind is the only merciful means we possess."

It was a messy business. Totton began by taking cups of rum in his hands, but soon became incapable and it had to be forcibly poured down his throat. He was tied fast with a band around his forehead to hold his head still, ankles and wrists bound tightly; he was trussed to avoid any movement but, although almost out of his mind with drink, his grunts and agonizing howls of pain rent the air as the surgeon made his cut and probed deep inside the chest cavity.

Jamie was terrified. His head ached, and he had no idea what had happened or what was happening. Bound as he was to the table, but now conscious, his face flat against the table top and facing away from what was going on in the cabin, the commotion sounded to him as if a man was being horrendously tortured. His mind raced to the conclusion that he was to be next. It seemed an age before the cries of agony ceased and when he heard the sound of footfalls coming closer he gritted his teeth and screwed his eyes, waiting for whatever was to befall.

"Hello, Jamie lad." The captain went down on one knee, his eyes close to Jamie's bandaged face. "You have had a troublesome time. We were attacked, Jamie. A cannonball hit the aft cabin and you were rendered insensible. We have a surgeon on board now and he has performed surgery on you. You are bound so you cannot touch your head when you awaken. Do you understand me? You must not interfere with your bandages. If you understand me, blink twice." He nodded when Jamie blinked and released the bindings. Both the patients were carefully carried out of the aft cabin to be made as comfortable as possible in their respective bunks.

The following morning Captain Christopher retired to his cabin, his eyes heavy and body weary. He had been on duty almost all of the night and shortage of crew was beginning to take its toll. Shorthanded before taking the prize and now with five men wounded and the remainder split between the two ships, everybody worked more watches. Fully dressed, he climbed laboriously into his bunk, pillowed his head and closed his eyes. Suddenly the sound of a single, distant crack of cannon fire caused him to sit upright. He rushed out on deck to see Tarquin holding a telescope to his eye and looking in the direction of the Brierley Maid.

"What is it," the captain bawled.

"You had better take a look at this, Captain." Tarquin waited for him to approach and handed him the telescope. "I think justice has being carried out – look to the mizzenmast mainsail yard"

Through the glass the captain could make out four figures hanging by the neck, swaying in unison with the roll of the ship.

"My God!" The captain exclaimed. "Fullerton has hung the wounded prisoners." He looked aghast at Tarquin. "He had no right to take matters into his own hands. I am the captain of this ship and only my word is law....."

"Yes, Captain," Tarquin ponted out, "but he is master of that ship - and on that ship his word is law."

The captain walked to the rail and called to a sailor, "you. Come here. What's your name?"

"Buckley, Captain," the man, answered. He stood motionless, as if he had been addressed by God. Never before had the captain paid him any attention.

Well, Buckley. I shall expect you to have the five prisoners paraded before me in five minutes time."

Buckley remained, unmoving. "What prisoners is them?"

"The men we took from the prize. Come on, man. Make haste to your duty." The captain showed his impatience.

"There ain't no prisoners, Captain." Buckley raised his eyes sheepishly. "They's gone. They's all – er – escaped.

Captain Christopher was about to question when he realised the meaning of the sailor's words. There had been judgement and sentence carried out - the prisoners had gone to a watery grave. "Damn me!" He turned to Tarquin. "Does my word count for nothing? You know what the crew have done, don't you?"

"The crew of any ship become a close-knit lot. So what did you expect? They have lost several of their mates because of those men, and they have seen the condition of the soldiers, and know how they have been treated..."

"Yes, yes." The captain waved a hand, dismissing Buckley. He said to Tarquin, "I shall retire to my berth before further distractions rob me of sleep." No sooner had he uttered the words than Tilly's head appeared above the deck as she climbed the steps of the companion ladder to the poop deck.

"Captain, may I have your ear?" She looked agitated. As he ushered her to the taffrail she said, "as captain of this ship I understand you have authority to speak in God's name at funerals and take religious services. Does your authority go as far as conducting a legal marriage ceremony?"

"Yes, it does. Why do you ask?"

Tilly moved closer to him as if she feared eavesdroppers. "Mr Roulette and I wish to be married as soon as possible. And we would be obliged to you, sir, if you would conduct the service for us."

"Mrs Dickinson," the captain sighed. "In two days' time we shall be in Antigua where there are fine Christian churches, with a passionate priesthood only too willing to unite yourself and Mr Roulette in holy matrimony."

"Two days may be too long, Captain." Tilly said, urgently. "The surgeon told me that Mr Roulette has lost much blood. Since he was wounded he has bled inwardly and the operation has taken from him even more. He said the body had been losing blood faster than it could produce it, and he warned me of the consequences." She paused, then said, in a whisper, "I must tell you that I carry Mr Roulette's unborn child and he urgently wishes to give the child his name. He is the only son of Sir Marcus Roulette and if the child I carry in my belly is male, should Mr Roulette not recover from his wounds, the child could well inherit the baronetcy. Please, Captain. We do not want our child to be born without the blessing of God.

A chair was placed on deck for Totton. Gunner gently carried him from his cabin but the slightest movement brought a wince of pain. He was ashen and his eyes, barely open, looked around for Tilly. She appeared dressed in her favourite dress and bonnet and stood by him, taking his hand in hers.

It was a solemn occasion. Totton was well liked by the crew. They regarded him as one of their own; so all those who could be spared from duty lined the deck as Captain Christopher went through the wedding ceremony. When he pronounced them man and wife Tilly leant forward and kissed Totton on the forehead. She squeezed his hand and a faint flicker of a smile briefly erased the agony he endured.

The captain had previously prepared a certificate of marriage and it was brought on deck with quill and ink and duly signed. Gunner then carefully lifted Totton and carried him back to his cabin.

A few moments later, Lieutenant Jack Battle spoke with the captain, "it is the way of life that happy occasions are commonly followed by sorrowful ones. A wedding in the morning and now I bring news of funerals. I regret having to tell you myself that three of the soldiers have succumbed to the devilish treatment they endured. Of the two remaining, one is near to death and the other, an officer, has a strong constitution and may yet pull through. Should he survive, I ask you to accord him the recognition due to his rank."

"Of course, of course." The captain wiped his eyes with thumb and forefinger. "I will conduct a service for the dead before nightfall but now, Lieutenant, I am going to get some sleep.

"Aaahweeooayow!"

"What in hell's name is that? The captain glanced about to see where the noise came from.

"Don't worry." Jack Battle smiled. "It's our Mr Pitchforth airing his views. Now he has found the secret of sound he is making the best of it." He left the deck and entered the gunroom where Jamie had his bunk.

"Ooooweeaaah."

As Jamie mouthed the unintelligible noise, Jack Battle laughed. "You sound like a castrated bull, lad. But don't worry, I am encouraged by your effort. I have known men suffering a rupture of the brain make noises just as you do, and some have completely recovered their speech. There is hope for you yet, lad." He examined the bandages and then went on, "you can sit up now but do not under any circumstances bump your head." He helped Jamie to a sitting position. "I understand you had no use of your left leg or arm. Can you move your fingers?"

To Jamie's surprise he could clench his fingers to a fist. Upon the surgeon's instructions he tried to wiggle his toes, but without success.

"Early days, early days." Jack Battle was pleased. "Every second day I shall remove the bandages and inspect the wound to make sure no infection sets in. In a few weeks the plate can come off and the bandages removed altogether." He patted Jamie on his shoulder. "I think you are doing well."

The captain had to be roused and reminded he was to conduct a funeral ceremony. The bodies of the three soldiers had been reverently wrapped and stitched in canvas with chain wrapped around their ankles. One by one they were carried to the side of the ship and placed on a board. The captain said a prayer as sailors stood about bareheaded. As the board was tipped he committed their bodies to the deep and a crewman fired a musket in honour of the dead.

It took three more days to reach Antigua. Everybody aboard felt frustrated at the slow progress. Totton was hanging on to life, and Jamie was still making strange noises. When the two ships lay at anchor John Fullerton came aboard the Branston Silver.

"You hanged those wounded men without my permission." Captain Christopher welcomed him with harsh words.

"I could do no other, Captain." John Fullerton was unperturbed. "I thought it wise to do an inventory of what was aboard. During our search the men came across the bones and skulls of imprisoned soldiers who had been starved to death. They also learned from the wounded pirates how the original crew had been murdered by casting them over the side – a sailor's greatest fear. We gave the bones of the men a service and committed them to the sea. Had I not acted in bringing those men to justice, my crew would have taken matters into their own hands. I conducted a trial where each had a fair hearing and then I pronounced them guilty and hanged them."

They had a fair hearing, you say?"

"Yes, Captain."

"And what did they say in their defence?"

John Fullerton hesitated, then he said, "I fear I cannot tell you that, sir. Two were Spanish and the others Mohammedans. I do not speak their language and neither do any of my crew. But I did allow them to speak up in their defence, according to law."

"You allowed them to defend themselves, without understanding a word they said, and then executed them?" The captain expressed astonishment.

"The evidence against them was overwhelming, Captain."

"You had no right to...."

"With due respect, Captain, I had every right. I was master of the ship and in those circumstances my – word – was – law!" He quoted the captain's favourite dictum.

"Yes, yes." The captain blustered. "What about this inventory? Anything worth the pickings?"

"Upon my word, Captain." John Fullerton was grateful for the change of subject. "The Brierly Maid was a naval supply ship. In the holds we found much military equipment, including a thousand of the newly issued muskets. Apart from the arms and accoutrements it was also carrying money, probably to pay the troops. I have not counted it but could amount to a significant sum. As we have performed the rescue of both ship and cargo, I presume, sir, this treasure is included as part of the prize."

"It does indeed, Mr Fullerton. Ship and cargo, as you say." The captain beamed. "I shall ask you to go ashore with me and we will register the ship as a prize. The Royal Navy here will be pleased to take charge of it and receipt the lot. Unfortunately for the crew we will not be paid until it is signed and sealed by the Admiralty in London. We'll all have to wait, but it seems it will be well worth waiting for"

"Will you allow the crew ashore, sir?" John Fullerton asked, but before the captain could answer he continued, "they will not desert the ship with prize money in the offing but they could be pressed, even here, into Royal Navy service. As for going ashore with you, I would ask permission to remain aboard, using the name John Smith, while in these waters."

"How so?" The captain was bemused.

"Because I am still on the reserve list. I was discharged when my hearing deserted me. Now my hearing has returned I may be called back into service. I shall have no excuse – they will presume that if I can be master of a ship – albeit an acting master - then why should I not be instructing gunnery again for His Majesty's navy. I have no wish to return to the service, so I would prefer to remain anonymous."

As they spoke a hunched figure came towards them along the deck. The man walked with the aid of a stick with a sailor on either side assisting him. He wore clothes given him by members of the crew that hung from his gaunt frame like rags about a scarecrow.

"Aaah!" Captain Christopher exclaimed. "An officer of the military, I am told." He and John Fullerton went to meet the man. "Jacob Christopher," he offered. "I am the master of this ship and this is my first officer John – er – Smith." He made a slight almost imperceptible nod of his head. "And you sir?"

The man turned his head away and coughed. Then he said in a weak voice, "Captain..." He turned and coughed again. "Do please excuse me gentlemen." He took several deep breaths, then, "I am Captain Valiant Halgalleon, at your service, sir."

The Brierly Maid was accepted by the Royal Navy and naval surveyors went aboard to check the vessel and the contents of its cargo, allowing all the Branston Silver crew to return. Totton was told of Val Halgalleon's presence and insisted that he be taken on deck to meet him. Two chairs were placed on the quarterdeck and Gunner carried the weakening Totton from his bunk to sit him in the Caribbean sunshine along with Val Halgalleon. They spoke of the times they had at Nestwith and Val told him of his fury when dressed down by Sir Marcus in front of his men. And how he schemed revenge and confessed that it was he who opened Lady Mary's bedchamber door on the night of the ball. He swore to Totton he knew nothing of her penchant for nudity. It brought a smile from Totton but he spoke few words and those he did utter came as stammered whispers, his face screwed in agony with each breath he took.

Tilly joined the two men and held a conversation with Val Halgalleon. Surgeon Jack Battle came to see his patients and to say goodbye. He had been summoned to appear at the Royal Navy offices to be questioned on the capture of the Brierley Maid by the pirates. He checked Val Halgalleon, placing a horn against his chest listening to the heartbeat. He looked closely into his eyes.

" You will survive, Captain," he said. "Eat well and you will be well." He turned to Totton and leaned over him, placing fingers against his neck. He then straightened up and spoke to Tilly, his voice low and sombre, "I am so sorry Mrs Roulette. I did all I could but I'm afraid your husband is now with God."

Chapter Thirty Nine

The Branston Silver lay at anchor in Antigua for twenty-two days. Captain Christopher was a busy man. With Jamie unable to help, he had not only to keep the ship's log but had to write a detailed report of the taking of the prize, for the attention of the Admiralty. A frigate was to embark for England so he speedily penned a letter to Lord Doulain, explaining the situation and included a report of Totton's death.

All but a few members of the crew attended the funeral of Totton. Tilly arranged and paid for a tombstone to be erected at a later date. It was an occasion of deep sorrow.

After the funeral, Tarquin departed for the interior where he continued his mission, but without success. Gunner had acquired a notorious reputation. The sailors, those allowed ashore, frequented the alehouses and spoke of Gunner charging down the deck of the Brierly Maid, slaying all before him. Alcohol stirred imaginations and stories abounded of him having taken the prize single-handedly; fictitious accounts added to his fame and he became known, and referred to, as 'The Gunner'.

Jamie improved slowly. Tilly tended him, removing his bandages every second day, as instructed by Jack Battle. He was beginning to form words but still sounded as if has tongue was glued to the roof of his mouth. He could move his toes and clench the muscle in his thigh, but Tilly forbade him to attempt to walk for fear of falling. When the ship set sail for Liverpool, Jamie returned to his duties as Master of the

Purse. Now, almost four weeks since the taking of the Brierly Maid, Tilly removed the bandages leaving the silver plate conspicuous above the mat of bristle that covered his scalp. She had shaved his beard and his facial appearance was markedly changed. His lower eyelid no longer drooped, his cheek muscles had almost returned to normality; only the corner of his mouth sagged crookedly. As days became weeks Tilly insisted he practise his walk along the deck. He improved so much he discarded his splint, but infuriatingly he could not discard his limp. He could muster little control below the knee and although the ankle stayed firm he had to kick forward the lower part of his leg with every step. When the time came to remove the plate from his head, Tilly carefully cut the sutures and the gut and eased it away from the scalp. Jamie grunted as it came away. One by one she snipped and pulled the stitches from the wounds left by the surgeon's knife, and pressed her fingers gently on the scalp. Jamie gave no sign of pain. As time passed he found he could recall moments of his past. Snippets of memory came to him. At first it was childhood happenings, then vague incidents of his youth, but huge gaps still remained.

At Branston House, his home in London, Lord Doulain relaxed in his sitting room sipping his morning coffee and going through the pile of dispatches that had arrived that morning. Many were pledges; donations promised for his shipbuilding scheme. He chuckled as he thought of Tarquin Willoughby in the Indies, going from plantation to plantation speaking to managers only he Doulain knew had no authority to pledge their masters' money. Presently, he came to a sealed packet of a different nature and breaking the seal began to read. Suddenly he leapt to his feet "Oh my God!" he exclaimed. "Oh God in heaven! Oh, the poor, poor fellow!" He began giving orders and the whole household ran to carry out his instructions. "Quickly," he said. "Quickly - with luck we can reach Oxford by nightfall."

Lawyer Branscombe alighted from his two-wheeled carriage and giving the reins to a groom he approached the front of Nestwith Hall. He climbed daintily and laboriously up the steps to the doors of the Hall where he was admitted. He removed his hat to reveal a scruffy, matted grey wig that perched on his head like a grain of corn on a cabbage. Not only was the wig too small for his head but its curls had unravelled and stuck out on either side like the horns of a mythical demon. He was ushered into the study and walked with tiny steps, placing a foot only the length of his buckled shoe in front of the other. It was a most effeminate gait, holding a folder under one arm and the other arm held wide, hand and fingers splayed, hips swaying with every step.

"I am Joseph Branscombe, attorney at law. I am here to attend and speak to one Russet Roulette." His voice boomed. Sir Marcus had almost forgotten the little prosecutor with the stentorian voice.

"My daughter is indisposed. State your business." Sir Marcus spoke curtly. The man had arrived uninvited and unannounced, and what possible reason could he have to speak to Russet.

"I am instructed to speak only with Russet Roulette" The voice seemed to fill the room.

"I am Sir Marcus Roulette. Russet is my daughter and any business you wish to discuss with her, you may confide to me."

"I have strict instructions to....."

"State you business or begone!" Sir Marcus lost patience. He had no liking for this pompous, self-important pettifogger.

Lawyer Branscombe relented. "I am instructed by Squire William Bull of Bullington House," he said. "I am to disclose certain facts to Russet Roulette regarding the will and testament of said William Bull. The squire is not deceased but it is his wish that Miss Roulette should know his intention.

"As Squire William Bull has no living relatives and no issue, nor is likely to have, he has made a bequest that upon his death, the Estate of Bullington, including Bullington House, the hamlet of Bullington and all lands, buildings thereon, and all his worldly possessions shall become the property of Russet Roulette. It is his purpose to disclose his wish at this time in the hope it will bring her cheer."

"Thank you for bearing good tidings, Lawyer Branscombe." Sir Marcus went to the door and opened it wide, a gesture that could not be mistaken other than that the lawyer's visit was over. "Good day to you." He offered a hand as a pointer to the open doorway and the little man resumed his unmanly shuffle and departed without saying another word.

Russet was writing when Sir Marcus knocked on her bedchamber door. She hurriedly put down her quill. The bump of her pregnancy was discernable now and she moved slowly from her chair to greet him. She wore no veil but had combed her hair forward over her forehead, hiding the left side of her face.

"Do you recall that peculiar little lawyer with the loud voice who acted for the prosecution against you in Loylton?" Sir Marcus asked.

"Could I ever forget him?" Russet looked questioningly at her father.

"He came to say that Willy Bull is leaving you Bullington House and the estate, upon his death. Now is that not uncommonly charitable of the good fellow?"

Russet frowned. Why has he done that? And why tell me now – is he ill?"

"Branscombe says he wishes you to know his intent in the hope it will bring you good cheer." Sir Marcus looked away and frowned. Then he said, "I may be a rustic at heart, Russy, but I have a suspicious mind when it comes to gifts and favours. I have never known a man promise his all without wanting something in return. And even for a friend like Willy, is it not a strange act to disclose such a last bequest while still alive?"

"What could he possibly want?" Russet asked.

"*You Russet!*" Sir Marcus laughed. "I can imagine the way old Willy's mind is working. I shall be cruel to you when I say he covets you – he wants *you*. Our Willy is a lonely man who will seek any opportunity to fill his bed. It is possible that he considers all and sundry will view you as the soiled maiden no other man will marry. Your injuries - your fatherless child to be." He paused and then said, "it would be no surprise to me should Squire Bull ask me for your hand in marriage."

"Never!" Russet stamped a foot. "Never! Never! Never! William Bull is a fine country gentleman but I would slit my own throat rather than be an old man's plaything. If you were to give him permission to ask me I would say no. No! No! No!"

I have no intention of doing any such thing." Sir Marcus was shaking with mirth. "Never would I force a daughter of mine into a union not to her liking."

"Father, I have no intention of ever being married." Russet came forward and hugged him. "I have given great thought to the matter," she said. "I am persuaded that my future shall be that of a spinster. I shall content myself with your gracious company and bring up my child with the help of God and the guidance of its grandfather."

Lord Doulain arrived unannounced at Nestwith Hall tired and dishevelled. His hair was uncombed and he was unshaven. Sir Marcus went out to meet him, accompanied by Charlotte and Katherine.

"Good day to you My Lord, and welcome." Sir Marcus greeted his visitor with outstretched arms. "To what do we owe this pleasant surprise?"

Lord Doulain climbed the steps, straight-faced, unsmiling. "I would speak with you, Marcus." He greeted Charlotte and Katherine then he added, "in your own room, if may be?"

In the study Lord Doulain appeared hesitant.

"Are you not well, Frank?" Sir Marcus said, with concern.

"Marcus." Lord Doulain began but hesitated once more. He was trying to find words to soften the blow but could not bring any to mind.

"Marcus." He tried again. "I have received a missive from Captain Christopher, master of the Branston Silver and I fear I am the bearer of the most saddening news. It is your son, Totton." he shook his head as he stepped forward. He spread his arms in a gesture of hopelessness "Marcus, Totton is dead."

Russet had donned her veil and was descending the stairs when she heard her father's cry of despair. Charlotte and Katherine stood waiting outside the study but Russet pushed past them.

"You are not to go in until you have permission." Charlotte snapped.

"Oh tish, Lottie. Did you not hear Father's cry." Russet entered the study, her eyes going to her father who sat with his head in his hands. Lord Doulain was at his side, an arm about his shoulders. "What is it?" She asked Lord Doulain.

Sir Marcus lifted his head, tears streamed from his eyes. "It's your brother, Russy. He's dead."

Russet went to her father. She discarded her veil and threw her arms about him "Oh, tell me it's not true. Tell me it's not true. Oh it can't be true." She wept as she clung to him. Katherine was sobbing and trembling and she too put her arms about her father.

Charlotte stood in the centre of the room, hands on hips, staring at Lord Doulain with unmistakable hostility. "Swine!" She spat out the word with venom. "Swine!" she repeated.

Lord Doulain, eyes red and misty stood aghast at the outburst undeniably directed at him.

"Those damnable pigs." Charlotte went on. "Where it not for those filthy animals Totton would still be with us." She pointed a finger at His Lordship. "This is your doing," she accused. "You may be a Lord of the Realm but I wonder you have the audacity to come here. Was it not *your* men, in *your* employ, who pressed Totton on to *your* ship." Charlotte showed her fury as she went on, "had it not been for those stinking swine, which you encouraged him to keep, my brother would yet be alive and here with us now."

Francis Doulain said nothing. In the midst of the family grief he had no answer to Charlotte's accusation. He stood with his head bowed. Sir Marcus gently pushed Russet and Katherine aside and got to his feet, his tear-stained face masked in fury. "How dare you, Charlotte! How dare you!" He was about to admonish her for her indecorum when Lord Doulain spoke out, "Marcus, I realise I must bear blame for Totton's visit to Liverpool but I swear to you I had no knowledge of them being pressed aboard my ship." He turned to Charlotte. "The weight of grief strikes in diverse form. I fully understand the way Charlotte sees my role, and if it will ease her grief then I shall willingly bear the burden of guilt, just as I blame myself for the death of my own son. It was I who sent him aboard a ship that sank with all hands. These are actions that once done become possessions of the past and cannot be undone" He went up to Sir Marcus and spread his arms towards him. "Marcus I am so very, very sorry. I shall go now and leave you to mourn your son. I hope that in future we may resume our friendship, for I hold my association with you and your family very dear to my heart."

"No!" Russet stamped a foot. "How could we behave so disrespectfully? His Lordship has come far to give us news and we dismiss him out of hand. Are the Roulettes bereft of all etiquette? Because my sister has a bout of churlishness are we all to let ourselves be tarred with the same brush? We are all shocked by the news but I am sure my father, indeed the whole family, would wish you to remain with us, and we are grateful that it is no other but you, our dear friend, who comes to us with this terrible news."

Katherine was sobbing uncontrollably and still clinging to her father. Russet held Lord Doulain by the arm, as if to emphasise her wish that he remain with them. Charlotte took a deep breath and exhaled with a pursed-lipped whoosh. Then as if coming out of a trance she went across the room to Lord Doulain. "I am so sorry, My Lord. I know not what came about me. I….."

"Words that brings forth shock, oft bring forth shocking words." Lord Doulain reached out and took Charlotte's hand. "I cannot put into words my feelings for all of you at this most grievous time. I can only say that I grieve with you and for you, and I offer you all my true friendship and deepest affection."

Russet squeezed his arm. "I will ask servants to prepare a room for you. Come." She led him towards the door but he held back.

"I almost forgot. I have other news." He fumbled in a pocket and produced a crumpled paper. He paused for a few moments as he perused the writing then he said, "Captain Christopher informs me that Totton took a wife..."

"A Wife?" Three voices questioned in unison. Only Katherine remained silent. She was inconsolable. She could not release her mind to other matters. News of her big brother's death dominated her perception.

Lord Doulain continued, "it would appear that when Totton knew he was dying he insisted on marrying a widow – Mrs Tilly Dickinson. As master of the ship, Captain Christopher conducted the ceremony, as church law allows. The reason for the hasty union seems to be that Mrs Dickinson is pregnant with Totton's child, and your son insisted it should bear the name Roulette. I must also tell you that she is aboard the Branston Silver and is on her way here."

Chapter Forty

It was a place of silence. The servants spoke in whispers. The atmosphere of sorrow enveloped the region as the entire village of Nestwith mourned its loss. Totton's death affected everybody. Sir Marcus was overcome with grief; spending much time at his desk, head in hands. Charlotte did not shed a tear but mourned in her own self-centred way. Russet busied herself consoling her father and caring for Katherine who was utterly disconsolate; from earliest childhood she had looked up to her brother with love and awe, and now found difficulty in coming to terms with the knowledge that he would not come back and that she would never again see him.

Lord Francis Doulain remained as a guest at Nestwith Hall. It was not his inclination to intrude in the family bereavement but Sir Marcus and Russet insisted he stay. He dispatched his coach and horsemen to Liverpool to await the arrival of the Branston Silver with letters to Captain Christopher, Tarquin and John Fullerton.

Sir Marcus was so engrossed coping with his own grief he paid no heed to the anguish of his daughters. Not so Lord Doulain, he spent time with each one, consoling and supporting them as best he could. He walked in the garden with Katherine, saying little of Totton's death. His attempts to change the topic of their conversation to happier matters found limited brief, their exchanges always returned to the sadness they felt.

"Why Tott?" Katherine asked, not looking to Lord Doulain for an answer. "What has this family done to deserve the cruelty of it all? First Russy is attacked and her future ruined, and now our brother is taken from us." She began to weep and covered her face with a handkerchief. Lord Doulain put an arm about her and spoke words of comfort.

The Reverend Butler called and suggested a private offering of prayer for members of the family at the Nestwith Parish church, with a memorial service for Totton to be held later when his wife could attend and all the facts were known.

On the day of the service while the whole family attended church, a messenger arrived at Nestwith Hall with dispatches for Lord Doulain. His Lordship had declined the invitation to be present at the prayers for Totton, insisting that it was a family matter and he had no wish to intrude. Upon opening his letters he discovered that his presence was requested urgently in London on matters requiring his personal attention. His coach and servants were in Liverpool so he ordered that a horse be saddled and said he would accompany the messenger back to London. He left almost immediately, leaving a note for Sir Marcus excusing his departure.

One day in the saddle was enough for Francis Doulain. The luxury of a carriage had softened him and he was so sore he hired a coach for the remainder of the journey. Arriving at his office he was surprised to see extra guards on duty at the door. Everybody seeking entrance was checked before being allowed in, and he himself was held up until he was recognised. He climbed the stairs to the office he had handed over to John Critchley and again an arm was held in front of him barring his way. Two burly guards stood at the door and as one of them prepared to perform a search, Lord Doulain pushed the man's arm away, I am Lord Doulain, "he pronounced. "I will not be subjected to such indignity on my own premises. Out of my way!" He pushed past, opened the door and entered.

Although the door had been tightly closed, John Critchley had heard the muffled sound of Lord Doulain's angry outburst but he did not recognise the voice. Now, as Lord Doulain entered he cringed with terror behind the desk, arms held up, as if to ward off a blow. When he recognised Lord Doulain he slumped back into the chair like a deflated balloon.

"My Lord," he gasped. "For one moment I thought......"

"What is happening, John?" Lord Doulain snapped the question. "Attempts have been made to deny me entrance to my own domain."

"I am glad to see you here, My Lord. I have received dire threats. I fear my very life is in danger."

"Oh, come now, John." Lord Doulain could see the man was deeply distressed. He went on, "how can your life be threatened when you have the protection I have just encountered?"

"It is my stepson Isaac. He has returned and threatened me. He confessed to me it was he who killed his mother," John Critchley was almost beside himself with fright as he jabbered on, "I too have a confession to make, My Lord. Some time ago, to enable me to see the heels of the rogue, I gave my stepson money and arranged work for him within this company in the West Indies. He has told me he was compelled to leave Jamaica in all haste because he had committed murder, and said that killing me would be of no consequence, one more would be of little matter for he would hang for the others anyway." He paused and sighed deeply, then said, "he came to me for money, I was about to submit to his demand when I foolishly let him have sight of my purse. He took it from me and told me it would be no good reporting the incident or trying to trace him for he was living under a changed name and would travel to meet a fellow of his acquaintance who would offer him concealment." He shivered, his shoulders hunched as if a cold wind had swept over him. "I do not for one moment believe him," he said. He is the very epitome of evil and cares too much for the swill-pots of this city. I do not doubt that when he has gambled away the contents of my purse, he will return and demand more."

Lord Doulain walked past the wretched John Critchley and looked out of the window at the bustling, crowded street below. He saw runners delivering dispatches, horse-drawn carriages transporting men of importance, sedan chairs being carried by lung-blown bearers, and others walking to discharge their business, with minders in attendance. His thoughts went back to the peaceful fields and woodlands of Nestwith and he seethed within at the thought that he might now have to return to the restless commotion of the city.

"I have great sympathy for you Critchley," he began. John Critchley immediately took note that the familiarity of his first name had been dropped. Lord Doulain continued, "however, you have committed one of the cardinal sins of commerce by allowing your personal affairs to interfere in matters of business." He left the window and stood before the desk looking down on his terrified manager. "I blame myself for promoting you. I thought you the right man to take charge, but I see I was wrong. You have guards on the main door, minders outside your own door refusing entry to all and sundry, while you sit behind your desk like a cowardly, frightened mouse. What sort of leadership does that convey to the people under your control?" He turned and walked to the centre of the room and looked up at the portrait of his late wife. "You give me no alternative – I will relieve of your post and you must return to the duties you discharged prior to your promotion."

"But I have…"

"It does not matter a jot what you have." Lord Doulain interrupted. He kept his eye on the painting. "What I need is a man of discipline, a man who can command respect. There are many in the Company who show promise but are not yet ready. I can think of no man who could fill the post and relieve me of this burden. He began to repeat the words in a whisper. "I can think of no man….." He paused, and frowned. Then as if struck by some mystical perception, he declared, yes I can! By George! Yes I can!"

The coach entered the village of Nestwith and came to a halt in front of the Rose and Crown Inn. Steam rose from the four sweating animals as they answered to the reins, nostrils flared, hooves stamping restlessly as tensed muscles relaxed. A footman climbed down and hurried to open a door. Seconds later Gunner, hat in hand, squeezed his mighty frame through the gap and looked around at familiar sights. He was instantly recognised by several villagers and children who crowded inquisitively to see the arrivals. Next out of the coach was Jamie Pitchforth attired in a smart new outfit. His face, now back to normality, was unknown to the curious locals and his limp barely noticeable. The other three occupants, Tarquin Willoughby, Tilly Roulette, and the gaunt Valiant Halgalleon alighted and entered the inn to rid themselves of the wearisome effects of travel before making their appearance at Nestwith Hall.

Gunner departed to the smithy while Jamie set off to walk along the Loylton road to his mother's cottage. When he arrived at the gate he felt a sense of trepidation. Would she recognise him? Would she accept that he was her Jamie? He walked round the cottage to enter by the rear door, but as he reached a corner of the building he saw Maisy, fork in hand, tending her kitchen garden. He put a hand against the cottage wall and leant with one leg across the other. For a few moments he stood watching her, then she straightened her back and as she did so she saw him standing there.

"Sir?" she inquired. "Can I be of help to you?" She stared inquisitively at the well dressed, ruggedly handsome young man leaning nonchalantly against the wall.

"Do you not recognise me, Mother? It is Jamie, at last I am home from the sea." He took off his hat, a huge smile creasing his face.

Maisy frowned and let her eyes wander over him. She leaned to her right to look at his left cheek then down to his leg. Her eyes widened as if she were looking at a ghost. "Aaaag!" She let out a yell of delight. "Jamie! It is you! Oh my Jamie!" Recognition brought tears of joy. The fork fell out of her hands as she lifted her skirts and ran to him. Her arms went about him. "Oh Jamie," she cried. "Oh Jamie." It was as if she could find no other words. Then suddenly she pushed him away. "You spoke!" she exclaimed. "You spoke to me. My Jamie has no voice."

"It is all the work of a clever naval surgeon who happened to be at a certain place at a certain time." He held her by the shoulders then brought her to him and hugged her. "With the help of God, that man performed a miracle. He not only gave me back my voice but also returned to me my face and ambulation."

"Ambu what?" She looked puzzled. I shall have to become accustomed to the way you speak." Maisy excitedly ushered him towards the porch.

Jamie was astonished at his own vocabulary. He would have to remember in future to be careful, using only words of few syllables. He answered, "it is a word I learned from the surgeon, I think it means to walk."

Inside, Jamie looked at the familiar room, the same furniture, the beamed ceiling and the huge pot by the fireplace. It brought back memories to a mind that could now recall events previous to his awakening as James Pitchforth.

"Now," Maisy said. "You can tell me all about your wanderings. She pulled a chair from the table and indicated for him to be seated. Sitting opposite she waited for him to begin.

He told her of his abduction and of the voyage, of slaves and of life aboard ship. He related what he had been told of the capture of the Brierly Maid and explained that he had no personal knowledge of the engagement as he had been rendered unconscious by the very first cannonball fired during the battle. He spoke of Gunner and of the attack on Totton and his marriage to Tilly Dickinson. He told how Totton died and he briefly mentioned John Fullerton and also expressed respect and admiration when speaking of Captain Christopher.

"I must tell you, Mother, that my memory is returning. Bit by bit, little by little, my past is coming back to me." He leaned forward and took both her hands in his, he looked into her eyes and went on, "I can remember a journey and being accosted three times on that day. I can remember riding through a forest and I can remember a great storm with branches cracking and crashing about me. There was thunder, and as lightning lit the forest I thought I had a glimpse of a face, an impression, but the features of that face are just a blur in my mind. I can remember that my mount was on the point of exhaustion, but nothing else, not until I awoke in this room. I awoke as your son, Jamie Pitchforth.

Maisy looked wide-eyed and frightened. She dropped her head and when she looked up her eyes were filled with tears. "I lost my husband and my three sons in but one year and now I am going to lose you."

"No, no." Jamie squeezed her hands. "You will never lose me. I shall never forsake you." Again he squeezed her hands reassuringly. "I promise, I will always be a son to you. But I must know how I came to be that son."

Maisy freed her hands and took a handkerchief from her sleeve and blew her nose. She wiped her eyes and then related the events of the night Gunner, Walter and Wriggly brought him to her. She told of her own son's death and how they buried him in the garden, and how the new Jamie took his place in the bed.

"Whoever attacked you meant that you should die, and we were frightened that those who did it would come back to finish you off. We didn't know if you would live, but when you did come to your senses you had no memory of the past. I didn't know what to do other than to carry on as if my Jamie lived."

"You buried your own son in the garden? You denied him a Christian burial for my sake? You did that for me?" Jamie said incredulously.

"I did that for all of us. And at least I know where he is." Maisy's voice then changed to one of bitterness as she said, that rector insisted that my husband and my two younger boys be buried in the paupers plot at the back of the church, with no mark to say where." She began to weep. Then suddenly she said, "do you know who you are?"

Jamie answered her question, "I am Jamie Pitchforth," he said. And I shall remain so until I can fully recall my past. Until then I shall not visit you again here, Mother. I intend to go to the Hall and continue working as a stable lad." Then he asked, How are the Roulettes. Is Sir Marcus well? Charlotte and Katherine? And how is Russet – not married, is she?

"No." Maisy wrung her hands. "Of course, you could not know." She went on to tell him of the attack on Russet and of the scars that marred her beauty. She told how Russet now wore a heavy veil and kept to her room, then, "the unknown attacker not only knifed her but had his way with her while she was unconscious." She looked away and added, "Russet is pregnant and her life is in ruins."

Jamie sat as if stunned. He clasped and unclasped his hands, then clenched his fists until the knuckles showed white. His face was ashen. He trembled with fury.

Three long blasts of the coachman's horn heralded the coming of Mrs Tilly Roulette. Everybody at Nestwith Hall knew of her impending arrival and servants peered inquisitively from windows. Sir Marcus went down the steps to welcome his daughter-in-law while Charlotte, Katherine and the veiled Russet waited at the head of the steps by the entrance. First out of the coach, Tarquin Willoughby shook Sir Marcus by the hand and turned to help Valiant Halgalleon. Katherine gasped when she saw him, her face reddening perceptibly. The two men then stood either side of the coach door as Tilly stepped out, offered a hand and curtsied to Sir Marcus.

At the top of the steps Charlotte stared in amazement. "Oh saints of heaven!" she exclaimed, loudly. "She's black!"

Chapter Forty One

"She's after money, that's what I think." Charlotte made the statement bitterly. "How do we know Totton wanted to marry her – he was ill wasn't he? And how can we be sure Totton is the father of her unborn child?"

The three Roulette sisters were in the drawing room going about their various interests. Charlotte was seated before an easel, painting a watercolour scene of the parkland. Katherine held an embroidery frame as she performed delicate needlework on a fire screen she was making for her bedchamber. Russet sat apart, with needle in hand, sewing a heavy veil to a sun hat.

"What money?" Katherine asked. "Father is always complaining that we have so little. What money could she possibly covet?"

"There is money in the estate." Charlotte insisted. "Now as the wife of the late heir she has come for no other reason but to claim her inheritance."

"Ah! Now we have it!" Katherine laughed aloud. She turned her head to face Russet, "our dear elder sister is jealous. At dinner she has insisted on sitting away from us at the foot of the table in all her glory as mistress of all she perceives. She will have to give up her position to Tilly, for it is she who is the matron of the house now, and it is she who will bear the Roulette heir. And another thing, Totton was the end of the Roulette line and if we have children they will not be Roulettes, they will take the name of their respective fathers. Should Tilly give birth to a boy child, then the

Roulettes go on. You don't like that, do you Lottie?"

"Who is to know the truth?" Charlotte refused to give up. "How do we know she is pregnant? She could well be lying to get Father's approval.

"She already has that." Russet spoke up. "And I like her very much. She adds colour to our drab lives for she is well read and a most intelligent lady. I for one welcome her company and I am pleased to hear that she will stay with us until her child is born."

"May I join you?" All three turned as Tilly put her head round the door then entered without waiting for the invitation. "I am to see your father at ten o'clock so I have time to spare to better know my new sisters." She was dressed not in the fashion of the day but in a style worn in England many years previously, the waistline high and tight below her bosom allowing the skirt to billow out. "Ah, I see you look at my habit," she said. "I fear we are always behind the times in the Indies. What is fashion here does not swim the ocean to become fashionable in Jamaica for many years. I would be so pleased if, in time, you would all help me improve my wardrobe."

"Charlotte thinks you married Totton for money - so you would inherit this estate." Katherine came straight out with it.

"Katherine. How could you say such a thing?" Charlotte blushed. She stared open-mouthed at her sister, as if a confidence had been dishonoured.

"I did not say it – you did." Katherine chuckled, she was enjoying seeing her elder sister squirm.

Tilly did not appear in the least perturbed "I assure you

money is of no consequence." She smiled. "As for this estate, well, my plantation in Jamaica is almost as large and far more productive than these empty fields. I married your brother because I loved him and he loved me. No other reason than that." She turned about and walked to the door with her parting words, "I am sure we will all get on just fine."

When she had departed and out of earshot Charlotte turned on Katherine. "You horrible girl. There was no need for you to repeat my words. What I said was between ourselves."

"Then you should be prepared to say to the face what you say to the back, dear sister." Katherine was growing up, and as age engendered wisdom, her opinion of her sister's attitude matured. She decided her own room was a better place to continue her sewing and got to her feet. "I have had enough of this silly talk," she said. "I wish you both a good day."

"And I suppose you will also leave me on my own, Russet." Charlotte appeared completely unaware that words she uttered could be insulting.

Russet also stood and put away the needle and thread. "Pitchforth is back," she said. "I have sent for him and I will have him drive me, as before."

Katherine was at the door about to leave. "Oh I am so pleased, Russy." She beamed her pleasure. "At least you will get out and about a bit now he has returned. He...."

"Yes, how nice for you indeed, Russy." Charlotte interrupted. "You will not be shy to remove your veil in his company, will you? You with your scars, and he with his crooked face. What fun you will have, the two of you, - comparing your ugliness."

"Thank God the man is a mute." Russet sighed. "At least I won't have to listen to the ugliness of *his* words."

Sir Marcus welcomed Tilly into his study and closed the door. He ushered her to two chairs he had placed by the window.

"Now, my new daughter," he began. "I am assuming you know of Totton's abduction and what immediately followed, so I would have you tell me what occurred in Jamaica and how my dear son came by his death.

Tilly told how Totton came to her rescue and received the knife wound to his chest. She said nothing of Mgumbi, thinking it better not to exacerbate matters. "The name of the man who murdered Totton is Isaac Critchley," she said. "The authorities hunted high and low for him but it was thought he had escaped from Jamaica and his whereabouts was unknown at the time we left Kingston."

Sir Marcus felt hot with rage. "I have a mind to go myself to find this man – Critchley you say?"

"It would not be wise, Father." Tilly shook her head. "If the military and the civic authorities cannot find the man, what chance have you?"

"Of course you are right, my dear, but I feel so helpless." Sir Marcus felt uncomfortable with Tilly calling him Father and he said, "when you refer to me as Father it makes me feel so old. I would prefer you to call me Marcus." She smiled and nodded as he went on, "I know your plan is to stay until your child is born but after that it would delight me to have you stay here as long as you wish."

Jamie held the horse by the bridle and waited at the foot of the steps leading up to the hall. His heart missed a beat when Russet appeared and he felt a glow of excitement at the prospect of her company. She was hatless but wore a veil draped over her head that reached down almost to her waist. As she descended the wide stone steps she held the veil out and away from her body to see her way down the steps. When she reached the last step she raised her head and looked towards the figure holding the horse. Jamie allowed the reins to slip through his hands as he went to help her into the carriage. He walked with his old pronounced limp, throwing his left leg in an arc, as he pretended to imitate his style of the past. He screwed his face, mouth open, jaw deliberately held askew. Head down, he took her hand to assist her climb into the carriage.

"A very good morning to you, Jamie. It is so good to see you back." As he took his seat next to her Jamie sensed her eyes upon him. She sat to his right and throughout the journey to the fallen oak he looked ahead, hiding the left side of his face. Thoughts raced through his mind; how was he to explain that he could now speak and that his facial disfigurement was a thing of the past.

When they reached their destination Jamie climbed down and tethered the horse in the usual place. He put on his stiff-legged limp and again screwed his face. Because of her condition, Russet turned to descend the steps facing the carriage. The veil hampered her view and her foot slipped on the last step.

"Careful!" Jamie placed his hands on her waist to steady her but the expletive escaped his lips in the confusion of the moment.

Russet faced him. "You spoke," she said, holding her hands before her as if to ward him off. "You are not Pitchforth. Where is Jamie Pitchforth? And who are you?"

"I am he," Jamie said.

"You are not Jamie Pitchforth. Jamie Pitchforth cannot speak" Russet was adamant and she felt anger rising inside. "I summoned Pitchforth and no other."

"I assure you, Miss Russet, I am Jamie Pitchforth. By the will of God and a good surgeon I have regained the power of speech. My face has lost its droop and I have better use of my limbs. I may look different but I am the Jamie Pitchforth you always knew. The Jamie Pitchforth that brought you to this place so many times."

Russet was bewildered. "You will have to do better than that," she said. "How do I know you are Pitchforth?"

How do I know you are Miss Russet? Jamie made reference to her veil but bit his lip, thinking he had gone too far.

"Your impertinence appals me." Russet was not convinced. "Tell me something known only to Jamie Pitchforth and myself.

Jamie thought for a moment. Then he said, "did you discover the identity of your poet, Miss Russet?"

Russet stood silent weighing the significance of the question. She said, "show me your hands." She took both his hands in hers and turned them over, palms up. She stared at the healed wound in the centre of his left hand and then the six-pointed star-shaped scar on his right palm. "Then you are who you say." She walked all the way round him looking him up and down. "Other than myself only Jamie Pitchforth has knowledge of that poem." She stopped before him and said, "no, I never discovered who wrote it. It remains a mystery that leaves me with a bitter taste. I find no respect for a simpering coward who skulks behind his own-penned words."

"Why do you cover yourself so?" Jamie asked.

"You know full well why. I am sure your mother will have told you of my misfortune. My looks are no longer for the eyes of others, I am sorely disfigured and not a pleasant sight upon which to dwell." She wandered over to the oak and sat down.

"Take it off Russet – er - Miss Russet." Jamie corrected himself. "It does not become you."

"How dare you!" Russet replied with anger. "Because you have regained your voice does not give you the right to rise above your station."

The only thing I want to see rise is that abominable veil from your head." Jamie did not care any more. Remembering Russet as she was and seeing her now was shocking to him. "Throw it off, Russet. Cast it away. Why cover yourself to look like a mushroom when there is a rose hiding beneath? Take it off and be yourself."

Russet began to rise from the oak. "Take me home," she said. "I will not be spoken to in that manner by a - a stable lad. Take me home at once."

"Not until you have heard me out." He stood in front of her stopping her from rising. "If I am to be dismissed from your service for relaying the truth, then so be it. You are my dearest friend, Russet and I hope you regard me with friendship for it is as a friend I now speak. My mother told me how you keep to your room and shun company. She told me of your reclusion, of your loss of interest in those about you. Well, that is not the Russet Roulette I know. You talk of a poet being a coward hiding behind his own words, but you are doing the same, concealing yourself behind that veil. Cast it off and cast off your self-pity with it. You are a woman of character, a beautiful woman that mere surface scars cannot efface. You are Russet Roulette so stand up and be Russet Roulette. If there are those who do not like what they see, well, let them all go to hell and damnation."

For a few moments Russet was rendered speechless. Not since her father had scolded her as a child for jumping off the rafters of a hay barn had anybody spoken to her with such reproach. She looked up at this peasant and at that moment she felt a sense of disquiet. He was right in every way. She put out a hand. He took it and helped her to her feet. They stood close to each other as she slowly raised an arm and lifted the veil. She held it for a second above her head then tossed it over her shoulder.

"There Master Pitchforth," she whispered. "Does that satisfy you?"

"It satisfies me greatly, Miss Russet."

She put a finger to his cheek and wiped away a tear. "Do you know, my friend, I do believe you are crying."

Adam Gunner sat on the anvil and looked around at the tools of his trade lined in rows on rails attached to the smithy walls. His eyes followed the lines of racked metal to the huge bellows and the forge over which he had sweated for the most part of his working life.

"Well, is your mind set, Gunner?" Walter Lupton leant on the shaft of a hammer. "Are you stayin' or leavin'?"

Gunner shook his head and said, "until I went to Liverpool, I'd seen nothing and nobody but the folks in Nestwith and hereabouts. Now I've seen some of the outside world and I have a yearning for more. I'm going, Walter. I don't know where, but I don't mean to spend the rest of my life hammering away here when there's adventures to be had out there."

"You let me 'ave the smithy then?"

"I won't be selling it 'cos the land it's on is mine by law. I'll rent it to you, Walter, tools an' all so's I have something to live on when age creeps up on me – if I lives, that is."

In the study at Nestwith Hall both Sir Marcus and Tarquin Willoughby studied letters they had received by express from London.

"His Lordship has taken it upon himself to instruct me to instruct you, Tarquin. The audacity of the man astounds me." Sir Marcus laughed and went on. "He requires your presence in London with all haste. You are to take his coach and leave immediately. Then he goes on to ask me to accommodate Captain Christopher until His Lordship arrives here - whenever that may be. He says it will take some days for Christopher to unload his cargo and deal with Customs and Excise and he has dispatched instructions for him to come here. Can you imagine a man with such gall – he treats my home like a common tavern – and we as his lackeys."

Tarquin looked grim. "That is more or less what he states in his note to me. I presume I am to go before him to explain my failure." He shook his head and added, "I doubt I shall receive any payment for my puny efforts, but I shall go there with my head held high and ask why he sent me on such a futile errand."

Russet knocked and entered the study. She held a neckerchief in her hand and waved it as she said, "good day to you, Father Roulette. Good day to you Mr Tarquin Willoughby." She strode across to her father and kissed his cheek then performed a fleeting curtsey to Tarquin and went to the window. "I hope the weather keeps fair." She stared at the sky. "Oh tish!" she exclaimed, and stamped a foot. "I fear the clouds are closing in. I did so hope rain would not attend this day."

Sir Marcus stood amazed. Russet had discarded the veil; she had tied her hair back to reveal her scars and her eyes shone brightly.

"And a very good day to you, Russy." Sir Marcus uttered his wish as if it was an afterthought. He remained standing in shock at the change that had come over his daughter.

"Ah, there he is! There he is!" Russet left the window and headed for the door.

"There is who?" Sir Marcus enquired.

"Pitchforth, Father. - I must go" Russet went to the door and with a wave of her neckerchief she departed, leaving her father open-mouthed and bewildered.

That night Russet sat in her bed, back propped up against pillows, arms clasping her tucked knees. Her eyes were fixed on a point of nowhere between herself and the ceiling. Why were things so different now Jamie had returned? What was it about him she found so attractive – no – not attractive – likeable – that was it – likeable? He was quite handsome – no, not handsome – manly – yes, manly. But he had one leg thinner than the other and he limped. Her thoughts raced. That did not really matter. He can speak now but he does not sound a bit like the peasantry. How can it be that his mother has the local dialect but Jamie, her son, speaks as we do? I must remember to ask him. She opened the drawer of her bedside table and took out a well-creased paper. She knew the poem by heart but she read it yet again. Who? Who? Who? She had come to hate the mystery and now she spoke aloud to the poem, "whoever you are I thank you for composing such wondrous words, but I doubt you would write verse to me could you see me now." Her restless thoughts kept her awake far into the night.

For the next few days Jamie was at the foot of the entrance steps waiting to take Russet for her morning drive. This particular morning she was ready and waiting as usual and, as she began her descent, a groom held the reins while he went to meet her. He took her hand and helped her negotiate the steps and into the open carriage.

Within a few minutes of their departure another coach arrived from the direction of Nestwith village. It was followed by a contingent of troopers on horseback and later a platoon of foot soldiers in their red tunics, marching in time, muskets shouldered, and bayonets fixed.

The coach carried two civic dignitaries who alighted,

adjusted wigs, and put on their braided hats to display the badge of their officialdom.

"To what do I owe this visitation?" Sir Marcus had little time for what he referred to as 'pretentious pomp'.

The larger of the two answered, "I have the authority of the court to search all buildings and properties within the parishes of Loylton-cum-Nestwith, and all woodlands, fields and other land in this locality. It is my wish that you will permit this intrusion, but I must warn you, Sir Marcus, I am ordered by law to carry out the wishes of the court. Should entrance be denied then I have warrant to enter your premises uninvited and with force if necessary."

"Of course you can enter, but I surely have the right to know why?" Sir Marcus placed himself in front of the two, blocking their way.

The shorter man came forward and took off his hat. "Sir Marcus," he said. "I apologise for this intrusion but there have been robberies and dastardly murders done. We search for the murderer and we must leave no stone unturned. Yesterday morning, three miles south of Loylton, a post chaise was brought to a halt by a masked man at pistol point and the driver shot dead. The mail was taken and passengers robbed. The attacker escaped. Yesterday afternoon another coach was found with the driver and all occupants robbed and killed. Two were shot and the other three dead of sword wounds. If you venture forth, Sir Marcus, you would do well to go accompanied and armed."

"Is there a description of the attacker?" Sir Marcus stood aside to allow the search.

The man shook his head. "We have little to go on. A passenger who survived the attack said she could not see his face but that his legs were long in the saddle, so we could be looking for a tall man."

Soldiers entered Nestwith Hall and searched every room, moving furniture searching cupboards and wardrobes, tapping walls with muskets butts, lifting rugs and carpets, even probing up the chimneys with their bayonets. When they had finished they trundled off to the stables and outhouses to continue the search.

Russet and Jamie were oblivious to what was going on at the hall. Jamie was performing an imitation of his old self. With fingers pulling down the left side of his face he walked with a stiff-legged gait round and round to laughter and applause from Russet.

He sat beside her and looked up at the sky. "I think, perhaps I should take you home, Miss Russet," he said. "The sky is darkening before time. Even though we make way now I doubt we will escape a soaking."

"I am not yet ready to go home." She spread her arms." I spend so much time at home and I just love being here with…."

"With me?" Jamie waited for her reply.

"I was going to say with – with – with. Oh very well, with you. But only because you make me laugh."

As they set off the rain began to fall. He took off his coat and put it across her shoulders. Then he took his hat and pulled it down over her head with both hands Her hair was tied back and as he squeezed the hat onto her head it rested on her ears, pushing them outward. He laughed. "You look like a little lost goblin," he said.

Soon the rain became heavier, shafting vertically in the windless air until they both became very wet. Because of Russet's condition Jamie could not hurry and kept the horse to a walk. He was worried she might catch a chill but Russet appeared unperturbed. She kept turning to look at him. She sat close and the touch of him sent shivers up her spine and gave her a strange feeling of excitement in the pit of her stomach. She laughed at herself and began to sing.

Sir Marcus was becoming increasingly worried for Russet's safety now he had news of a murderer at large. He stood at the open door attempting to peer through the mist thrown up by the pouring rain. He was joined by Charlotte who came to him with a shawl about her shoulders and holding out another for him.

"She is a fool going out in this weather in her condition." Charlotte pulled the shawl tighter round her shoulders.

"It was fine when she set off." Sir Marcus made the excuse. "Another five minutes and I shall send for a mount and start a search."

"Listen!" Charlotte put a hand up and cupped an ear. "What is that?"

They stood silently as the strains of Greensleeves came through the mist. It was a duet as Jamie and Russet sang in harmony. As they came into sight, Sir Marcus and Charlotte saw the pair, Russet wearing Jamie's hat, brim drooping with the weight of water, her wet clothes clinging to her body and clearly showing the bump of her pregnancy. He, in only a shirt and breeches, both wet to the skin, and each holding high an arm as they ended the ballad and broke into fits of laughter.

"Just look at her, Father," Charlotte said with disdain. "She sang to a king, then to a pig and now she sings to a horse. I tell you, her mind is crazed and she will finish up like Mother. I do not know why on this Earth you allow her to go with that ignorant oaf."

Sir Marcus handed back the shawl to Charlotte and said, "he might be a peasant and a mere stable lad, Lottie, but this is the second time that fellow has given me back my daughter.

Chapter Forty Two

Valliant Halgalleon was not a well man. His physical condition had improved but his mental health remained in a state of depression. Nightmares persisted and even during daylight hours his mind was fixed on the horrors of his imprisonment. He knew he could not stay at Nestwith Hall. He had no wealth or other assets, and as a soldier of the King he had only a meagre annual gratuity, so his fondness for Katherine could come to nothing. He left Nestwith with Tarquin, bound for London and a new life.

Tarquin helped Halgalleon settle into lodgings and now he climbed the stairs of the Company Doulain offices in low spirit. He had to face Lord Doulain to report his failure to carry out his assignment. He paused at the door before knocking. Money was his foremost thought, and he was sure that the noble lord would reduce, or even cancel, his promised gratuity. He knocked and waited for an invitation to enter. Briefly, he hoped his request for entry would be declined. He felt an urge to turn and walk away.

"Enter!" The voice from within resonated authority.

Tarquin entered to see Lord Doulain behind his desk, head down, perusing papers. He looked up and when recognition dawned he almost leapt to his feet.

"Tarquin, my boy. How good it is to see you." He came around the desk with both arms outstretched. "Well done, young man, well done indeed."

Tarquin was taken aback. Perhaps His Lordship was not aware of the fruitless result of his mission. "My Lord," he began. "I apologise to you for my ineptness. I have failed you and…"

"Failed me? Failed me?" Lord Doulain interrupted. "Tarquin, my boy, your mission has been an astounding success."

"But My Lord, I did not bring any accretion to your cause. My time was wasted in discussion with managers and overseers who had no authority to donate." Tarquin shook his head in dismay. He was now sure the man standing before him had no knowledge of his fruitless efforts.

Lord Doulain produced a claret jug and two silver goblets, putting them down on a small table. "It was my intention that you would come home with the purse empty," he said. "I sent you on an impossible mission since I could not tell you of the plan I had in mind lest you inadvertently revealed my purpose." He made a gesture towards a chair and Tarquin sat down, still feeling uncomfortable.

"I knew you would speak only to managers of the plantations, but that is exactly what I required of you." Lord Doulain filled the two goblets, then continued, "let me explain." He took hold of the claret jug. "Here we have Lord George." He took a sip of claret and pushed his goblet to the centre of the table. "And here we have Sir Henry, both owners of plantations in the Indies. I could not approach either of these gentlemen personally, or for the matter, any other wealthy men for donations; never would I go cap in hand to ask for money. In the first place I would debase myself by holding out a begging bowl, and secondly, they would without doubt, take great delight in sending me packing. And that is not to mention the tales they would tell of how they were able to put down the Lord Doulain. It would have lowered my standing, and I would have come away with nothing.

"With great care I planned my course and spun a web of mendacity." He chuckled with pleasure. "All I wanted was a bright young fellow and a few trusted whisperers. The whisperers were easy to come by, and then you came along to look after Russet and I knew you were the man for the job. Your integrity and incorruptibility brought about the desired effect. You spoke to the managers of plantations and you thought you had not succeeded, but as soon as you departed their company what did they do? They did their duty and put quill to paper to inform their masters that an emissary of Doulain had paid them a call – and wrote to them of your request.

"Now we come to these two gentlemen of note." He pointed to the claret jug and the goblet in turn. "Lord George would dearly wish to deserve an earldom and Sir Henry desires more than anything to be created a peer of the realm. Both ambitious men, dwelling in large country houses filled to the brim with expensive furniture and exotic artefacts. They throw parties and balls to show off their affluence, and invite, not their friends, but people of note who are likely to further their aspirations. Improving their station in society is the corpus of their desire - that above all else. So, I choose Sir Henry. My whisperer conveys to his ear that he is being spoken of as a cheapskate because he has not donated to the building of ships to protect his cargoes. He is also told that

Lord George and many others have already given pledges –
which, of course is not true - but he does not know that.
Rather than be disgraced in society Sir Henry sends me a note
pledging his gift. I then send another teller of tales to the
broadsheet writers, and low and behold there it is in print for
all to see, Sir Henry has donated, not the true amount, but
through my instruction, printed as treble his promise. Lord
George reads of Sir Henry's charitable patriotism and follows
suit for he has no option but to do so, or fall from grace. Many
others followed and Sir Henry, seeing the false account of his
generosity ups his pledge to the broadsheet printed amount.
You thought your endeavours had fallen short but were it not
for you my effort would have failed miserably." Lord Doulain
took a drink and continued, as it stands at this time I have
received pledges enough to build a seventy-four gun ship of
the line and half a frigate. What say you to that, Tarquin
Willoughby?"

Tarquin was speechless. He shook his head in disbelief.
He was overawed by the sheer cunning of the man. No
wonder, he thought, this shrewd, likeable fox was one of the
most respected and wealthiest men in England.

Lord Doulain raised his glass. "A toast to you Tarquin, my
boy, and might I say - to us - for it is my wish that you will
assist me in other ventures. The Orient is ripe for the picking
and, I believe, undiscovered treasure abounds there." He
smiled and went on, "I promise never again to send you
chasing a barren purpose, and if you will offer your service
we shall go about making you a man of wealth."

Lord Doulain sat back in his chair and Tarquin was

amazed at the change that came over him. His mood of exuberance changed to one of melancholy.

"You may think I look with disdain upon those from whom I have perfidiously extracted monies for this cause. That is not so. I have the greatest respect for the Lord Georges and Sir Henrys of this world and I envy them."

You! - Envy *them*?" Tarquin was about to drink his wine, his lips spluttering at the rim. "How could you possibly envy such men?"

Lord Doulain sighed and said, "until recently I thought I was lord of all I surveyed. Then I lost my son and I realised that wealth alone cannot bring happiness. It also came to me that although I have many acquaintances, I have no true friends. The house I live in was purchased by my grandfather, my father lived there and I was born there. I spent most of my life in this very room and while the Lord Georges and Sir Henrys put their riches into stately homes the Doulains bought and built ships and invested money where it would make more. I meet many men, but they come to me for reasons of business. There are those who wish me to invest in their schemes. There are those who ask to borrow money. Some I oblige, others I shun. The ones I turn away I see no more, the ones who borrow I see blatantly avoiding me for fear I shall call in their debt. Then I paid a visit to Nestwith Hall and met Marcus Roulette."

Lord Doulain filled the goblets again and continued to speak, "I am ashamed to say that the purpose of my visit was to deprive this good gentleman of his home and his living, yet to my surprise I found this honest fellow wanted nothing from me but my friendship. I have come to have a great fondness for the Roulette family and they have invited me to visit again. That is why I now envy those with their country homes. It is an escape from a life of small and gross deceptions to downright honesty, and I long to go back for more."

Captain Jacob Christopher was embarrassed. He stood at the foot of the steps leading up to the doorway of Nestwith Hall with a feeling that he was rudely imposing on the hospitality of Sir Marcus Roulette – a man he had never met. He had dismissed his hired coach and watched for a moment as the coachman steered the two horses round the carriage turnabout by the stables and came past him on the way out. His sea chest by his side and gunnysack in hand he glanced around for help. All was quiet and after spending most of his working life sailing vast oceans he could not recall ever before feeling such a sense of distraction. He had been commanded by Lord Doulain to go to Nestwith Hall and remain there until ordered otherwise, but this was the home of another and he felt he was an intruder without an invitation.

"Captain Christopher!" The call came from the doorway and the captain looked up to see a figure hurrying down the steps, hand stretched out and followed by a host of servants. "Captain Christopher, I do beg your pardon, sir. We did not expect you until later. I am Marcus Roulette."

"And I beg your pardon, Sir Marcus" The captain shook the offered hand. "I hired a coach to get here and the owner insisted on an early start in order make the best of what daylight he could for his return." At the head of the steps the captain stopped. He said, "Sir Marcus I find my position embarrassing but my orders from Lord Doulain were that I should remain here until his arrival. I do feel acutely embarrassed that I am here uninvited by your good self."

"Think nothing of it, sir." Sir Marcus patted the captain on the back. "You are very welcome here and we are delighted to have you to stay with us. I assure you we are all looking forward to your account of events aboard the Branston Silver."

At dinner that evening Charlotte claimed her usual place at the foot of the table. Sir Marcus took the head with Tilly and Russet on his right and Captain Christopher and Katherine to his left. With the eating done it was usual for the ladies to withdraw, but on this occasion Sir Marcus allowed them to stay to hear what Captain Christopher could tell them of Totton's part in the voyage of the Branston Silver.

Pipes were lit and port served to the men, then the captain began, "firstly, sir," he addressed Sir Marcus, "may I offer my deepest and most sincere condolences on the death of your son. It is a guilt I will bear for the rest of my life, had I not given orders to press men in to my service, your son could well be alive this day." He paused then went on, "my bosun informed me that he had been told by a harlot – a certain method of seeking out sailors – that four sailors lurked in a nearby tavern. He took your son and the other three men and brought them aboard. It is usual practice to lock men away until we are well to sea before releasing them. Because my crewmen were a'feared of the one they call Gunner, I kept them shut down for two days. It was only then discovered that three of the pressed were men of substance. The other appeared to be a cripple." Again he paused and puffed on his pipe and took a sip of port. "We suffered strong winds and it was not possible to think of turning back. As it was, I had taken aboard four of the most admirable men a ship's master could wish for.

"Because of his rank as a naval officer I appointed John Fullerton my first mate. Gunner is a skilled metal worker so he joined the carpenters and sail makers. Totton was unskilled so he became one of the crew. By the time we reached Jamaica he was as adept as any and scaled the rigging and shinned up the footropes out onto the yardarms as good as any well-seasoned mariner.

"I was not present at the attack upon your son but Mrs Roulette will no doubt have recounted the details of that foul deed. After we left Jamaica we were attacked by a pirate ship. I am not ashamed to say that as master of a merchantman my knowledge of naval strategy is small, so I promoted John Fullerton in my place whilst I played my part in other ways. He, meantime, is a fine man to have in such a situation. He had trained the crew in gunnery during the voyage until they were honed to an edge that would have matched any disciplined naval gun crew. Fullerton fooled the pirates, made them think we were surrendering to them, then blasted them to hell – if you will pardon the expression ladies. It was then that Gunner jumped aboard and charged into the rogues cutting them down like a scythe through corn stalks. But the hero of the engagement was Totton Roulette who stood on deck with musket balls flying about his head and kept up a barrage of the most accurate shooting I ever witnessed. Such was his marksmanship that none of the pirate crew dared approach the helm and their ship went out of control. I am sad to say that I later learned from the surgeon we rescued, that the constant recoil of the muskets against Totton's shoulder opened up the old wound to his lung from which he did not then recover."

As the captain paused there was a silence around the table as if everyone paid reverence to son, brother, husband and friend. Then the captain went on, there was also another I should mention – a heroine of the hour, I would say. While Totton kept the wheel deck clear, Mrs Roulette was behind him, risking her life to load and reload the muskets for her man. I have never seen the like, nor shall I ever again. There she was, kneeling on the deck, ramrod between her teeth, loading powder and shot again and again with musket balls coming at her but never once did I see her flinch or be distracted from her self-imposed task."

All eyes went to Tilly but she said nothing and sat with her head bowed, hands clasped.

"You mentioned four admirable men." Russet said. "What could possibly be admirable about Jamie Pitchforth?"

"Aaah!" The captain puffed his pipe then said, "when I saw Pitchforth I knew not what to do with the man. He was so crippled he could not stand on a rolling deck but had to crawl his way for fear of going over the rail and into the sea. I gave him what menial work I could but he was no more than a passenger – a non-paying one at that! One day he was cleaning the aft cabin, I had taken the noon sighting and was about to calculate our position – a task I have never relished – when, by signs, he indicated that he would do it, and by George, he did. I found he could write down the figures I gave him and calculate our position in a fraction of the time it took me. From that time on Jamie became our navigator and I tell you a more skilled pilot never sailed the seas. At landfall, it is the usual practice to take sights to establish the ship's position and then steer a course along the coast to the port or harbour of destination. Not so when Jamie navigated. We came over the horizon and there in front of us was the port. The same when we sailed to Kingston – there was the harbour and we sailed straight in. So good was he that I appointed him Master of the Purse. A position he filled to good account."

"But Captain," Russet insisted. "Jamie Pitchforth is an illiterate peasant worker he can neither read nor write. How could such a person navigate a ship when he has never been to sea?"

"Not write? Not read?" The captain put down his pipe. "I can assure you that the Jamie Pitchforth I know is not only literate, the man is a scholar. We held converse on many topics and he is a far more educated man than I."

"Then we must be speaking of two different people for the Jamie Pitchforth we know was mute and could not hold a conversation with anybody." Russet thought she had found the answer.

"We conversed by my voice – I asked the questions, he wrote down the answers to my questions and vice versa. By the time we reached Jamaica there was hardly a scrap of clear paper left aboard. However, with the very first salvo of the engagement with the pirates Jamie was struck on the head and rendered unconscious. We thought him lost, but on board the Brierly Maid, the pirate ship we captured, we found imprisoned a naval surgeon who operated on Jamie's head and gave him back, not only his senses but also his speech and his appearance."

Russet shook her head. "I cannot believe that Jamie Pitchforth is literate. I have been in his company so many times and he has given no indication that he possesses such a skill."

"I assure you Miss Roulette, Jamie Pitchforth is a learned young man. Not only can he write but he has a gift for writing poetry. So much so th......"

"Poetry!" Russet stared wide-eyed at the captain.

"Why yes. I read some of his verse but I fear it was a little too deep for my thoughts. When the cannon ball hit the aft cabin it tossed the furniture about and Jamie's papers were strewn across the deck. I spent some time sorting them and I came across a poem he had not shown me. I intended to return it to him but it went from my mind. I do believe I have it here" He fumbled in a pocket and withdrew a leather wallet. From it he took a piece of paper and unfolded it.

"I surmise he wrote this before he regained his voice. It seems to be a prayer of sorts. It is as if he is asking the gods to help him speak to the woman he loves. I feel sure Jamie would not mind me reading it to you. He reached over and pulled a candelabra closer and held the paper under the light.

"It reads thus." He began...

Oh soul of guile why dost thou cast me in a cloak of shade
And cover me in pain of trouble due.
When practiced vent doth preach such great resolve,
In truth, I fail to overcome a fear of that which I would
do.
So take my hand and turn aside capricious nerve
That I may bite the lip of wanton rhyme,
And falter not to temper words that shape my cautious
tongue.
Come, free my mind, my heart, my love,
For there may be no other time.

Russet put her hands on the table and pushed her chair back. She held out a hand to the captain. "You say Pitchforth penned the poem?"

"I did say that, and I know his hand so well I can vouch for it." The captain held up the piece of paper and with a quick movement of her hand Russet took it from him.

"It is such a beautiful poem I must copy it." She headed for the door.

"Russet!" Sir Marcus called after her. "How dare you leave the table without my permission? And do you think it not rude to leave our guest..." He might just as well have spoken to the walls, for Russet was gone.

She climbed the stairs quickly and entered her bedchamber. Rain rattled against the open window and wind billowed the curtains into the room. She went to the window and closed it and by the dim light of one candle she went to her bedside table and took out her poem. She lit another candle and placed it with the other to give more light, and then she held the two pieces of paper side by side and compared the writing.

For a few seconds she stared at the written words then she looked up "Jamie Pitchforth?" she asked herself. "Jamie Pitchforth?" she repeated incredulously. Then with venom in her voice, "Jamie Pitchforth!"

Chapter Forty Three

It had rained incessantly for four days. The earth could take no more and the parkland was dotted with pools of water. Sir Marcus rubbed condensation from the window and peered through into the gloom.

"Is there no end to it?" He turned from the window and spoke to Tilly. "I doubt you will ever have seen such weather, my dear. I had words with Thomas Chatterton, yesterday, and he tells me the river is running at such a height he is a worried that it will flood the piggeries."

"There is nothing you can do about it, but wait until it ends, Marcus." Tilly gave him one of her radiant smiles. "There is a beginning and an end to everything in this world. We have seen the beginning so now we must exercise our patience until the end."

"I cannot find enough patience, Tilly. Since you told me my son was murdered, the name Isaac Critchley is etched forever on my brain. I cannot exercise patience until I see the man hang. I had a mind to go to the Indies to search for him, but as you keep telling me, if the authorities there cannot trace him, what chance have I?" He rubbed again at the window with his sleeve. "My God," he exclaimed. "A rider comes. On a donkey. In such a rainstorm. He must be out of his mind and wet to the very skin."

Ten minutes later a houseman knocked on the study door and entered. "There is a man come with a message for you, Sir Marcus. He will speak to no other, and he is in a wet and filthy state."

"I will see him shortly. Ask cook to see that he has food and drink. Any man who rides through this weather deserves a reward." He busied himself for no more than a minute, pretending to sort papers on his desk, then said, "please excuse me Tilly, I must see what this fellow is about."

The messenger stood near the kitchen door, not daring to venture further for fear of dripping water from his coat or spreading mud from his boots on Jossy's clean flagged floor. The relief on his face was obvious when Sir Marcus appeared and he could turn away from Jossy's forbidding glare.

"I got a message for you, Sir Marcus," the man said. "I been told to ask a priest to attend Squire Bull and to tell you of his accident, like."

"Accident?" Sir Marcus frowned, inquiringly.

"Aye, his housekeeper says he fell from his horse and 'is life's ebbing. She said to get the vicar from Loylton but when I asks for him, I be told he's away somewheres. I rode up to Nestwith 'cos the squire needs to confess his sins and wants absolvin', like. The curate said the rector was ill with boils on his tender – his – well, down there." He nodded several times, then went on, "the curate says the doctor can't get to see the rector 'cos the beck's a'flood. When I asks the curate if he'll go to see the squire he said he would on the morrow. I told him he wouldn't get up the road from Loylton bridge to Bullington with a horse and carriage because of the state of the road. He said he would with God's help." The man ceased his gabble and paused for breath.

Sir Marcus said, "if my friend William Bull is in need of succour then I too shall visit with him on the morrow." He turned to leave then took some coins from his pocket and handed them to the man. He frowned and asked, "you say the way is not good from Loylton to Bullington?"

"Aye, sir." The messenger pocketed the coins and touched his forehead. "The squire never spent a penny on that track and it was bad afore the rain. Now, with the river in such spate as I have never seen, the roadway is under water and runnin' a mighty torrent. I kept m'self to the high ground to get as far as the Loylton bridge." He sniggered, then said, "if that Snufty goes by carriage he'll be needin' more than God's help to get 'imsel along that track."

It rained continually through the night. In the morning Sir Marcus donned a caped, oiled canvas raincoat and high knee-boots. Katherine called out to him as he was about to leave. She was still in her night attire with a blanket about her shoulders and she held out an object, "father," she said, "your pistol."

"I won't be needing any pistol." He laughed. "What fool would venture out in this weather, awaiting some other fool to ride by? And by what wizardry would a highwayman keep his powder dry?" He took another coat from the stand and draped it over his head and shoulders. "I have a knife" He patted his side as if to assure himself the weapon was there. "That should guarantee protection enough."

"Russy thought she was safe and look what happened to her." Katherine was adamant. "Here," she said. "I have loaded it for you and it's not cocked. You could wrap it well and put it in your saddlebag. Please, Father."

Sir Marcus reluctantly took the pistol, tucked it under his

coat and then he took his leave and walked through the downpour to the stables. Dawn was breaking as he discarded the cover over his head, put on a wide-brimmed hat, mounted his horse and set off.

There was not a breath of wind as he made his way through the teeming rain. Riding along the Loylton road he noticed murky mud-disturbed tracks, signifying the recent passing of a wheeled cart or carriage. Wet and now miserable, wishing he had postponed his journey, he approached the Loylton bridge. Here the river overflowed to form a lake that covered the road and spread wide, devouring fields and hedges like some ravenous monster of nature. Ahead of him a man stood in an open carriage cracking a horsewhip, bringing the lash down again and again on the back of a distressed animal as it strained in the traces. The carriage was held fast, one wheel almost covered by water, the other up to the axle in the overflow.   The man had steered the horse off the waterlogged road and into a ditch. Now he blamed the animal and punished it for his own failings.

Sir Marcus gave the stranded carriage a wide berth as his mount waded through the high water. He recognised the driver as the curate, Isiah Snufty, but lowered his head and hid his face behind the brim of his hat.

As he approached the bridge the curate called to him, "you!" The squeaky utterance was almost inaudible. "You!" The curate repeated his call for attention. "I am a man of God about God's business."

"You!" Snufty called again, a note of desperation in his voice. "I am to give a dying man absolution….." His voice was then lost in the roar of rushing water.

Sir Marcus said nothing. Not even for a man of God did he intend to dismount and wade up to his waist in water. He kept his head down and urged his horse up the cobbled slope of the bridge. As he reached the crown he felt the old structure tremble and fear struck him as he glanced over the stone parapet at the gushing water below. The river was a raging torrent; the two stanchions of the bridge cutting the rushing flow like the bows of a boat. The horse was reluctant to go further. It tossed its head and backed down the slope of the bridge. Sir Marcus then saw upriver a monster, uprooted tree surging towards him. He heeled the horse violently, urging it forward over the crown of the bridge, down the slope and into the floodwater on the opposite bank. No sooner had he left the cobbled surface than the tree hit the bridge like a great battering ram. He watched in wonder at the power of nature. It was as if the incident was happening in slow time; water piled up behind the tree and it was swept sideways against the bridge. The weight of water and tree proved too much for the ancient structure. It began to bend and crumble then succumbed and collapsed, crashing into the swirling torrent in a surge of spray. The tree, turned with the force of the current, slowly made its way through the breach to continue on its way, leaving behind a great gap where the span had been.

Peering across the river Sir Marcus could just make out the figure of Isiah Snufty, arms held high to the heavens, praying to his God and still upright in the bogged-down carriage. He turned away and made his way to higher ground, and continued towards Bullington. In his mind he was thinking that William Bull would not find absolution this day.

Bullington House was in a state of dilapidation. The original building had been built of timber and wattle but the wood had long since rotted away and constant remedial work and additions over the centuries had produced a hotchpotch structure that denied it period status.

As the hooves of the horse clattered on the cobbles of the open courtyard the rain eased to a drizzle. Sir Marcus dismounted and led the animal to cover in the stables. He took off the saddle and blanket and when curiosity got the better of him he opened the saddlebag and checked the pistol. It was dry. He put it back, fastened the straps, then ran across the courtyard and hammered on the door.

A dowdy little woman opened the door. "Yes?" she said

"I am Sir Marcus Roulette of Nestwith and I am here to visit my friend Squire Bull." Sir Marcus was not going to wait for the permission of a serving woman to enter so he pushed the door and went in.

"Is there a priest with you?"

"No, The bridge is down at Loylton and I fear no priest will get here for days."

"Days'll be too late." The woman adjusted her bonnet and closed the door. "He's first door on't offside at top o't stairs." She shuffled away, signifying the conversation was over.

Sir Marcus entered the darkened room and found the stench almost overpowering. William Bull lay in the bed, his head propped up on pillows and the covers pulled up to his chin.

"Willy," Sir Marcus whispered. "My friend, it is Marcus. I

am indeed sorry to see you so indisposed."

"Marcus." Willy Bull tried to push himself up but gave up and flopped back on his pillows. "I fear I am badly. Is there a priest with you?"

"I am afraid not, Willy. I doubt a priest will get here for some time. I only managed to cross the Loylton Bridge just before it fell into the flood." Sir Marcus was about to sit on the edge of the bed but changed his mind.

"I must confess my sins, Marcus. I must. I must." Willy Bull's face was crimson with effort. "I have sinned most grievously. I must ask for absolution. I must. I must. I fear the fires of Hell, Marcus. I greatly fear the fires of Hell"

"I am not acquainted with church law about such matters, Willy. All I can suggest is that I hear your confession and repeat it to a churchman as soon as may be." Sir Marcus had a great affection for his friend and was sure the confession would be of trivial misdemeanours.

"I killed my own wife, Marcus. I poisoned her. I gave it her in her food until she died." Willy Bull blurted out the confession. "I must be absolved from my sins and I fear there is little time."

"My God, Willy. I think you do need a priest." Astounded, Sir Marcus thought perhaps this was only the ravings of a dying man.

Willy Bull kept on talking, "remember I told you once that when I married Agatha she said that she would not perform like the beasts of the field?" Sir Marcus nodded. Willy Bull continued, "I went to London with your brother, Oliver, and he introduced me to gambling and whoring. He had money and I had little. I lost what I had at the tables and there was a man at the same table who also lost. I was in my cups and this fellow persuaded me to join him. We acted feloniously, Marcus. We committed highway robbery – many times. I wanted to give up but he discovered where I live and that I am a magistrate. He threatened to tell.

"Who is this fellow?" Being told his brother was involved aroused Sir Marcus' interest.

"His name is Isaac Critchley."

At the pronouncement of the name Sir Marcus felt a chill up his spine and the hairs rose at the nape of his neck. "And where is this fellow now? Do you know?" he tried to make his voice sound natural.

"He's here. He came but two weeks gone. Calls himself Isaac Craven now. He's living in the keeper's cottage. He asked for money. I put him off and told him I would have some for him later." He inhaled deeply, then said, "he is the cruellest devil I ever met. Not only does he rob, he takes delight in killing men in a strange manner. He strips his victims and then pegs them out like a crucifixion and leaves them to die. He did it to a man in Black Wood but I think the foxes and badgers got him 'cos I heard no more of that fellow." He coughed, a deep raking bark, cleared his throat then reached for a cloth and spat into it. "I must go on Marcus," he insisted. "There is more - I must confess everything.

"I satisfied myself with a harlot, in Nestwith and I slit her throat in case she'd recognised me. I did the same thing to another in Black Wood not long gone."

Sir Marcus was trembling now. "And Russet?" He whispered.

"God forgive me Marcus it was a mistake. I have seen my lawyer and left everything I have to her. It is the least I can do to atone. I swear it was a mistake. I had my eyes on a serving wench who works at The Rose and Crown. She was in the habit of visiting the Pitchforth woman and I thought it was she. I have suffered Marcus and now I'm dying with syphilis. I swear to you on my soul I would never knowingly have done that to Russet."

"But you helped with the search, Willy. We spent the whole day looking for her and yet during that time you knew where she lay." Sir Marcus felt a cool calmness come over him. "You could have led us to her

"I know Marcus, I know. I thought she was dead. It is something I shall regret for the rest of my life."

"Then you will not regret it for long." Sir Marcus snatched the pillow from beneath the sick man's head and slammed it down over the startled face. He held it as the man wriggled in an attempt to get free. Sir Marcus glanced towards the door then pushed his elbows into the bed at either side of the writhing form to hold down the threshing arms. He looked again towards the door for fear the housekeeper might enter. The movement beneath him got less, and less, until the figure lay still. Sir Marcus held the pillow over the face until he was sure the man was dead. He then lifted the head and pushed the pillow back in place, straightened the bedding, and left the room.

When he reached the foot of the stairs he met the

housekeeper who held a tray on which stood a steaming bowl of soup.

"My friend sleeps," Sir Marcus informed her. "Best leave him to rest." He placed a hand on the woman's shoulder to guide her away from the stairs. "Do you know," he said. The Squire has just made a strange request. He has asked me to shoot some ducks and give them to you. He said you would roast them and......"

"And fry the breasts in duck fat." The woman interrupted. "It's his favourite fare."

"Then I must see to it. I fear he is very ill and if that is his wish, then I shall endeavour to do his bidding. Could you direct me to the keeper's cottage?"

"Him!" The woman screwed up her nose. "He's new and I don't care for the man. There's something evil about him."

"Yes, but where can I find him?"

"You goes back towards Loylton for 'bout half a mile and you'll see a ride goin' up through the woods. It's up there. Can't miss it."

Sir Marcus saddled his horse. His mind was infused with a fierce but cool determination. He took the pistol from the saddlebag, checked it thoroughly then pushed it, uncocked, into the belt holding up his breeches. As he set off the heavens opened up again and he could hear the distant rumble of thunder.

The keeper's cottage stood back from the track. He dismounted and tied the reins fast to a gatepost. Under his coat he cocked the pistol then walked up the path and rapped his knuckles on the door.

A voice called, "go to the back."

Sir Marcus walked round the side of the cottage to an open porch. A door beyond opened and a man came out. He was tall, with a mop of mousy hair, long nose and sinister blue eyes of such paleness the irises seemed to merge with the whites. Sir Marcus had an eerie feeling those eyes were penetrating his very soul.

"Mr Craven?" Sir Marcus asked

"Who wants to know?" It was a southern dialect

"I am come from Squire Bull," said Sir Marcus, innocently. "Are you Mr Craven?"

"Aye, I am he. What of it?"

"The Squire is ill in his bed and has asked me to give you a purse. Wages I suppose, though it weighs heavy to be sure."

"Well where is it?" He held out a hand.

"I have it in my saddlebag if you would….." He got no further. The man, ignoring the rain, pushed past him and strode down the path. Sir Marcus followed, taking the pistol from his belt and holding it behind his back and under his coat. He was shaking with excitement. Trepidation crept into his mind. Had Katherine loaded the pistol properly? Had the powder become damp? What if it got wet when he took it from under his coat? What if it misfired? If he failed the man would surely kill him.

The man began opening the straps of the saddlebag, his greedy mind concentrating on his objective.

"Isaac Critchley!" Sir Marcus shouted the name.

The man swung about, his startled eyes staring into the barrel of the pistol. Sir Marcus pulled the trigger and the charge went off. For what seemed an age the man remained standing but a black hole had appeared in place of his right eye. The back of his head exploded in a mass of blood, bone and brains as the ball sped on. Slowly he crumpled to his knees and remained in that position, head slightly cocked, shoulder resting against the hedge, with what was left of the grey, bloody soup of his brains draining away to mingle and discolour the rivulets flowing down the track. Startled by the report the horse shied only for its head to be dragged down by the fastened reins; its eyes wide, nostrils flared and pulling to get free. Sir Marcus calmed the animal and once it had settled he turned back to his task.

It was done. Sir Marcus stared down at the kneeling figure. He felt neither regret nor remorse, his mind likened it to exterminating a rabid rat. He kicked the kneeling body and it toppled over. He removed Critchley's shoes and stockings and returned to the cottage. There he placed the shoes near the door and the stockings in the parlour, over the back of a chair. He checked the front door and bolted it from the inside. His mind was cool and calculating, a man would not go out without his hat, so he picked up the one hat from the stand screwed it up and stuffed it in the pocket of his coat. Nobody would know how many pairs of shoes a man possessed, so leaving the shoes created no problem. Keys? A search and he found keys to the cottage near the front door. Rope? He found what he wanted in an outhouse so he locked the rear door, and went back to Critchley's corpse. He tied one end of the rope around the chest and threaded the other through a ring on the saddle then mounted and set off dragging the body behind.

The rain was now torrential and the flow of water down the track made dragging the body an easy task. Flashes of forked lightning breached the gloom, claps of thunder exploded to the ear like bellows from Hell. Sir Marcus, head down steered the horse in the direction of the river. Periodically he glanced back to be sure the body was still there and he silently congratulated himself for thinking of removing the shoes and stockings. They would have been the first objects to be dragged off and he had no wish to leave a trail.

The roar of the flooded river could be heard long before he saw the rushing torrent. Sir Marcus dragged Critchley to where the bank was high and the water gushed in great waves between two rocky outcrops. He untied the rope and rolled the body to the edge of the bank. Searching through the pockets he threw whatever he found into the river. He took a ring from the man's finger and tossed that into the flood. The hat and the keys he removed from his own pocket and cast them far into the murky water. Then he stood back and put his foot to the corpse and pushed it over the bank. He watched as it rolled over the rocky surface to be swept away by the raging current. It disappeared from sight. An arm broke the surface, then it was gone.

Sir Marcus turned away from the river. He felt drained of all strength and emotion. After taking a few steps he fell to his knees and clasped his hands. A tremendous flash of lightning cracked like an enormous explosion of gunpowder. The lightning bolt struck a nearby tree and it came crashing down, hitting the ground with a resounding crunch. It was followed by an ear-splitting crack of thunder. Sir Marcus took off his hat and lifted his face to the sky. Rain lashed his eyes but he kept them open, ignoring the stinging shafts. "Oh Lord," he called out. "I have sinned greatly this day. I have taken it upon myself to take revenge, when vengeance is thy due and solely thy preserve. I ask for thy merciful forgiveness, oh Lord. What I have done this day no man shall ever know. What I have learned this day will go with me to my grave."

Flashes of forked lightning lit the gloom. The heavens crashed with thunder. The deluge and the roar of the torrent added to cacophony of sound. The noise was deafening, but Marcus Roulette heard none of it as he clasped his hands and bowed his head in silent prayer.

Chapter Forty Four

It was a period of frustration for Russet. At first she resolved to face Jamie and chastise him for leaving her to guess who had written the poem, but the constant downpour forced her to put it off. Her condition prohibited her from leaving the hall, and she had no wish to venture forth while the dreadful weather prevailed. As the days passed she came to look upon her discovery in a more positive frame of mind. The poem was, after all, an expression of love - but Jamie Pitchforth? Her thoughts raced; firstly, disappointment that it was not some gallant, wealthy suitor who would carry her off to a life of bliss and everlasting love. Then she came back to reality; what man of substance would want her; scarred, used, and pregnant with the child of some unknown blackguard. But Jamie Pitchforth? The captain had spoken very highly of him and called him a man of letters. How could a peasant quarry worker write such words? How could he have learnt to navigate a ship? She paced back and forth, hand on chin, trying to fathom an answer. Suddenly she stopped, looked around at the walls and then summoned a chambermaid and ordered that all her mirrors be reinstalled.

"You are very restless, Tilly." Katherine attended to her embroidery while her sister-in-law sat opposite, reading a book. Every now and then Tilly would place the book down, rise, and go to the window to hold back a curtain and peer out. "I worry for your father," she said. "He was expected back before nightfall. Darkness is drawing in and there is no sign of him. With a murderer, or murderers, afoot it is not safe for any man to travel alone."

"He has his pistol," Katherine made her statement as if she were trying to convince herself of her father's safety. She added, "Father is no fool, he can look after himself."

A maid knocked and entered "With the master away, cook wants to know what time you will take dinner, and where to serve it, Ma'am. In the dining room or on trays?" The woman waited by the door.

"How do you know the master will be away?" Tilly asked.

"'Cos Jossy told how he'd gone to Bullington, and there's news the Loylton bridge is down - swept away in the flood. If he's comin' back from Bullington he'd 'ave to go another nine miles downriver to cross ower to this side. That's another, er, er, lot further"

"We shall have dinner served at the table as usual, and thank you." Tilly took the decision and dismissed the girl.

"That is that then," Katherine declared. "Father won't be back until tomorrow. He will stay with his friend, William Bull, and I have no doubt they will empty a few bottles between them tonight."

Sir Marcus Roulette had, in fact, other matters on his mind. He had returned to Bullington House to be told by the housekeeper that while he had been away, seeking the gamekeeper, Squire Bull had passed away in his sleep. He was invited to stay the night but declined the offer. He lied to the housekeeper, telling her he had searched but could find no sign of the man in the keeper's cottage, and then he set off for home. A distance of fifteen miles separated Bullington from the packhorse bridge near the hamlet of Grassworth. Darkness was closing in as he dismounted and led his horse across the narrow span. In the evening gloom he glanced over the parapet almost expecting to see the body of Critchley floating by in the turbulent current.

At the other side he mounted once more and pointed his mount in the direction of Loylton. He had travelled but a short distance when a man stood out in the highway, hand held high. Sir Marcus hauled on the reins, his hand going to the straps of his saddlebag where his unloaded pistol lay.

"It be all right Your Worship" the man called. "I be 'ere to warn 'ee. There be felons about 'tween here and Loylton and, with respect, Your Worship, 'tis but a fool what travels alone."

"Are you offering protection," Sir Marcus asked. He knew no felons would bar his way this day.

"Aye, sir." The man shouted his eagerness. "I 'ave a lantern." He held the lamp high. "I could lead the way wi' this."

"Then do so." Sir Marcus commanded him. "Take hold of the bridle and lead me to Loylton and I will give you thruppence."

The man hesitated then he said, "my charge is sixpence, Your Worship, thruppence to Loylton and thruppence back."

"But I am not coming back." Sir Marcus knew what was coming.

"No, Your Worship, but I is. You be askin' me to walk you there for thruppence, and walk back for nowt?

"Thruppence it is or I go alone." Sir Marcus eased his mount to one side to pass but the man moved across to block the way. At that Sir Marcus took the unloaded pistol from his saddlebag.

"Thruppence it be then sir." At sight of the pistol the bartering had ceased abruptly. The man took hold of the bridle and set off.

Sir Marcus attempted to relax but found he could not do so. He began to shiver, not because he was wet and cold, but from delayed shock at the thought of the enormity of his own actions. He had killed two men and although he was sure they fully deserved their fate, he had, nevertheless, taken the law into his own hands and twice committed murder.

Upon arriving at Loylton he directed his guide to the George and Dragon Inn. There he took a room, but first paid the guide the sixpence fee he had demanded. He ordered hot water, rum, and sugar to be brought. When alone he sat before a blazing fire and sipped the rum laced with hot water and sugar. He topped up his drink again and again and, as the fire burned down to embers, his alcohol-befuddled mind dismissed the deeds of the day. Eventually, he lurched across the room and flopped onto the bed and slept.

Russet carefully questioned Maisy about Jamie's education but all she got was that 'he had always been a bright boy'. Maisy shrugged off further probing and would say no more. The rain had ceased; Sir Marcus was home but in such a subdued mood that the whole household found difficulty in approaching him. He either sat with his head in his hands or paced back and forth, head down as if in a trance. Russet knew that Lord Doulain was due to visit and she hoped he would shake her father out of his state of torpidity.

At last she could venture out. The sun had been shining for several days and dried the land, so she sent for Jamie and her carriage. She stood at the head of the steps looking down as he handed the reins to a groom and awaited her. It was as if her heart missed a beat at the sight of him but she dismissed the feeling, putting it down to her excitement at being able to tell him she knew he wrote the poem. He took her hand to assist her climb into the carriage and at the touch she felt a fluttering, a thrill of excitement as a strange sensation gripped her. She ordered him to drive over the hill to the fallen oak.

Russet chatted away about the weather and how she had longed to be out once more after the storms. As he handled the reins he looked ahead, but she kept glancing sideways at him, wondering why she had so looked forward to seeing him, and why she enjoyed the company of a man of such humble origins. Upon reaching their destination Jamie helped her down from the carriage and they walked to the fallen oak. He threw a blanket over the timber for her but before she took her seat she turned to him.

"Jamie," she began. "You have been my confidant since you first came to my acquaintance, so you must be the very first to know - I have discovered the writer of the poem."

Jamie looked at her with eyes wide, his expression one of surprise. "Well," he began. "I…"

"Yes," she interrupted him. "I am so happy, Jamie. I thought I had only a life of spinsterhood before me and now I am to be married."

"Married? To whom?" Jamie was lost

She ignored his question and went on, exuberantly, "it

means my child will have a father. Oh Jamie, I have never known such happiness."

"But –er -Russet," Jamie stammered. "It was…"

"The Reverend Alexander Butler," she interrupted. "I obtained a copy of his writing and compared it with the writing of the poem. It was he without doubt. Just think of it Jamie, I shall be Mrs Butler the Rector's wife. Mrs Butler! Oh joy! And if we are speedy with our arrangements my child will be born in wedlock. What do you think of that, Jamie Pitchforth?"

Jaimie was dumfounded. "You cannot marry – that – that - man," he stammered. "The Reverend Butler – never! It was not he that wrote the poem."

She came close to him, her fists clenched. "No Jamie Pitchforth!" Through clenched teeth her voice hissed, "because it was you! – You! – You! – You! – You! – You!" As she uttered each word she thumped a clenched fist against his chest. "You deliberately left me mystified. Are you not aware of the unease you occasioned me? Did you not think to tell me of your contrivance?"

She was standing close to him and he placed his hands on her shoulders "I could not tell you," he replied. "I could not speak to you then – remember? I did once try to admit the sin of attempting to tell you of my affection for you, but you took my meaning to the vantage of others."

Russet did not try to dislodge his hands, nor did she move away from him. She felt strangely secure with his hands upon her. "Your poem was sad but it was written of a love that could never be returned." She looked up into his eyes. "Do you account me so highly, Jamie?"

A flicker of a smile crossed his lips as he said, "I have loved you, Russet, since my lips first touched yours."

She thrust herself away from him. "You take too much upon yourself, sir. Your lips have never touched mine. I cannot imagine any such horror." As soon as the words came out she regretted having uttered them.

Jamie noted the title, 'sir'. "Yes," he said. "It was horror indeed. My lips did touch yours but you knew naught of it"

"Oh, I am so sorry, Jamie." She moved closer to him. "It had for a moment slipped my mind that you breathed life back into me." Again, the closeness of him filled her with a strange infatuation. "I read your other poem and it…"

"What other poem?" he looked bewildered. "I wrote but one to you, and placed that very one on your pillow. I wrote no other. You say you received a second?" He was speaking sharply.

"Ha! I have you worried now." She laughed, and without thinking she put her arms around his waist, the bump of her pregnancy pressing into him. "You think perchance I have another suitor?" Then realising her brazen behaviour, she pushed herself from him and turned away. "I think you had better take me home now," she said.

Below the entrance Jamie helped her down from the carriage and she took his arm to assist her ascent of the steps up to the hall door. "Same time tomorrow," she said, as he turned to go. She remained just inside the door and watched him as he drove away. "What are you doing?" she said aloud to herself. "Russet Roulette, what are you doing? Surely you have not fallen in love with a stable lad."

She spent a restless night. Thoughts of Jamie filled her mind; her imagination ran wild. She could never marry him, but why not promote and develop a secret affair with him? - Yes. - Why not? - She would now be compelled to remain unmarried so why not encourage him. - He was, after all, the only man she could trust with such a secret - and nobody would ever know. After the baby is born why should I not enjoy a passionate relationship? - If not, I risk going through life without knowing the joys of love. – Love? – Could it be that I am in love with him? Yes, she determined, I do believe I am. But, what if he were to beget me a child? - How would I explain that? Her mind accepted her musings at first, and then almost immediately denied them. So confused was she that morning light was bursting through the curtained window before she finally slept.

She was late rising and hurriedly dressed to go out. In the entrance hall she peered out of the doorway but Jamie had not arrived. Sir Marcus was about to enter his study when he saw her silhouetted against the light of the open door.

"It would be wise for you venture forth for only a short period, Russy." He came forward and looked past her. "If your driver is late I shall punish him. I will not tolerate tardiness with regard to you."

"No Father," she quickly assured him. "I am early, not he late."

"You are in great hast to take your leave." Sir Marcus, smiling, looked at his watch. "What time is your man expected?"

"I have already admitted to being early, Father. My enthusiasm may be marked down to my being only four weeks from the arrival of this." She patted her abdomen. "I shall be confined for a period of time, so I shall make the most of it now and get out in the open while I may." She tried to hide her excitement and was pleased when she heard the rumble of wheels and the creaking of leather harness as her carriage arrived.

They travelled to the fallen oak and when it came to alighting Jamie held her hand to help her down, but once her feet touched the ground she put her arm through his and held him close as they walked the short distance to the old tree.

When seated she began the conversation, "Jamie, I have but four weeks to go before I give birth to this child I carry. I shall be in confinement for some time and I shall have to feed it regularly so I will not see you, - unless I can find a wet nurse – but when my confinement is over I would wish that you and I...." She faltered.

"You and I, what?" Jamie was smiling.

"That you and I could – secretly of course – could – could be...."

"Wanton?" Jamie offered. His smile had become a wide grin, but he was astounded at her suggestion.

"I was not going to say that." She pouted her lips.

"Are you suggesting that you, Russet Roulette, the daughter of Sir Marcus Roulette, would seek passions of the flesh out of wedlock?" Jamie could hardly keep a straight face.

"You make it sound dirty," she answered.

"It is not exactly a lily-white activity. To flaunt your wares as a single woman." He laughed aloud and stood to face her.

Her voice was tinged with misery as she said, "you may well laugh, Jamie Pitchforth, but circumstances prevail that make it unlikely I shall ever marry."

"You could marry me." The words came out with such eagerness he knew he had acted too swiftly.

"Ha! Marry you! Oh my God! Jamie you amaze me. How could I possibly marry you? The lady of the manor and the stable lad? I ask you." Russet threw back her head and laughed. She mocked him, and secretly she was pleased; her suggestion had placed her as the petitioner but now she could take the initiative. She continued with her rejection of his offer, "You ask the unthinkable. Mrs Butler would have been bad enough but - Mrs Pitchforth?" Then with her face screwed with mock revulsion, "Mrs Pitchforth!" She thought she had settled the argument but Jamie was standing before her, hands on knees, doubled over with laughter.

"You may well laugh," she said, "but you are also forgetting the essential detail. In your class - I mean the peasant class – a daughter brings little income in to a family household and providing a suitor is somewhat acceptable, the parents are only too pleased to get her off their hands and into marriage. In my station it is very different. A daughter cannot marry without the consent and blessing of her father, guardian, or in some cases, when the parents have died, the brother."

She began to rise and as Jamie went to help her he said, "that is the trouble with your class. The daughter of a family of - er – my class can marry who she chooses. The father will usually agree. In your case you are the prisoner of your father's will – not the freedom of your own. You will marry a man, not for what he is, but for what he has. If I were a man of wealth would you accept me, Russet?"

"Well, you are not a man of wealth. How much do you earn as a stable lad – sixpence a day or eight pence? What home could you provide for me – a hovel by the river where we could live on pig offal and bring up my child in penury? Be realistic, Jamie, asking me to forego privilege for poverty is an implausible proposal. And could you ever, in your wildest dreams, imagine my father giving *you* his consent and his blessing to marry *me*?"

"If I ask your father and he gives his consent, will you marry me Russet?"

"That is silly talk and I will have none of it." She began to walk towards the carriage.

"You have not answered my question," he insisted. "If your father gives his consent and blessing, will you marry me?"

She stopped and looked at the serious expression on his face. "Oh yes." She laughed. "Were my father to give his consent for me to marry you, a peasant, then yes, I would gladly marry you. But it can never come to pass. Why, even in your poem you admit that we live on opposite sides of the hill. And if you did have the feather-brained impudence to ask my father, he would have you thrown off the estate."

On the way back Jamie whistled and hummed happily but Russet felt uneasy. She had put him in his place and yet he appeared to be in a joyous mood.

"What have you to sing about," she asked.

"Because I am happy," he replied. "What man would not be happy when the woman he loves has accepted his proposal of marriage?"

"I did not accept…"

"Oh yes you did." He was emphatic. "You said you would marry me if your father approved."

"I have told you Jamie, that can never be. It is out of the question, he would never give his consent."

"We will see when I ask him, then." Jamie did not have to wait for her reply. It was instant.

"Don't you dare! Oh my God! Don't you dare! You wouldn't do that to me, Jamie." She was pleading now but annoyed by the smile on his face. She was not sure if he teased or not. "You would make me a laughing stock if you ask him."

He did not answer her but pointed a finger. "Look," he said. "His Lordship has arrived." As the black coach with its footmen and outriders pulled in front of the entrance, Jamie steered off the drive and onto the grass to negotiate a circle and come up behind the larger coach.

"Well, Russet, "Jamie grinned. "Now is as good a time as any."

"Don't you dare ask Father." She gritted her teeth and gave him the darkest of looks. "Don't you dare, Jamie Pitchforth."

With attendants ranged behind, Sir Marcus, Tilly, Charlotte, and Katherine waited at the foot of the steps to welcome their visitors. Lord Doulain emerged from his coach and turned to assist Emma Fitzhamilton. His Lordship saw Russet seated in the carriage and waved his coach on for Jamie to come up to the steps. Sir Marcus and Lord Doulain assisted Russet and they began to make their way up the steps. Russet glanced over her shoulder to see Jamie following. She shook her head at him with gritted teeth, her whole being expressing fear of what he might do. She was aghast when Jamie did not approach Sir Marcus but came up behind Lord Doulain.

"My Lord." Jamie called.

Lord Doulain turned, one foot above the other on the steps. "What is it?" He demanded, impatiently.

Jamie stood before him and with an exaggerated flourish took hold of the brim of his hat and swept it off his head. "Good day, Father," he said. "I fear you are going to have to kill the fatted calf."

Chapter Forty Five

It was as if time stood still on the steps of Nestwith Hall. At most four or five seconds passed, but to all present it seemed an age. Everybody stared at the man standing before Lord Doulain. Nobody moved; it was like a tableau in stone. Charlotte stood with arms folded, lips compressed with an 'I-knew-it-all-the-time' expression on her face. Tilly and Katherine stood on either side of Russet, their assistance in check. Russet paused, mouth open, her hair had come unravelled and now fell over the left side of her face. She tossed her head and attempted to blow it away through the side of her mouth. Sir Marcus was level on the steps with Jamie. The content of the spoken words had not penetrated his mind and his face expressed annoyance that a mere stable lad in his employ should address his noble guest so brusquely.

Lord Doulain looked down on the figure before him, but it was Emma Fitzhamilton who broke the silence, "it's James!" she exclaimed. "Oh heaven preserve us! Frank, it's James!"

"James?" For a second Francis Doulain appeared not to understand, then, "James?" He came down a step and looked into the face. "James?" It was as if he could not apprehend the significance of the moment. Then recognition dawned. His arms went out, all composure gone. "James! James! My son! My son! Oh my son!" He was like a man possessed. He threw his arms about Jamie and hugged him. Tears streamed from his eyes. "It's James, Marcus. Emma it's – it's. He stammered. "Oh, I don't understand any of this, and I don't care. I have my son again. He's alive! He's alive!"

Questions flew around in the sitting room at Nestwith Hall, but Jamie insisted on the presence of Maisy, Captain Christopher, Gunner, Albert Wrigglesworth and Walter Lupton before he began his explanation. They were sent for and when all were assembled James Doulain took the centre of the room and began by addressing his father, "you may recall, Father, a decision was taken at short notice that I should travel to the Port of Liverpool to join the Branston Gold and sail in her to the West Indies with the intention of purchasing land adjacent to our own. I carried with me a deal of money for that exchange. As it turned out, the plantation in question was the very property owned by Mrs Roulette - who was then Mrs Dickinson. We acted on news that her husband had died in a riding accident and we wanted to add the property to our own.

"I set off by coach but we were attacked on two occasions. On the second encounter I made my escape on one of the coach horses. My attackers were indeed resolute in their intent, as if they knew I carried riches. I was pursued and I left the main highway in the hope of shaking them off. I can remember a great storm and recall entering woodland I now know as Black Wood. I presume my pursuers caught up with me but I have no recollection of it. And as that is all I can tell you of the incident, I will ask Gunner to relate to you what then followed.

Adam Gunner told of finding a man in Black Wood and explained the circumstances. He spoke of how he discovered the man was alive and took him to the nearest shelter; Maisy Pitchforth's cottage. All eyes turned to Maisy as Gunner recounted the events of that night; of the death of her son Jamie; of his burial in the garden and of the injured man taking her son's place. He ended, "Mistress Pitchforth swore us to secrecy and none of us has spoken of it since. For her sake I petition you all to hold in trust what I have said."

James Doulain spoke again, "I awakened as Jamie Pitchforth. The blow to my head erased all memory of my past life. As far as I knew I was Jamie Pitchforth and Maisy was my mother." He turned to Lord Doulain, who sat red-eyed and in awe as events of that night unfolded. "Maisy Pitchforth saved my life and I will be forever grateful to her, and I shall always regard her with great affection."

He turned and faced the assemblage. "I thank Jacob Christopher for his friendship and I shall be eternally grateful to Surgeon Jack Battle, who performed a miracle and not only gave me back my limbs and my looks, but also restored my memory. You may all ponder why I did not disclose my identity, but I had good reason to remain silent. Since my return I have slept in the stable barn and not ventured into the village. I have done this to safeguard Maisy, because of her incredible generosity in sacrificing a Christian burial for her own son to favour me, and this is a matter that must be resolved with all haste," he concluded.

Lord Doulain and his son spent an hour on their own in the study as James recounted his experiences in detail, concluding with his intentions regarding Russet.

"She turned me down, you know." Lord Doulain laughed. "After her abominable, er, accident, I was willing to give her my name, and now I find, that by the providence of God, she shall have it."

Later, Russet stood on the terrace overlooking the parkland trying to come to terms with the surprising revelations. Jamie found her there and when she saw him her eyes twinkled with amusement.

"I must call for a chaperone, sir," she said with mock indignity. "I do not have your acquaintance and we most certainly have not been introduced." She grinned then said, haughtily, "I once owned a friendship with a fellow by the name of Jamie Pitchforth, but it would appear he has vanished into the mists of convenience. His looks compared favourably to your own, sir, so is this Jamie Pitchforth or James Doulain I see before me, or is it yet another pseudonymous pretender?"

"Russet, I must be serious." He looked down into her face and the greenness of her eyes shone up at him. "I asked you to marry me and...."

"You tricked me!" She came close to him. "What sort of a man would deceive a lady so?"

"I did not deceive you." He denied her suggestion. "I have never been more truthful in my life. I will ask you again. - Russet Roulette, will you be my wife?"

Again she laughed. "Am I not the most fortunate person – two proposals in one day? Now which shall I choose? The stable lad, or the son of a noble lord? If I play my cards with guile, maybe I shall acquire both." She put a finger to her cheek and said coquettishly, "I shall give it some thought, kind sir."

"Well, don't think for too long," he advised. "The banns

must be read on three consecutive Sabbath days and if that," he pointed a finger at her abdomen, "is going to be born in wedlock, this coming Sunday must be the first."

"Is that so important," she said.

"If it is a girl, not so very much. If it is a boy then it matters greatly. I have seen it happen before. Would you have him referred to behind his back as The Bastard Roulette?"

It was a long walk for Russet. From the lichgate up the steep path to the church door proved an effort for her. She leant on her father's arm and paused to catch her breath before entering. Maisy was in attendance, and they were followed by Jamie and Lord Doulain.

"I do hope the Rector is in a good humour today. Russet gasped for air.

"Why should we worry what mood he is in?" Lord Doulain asked.

"You don't know the man, Father." Jamie spoke up. "He considers himself Lord of Retribution, and he can be very awkward if it so pleases his purpose."

The stone-flagged aisle led up to the altar. Here it met with the transept; a stone walk running the width of the nave in the form of a cross. To the right was the vestry, the left to a doorway leading to the churchyard and on to the rectory. The group moved silently down the aisle then eased into the enclosed Roulette pews at the front and knelt in prayer.

The curate, Isaiah Snufty, busied himself at the altar, but kept a watchful eye on the worshippers.

"Curate." Sir Marcus whispered. "We shall take pleasure in a word with the Rector."

The curate sniffed and said, "the Reverend Butler is indisposed. I...."

"Then un-dispose him!" Lord Doulain interrupted and demanded loudly.

The curate ran off and within minutes a harassed looking Reverend Butler appeared walking awkwardly, legs as far apart as they would go, an expression of pain and exasperation creasing his face.

"What is this about?" He questioned angrily. Then he caught sight of Maisy "What is that woman doing here, without my permission?"

"Reverend," Sir Marcus ignored the rector's words and went on, "my daughter and this gentleman wish to be married. It is a delicate matter, as you may well see, so I require you to take note and read the banns this coming Sabbath."

The Rector glanced at Russet and at her distended abdomen. "This woman has sinned in the eyes of God," he declared. "She has fallen to the sins of the flesh without the blessing..."

"Priest! A word with you!" His voice reverberated from the walls of the church as Lord Doulain took hold of the Rector by the shoulder and ushered him through the side door and out into the churchyard.

Cries of protest issued from the Rector. "Unhand me! Unhand me this minute!" His cries of protest and moans of agony, as the pain of his boils chafed his groin faded to nothing as he was bundled out into the open.

Sir Marcus moved to follow but Jamie raised an arm to bar his way. "It would better my father deals with this," he said.

"Reverend Butler rules his parishioners with fear. My father is not so easily frightened and this Rector will not have encountered his like."

The group remained expectant with all eyes on the open door. They saw the two men walk by along the churchyard path, Lord Doulain's hand still grasping the Reverend Butler by the shoulder. They came past the doorway from the other direction, this time Lord Doulain had his hand on the other shoulder, no longer pushing the distressed priest. Once more they briefly came into view, and this time the man of God was nodding his head vigorously.

When the two men re-entered the nave the attitude of the Reverend Alexander Butler was an unbelievable transformation. He laid hands on the heads of James and Russet and blessed them. The promise of the first reading of the banns on the following Sabbath and his suggestion that the wedding take place quietly on the Monday following the third Sunday were welcomed with astonishment.

After dinner, when the ladies had withdrawn, Sir Marcus addressed Lord Doulain, "Frank, curiosity is killing me," he said. "What in this world did you say to the Rector that brought about such a change in the man?"

Lord Doulain looked smugly into his wine glass and swirled the contents before taking a sip. "You may recall that the deeds of the Nestwith Hall Estate were in my keeping for some time. Well, while in my possession I read every single word therein. I came across some very interesting information. The Reverend Butler afforded further to this when I spoke to him this morning. It would appear he became

Rector of the parish of Nestwith during the last week of your father's life, but was never officially appointed. Your brother, Oliver, it would seem, attempted to push responsibility for the 'living' on to the church authority to avoid paying for the upkeep of any church properties. Nothing more has been done and although not officially appointed, the rector carried on with the duties.

"He has thirty two acres of land and use of the rectory; an income from tithes and the rent from twenty acres of the meadow included in the 'living'. His only real expenditure is that he pays his curate twenty-two pounds a year. In fact, The Reverend Alexander Butler has a very agreeable existence. I gave him to understand that I have the ear of the Archbishop of Canterbury and I advised him not to act in a manner inconsistent with his circumstances."

"You must have impressed him verily when you mentioned the Archbishop of Canterbury," Sir Marcus said. "I suppose that would frighten any ecclesiastical journeyman."

"Ah yes, but that was not the butt that took the arrow." Lord Doulain smiled. "You should read those deeds thoroughly some time, Marcus. You will find that the 'living' of Nestwith is entirely within your gift. You can appoint or dismiss the clerical personage at your will. The Reverend Butler knows he is afforded a good benefice, and fear of losing one's livelihood can change the attitude of better men than our ecclesiastical brother. I just happened to point this out to him, and the Lord must have intervened also, for the change in the fellow was immediate and drastic. In truth, I feel the man was all bluster, hiding behind a display of exaggerated importance to cover his inferior capabilities."

There was much laughter and the wine and brandy flowed freely. Captain Christopher was still feeling like an interloper in the family matters of others, but he used the occasion to ask Lord Doulain why he had been asked to remain at Nestwith.

"Ah, yes." The laughter ceased and Lord Doulain became serious. "I have relieved you of your duties as master of the Branston Silver. When I am away, I find there is a lack of discipline among my staff in London. What I need is a man of iron – a man who will not tolerate lack of will and purpose; a man who's word is law." There was a pause as Jamie muffled a laugh. Then, Lord Doulain leant across the table and stared for a few moments into the unflinching eyes of the captain. "I have a mind to appoint you to the post of Master of the Fleet and place you in charge of the running of the Doulain shipping and the Doulain Company - a sort of commercial manager. What say you, Jacob?"

"I say aye to that, My Lord. I shall accept your offer with gratitude."

Lord Doulain raised his glass. "Then we shall all drink a toast to your appointment, and wish you success."

Three days later, in the early hours of the morning, four hooded figures arrived at the Pitchforth cottage with a horse and covered cart in which lay concealed four empty coffins. Lord Doulain and Sir Marcus conspired to have Maisy stay the night at Nestwith Hall and it was Gunner who led the men to the herb garden. By lantern light they exhumed the body of Jamie Pitchforth, placed the corpse in a coffin, sealed the lid with resin, and departed with it in the cart in the direction of

Nestwith Parish Church. There, under the direction of a reformed Reverend Butler, further exhumations were carried out and the bodies of Sam Pitchforth and his two boys were removed from their paupers' graves and placed in the remaining coffins. These were transferred to, and interred in a deep ready-dug grave in a prominent position at the side of the church. The men then departed in the direction of Loylton with the coffin containing the corpse of Jamie Pitchforth.

Later the same day, all work ceased and the whole population of the village of Nestwith turned out to pay their respect at the Christian service and burial of Maisy Pitchforth's eldest son. It was understood that he had finally succumbed to the head injuries incurred as a quarry worker.

Weeks of dismal wet weather had come to an end and the sun shone warmly, drying the earth, and allowing Russet and James to venture forth in an open carriage for the last time before the wedding and probably, her confinement. Her mind was still in turmoil and again and again she looked sideways at him and the more she looked at him the more she realised the depth of her love for him. When they reached the fallen oak he would not allow her to step down because of her condition.

"Have you decided where we shall live, Jamie?" She glanced at him quizzically.

"I am James now," he began.

"Oh no you are not." She laughed at him. "In my condition I have no intention of changing horses in mid-stream. You *were* Jamie to me and you will always *be* Jamie to me. So you will have to accept that."

He did not argue. But went on, "we shall live at Bullington House..."

"Bullington House is mine, it was left to me." She teased him. "And have you ever seen the place. It is not by the river, but it is nevertheless a hovel."

"Then we shall have it demolished and a new house built to our requirements." He turned and kissed her cheek. "And I would remind you, Russy dear, when a woman marries, her possessions pass to her husband to do with as he sees fit. And if she be a scolding wife, the law states the husband can beat her for her fractious behaviour."

"You wouldn't dare!" She leaned towards him and put her head on his shoulder. "I love you Jamie." It was the first time she had spoken the words. He turned to her and put his arms about her shoulders. He kissed her forehead, then the scars on her cheek, the tip of her nose and then his lips found hers. For a few seconds they kissed passionately, then the moment was gone and they both began to laugh.

"If anybody could see us," Russet squeezed his arm. "What would they think? A young, handsome suitor, and a pregnant woman almost about to give birth, kissing and cuddling like a couple of youngsters having a first affair." She giggled at the thought. His lips found hers once more, a long lingering kiss; she felt content, secure, and in love. She had never known such happiness.

The parishioners of Nestwith sat mesmerised as the rector delivered his sermon. Not once did he threaten. No mention of sin or sinners, only of God's love for his children. Never had he spoken such words from the pulpit and he was astonished at the results of it. Whereas previously when standing at the door of the church as his flock departed there had been nods and polite wishes of good health. Now they lingered, coming up to talk to him and telling him of family matters, volunteering help for church improvements, and speaking in words of friendship rather than fear.

Quietly, on the Monday following the third reading of the banns, the coaches and carriages arrived at the rear of the rectory stables and Russet alighted to walk the short distance to the side door of the church. If the truth were known, she was now experiencing considerable discomfort. Apart from members of the immediate families, Jamie's friends, Gunner, Walter, Wrigley and Gertrude were present, together with Maisy, and Captain Christopher. Maisy to attend Russet; the Captain as a witness and signatory to the marriage.

When it came to Russet's turn to recite her marriage vows, she began, "I Russet Roulette oooooooh!" She gasped and looked down at the pool that was spreading from beneath her gown.

"Her waters have broke!" Maisy cried.

"Hasten your words, priest," Lord Doulain roared," lest you be obliged to commute this marriage to a Christening."

In her bedchamber at Nestwith Hall, at ten minutes to midnight on her wedding day, Russet Doulain gave birth to a healthy son.

Propriety of the age forbade the presence of men in the room at times of birth, so James Doulain had to wait for permission before he could see his bride. Maisy tidied everything and, at last, with the newborn infant fed, asleep and taken from the room in the care of nursemaids, she left the bedchamber to tell Jamie he could see his wife.

Alone in the room, Russet took hold of a hand mirror from her bedside table and looked at herself in the glass.

"Well, Russet Doulain," she said to her image in the mirror. "What an interesting life you do lead." She turned her head and peered at the scars that marred her cheek, "Jamie Doulain," she murmured, "I must say I have to admire your impeccable taste when it comes to choosing a wife." She laughed aloud at her own facetiousness. Then, "if my wounds are not a worry to you, husband, then to me they no longer exist." She opened the drawer of her bedside table and took out the poem. She read it yet again and for the first time she grasped the deeper meaning of the words. She had spent many hours with Jamie, over the hill at the fallen oak, and because he loved her when he wrote the poem he wrote in truth that he was clutching straws of hope for a love that could never be returned. She continued to read on and understanding became clearer in her mind. He truly loved me and dreamed that the disparity that kept us apart would vanish; but he knew that in reality our seasons – our lives – could never be as one. He accepted that for the rest of his life he would have to endure frustration and loneliness because convention prevented me from responding. He was telling me in the poem that we lived on different sides of a great divide, and that it would always be so. She felt a lump rising in her throat as she thought how he must have suffered; not being able to speak his love and yet having to spend time in the company of the one he loved. She put a hand over her mouth as she felt she was about to burst into tears. Quickly, she composed herself and said aloud, as if speaking to the written words, "oh Jamie, it is of no consequence. I know I was in love with you when I thought you a peasant and I shall love you for ever."

She folded the paper and put it back in the drawer. With a hairbrush she tidied her hair, then straightened the bedclothes and pinched her cheeks to give them a rosy glow as she settled back on her pillows to await her husband.

When James Doulain entered the bedchamber he expected to see a woman in distress. Instead he was surprised to see Russet propped up on pillows, hair combed, eyes bright and looking radiant.

"Good night to you, Mrs James Doulain," he said. He sat on the edge of the bed, smiling as he took her hand in his and put it against his cheek. "I am told you have been a very clever girl – but Maisy will not allow me to see the boy till morning.."

"It was a near run thing," she giggled. "I thought I was going to birth it on the church floor." They both laughed and she looked up at him lovingly. "If you are a good husband I will allow you to give me some more of those."

He took her in his arms. "I love you Russy. I will always love you." Her eyes were beginning to fill as he said, "I will do everything I can to make you happy."

"I have never been so happy." She put her arms about his neck and whispered, "you realise that the prophesy in your poem has been completely dispelled. We have no reason to be over the hill for the grass could not be greener than it is right here."

Lord Doulain stood with hands clasped behind his back as he stared unseeing into the glowing embers in the hearth.

"You are very quiet, Frank." Sir Marcus observed. "A wedding and an addition to the family all in one day. Surely this is an occasion of joy, not one for a sombre mood.

Lord Doulain turned away from the fire to face Sir Marcus. "Had the child been born a girl then I would be the first to rejoice, but I fear the birth of this boy can open up a direful bag of worms." He shook his head and then went on as if the true meaning of the events of the previous day had just come to mind; he tried to put his fears to one side and said, "I understand Russet has chosen to name the boy William – after the fellow William Bull who bequeathed his estate to her." He heard a gasp of surprise and looked closer through the candle-lit gloom to see Sir Marcus sitting, ashen faced, wide eyed, mouth open.

"My God, Marcus. Are you not well?

Sir Marcus pulled himself together. "I am well enough. Just a little light-headed. The happenings of the day. Perhaps a brandy," he stammered. "You - you were saying, Frank?"

"I was about to say that I have a strange feeling of foreboding. The birth of this boy can cause many problems of dire consequence. He is not a true Doulain and without Doulain blood running through his veins he is not eligible, under the law of the crown, to inherit my peerage. If James and Russet have other sons through their marriage then those sons will take precedence and William, although the eldest, will move down the pecking order of family inheritance. As he grows up, how in God's name can that be explained to the boy? - that his father is not his true father – that his real father was a murderous cutthroat." He shook his head and muttered solemnly, "I foresee dissention within the family, Marcus. I see only trouble and dissention.

Lightning Source UK Ltd.
Milton Keynes UK
UKOW05f1709280813

216129UK00001B/2/P